THE AFGHAN WIFE

CINDY DAVIES

Published by Odyssey Books in 2017

Copyright © by Cindy Davies

All rights reserved. No part of this book may be reproduced or transmitted by any person or entity, including internet search engines or retailers, in any form or by any means, electronic or mechanical, including photocopying (except under the statutory exceptions provisions of the *Australian Copyright Act* 1968), recording, scanning or by any information storage and retrieval system without the prior written permission of the publisher.

www.odysseybooks.com.au

A Cataloguing-in-Publication entry is available from the National Library of Australia

ISBN: 978-1-925652-31-4 (pbk)

ISBN: 978-1-925652-32-1 (ebook)

Cover design by Simon Critchell

*To my dear husband Harvey
for his patience and wisdom,
and for our friend the late Bert ten Broeke*

AUTHOR'S NOTE

As this is a work of fiction, none of the characters I have imagined are based on actual people. When I was an English language teacher my students shared their stories with me, and I have drawn on these for this book. Ahmad getting lost in the mountains, for example, was a real incident. One of my Laotian students told me of escaping at night over the border to Thailand. Her family spent twenty terrifying minutes searching in the dark for her three-year-old son who had wandered away.

According to Afghani women I spoke to, life in Afghanistan in the 1970s was very different. Many older Afghani students had photographs of themselves as young women wearing Western clothes. Many of the younger ones had escaped just before the Taliban took over.

In the early days of the revolution in Iran, women were targeted by the authorities. Several young Iranian students told of being arrested and taken to the local police station. They were often threatened with a beating for showing strands of hair from under a headscarf. Another student arrived in Australia from Iran in 1980.

She was traumatised after several of her young female friends had been hanged.

I visited Iran a couple of years ago as part of my research for the book. It is a physically beautiful country, with extremely friendly people and amazing historical sites. The strict dress codes described in the novel have been relaxed somewhat and women can now wear make-up. They can choose to wear a chador, but must always wear 'respectable' clothes in public, clothes that cover the whole body. A headscarf is still mandatory for all women, including those from overseas.

It is an historical fact that sixty-six American hostages were seized on 4 November 1979, and fifty-two of them were held captive in Iran for 444 days.

Shortly after the revolution, several Iranian counter-revolutionary groups were organised. As far as I know, none of them tried to rescue the American hostages. The rescue attempt in the novel, which was organised by Firzun, is purely imaginary.

I have researched the background for this novel thoroughly and have the experience of living and visiting in a Muslim country over a number of years. I apologise for any inadvertent inaccuracies that may be present in this fictional story.

It's my wish that you enjoy reading *The Afghan Wife* and eventually its sequel, which is due to be published in 2019.

1

THE REVOLUTIONARY

Herat, Afghanistan, September 1979

The hot, dry lands around Herat were cooling quickly. The autumn fruit had been harvested and winter was on its way. Firzun could smell the change of season on the dusty breeze as he crouched behind the wall. From here he had an uninterrupted view of the lunch party.

Behind the barred gates of the Soviet consulate, the guests were enjoying themselves. They spilled out of the French doors and onto the lawns. Diplomats, advisers, military men, and their dumpy wives held champagne glasses. *Arrogant bastards!* Firzun thought. They believed their own propaganda about the invincible USSR. He'd show them—this was his country, not theirs!

He checked his watch. Next to him he could hear Osman breathing heavily. 'Two minutes,' he whispered.

He squinted through a gap in the wall. Even from this distance he could see the cake. It was a centrepiece in the middle of a white-clothed table. They'd delivered it over an hour ago, dressed as bakers. The two sentries who'd waved them through had already reeked of alcohol. *Idiots!* He and Osman had staggered towards the main reception room and put their heavy carton on the table.

He focused on the scene in front of him. It was like looking at a movie with actors playing out their parts, smiling, chatting, putting glasses back on trays.

He muttered the prayers for the dead and his heart hammered in his chest as he counted backwards. Three ... two ... he held his breath ... one! Nothing happened. They were still there, all of them. Still laughing, still drinking.

Osman turned to him and their widened eyes met. They didn't dare speak. Firzun looked back at the building. The lunch party had turned into a tableau. The guests watched as a couple of soldiers in combat gear kneeled behind the cake. One of them had his head bent forward and Firzun could see his arms moving, defusing the device. The cake should have exploded by now and sent them all to hell!

Then someone flung open the gates and more soldiers in combat gear poured out of the building, spraying bullets from sub-machine guns as they ran into the street. Guests screamed as they rushed to safety. Behind the wall, Firzun and Osman scrabbled along on all fours.

The van was waiting, the backdoors flapping open. Bullets ricocheted off it. A hand grenade exploded behind him, making his ears sing and pop. He threw himself into the van and rolled along the metal floor. Osman hurled himself in as the van gathered speed. Choking on the dust, Firzun yanked the doors shut; he shouldn't have waited ... he'd wanted to be sure and now they'd seen the van. It tore through the streets until they got to a courtyard, scattering chickens and children.

'Get out tonight!' he said to Osman as they tumbled onto the ground.

'*Allah u Akbar!*' Osman mumbled.

Firzun nodded. *Allah u Akbar*—God is great. This had nothing to do with God, he thought as he changed quickly from his dirty clothes. He pulled a fresh *shalwaar kameez* over his head and rammed his flat *pakul* on his dusty hair. He had to get out of town fast and he couldn't do it without his cousin Zahra, and—he spat on the ground—her vile husband Mahmoud.

Zahra sat her desk in the empty classroom, marking her students exercise books as fast as she could. She jumped when she heard the light tap on the door, but before she could get up to open it, her cousin was in the room. She frowned; he looked more dishevelled than usual. His long *shalwaar kameez* was crumpled, his pants were grimy. To her surprise he'd grown a beard.

He glanced round restlessly, his deep-set dark eyes darting back to her face as he greeted her quickly. '*Salaam alaikum*, cousin Zahra. Are you alone?'

'*Wa alaikum as-salaam*,' she replied automatically. 'The other teachers have gone home, but the caretaker's here somewhere. What's wrong?'

She knew about his anti-communist activities. When things got rough he went to ground. Once he'd hidden in the wood store of her apartment block for three days and she'd taken him food and water. If Mahmoud had found out he would have punished her, but Firzun was family, more like a brother than a cousin. If he was in trouble again she had to help him.

'I have to get out of Herat,' he said urgently. 'I need you and Mahmoud and little Ahmad to come with me. We can escape as a family—it's a good cover. It won't be for long.'

She put her hand over her mouth and looked at him. He was stocky and strong, but only a head and shoulder taller than her. His thick black hair had already dislodged his *pakul* and he rubbed his new beard distractedly.

'Is it bad?' she asked.

He frowned, then told her what had happened. It *was* bad this time, she thought fearfully. If the authorities arrested him, he'd be executed.

The latest news from Kabul, Firzun went on, was that Afghan communist President Taraki had been arrested and 'disappeared'.

She stared at her cousin—he was making her feel extremely nervous. In March, a resistance group had killed more than a hundred Soviet citizens living here in Herat. Now he was attempting to kill even more of them. Why?

'I'm not a communist, Zahra, you know that,' he said defiantly, as if reading her thoughts. 'I want a democratically elected government. If we continue to harbour the Soviets, they'll invade and take over.'

'Firzun ...' she began, but he interrupted her.

'I'll come and see Mahmoud tonight about the arrangements. I thought you should know first.'

She hardly had time to say goodbye before he wrenched open the door and she heard him running down the corridor. She didn't see him cross the open playground, but he knew the back way out of the school. She gathered her books together quickly and put them to one side on her desk; she'd have to come in early tomorrow and finish them. Mahmoud didn't like her working at home. She was glad Firzun had warned her—most Afghan men wouldn't consider telling a woman anything before her husband knew, but Firzun despised her husband. He knew that Mahmoud hit her, but there was nothing he could do about it. She paused as she collected her pens together. She had no idea where they were going—he'd forgotten to tell her.

The shadows were lengthening and she heard the start of the afternoon prayer call as she hurried towards the bus stop. She enjoyed her status as a teacher of English and Persian language at the prestigious girl's school, but she knew her job would be in jeopardy if she'd been seen alone with a man in her classroom—even a male cousin. The communist government had lifted restrictions on women's dress—she wore a suit for work with a skirt below her knees

—but many customs were still ingrained in Afghan society. At her husband's insistence, she also wore a lose headscarf over her long brown hair.

'You're the wife of a Muslim man, you should show some respect for your religion,' he'd said righteously more than once.

She would always turn her head away from the smell of alcohol on his breath, infuriated by his hypocrisy. Good Muslims never touched alcohol, and he had no right to grow a beard and allow people to refer to him as *'Haji'*, a title reserved for people who had performed the 'Haj'—the pilgrimage to Mecca. In a drunken moment, he'd laughed and told her he'd never been to Mecca but the beard gained him a lot of respect. Now her cousin had grown a beard. She was absolutely sure he'd never been on the 'Haj' either.

The main street was busy as usual and the smell of diesel fumes hung on the warm air. As she walked she thought of Firzun. They'd been brought up together in the same extended family and had always been close. As she hurried along, one memory connected to another: her Afghan father dying when she was ten, her Iranian mother tolerated by the family until that wonderful day when Zahra was seventeen and they'd left to start a new life in Tehran, the capital city of Iran.

She sighed. What was the point in going over the past and the terrible ending of their journey to Iran? It had been Firzun who'd escorted her home. Firzun who'd ordered his mother, her aunt, to be kind to her.

Zahra got onto the hot, overcrowded bus and managed to find a seat. The vehicle moved off then jerked to a stop when two police cars, sirens screaming, rushed passed. Her heart sank—had they found Firzun? She looked out the grimy window again in time to see several Russian jeeps full of armed soldiers following the police cars.

'Someone tried to blow up the Russian Consulate,' one of the other passengers said.

Zahra felt as if a hand was squeezing her heart, making it hard to breathe. Firzun had done this, and now he expected her husband to help him leave town. She wondered if he had gone home to his mother, her Aunt Mina. She doubted it. Mina never knew where he was; she probably thought he was still in Iran. He'd won a scholarship and completed a degree in chemical engineering at Tehran University. Now he often got contracted work in different parts of Iran.

Zahra stared at the crowds thronging the streets as the heat of the day eased. Shopkeepers were lounging in their doorways, resting after they'd dragged sacks of dried lentils, beans and spices out onto the footpaths for the evening trade.

The bus stalled and she watched as a man and his young helper heaved boxes of fruit out of their shop, then arranged them carefully, waving away the begging children gathered around them.

The memories flooded back again—they always did when Firzun showed up. It was her Aunt Mina who had pushed her into marrying Mahmoud. If her mother had been alive she would have vehemently opposed the match and told her she could do better. Zahra would never forget the day he'd visited, bringing sweets and gifts. She'd been told to wait in her room while Mina 'negotiated' with him. But the walls were thin and she'd heard everything.

'Of course, you know her mother was Iranian?' Aunt Mina had said. Zahra could imagine the sneer on her aunt's face. 'After my brother-in-law died, she had nowhere to go. She had to stay here with Zahra ... her family cut her off. Next thing, her mother rushes off to a long lost sister in Tehran and dies there. It was left to me and my husband to look after the daughter. We even let her go to university."

'You were very good to her!' Mahmoud had answered smoothly. 'Now I'm in a position to take her off your hands.'

'Well, she does have a choice,' Aunt Mina had replied. 'My son, her cousin Firzun, would marry her, but she prefers you.'

Zahra stared unseeing out the window of the bus—if she'd married Firzun, she would have been trapped with vindictive Aunt Mina and forced to live with the extended family in their house.

Firzun had no intention of marrying anyone, he'd told her that. She'd chosen Mahmoud hoping for freedom, but she'd been bitterly disappointed. She could recall every word he'd said to Aunt Mina. They'd arranged a 'bride price' and she'd ended up with no money of her own and none of the land that had belonged to her father. Mahmoud was a widower and he'd offered his first wife's jewellery to Zahra as a wedding present. It was a parsimonious gesture, but it satisfied her aunt.

His parents were also dead and his sister lived in Kabul. At forty-two he was twice Zahra's age. He'd asked for the wedding to be arranged as quickly as possible.

The bus driver's voice broke into Zahra's reverie as he called out her stop. She pushed her way off and started walking quickly down a narrow street bordered on both sides by mud brick houses. The road was unsealed and her smart work shoes were soon covered in dust. She pushed open a gate into a square courtyard of baked earth where several children including her son, Ahmad, were playing ball.

'Mummy!' He ran and threw his arms round her and she smiled down at him. Her lovely son, her only compensation for being married to Mahmoud. She tousled his dark hair, he'd turned five recently—in a year he'd be going to school.

She paid the young woman who ran the small kindergarten and carried on walking down the long alleyway with Ahmad chatting brightly at her side. A man leading a donkey with panniers on either side of its body pushed past them and several ragged children skipped alongside them, trying to talk to her and pulling at her sleeve. She stopped as she often did and gave them a few coins.

Even though Mahmoud worked as a lecturer in engineering at the University, of Herat, he insisted on living in the apartment that had belonged to his parents in a run-down neighbourhood. It was here that his first wife had fallen to her death on the outside stairs. Zahra had been appalled when she'd seen the apartment—such a far cry from the extended family compound where she'd been brought up on the other side of the city. Garbage and dust were a constant problem. When she'd suggested moving, her new husband had flown into such a terrible rage that she'd never raised the subject again.

The alleyway opened up and she turned to where the small apartment block stood. In front was an open space with cracked paving stones. It was full of litter, old newspapers, and household garbage tossed by passers-by. She climbed the stone stairs to the third floor, keeping her eyes lowered as Mahmoud had forbidden contact with the neighbours.

While Ahmad played with his toys, Zahra prepared the evening meal. Her hands trembled as she collected the plates and cutlery. Her cousin was in serious trouble. If the police found him he'd be tried and executed. He was putting them all in danger by even visiting their flat. Why would he think Mahmoud would help him? He must be desperate to even ask. Firzun knew about her husband's savage temper, and Zahra dreaded a confrontation. She might even be dragged into a fight between the two of them. There'd been a tussle between the men a couple of months earlier and Mahmoud had grabbed Firzun by the throat. She'd ended up with a black eye after that, just for being there. This time she'd make herself scarce, watch and listen from behind the kitchen door, and hope that things didn't get violent.

2
THE VISIT

Mahmoud scowled at her when he came home, slamming the door behind him.

'Your *haramzadeh* cousin is coming to see me tonight,' he said with a sneer. She looked down at the floor and tried to keep her face impassive. Calling her cousin a bastard was insulting, but she knew there was worse to come. It was his little game; he liked using foul language in front of her and watching intently for the slightest change in her expression. If she didn't react he'd pounce and call her a whore who loved dirty talk.

'He's a shit-eating child of a dog like the rest of your family.' His spittle sprayed across her hair as he said the disgusting words.

She didn't respond.

'Aren't you going to ask me *why* he's coming?' Mahmoud mocked. 'Maybe he needs my help.' He paused. 'Perhaps he needs to get out of town.'

Zahra kept her eyes lowered, not sure of how much Mahmoud knew. After she'd brought him a beer and a wet cloth for his hands and face, she went back to the kitchen. She quickly coiled her hair into a tight knot at the back of her neck, then added spices, carrots, sultanas and almonds to the steamed rice. She could hear Mahmoud interrogating Ahmad in the living room, asking him what he'd learned, getting him to count to twenty and say his letters. The child was tired and as usual he made mistakes. Each time he did, his father banged a book on a small table and Ahmad whimpered fearfully. She went into the living room and took Ahmad by the hand.

'I'll give him his meal in the kitchen,' she said firmly.

'He's an idiot mummy's boy,' Mahmoud said in disgust. 'Take him out of my sight.'

Zahra kept Ahmad with her and he soon recovered, telling her in whispers about his day. She spooned rice into his dish and gave him one of the minced lamb kabobs she was making for the adults. Mahmoud called for another beer. He ignored her when she put it next to him. He was intent on reading the evening paper and the room was full of smoke from his foul-smelling cigarette. After she'd fed her son, she took him to the tiny bathroom, washed him and helped him into his pyjamas. She told him that cousin Firzun was coming and that he'd have to go to bed early. She left him in the bedroom turning the pages of his book about trucks. If there was going to be any violence between the men, she wanted Ahmad out of the way. She emptied the overflowing ashtray and put plates and spoons ready on a cloth she'd spread on the floor.

As soon as her cousin arrived, Zahra settled Ahmad for the night then retreated to the kitchen. She heard Firzun greet her husband. After she'd brought him a beer and a warm cloth for his hands and face, she went back into the kitchen, held the door ajar slightly and listened as Firzun started to talk. She could see the men in profile as they sat opposite each other on the floor. Mahmoud leaned aggressively towards her cousin, but Firzun was his usual solid and defiant self. They looked similar now that Firzun had grown a beard. Zahra picked up a large platter of salad and a basket of bread, nudged the door open and laid the food on the floor cloth. The men ignored her as she put salad on their plates.

'It's time to go, Mahmoud. I've organised the passports,' Firzun began.

Zahra caught her breath. Passports?

'So you're on the run again. You botched that job at the Soviet consulate, didn't you?' Mahmoud sneered. 'You can clear off across the border to Iran on your own. I've got a wife and a child to think of.'

He flicked his hand at Zahra, waving her back to the kitchen.

Zahra felt a rush of anger towards both men—why hadn't Firzun told her they were going to Iran? She'd thought they might head for Kabul or another big city. She'd thought Mahmoud knew nothing about Firzun's activities, but she'd been wrong.

'We can get out as a family,' Firzun said.

Zahra moved nearer to the kitchen door and opened it further.

'You!' Mahmood jabbed his finger a Firzun. 'You …' he spat a foul insult in her cousin's face, and she was surprised her cousin didn't hit him, '… and your stupid revolutionary ideas.'

'I'm fighting for democracy!' Firzun raised his voice.

'Anything that's going, you just jump on the bandwagon. I know all about you helping those rich friends of yours in Iran. Well, they got rid of the shah. Now they don't like the religious mob and the Ayatollah Khomeini and you're right there in the front line … you … you bloody stupid anarchist. You're a waste of space. Why don't you get a proper job?'

'I've got a job,' Firzun spat. 'But when the commies take over here, *you* won't have one. You'll have to live on Zahra's money. You wouldn't like that, would you?'

Mahmoud started to get up.

'Settle down,' Firzun said calmly. 'I've got you a teaching job at Tehran University.'

Zahra frowned—that had to be a lie. Firzun had told her that Mahmoud was a third rate engineer and a worse teacher. Why would a prestigious school like Tehran University offer him a job?

'Forget it, I'm not going,' Mahmoud said, stuffing bread into his mouth.

Firzun reached into his pocket and laid out photographs on the floor in front her husband like a winning hand of cards.

'You're in all of these. You're lucky you haven't been arrested like some of the others,' Firzun said.

'You bastard!' Mahmoud said angrily.

He grabbed a photograph, crumpled it in his hand and threw it across the room.

'You're on the commies' list, Mahmoud. Get out while you can.' Firzun smiled insolently at Mahmoud as he put the photos in his shirt pocket and tapped it.

Zahra picked up the dishes of rice and meat and held the door open with her foot. She kept her eyes lowered as she knelt and served the food onto their plates. She wouldn't give her husband the satisfaction of seeing fear in them.

Back in the kitchen she ate her own food standing up and squinting through the crack in the door as she listened to Firzun's plans.

'We leave on Thursday. One small bag each, that's all.'

'I'm not going! You're an anarchist and a liar!'

Firzun leaned forward. 'Listen, Mahmoud, they know we met in your room at the university,' he said testily. 'You're in this up to your neck like me. I paid you well, didn't I? They'll get you sooner or later.'

Mahmoud balled his fists. Would he hit her cousin as he sat there smirking? He wouldn't dare, she thought. He knows he'd come off worse like last time. But she hadn't known that Firzun had manipulated him with money.

'I'll tell them it was you!' Mahmoud shouted, his voice rising a pitch. 'You dragged me into this. I'm not a fighter!'

Only in your own home, Zahra thought.

'You do that. I'll be in Tehran by then.' Firzun shrugged. 'Face it, you've got no choice. I've arranged Iranian papers, they're good copies. We'll pick them up after we cross the border.' Firzun started to eat.

Back in the kitchen, Zahra's alarm grew. Passports, visas, forged papers? Wouldn't they be arrested? Now Firzun was saying something about a refugee camp if the papers weren't right. Then she caught her breath. He was talking about Nasim and her husband Rashid, his wealthy friends—names from her own past. He'd organised for everyone to stay in their house. The house where she'd heard about her mother's death ten years ago. The house where she'd first seen Karim Konari. Her heart contracted and for an instant she was seventeen again.

She'd never forget seeing Karim for the first time as he stood in the doorway of Nasim's huge salon, scanning the room. Was he still as handsome and urbane with easy manners and American-style clothes? If she saw him again, would she still feel that overwhelming rush of ... what was it? Love? Infatuation? The thought of him still made her feel weak inside. She shook her head, trying to rid herself of the bittersweet memories as she opened the kitchen door and walked quietly into the living room. The men ignored her. She collected the plates, made the coffee, and later stood near the door to wish her cousin goodnight. When her husband flung it open, she smelled wood smoke.

'Leave the house when you hear the *azan-e mahgreb*, Mahmoud. Wait by the side of the mosque in Salaam Street,' Firzun shook their hands. 'Dress warmly.'

As he clattered down the concrete stairs, Zahra shivered involuntarily. The *azan-e mahgreb*—the sunset prayer call—on Thursday! She felt desperate. How could she pack up her life in such a short time? Mahmoud slammed the door shut. She stood back as he performed the nightly ritual, locking, testing, bolting.

'Did Firzun say we're leaving on Thursday?' she asked when he'd finished.

She knew she would regret saying anything to him. He turned sharply, grabbed her arms, and squeezed them hard above her elbows. He shook her violently, his jagged nails biting into her flesh.

'This is how your *respectable* family repays me for taking you off their hands.' His spittle hit her face. 'Your useless cousin's dragged me into one of his botched plans. Now we're on the run!'

Her head hit the wall when he threw her back against it, cursing loudly. He slapped her hard across the face. With another curse he stomped away. She massaged her face, trying to soothe the stinging flesh. Her neck felt sore where it had snapped back. Once again her thick knot of hair had saved her skull. Her arms ached and stung from the pressure of his fingers. She clenched her fists, hating him, wishing him dead. She stood in the kitchen and waited till he'd used the bathroom and she'd heard him close the bedroom door. Tomorrow, she thought miserably, she had to see the school principal and come up with a convincing lie for quitting the job she loved.

Fatima Gul, principal of Herat Girls College, wasn't pleased but bowed to the inevitable.

'We all have to do what our husbands say,' she sighed.

She believed Zahra's carefully constructed lie about going to Kabul to stay with Mahmoud's sister. Although Fatima pressed her for a return date, she couldn't give one. She hated lying to the woman who was her boss and her friend. She was one of the few people who knew how Mahmoud treated her.

Her students were dismayed when she told them. She hid her distress from them and said that no one was indispensable. She set them a writing task and let her mind wander. How would they manage in Iran without her income? It was bound to be more expensive there. Mahmoud always gambled his salary away each month. She had very little faith in Firzun's promise of a job for her husband. Her salary paid for rent and food, Ahmad's kindergarten fees, and for Ayshe to clean the house and mind Ahmad sometimes. She'd even managed to put some in the bank. She expected Mahmoud would have emptied the account by now.

That evening he ordered her to pack their personal things in boxes.

'Another family's moving in on Saturday,' he announced.

She bit back the angry response that if things went wrong they'd have nowhere to live. The following evening he reluctantly gave her half of the money from the bank to sew into her clothes.

'They won't search a woman,' he said. But who were 'they'? The communists or the lawless mountain gangs—the Mujahadeen?

'Why Iran?' she ventured. 'There's been a revolution; it's an Islamic State now with Sharia law!'

Mahmoud clenched his fists and she backed away from him. 'Shut up, stupid woman! They have Sharia law to control women like you!'

She said nothing; protesting to Mahmoud was a waste of time and she didn't want to be hurt again.

That night she lay awake next to her snoring husband and allowed herself to think about Karim Konari, the man she'd met briefly when she was a gauche schoolgirl of seventeen. Firzun had reluctantly allowed her to come to one of his political meetings at his friends' house. She'd been clutching a glass of Coca Cola, wondering how she could drink it without spilling all the ice, when she'd noticed Karim standing in the doorway. In the intervening years she'd gone over and over the same scene in her head—she knew by heart every word, every nuance. Like a favourite fairy story, it had sustained her through all her troubles.

She could still see him clearly in his jeans and dark polo shirt with his lightly tanned olive skin, but his eyes ... they were the colour of honey, with thick dark lashes. He was taller than her cousin and he looked slightly older. As she'd watched, he'd pushed his longish dark brown hair back with his right hand. There was much to admire—his determined jaw line, his sculptured lips. He'd smiled straight at her and her heart had lunged. He was coming over to speak to her!

'Hello Maryam,' he'd said, extending his hand to the young woman sitting next to her. Zahra had looked down at the carpet—he hadn't even noticed her.

'Hi Karim,' Maryam had answered. 'I haven't seen you for ages.'

'I've just got back from the States.' He'd smiled briefly at Zahra as he sat down. 'My parents have a house at Martha's Vineyard.'

His voice was cultured, as if he'd been to an expensive school. Parents with a house in a vineyard, how exotic! Zahra had glanced at him, trying not to stare.

'Are you going to introduce me to your friend?' he'd said to Maryam as he smiled at Zahra.

Maryam obliged and Zahra had hastily put her glass on the floor. She remembered his handshake, warm and firm. When he'd leaned forward slightly, she'd caught a scent of fresh linen and almonds.

'Oh,' he'd laughed, 'your tiny hand is frozen!'

'I'm so sorry, the glass is full of ice,' she'd replied, the words tripping over each other.

'She didn't get it, she's probably never seen an opera.' She recalled Maryam's broad smile. 'She's Firzun's cousin from Afghanistan.'

At the time Zahra had had no idea what they were talking about.

Karim had then smiled directly at her again. His teeth were even and white. 'Afghanistan's a long way from here, Zahra.' Her name had sounded warm on his lips. 'Welcome to Iran.'

She'd felt as if all the breath had left her body, but she'd managed an awkward nod. He'd asked if the man wearing the Ché Guevara tee shirt was her cousin. When she'd nodded again, he'd raised his eyebrows and remarked, 'That's odd; Nasim said he was an anti-communist.'

Now, ten years later, she understood what he'd meant, but then she'd frowned and said hesitantly, 'You mean he looks like the man on the tee shirt?'

'Give her a break, Karim,' Maryam had chided.

She'd felt as if they were sharing a private joke, then Karim had leaned forward slightly and patted her hand. She'd never forget the thrill that had run through her body.

'Look up Marxist ideology when you get back to school,' he'd said kindly.

Lying on the edge of the thin mattress, next to her odious husband, a tear rolled down her face, then another and another. Karim Konari had paid the airfare for the cousins to come back to Afghanistan after they'd buried her mother. He'd sent the tickets via Rashid, Firzun's friend. 'Karim can afford it,' Firzun had said when she'd questioned the gesture. 'He's from one of the richest families in Tehran.'

She'd written to Karim and thanked him, entrusting the letter with her cousin when he'd returned to Iran. But although she'd watched for the post every day, he'd never replied.

Thoughts of Karim still haunted her as she travelled on the bus for her last day at the school. She doubted that after all this time he would remember her even if they did meet again. He was probably married with a family by now, and in his early thirties, she thought. She sighed—not to mention, she was married and damaged goods at that. She was no longer the wide-eyed virgin she'd been then, and the shame of being a beaten wife hung heavy in her heart. She would never be able to look Karim in the face without him knowing all her dark secrets, all the humiliations she'd suffered in her marriage. As she walked across the school yard, smiling at her students, she hoped Karim had left Iran for good and that she would never see him again.

She came home early on her last day, laden with parting gifts. Her special gift from the tearful girls was a green cashmere scarf.

'I'll always think of you when I wear it,' she told them, knowing in her heart that it was the only gift she could take with her.

There was a bright yellow parka for Ahmad and countless handkerchiefs and cards. The good wishes from her students and colleagues echoed round her head as she cleared up from their last hasty meal. 'Khodafez! God protect you on your journey, Zahra Khanoum.'

She double-checked that she had all she needed for herself and Ahmad in her travel bag. She had also packed a bag for Mahmoud and put it next to hers near the front door of the apartment.

'Make sure you and the boy are ready on time. I have to rest,' Mahmoud ordered as he opened the bedroom door. Ahmad, still wearing his new yellow parka, followed her round, peppering her with questions. In the kitchen, she doused the fuel stove and swept up the dust. She got Ahmad to help her wrap the dishes in tea towels and carry them into the living room. She buried all her cards and gifts under the dishes, then stopped and looked round for the last time.

Mahmoud had torn all the pictures and photographs off the walls in a frenzy the previous night, then dumped them in a corner, breaking and splintering the glass. The room looked drab again, like the first time she'd seen it. She'd had so many plans for the dreary little flat when she first married him. But within days they'd been dashed. There wasn't a wall he hadn't thrown her against. Her gaze settled on the closed bedroom door. She recalled her wedding night and all the other nights with a shudder. He was even more violent in the bedroom.

She didn't want to go. But could life be any worse? Maybe she could divorce him in Tehran and get a job. It was a big cosmopolitan city. Perhaps Nasim and Rashid could help. Then she remembered the Ayatollah Khomeini and the Sharia law he had introduced. She'd read in an American magazine about the draconian restrictions on women in Iran. She shuddered; she had more freedom here in Afghanistan under the local communist government. In Iran she would be trapped forever with no one to help her.

3

THE JOURNEY

Zahra waited at the open front door with Ahmad. The sun was just setting and she shivered when she heard the beginning of the *azan-e mahgreb*. The first call was always from the minaret of the Masjid-i Jami, the Friday mosque, in the centre of Herat. The muezzin's voice echoed across the silent city from the ancient building. '*Alloooooh u Akbooooor!*' He drew out the syllables as he sang the words: 'God's mightiness is beyond description ...' Slowly the call was taken up by other mosques until it made the familiar circular sound she loved.

'Move,' Mahmoud ordered, throwing her bag at her.

Ahmad was excited and wide awake. He had his hand in one of the pockets of the parka, the other in hers. She pulled up the hood over his thick black hair and bent to fix it.

'Now, woman!' Mahmoud said irritably, pushing her and Ahmad out the door. He locked it and left the keys under a stone. She looked up at the small green packet that hung below the lintel. Inside were verses from the Koran. She'd chosen them when they first married; they were meant to protect the house and family. They didn't protect me, she thought bitterly. No one protected me.

As she scurried down the stairs after Mahmoud, she remembered running down them with baby Ahmad, swaddled in blankets. It wasn't her first attempt at escape, but when she got to the family home, Aunt Mina had slammed the door in her face. 'You married him!' she'd shouted through the closed door.

At the bottom of the stone steps she thought again of Mahmoud's first wife, found dead on this same spot ten years ago. 'It was a tragedy, she was so beautiful,' the neighbours had told her before he'd stopped her speaking to them.

She took a deep breath and smiled down at Ahmad. Surely my life and his can't get any worse, she thought. Firzun had said that Nasim and Rashid, his old friends in Tehran, were married now, but what would they think of Mahmoud? Could they help her? She felt a rush of shame; she could never tell anyone what he'd done to her. They might think it was her fault.

Her small bag felt heavy as she hurried behind her husband along the narrow alleyways. The prayer call still echoed mournfully off the walls of the closely packed houses.

'You got your passports and the money?' Mahmoud snapped over his shoulder for the third time. She nodded. She had hers and Ahmad's; he hadn't trusted her with his. Inside the shoulder bag slung across her body were a few rolls of paper money. More money, jewellery and some gold coins were sewn into the hem of her long coat, weighing it down. He had the rest of the money in his wallet.

As they emerged into the wider main road, she looked around nervously for signs of police patrols. They were extra vigilant now. What if they were stopped and questioned? She wanted to ask Mahmoud, but he was more concerned with Ahmad. He turned and pushed him roughly when the boy kicked stray pebbles along the dimly lit road.

'Stop that, we're here,' he said.

His voice sounded strained as he turned into Salaam Street at the side of the mosque. He scanned the deserted area and tutted, hissing through his teeth.

'Where's your useless cousin, for God's sake?'

The white painted walls of the mosque loomed silently behind them. In the distance she could hear the faint drone of prayers. There was no sign of Firzun or the van that was supposed to pick them up. She glanced at Mahmoud. He'd followed Firzun's instructions and dressed in traditional clothes. A dark *shalwaar kameez* fell below his knees over baggy trousers and thick sheepskin boots. A rough brown woollen coat kept out the sharp mountain wind and he wore a grey turban on his balding head.

She was dressed 'respectably' according to his instructions in a long black coat over warm black trousers and a thick grey sweater. She adjusted her new scarf over her hair and checked that it was still securely tucked into her collar. In spite of her thick clothes, she shivered and pulled her coat closer to her body.

'*Salaam*, cousins.' Firzun's voice startled her. He emerged from the shadows wearing similar clothes to her husband's. 'It's time. The driver's waiting.'

They followed Firzun round a dark corner. A shabbily dressed man emerged from the gloom, his flashlight trained on the ground. She could just make out his sharp features. He looked like one of the villagers who came into the city on market day with fruit and vegetables. He'd thrown a sheepskin coat with a frayed hem over his baggy pants and *shalwaar kameez*, and his thick boots were caked in mud. He stuck the flashlight in his pocket, reached up to his hat, extracted a cigarette from the folds of his *pakul,* and lit it. Firzun introduced the driver as Ali. He ignored Zahra and greeted the men.

'*Salaam alaikum,*' he lisped through broken teeth, the cigarette glowing in the corner of his mouth.

'*Wa alaikum as-salaam,*' they replied.

He jerked his head to one side and they followed him across the uneven road and round another corner to a black van the size of a minibus. Its paint was peeling and it was covered in dust and mud. When he wrenched open the rear doors, they creaked and sagged. Zahra's heart tightened with anxiety. She peered through the gloom.

How would this old wreck get them across the rough mountain roads?

The man pushed aside several boxes and looked round furtively. 'Quick, get in.'

She lifted Ahmad into the van; he hesitated and turned round nervously.

'It's okay!' she said, scrambling in after him. Her long coat caught under her feet and she bent double as she staggered into the van. Ahmad whimpered, able to stand up but unwilling to move. She pushed him forward gently along the narrow passageway through the boxes stacked on either side of the van. They got to a small clear space at the front. There were no seats.

'Move it, woman, for God's sake!' Ali hissed impatiently.

He slammed the doors shut and she heard the lock grate as he fastened it. Firzun and Mahmoud were already squashed on a bench seat in the front. She gathered her clothes together and sat down, coaxing Ahmad to join her. She tried to find a comfortable spot on the sacks that covered the uneven floor, but in spite of her thick clothes she could feel the cold from the metal seeping through to her skin. She felt around the floor for more sacks and adjusted herself and Ahmad so they could sit on them. Through the cracked Perspex screen between her and the driver's compartment she heard Ali talking to the men. He was edgy and his accent was thick and indistinct.

'What's the idiot saying?' Mahmoud hissed.

'It's five hours to the Iranian border,' Firzun translated. 'He's going on the back roads to avoid the Soviet patrols and the Mujahedin.'

'So what do we do if we're stopped?' Mahmoud asked irritably.

'You keep your mouths shut!' the man answered.

That much she understood before he started to gabble again.

'He says the back roads are rough, don't complain,' Firzun told them.

'God give us a good journey,' Mahmoud said automatically.

'*Enshallah*, God willing,' the driver grunted.

Her stomach clenched when they lurched off into the thick darkness. The potholes in the road jolted them and shook the van. Stones flew up and hit the sides and Ahmad jumped with fright. The van swayed from side to side as the driver coaxed the old vehicle round the bends. The boxes shifted constantly, often sliding towards them. The wind was cold now and whistled through gaps in the rear doors. She held Ahmad close to her. Eventually he fell asleep, lulled by the sound of Mahmoud and Firzun's low voices as they talked.

'Where are we crossing the border?' Mahmoud demanded.

'Further north. He's going through the mountain passes,' Firzun said.

'The man's an idiot ...' Mahmoud began.

'Know better than me? Want to get stopped on the main road?' the driver snarled.

Zahra listened nervously to the conversation. As well as patrolling the border, the Soviets were also flying reconnaissance missions into Afghanistan.

'I've got me own route—I can steer clear of the lot of 'em,' Ali added.

Zahra shivered. What madness had possessed her husband to agree to this journey? Was his name really on a 'list'? Mahmoud was a coward; she knew that he feared a Soviet invasion like everyone else. Somehow Firzun had manipulated him for his own reasons. But what exactly were they? She strained her ears to get snatches of their conversation.

'Okay, Mahmoud,' Firzun was saying, 'we pick up our papers at the safe house. We get a bus from the village to Mashhad—the nearest big town. From there, an overnight coach to Tehran. Rashid will meet us at the coach station.'

Zahra had checked the route in her old school atlas. From Mashhad to Tehran would take at least eight hours. A hint of impatience in Firzun's voice made her concentrate on the conversation again.

'The Iranian visas in the passports are only valid for three months,' he said. 'They'll get us across the border. We need the Iranian identity papers to get work. It's all arranged.'

'So we use them on the coaches?' Mahmoud asked.

'Of course!' Firzun sounded exasperated. 'We've got to pass as Iranian—refugee camps, remember?'

As she listened to the men, Zahra felt fearful, alienated, carried along by the whim of her cousin. Firzun must have arranged papers for them when he'd finished his job at Tehran University in June. All this had been done without her knowledge. Since the troubles in Herat, everyone had to have new identity papers with photographs. There were plenty of spares ones in the house. Mahmoud must have passed theirs on to Firzun without telling her and arranged passports for them all. He had balked at going to Iran a couple of days ago; maybe he'd intended to go to Pakistan if the Soviets invaded. Firzun's 'evidence' against him must have convinced him to get out quickly across the nearest border to Iran.

She sighed as the van bumped and strained over the mountain roads. Ahmad, lying across her lap, had slept deeply for the first couple of hours. Zahra, cramped among the shifting boxes, stayed awake. No one spoke to her. Then Ahmad woke suddenly. He fidgeted and said he needed the toilet.

The van was labouring hard in the mountainous terrain. At times it freewheeled down the rough roads, then struggled up as Ali ground the gears and cursed. Suddenly it lurched sideways, rocked down a slope and stopped. Ali slammed out of his cab and she heard his footsteps crunch across the ground. He flung the rear doors open. Outside the night was pitch black and a fierce cold wind rushed in.

'Get out and shut up,' the driver ordered.

He snapped off the van's lights, plunging them into blackness. Holding Ahmad firmly, she groped towards the thin beam of

Firzun's flashlight. The stranded van creaked and pinged as the engine cooled.

'I need a wee wee,' Ahmad wailed.

She helped him relieve himself at the back of the van, fumbling with his clothes in the darkness.

'I'm frightened Mummy,' he whispered.

'Move away from the van, Zahra,' Firzun's voice came out of the blackness. 'We've got to push it.'

It was a clear night, but there was little light from the thin crescent moon. She walked slowly, testing the ground ahead with each foot, unsure if her next step would plunge her and Ahmad over an unseen precipice. Her feet slipped on pebbles and stones. Her toe hit a rock; she stumbled and let go of Ahmad. She felt him fall sideways and she threw her hands out, desperately flailing round her body for him.

A MiG fighter jet screamed out of nowhere and distant explosions lit up the gloomy sky. For a second she saw Ahmad. He tripped as he ran towards her and then he disappeared.

'Firzun! Mahmoud! Help! Ahmad's gone!' She stumbled forward calling Ahmad's name.

'Stupid bastard child,' Mahmoud said as he gripped her arm.

'He's gone, he's gone!' she cried in terror. 'Over there ...'

'We'll find him, cousin.' Firzun sounded confident, reassuring.

She stumbled behind them, following the wavering flashlight, choking on the smell of the driver's cigarette close behind her.

'I told you to shut up,' Ali's voice came out of the dark. He pushed her in the back and then ran his hand over her buttocks. She recoiled and lashed out with her elbow. He grunted angrily, swearing at her under his breath. 'Better find the kid quick or I'm off.'

Firzun swung his flashlight low on the ground. 'Over there ... in the crater.'

He slithered down the sides of the hollow space, then staggered up the slope with the sobbing boy in his arms.

'He's all right,' he gasped. 'Get back to the van. We've got to push it out of the pothole.'

She sat awkwardly in the van while Ahmad sobbed and clung to her, begging to go home. Feeling desperate, she lay him down on the sacks and stroked his head. She heard the men arguing with each other, then the van jolted as they tried to right it. To her relief, Ahmad fell asleep and she covered him with more sacks. The vehicle was upright now and the men's voices were louder. Mahmoud was shouting in his high-pitched nasal voice. She recognised the tone; he was working himself up into a vicious tantrum. She crawled to the back of the van and peered through the film of dirt on the rear window. Firzun and Mahmoud were locked in a heated argument; the flashlight on the ground shone up at them making their faces look like eerie masks.

'This is madness, you bloody liar!' Mahmoud clenched a fist in Firzun's face.

'Listen, I've saved your damn life!' Firzun stepped back suddenly. Zahra gasped when she saw the glint of Mahmoud's knife.

'I'll slit everyone's throats and drive the van back myself,' Mahmoud screamed.

The men scuffled, grunting and gasping like animals. She cupped her hands against the glass, straining her eyes in the darkness. Someone kicked the flashlight and she saw Firzun grab Mahmoud's jacket.

'No one threatens me,' he snarled.

He raised his right arm as if warding off a blow and she saw Mahmoud fall sideways into the blackness.

The driver was still in the cab, urging the men to push the van.

'Something's wrong!' she yelled to him.

He ignored her and fiddled with the gear stick. He turned on the engine and then grated the gears. The van lurched up to the side of the road. As it righted itself, she was thrown backwards into the boxes. Ahmad woke up and crawled over to her, grabbing at her clothes. The driver revved the engine.

'Stop, stop!' Firzun shouted from the darkness.

Something terrible had happened, she knew it.

Ali got out, cursing. 'What the hell's going on?' He walked past the window and dropped down out of sight. 'God save us!' he said.

Zahra crawled back to the sacks with Ahmad, trying to reassure him. He started to cry when she told him she had to get out of the van. She pulled a bag of chocolate from her pocket, promising more when she got back. She tightened the scarf round her head, edged her way through the boxes and banged on the window. Firzun's face appeared, weirdly illuminated by the driver's flashlight.

'God protect us! It's Mahmoud,' he exclaimed.

'Let me out, Firzun!' The sour taste of panic stung her throat.

The door creaked as he opened it. He grabbed her arm as she half fell onto the stony ground. By the faint beam of the flashlight she saw Mahmoud lying on his back near the van. She gasped and Ali looked up from where he was squatting next to her husband.

'Put her back in the van,' he said roughly.

She ignored him and kneeled down next to Mahmoud. She touched his face. It was sticky with blood.

'Give me the light.'

She shone it on Mahmoud's face. There was a large gash on his right temple and he was completely still. The driver stood up and lit a cigarette.

'Mahmoud, Mahmoud.' She shook his arm. She looked up at Firzun, a deep sick feeling in her stomach. 'What happened?' she whispered.

Her cousin kneeled down next to her. 'It was an accident,' he answered.

She looked back at her husband's face. His glasses were gone. The wound was bloody, but no blood ran from it. She put her hand on his chest. There was no movement.

'Try the neck,' Ali said hoarsely from the darkness.

Firzun placed his fingers under Mahmoud's left ear. 'Nothing,' he said quietly.

'Give him a shake.' Ali walked over to them. He spat his lit cigarette onto the ground, then got hold of Mahmoud's shoulders and shook him roughly. 'Wake up, you, wake up!' he shouted.

Firzun pushed him away.

Ali lit another cigarette. 'He's dead. We've got to get rid of him,' he said. 'Stick him in that crater where the kid was.'

'No! He needs a doctor!' Zahra looked up at them as a wave of panic swept over her.

She couldn't do this journey without a husband! However bad he was, she needed a man to protect her and Ahmad. She took one of his hands in hers. It was warm. She felt for his pulse, playing her fingers on different parts of his wrist, convinced that she would feel a faint throb. She slid her hand inside his thick jacket, searching for his heart. There was no beat, no movement of his chest. She laid her cheek near his mouth, seeking his breath. He was completely still.

In the feeble light, Mahmoud's features looked like wax. His eyes were closed as if he were sleeping.

'He's not dead ... he can't be!' She looked up at her cousin. The stony ground cut into her knees and the cold air soaked through her coat. She staggered to her feet and a sense of unreality overwhelmed her.

Firzun kneeled down, and after he'd tapped his cheek and said his name, he felt inside Mahmoud's jacket, leaning low over his body. Her cousin stood up slowly. 'He's dead. You're free of him,' he murmured. 'God rest his soul.'

Mahmoud was dead! She couldn't believe it. She covered her face with her hands and concentrated on the throbbing darkness.

The driver pushed past her. 'Got to get rid of him,' he said.

'But ... he has to be washed ... we have to pray,' she remonstrated.

'Shut up, woman. You! Get the shoulders.' He jerked his head at Firzun.

They staggered as they picked up the body between them.

'The light, Zahra,' Firzun commanded.

Her hands shook as she walked ahead of them and lit the path. At the crater where they'd found Ahmad they knelt and rolled Mahmoud's body down. She heard it dislodging earth and pebbles, then silence. She tried to remember the prayers for the dead, but her mind was a blank. She repeated the opening words of the holy Koran like a mantra: '*Allah u Akbar b-ismi-llāhi r-raḥmāni r-raḥīmi ...*' (Praise be to God, the compassionate, the merciful) '*Allah u Akbar b-ismi-llāhi r-raḥmāni r-raḥīmi ...*'

She forced herself to look into the crater, faintly illuminated by the flashlight. She saw a huddle of clothes—Mahmoud. The men slithered down and she heard them gabbling. A prayer? She wasn't sure. Then they kicked loose stones and soil over the body. They scrabbled back up the slope and Firzun propelled her forward, holding her elbow.

'We've got to get out of here ...'

He bundled her inside the van and Ahmad clung to her, sobbing. Firzun shoved the boxes round to cover the back window. Zahra staggered forward on her knees, her son grasping at her like a wild animal. When Firzun slammed the door behind them, she collapsed on the heap of sacks, bottling up her fear as she tried to calm her son.

'I want to go home!' Ahmad wailed.

'Not long now,' she lied as she wiped his face.

She tried to unwind his arms from her neck, but he clung to her coat. The driver revved the engine and the van lurched sideways. She was trembling with fear and cold. Firzun turned to her from the front seat.

'It was an accident,' he said. He was out of breath. 'We're near the border. I need your passports.'

She fumbled for them and handed them over. She looked down at Ahmad—he'd fallen asleep in her arms. She laid him down carefully.

The van lunged forward, throwing her against one of the boxes, and she heard something fall out. She felt around the floor and her fingers closed around a hard stone in a hessian bag. She was an Afghan woman and she knew without looking that it was opium resin, hidden among the fruit.

What if they were stopped and searched at the border? Stupid, stupid men! She glanced at the driver's cab—they weren't looking. She put her hand in the box and moved it round. There were lots of tiny bags hidden among the apples. With Firzun, there was always a second agenda, but still, she was stunned. What did he need drug money for? Was it for one of Nasim and Rashid's radical causes? And what about her? Now that Mahmoud was dead, was there any future for her in Tehran? She'd get their passports back from Firzun once they were over the border and go home. She could live with Fatima Gul, her friend. She'd tell Firzun when they got to the safe house. Her head ached with plans and possibilities.

She leaned against the wall of the van feeling drained. She was a widow. A *widow*! She dozed, and then woke suddenly as the van veered across to the right and stopped. Ahmad stirred in his sleep.

'*Khanoum!*' the driver barked. 'Iranian border. Stay there and shut up.'

Her throat was dry with fear and dust as she squinted at the pale pre-dawn light that filtered through the window above the boxes. Someone was talking to Ali. She lay down on the sacking and curled Ahmad close into her body. Footsteps crunched on the dirt. A voice asked for names and passports.

'Ali, and I'm Mahmoud,' Firzun said.

Had she heard right? She strained her ears trying to catch what they were saying.

'Wife and kid in the back, Zahra and Ahmad.'

'We're taking fruit to the markets in Taybad,' Ali added casually.

She heard the man walk away. Nobody spoke. She jumped when she heard footsteps near the side of the van. Through a gap in the boxes she saw the outline of a man by the back window. He was muffled in a thick coat and fur hat. His rifle swung forward and hit the van as he peered through the dusty glass. She pulled Ahmad closer, her heart thudding in her chest.

'Just boxes and the woman and kid,' Ali said. She heard the rustle of papers.

'You got some stuff?' a man's voice asked quietly.

'Yes, I got,' Ali replied. 'Here ...'

The man grunted with pleasure. 'Okay, passports, keep the papers for when you leave,' he said in an official tone. '*Khodafez. Allah u Akbar! Salaam* to the Ayatollah!'

They drove away from the checkpoint into the pre-dawn of an Iranian day. She sat up and leaned back on the cold van, trembling with relief.

'We've made it, Zahra!' Firzun announced.

She adjusted her headscarf and clothes. There was only one thought thudding through her brain: Mahmoud was dead—buried in the mountains, and she was a widow with a young child. She shuddered—somehow she had to get back home.

4

THE HOUSE IN THE VILLAGE

Zahra stared ahead, dry eyed. She wanted to ask Firzun why he'd assumed Mahmoud's identity. It could only mean one thing: he was a wanted man in Iran as well as in their own country. He needed her and Ahmad to legitimise whatever he planned to do here. She leaned her head back against the cold metal of the van wall, trying to get her thoughts in order. Every time she closed her eyes she saw Mahmoud's bloodless face and still body. When the van slowed, she opened her eyes and moved Ahmad, who lay asleep on her lap. The boxes had shifted, and in the early dawn light she could see out of the rear window.

They were passing the mud brick walls of village houses, some with small windows cut into the adobe. The dawn prayer call began, echoing eerily round the deserted street. An untethered goat raised its head as they passed and a cockerel crowed loudly, startling her. She saw a few men shuffling through the courtyard door of the village mosque.

The van lurched down a slope into a narrow lane and stopped, and Ahmad woke with a start. Ali banged on the side of the van and told them to get out. He threw open the door as Zahra was fastening her headscarf.

'Quick!' he rasped, pulling Ahmad down while she struggled out with the bags. Firzun grabbed Mahmoud's bag from her and slung it over his shoulder. He strode ahead, jerking his head for her to follow him along the deserted lane.

The smell of wood smoke on the autumn air filled her nostrils and the pale morning light blinded her temporarily. She narrowed her eyes and looked round, half expecting to see Mahmoud ahead of her. The *azan-e sobh*, the first prayer call of the day, ended abruptly. In the sudden silence a dog started barking. Mahmoud's dead, she thought. She couldn't believe it.

They stopped outside a door in a high mud brick wall. Ali held it open with one hand, motioning them forward with the other as he looked furtively up and down the dusty yellow lane. She stepped down carefully with Ahmad into an earthen-floored courtyard surrounded by high walls. Ahead was a single-storey house completely hidden from the lane, with dark windows on either side of the wooden front door. The only sound was the wind scattering piles of old leaves across the empty courtyard. A rough wooden table and chairs stood unoccupied beneath a makeshift overhang, which bent under the weight of an overgrown green-leafed vine. She shivered as Ahmad nestled into her side, hiding his face in her clothes. She pulled him closer.

Ali banged on the front door. A woman's voice behind it told them to wait, she was finishing her prayers. The door opened slowly, revealing an old woman. She'd thrown a floral chador around her shoulders and head. The hem of her long black skirt was flecked with mud and her thick house shoes made her skinny ankles look like sticks. She glared at them and pulled the chador around her against the morning chill. The pink rose pattern on the voluminous garment emphasised her dark complexion and sharp nose.

'Fix her up,' Ali ordered, indicating to Zahra and motioning Firzun to follow him.

'Welcome,' the woman said reluctantly in a thick local accent. She pointed to the rows of slippers lined up near the door.

'Put them on,' she ordered, nudging them forward with her foot.

Zahra took off her shoes and slid her feet into the greasy brown vinyl slippers. As she bent to untie Ahmad's sneakers, she caught her breath—how bad he smelled! The woman watched them impassively, then she helped Ahmad down the step into the house.

'*Mashallah*! God protect him,' she said in a softer tone as Zahra steered her son ahead of her into the large kitchen.

Although she felt shaky and disoriented, Zahra glanced round curiously. Cotton *gelims* covered the earth floor, and the smell of baking bread from a large fuel stove made her stomach lurch with hunger.

'You've got to wash and change, hurry up,' the woman urged. 'This way.' She jerked her head impatiently towards the back of the house. Holding a door open with her body, she frowned as she waited for them to follow down a dark passageway.

'Take what you need. Leave your bag here.' She indicated a turquoise painted room full of mattresses and boxes of clothes. 'Washroom's this way.' She handed Zahra two rough towels, washcloths and a small piece of soap, and led them past tightly closed doors along a cold passageway to a primitive bathroom. 'Wash the child, send him to the kitchen. Hurry up, don't leave any clothes in there. Put that on when you've finished, no hair showing.' She shoved a large black headscarf and long chador into Zahra's arms.

The only light in the gloomy room came from a small high window and a chilly draft rattled the cracked glass. The freckled grey stone floor crumbled at the edges where it joined the wall. A chest-high earthenware urn of water stood in a corner with a pan attached to the side for washing. Zahra helped Ahmad out of his filthy clothes, then dipped the pan into the icy water and washed him. He yelled out loud when she ran the freezing washcloth over his body and whimpered when she rubbed him dry with the rough towel. When he was dressed she told him to go to the kitchen. He pouted and said he'd wait outside the door.

Zahra shook with delayed shock as she washed herself, then dressed quickly in pants and a light wool jumper. When she put on her fresh clothes, they smelled of home and she burst into silent tears. She stopped suddenly when the sound of men's voices drifted into the washroom through the high window. She wound the black headscarf quickly over her hair and moved closer to listen.

'I hid the stuff ... they wouldn't come here ...' It was Ali, the driver.

'You don't think so, idiot?' another voice said and he spat on the ground. 'They run this place!' Chairs scraped and they moved away.

Zahra shivered with fear. She was an Afghan; she knew who he was talking about. The Mujahedin roamed the mountainous border regions of Afghanistan and they controlled the opium trade. Was Ali trying to outwit them? He must be mad; no one ever outwitted the Mujahedin and survived.

She clamped her hair out of sight with a headband under the headscarf, and fastened her black chador by its two strings over her dark clothes. She opened the door, took Ahmad's hand and retraced their steps back to the kitchen. Although she'd felt hungry before, she had lost her appetite now as she forced herself to listen to Firzun's instructions.

'We eat now, then leave for the nearest town. We're catching the bus to a bigger town from there in a couple of hours.'

'What's going on?' she asked him, glancing over her shoulder at the old woman who had her back to them. 'You used Mahmoud's passport.'

'It's dangerous here for you—alone with a child,' he muttered. 'It's for your safety. I'm officially your husband Mahmoud now. Trust me, Zahra.'

She drew breath to protest, but he pushed an envelope across the table. 'Papers for you and the boy. I've got Mahmoud's. We'll separate on the bus. You'll be better with the women at the back.'

She stuffed the papers into her handbag. 'Firzun ...' she began.

A volley of shots from an automatic rifle hit the outside wall and he leapt to his feet. The courtyard door crashed open and she heard more shots. Food and dishes crashed to the floor as he threw the wooden table on its side and pulled them behind it. The old woman crouched for shelter with them.

'It's the Mujahedin!' she squawked.

Shuddering with fear, Zahra curled her body round Ahmad. Next to her, the old woman rocked and called on God to save them. A window shattered and Ahmad sobbed with fright.

'We lost time,' Firzun muttered. 'They followed us. They're shooting in the air to scare us.'

'Where is it?' a man's voice yelled. They heard Ali pleading.

'In the van, under the fruit, God protect me.'

There was a single gunshot then silence.

Heavy footsteps crunched across the courtyard and Zahra closed her eyes. She could hardly breathe, and bile rose in her throat. She held her breath, her senses heightened to pick up the slightest sound. Someone was walking around outside near the house. She heard a click, then bullets smashed through the windows and rebounded off the walls. Firzun was wrong: they weren't shooting in the air. Empty cartridges clinked as they hit the ground. Suddenly a car engine started up and tyres screeched. A deep stillness descended on the house.

'Zahra,' Firzun's voice was a hoarse whisper, 'are you all right?'

'Yes.' The word stuck in her dry throat.

She uncurled herself from the crouched position where she was holding her terrified child. Firzun stood up cautiously and looked round, blinking in the light. 'They've gone. Let's get out of here!'

Ahmad clung to her clothes, his face buried in her waist. The old woman stopped praying and started cursing.

'Zahra, now!' Firzun called over his shoulder as he headed for the door. They ran over broken glass, smashed crockery and spilled food. The *gelims* glittered with crystal shards; the curtains hung drunkenly and swung in the cold draught from the gaping windows. There was an eerie silence, then she heard voices: two men calling for their mother.

She pushed Ahmad into his parka and struggled to get his feet back into the sneakers. She pulled on her shoes. Two men were running across the courtyard. She looked up and saw Ali slumped in a pool of blood on the ground. She turned away, her stomach heaving with revulsion, and stood between Ahmad and the body. She recognised the voices of the rough, bearded village men. She'd heard them minutes ago through the washroom window.

They grabbed Firzun by the arm. 'The van's empty, burned - stuff gone. They shot Ali. We'll deal with them.'

'Just get us out,' Firzun said.

He grabbed Zahra's arm. 'Hurry up. Dariush can get us to the bus station.'

He dragged them past the smouldering wreck of the black van as they followed Dariush. She shuddered and looked away. A siren echoed in the distance.

'Quick, it's the police.' Firzun looked over his shoulder.

She half walked, half ran with Ahmad. They got to an old car hidden among some straggly trees near a chicken run.

'Woman and boy in the back,' Dariush ordered, flinging open the driver's door.

The car lurched up a slope, and then stopped suddenly, still hidden by the trees. Another car passed on the lane above them in front of the house. She heard doors slamming and a voice called out: 'Police, don't move!'

'Get down,' Dariush growled, inching the car slowly forward until he was parallel with the lane. 'They're in the house. They won't see us,' he muttered.

He swung the car up onto the road. As he accelerated, it careered from side to side. She raised her head and saw the police car outside the walls of the house, now receding in the distance. Dariush pulled his ramshackle vehicle onto the main street and raced through the village. People stared and jumped out of the way.

'Keep your head down woman,' he snarled.

Zahra obeyed quickly and lay down across the seat, her arm thrown protectively across her son. She clenched her fists, trying to control her trembling body. She pulled the end of the scarf across her face. The smell of oil, grease and stale body odour made her feel sick to her stomach.

She clung to Ahmad as they were thrown from side to side in the back seat. It was impossible to lie down for longer than a few seconds. She risked another look outside, then felt nauseous again as the car swung wildly round a battered-looking minibus. She stroked her son's head; his hair was flecked with dust from the old house. When he turned his face up to look at her, it was blotchy with tears and streaked with dirt. He wiped his sleeve across his runny nose.

'Are we going home?' he asked as she cleaned his face with her handkerchief. She shook her head. 'Not yet.'

She risked another look out of the window. They were coming down from the mountain village now towards a bare open plain. To her relief, the mountains were far behind them and the air whistling through the gaps in the windows felt warmer. The sun had risen and the sky was a harsh cloudless blue. Dariush drove fast, swinging round farm trucks and honking the horn. She tried to tuck herself and Ahmad into a corner of the seat. Every bump jarred their bodies and jolted them backwards and forwards.

In spite of the wild drive, Ahmad had drifted off to sleep. The car slowed down at last. She sat up, ignoring Firzun's glare from the front seat and looked out the window. Dariush was negotiating a traffic island with a dry fountain at its centre. Maybe this was where they'd catch the coach. The small town was already awake, its footpaths full of women scurrying along in ankle-length black chadors or sweeping in and out of the small shops along the main street. There was a teahouse where men drank and talked and smoked bubble pipes. Zahra put her hand across her eyes. It was hard to absorb the mundane street scenes. Every time she closed her eyes, she saw her dead husband and the murdered driver.

'Coach station,' Dariush said as he slammed the brakes.

Firzun flung open the car door and pulled Ahmad onto the footpath. She hardly had time to scramble out into the gutter before the car took off.

'Wait in the women's room.' Firzun pointed. 'Get some food. I'll buy the tickets. The coach leaves in an hour. Listen for the announcement for Mashhad.'

5
COACHES

People pushed past them speaking Farsi. Although she spoke it fluently, she felt nervous about her slight foreign accent. Would someone call the police if they picked her as different? She took a deep breath and adjusted her shoulder bag across her chest. She gripped her overnight bag tightly in one hand and Ahmad in the other. His hand in hers felt small and hot.

Her long black chador reached below her shoes and at every step she feared that she would trip on the hem. The hair band that clamped her hair back felt hot and uncomfortable under her voluminous scarf.

She looked up at a billboard with an image she recognised from the newspapers in Afghanistan. The Ayatollah Khomeini glared down at them, making her shiver. He was dressed in black with a black turban and grey beard. His fierce hard eyes stared out across the coach station. 'God bless the Ayatollah, saviour of our country' it said above his picture. None of the scurrying people gave the poster a second glance.

Several coaches were parked in front of the main building. A printed notice inside the windscreen of one of them said '*Mashhad*'.

On another it said '*Herat*'. Her heart flipped—she knew it! She could go home from here! She'd tell Firzun.

Suddenly, to her amazement, she saw Mahmoud across the street. Her heart sank. How had he got here? He was looking for them; he wasn't dead after all!

She hesitated, wondering whether to hide in the women's room, but if he turned and saw her, he'd think she was running away from him and punish her. Pulling Ahmad along with her, she stepped off the footpath. She weaved round the traffic to the other side of the road. She called his name quietly, then louder and more insistently.

'Mahmoud! Mahmoud, wait!'

'Zahra!' Firzun's voice brought her to her senses.

He swept Ahmad into his arms and grabbed her bag. He pushed her back across the busy road towards the women's waiting room.

'I ... I thought I saw Mahmoud over there!' She pointed.

Firzun stopped, put Ahmad down, and glared at her.

'He's dead, Zahra.' His face was tense.

She stared at him, lost for words.

'Pull yourself together. *I'm* your husband now. Don't wreck everything! Get in here.'

She stood on the threshold of the women's room, trying to clear her thoughts. A cacophony of women's voices and wailing children assaulted her ears.

'Get moving!' a harsh voice shouted. 'You're blocking the doorway!'

Someone pushed her in the back and she stumbled into the room. Ahmad clung to her as she staggered forward. She looked round at the rows of wooden benches crammed with women and children. The floor was bare stained boards. She put her hand over her mouth to quell a rising nausea. There was a terrible stench of body odour and urine, mingled with the smell of tea and cooked meat. She clutched her things and stepped aside quickly as a group of village women shoved past.

'There's space here,' a young woman holding a swaddled baby

called to her. She moved along the bench as Zahra took the place and sat Ahmad on her knee. The woman was garrulous but kind and offered to mind her bag. She pointed out a place to order food.

'The toilets are filthy,' she confided.

The woman was right about the toilets. Zahra gagged at the smell when she opened the door. Each cubicle with its stinking hole in the floor was wet and slippery. She helped Ahmad relieve himself, trying not to retch as she fastened his pants. On the way back she ordered some food at the counter, fumbling with the unfamiliar money Firzun had pushed into her hands.

She sat down again next to the young woman, but her friendly chatter sounded as if it was coming from another planet. It was an effort to eat the food, but she was thirsty and the tea was welcome. She was conscious of Ahmad standing next to her, talking and eating hungrily. She looked ahead unseeing, unhearing. God help me, we left Mahmoud in the mountains, she thought, the words drumming ceaselessly through her mind.

The woman pulled her sleeve. She blinked and the image of Mahmoud's dark shape dissolved.

'They're calling the coach to Mashhad now. *Khodafez!* God protect you. Have a good journey.'

Zahra stood up and was carried along by the tide of women heading for the door. She squinted in the brightness outside. When she saw Firzun waiting for them, relief washed over her. He pushed through the throng and picked up Ahmad.

'I've got your coach ticket,' he said. 'You and Ahmad sit with the women at the back. It's six hours to Mashhad.'

She grabbed his arm. 'I'm going back home. I can get a coach to Herat from here. You're better without us!'

He glared at her and a frisson of fear ran through her body.

'Listen,' he said quietly. 'You've got to get on that coach to Mashhad with me. You can't go home. The police are looking for Mahmoud and they're probably at your flat right now.'

'What?'

'You know nothing about what he was up to ...' Firzun began.

A loudspeaker announcement for the coach interrupted him.

'For God's sake, trust me, Zahra. You *can't* go home,' he finished.

She followed him reluctantly past shops that smelled of spices, rice cooked with saffron, greasy grilled lamb and strong cigarettes. When Firzun stopped at the coach, she made one last effort to refuse, but he took her arm and steered her towards the steps. She covered her mouth, trying to swallow the tears.

'Pull yourself together!' Firzun hissed under his breath. 'You'll wreck everything.'

'Don't cry, Mummy.' Ahmad looked up at her fearfully.

She heard Firzun's burst of exasperation close to her ear. 'Get on the damn coach! I'll fix up your luggage.'

She stumbled on her long chador as he forced her up the steps.

'Tickets,' Firzun said, pushing them at a young man.

'Welcome,' he said pleasantly, glancing at the tickets. 'Madam and the little fellow at the back, seat number 40 and 41. You're in the front, sir.'

She couldn't look at him, ashamed that he had seen the angry exchange between her and Firzun.

The coach was clean, but old and smelled of cigarettes and stale rosewater. She shuffled her way to their seats, avoiding eye contact with the other passengers. Ahmad climbed up onto the plush seat and pressed his nose to the window, his previous distress forgotten. She glanced round quickly; there were several other women with children and a couple of them smiled at her. She looked away, convinced that they'd seen her altercation with Firzun. There were village women who talked excitedly to each other in their harsh accents about a wedding they were going to.

As she sat down, she heard the woman behind her say urgently, 'Look out ... the Revolutionary Guard!'

There was a flurry as the women fiddled and pulled at their

head coverings and bunched their chadors closer to their necks. Zahra watched in alarm as four men walked purposefully across the car park towards the coach. Each man carried a semi-automatic weapon. They looked irritable and angry.

An older woman who was sitting across the aisle motioned to her urgently. 'I'm not showing any hair am I?' She leaned forward in her seat so that Zahra could check.

'No, what about me?'

'You're fine. We have to be careful, they're even stricter here than in the capital.' The woman dropped her voice to a low whisper. 'They're just village lads, not very bright.'

The woman had an educated accent and she looked nervously at Zahra from across the aisle. Like Zahra she wasn't wearing any makeup. Before she could say any more, the men boarded the coach and Zahra felt a cold shiver down her spine. The four bearded young men were dressed identically in light grey, loose-fitting tunics over baggy pants. They pushed their way down the narrow aisle, their weapons slung loosely over their shoulders. Rounds of bullets on low belts hung below their waists.

Their leader started shouting as soon as he got near the women. '*Allah u Akbar! Allah u Akbar!*'

Some of the terrified women replied, '*Allah u Akbar!*'

'All women,' the leader proclaimed loudly, 'must be decently dressed or they'll be arrested and put in prison.'

The women patted their headscarves, smoothed chadors and ran their fingers round their hairlines. The menacing group came nearer. Zahra jumped when the woman opposite her tapped her arm and handed her a mirror. 'Final check.'

Zahra looked in the tiny mirror, and was shocked when she saw her face. Her red-rimmed eyes had dark shadows under them, her skin was pale and drawn, and her lips bloodless. Even to herself she looked desperate. But no hair was showing from under the tightly drawn scarf. The long pants she wore under her chador came down to her ankles and her sensible walking shoes, her own shoes from home, fit snugly on her feet.

'Friends, I've got to leave now to keep on schedule,' the driver shouted down the coach to the intruders.

'Yes, go, go, go,' the leader replied. 'You can drop us at ...' He said a place name—it could have been minutes or hours away for all Zahra knew.

'You can't stand on the coach longer than ten minutes, that's the law,' replied the driver.

'We're the law now,' a young guard replied impudently. 'You drop us where we want.'

The driver didn't reply as he swung the coach out of the parking bay sharply, compelling the men to grip the headrests of the seats to keep their balance. As soon as the coach was on the highway, the men continued to the women's area at the back. Zahra's fellow passenger across the aisle gave her a nervous look as the group swaggered down the coach. Her travelling companion was right; they were teenage boys with wispy, badly cut beards. But the guns were real enough. What if they asked for passports or papers? At each seat they leaned forward and stared hard at the women. The village women pulled their shawls across their faces. Zahra's face was tense with fear, her hair was scraped back under the scarf but she felt totally unprotected from the insolent ogling. The teenagers were now only two rows in front of her and her heart was hammering in her chest.

Suddenly a large village woman on the opposite side of the coach threw her arms out.

'Mohammad!' the woman screeched.

The group leader looked closely at the woman and said nervously, 'Aunty Zohreh?'

'Aye, Ayeeeee! Your mother's worried to death about you.'

The young man straightened up. 'I'm a fighter in the Revolution now.'

'We're all so proud,' said his aunty. 'Go and see your mother. She thinks you're dead. Allah be praised, you're alive!'

She grasped hold of him and he raised her work-worn hands to his forehead. She stood up with difficulty in the narrow seat, gathering her clothes around her bosom and adjusting her large headscarf. She addressed the other women on the coach: 'Sisters, this is my nephew Mohammed. He was named after the Prophet. Peace be upon him. *Allah u Akbar!* My nephew's alive!'

'*Allah u Akbar!*' the other women answered quickly.

'Get off this coach, nephew, we're near our village. Go and see your mother,' croaked the old woman.

One by one the young men took her hands and put them to their foreheads. Then, led by Mohammad, they strutted back up the coach and told the driver to stop because they were getting out. Zahra watched in amazement as the armed men stood like school children, waving until it was out of sight.

Aunty Zohreh leaned round her seat. 'My nephew was the stupidest child at school,' she announced to the other women. 'He hasn't changed.' She cackled loudly.

She rearranged her bulk on her double seat, opened a bag of pistachio nuts, peeled their skins and cracked each nut open with her teeth. She ate noisily, discarding the pistachio shells on the floor of the coach. Zahra leaned back against the headrest and put her shaking hands over her face.

'Wasn't that awful?' a voice said.

She dropped her hands and looked across the aisle again at the woman who'd lent her the mirror.

'I'm Soeheila.' She smiled.

'I'm Zahra and this is Ahmad.' She pointed to her son, who was still looking out the window.

'I'm not travelling with my husband,' Soeheila said quietly. 'He was arrested four months ago because he was a government minister under the former shah.' She looked round nervously. 'I've been to visit my daughter in Taybad—it's an awful place. Her husband's a doctor, but he's been sent here to work by the new government—he used to work in a prestigious hospital in Tehran. He says the hospital here is dreadful—very run down. My daughter's depressed. She's just had a baby and she's longing to come back to Tehran.'

Soeheila's unburdening was into its stride. She looked round again and dropped her voice even lower.

'The whole family is being punished. My oldest son has lost his job. He's determined to get his father released. My younger son is with me. He's only fourteen. They made him sit up at the front of the bus. I'm so worried; my husband has a weak heart.'

Tears welled in her eyes and she raised her silver rimmed glasses and dabbed them away with a handkerchief.

'These are terrible times, terrible times.'

Zahra nodded sympathetically, close to tears herself. Soeheila smiled at Zahra and indicated Ahmad.

'Your little boy has fallen asleep. We'll talk later.'

Ahmad, still sitting on his cushion, had slipped sideways in his seat. Gently Zahra eased the pillow from under him and placed it on her lap. She arranged him comfortably and stroked his head.

'Mashallah, God protect him.' Her neighbour smiled again. 'This is the worst part of the trip, isn't it? The mountain roads are so bad. Was your husband working in Taybad?'

Zahra shook her head; she had anticipated the question and replied as smoothly as she could. 'No, we went to visit my grandmother—she's not very well.'

'I'm sorry to hear that ...'

To Zahra's relief, any further questions were interrupted by the driver telling people to sit down as the mountain roads were dangerous. With a smile at Soeheila, Zahra checked Ahmad again. Before she eased her seat back, she risked a look up the coach—she did not know if it was forbidden. She could see the back of Firzun's head and she felt better knowing that he was with her. She closed her eyes as the coach swayed from side to side, with the driver coaxing it round the bends in the rough roads. The smell of cigarette smoke drifted down from the men's area and lingered in her nostrils.

Once again the events of the previous night played relentlessly behind her eyelids. She shuddered; whatever sort of life was ahead of her, it couldn't be worse than the one she'd left. The coach hit a pothole, jolting her awake. She glanced across at Soeheila, who was reclining with her eyes closed. The story she'd told and the incident with the Revolutionary guards had alarmed her. Although she knew about the fall of the shah and the establishment of the Islamic Republic, being here and experiencing it firsthand was frightening. She closed her eyes again and tried to assemble her jumbled thoughts.

It sounded as if society in this country had been turned on its head. If government ministers could be arrested and put in prison, then what would happen to them if their false identity papers were challenged? What if the guards had suspected her? She stared out the window; the sun was high in the sky now and the bus was getting stuffy. Her mind wandered back to the day she'd accepted Mahmoud as a husband. She was unequipped for marriage, and now he was dead she would have to manage as a single mother.

She believed Firzun when he said he would look after them. Like the rest of the family, he knew how Mahmoud had treated her. Unlike them, he'd tried to help by giving her money for Ahmad. He usually came to her workplace to avoid contact with Mahmoud.

During the upheaval of finding the right coach to Tehran at the Mashhad terminal, she lost sight of Soeheila. She was travelling with a different coach line. Zahra sighed; her chance of learning more about life in Tehran from a kindred spirit had gone. She looked out the window at the darkening sky as their new coach started up and headed west towards the capital. As the coach raced along the road away from the lights of Mashhad, she saw a mosque and heard the *azan-e mahgreb*, the sunset prayer call. She shook her head; had it been only twenty-four hours since they'd got in the van in Herat?

That city was already fading into her past. As the sky slowly turned black and the coach started to grind its way upwards through more mountainous roads, she wondered what lay ahead. She hoped for a better life for her and Ahmad, and vowed never to be a victim again. She looked down and noticed that she was clenching her fists tightly. She prayed that such determination would be enough in a new country.

6

TEHRAN

Zahra slept deeply. When she woke, her eyes stung and her neck ached. The mountain landscape had given way to desert, then fields of crops. They were now in the outer suburbs of Tehran. Her memories of coming here with her mother were hazy. But the huge posters of the Ayatollah Khomeini on most of the sand-coloured apartment blocks weren't there ten years ago. Zahra shuddered; he looked like Mahmoud, stern and uncompromising.

When the coach stopped, she pushed her way off with the other women. Ahmad clutched her hand, making her fingers ache. Firzun was waiting for them on the footpath, smoking a cigarette. He wasn't carrying Mahmoud's bag, she noticed, only his own. He must have dumped it somewhere, she thought, but she was too tired to care.

'Rashid should be here. I told him ten o'clock,' he said, looking round restlessly when she joined him.

'Firzun, my friend, welcome, welcome!' a voice called out.

The men embraced each other, then Rashid turned to Zahra and she sensed his kindness, his concern. She lowered her eyes and returned his greeting, feeling as if she were watching the scene from a great distance. A handsome, well-spoken man in a short-sleeved shirt and jeans was greeting a shabby refugee in a black chador and headscarf who held a grubby child by the hand.

'I only met you briefly before,' Rashid said. 'It's good to make your acquaintance again, Zahra Khanoum.'

'Where's Daddy?' Ahmad said suddenly.

She looked up and saw the men exchange glances. Rashid raised his eyebrows—so he already knew about Mahmoud. Firzun must have phoned him, maybe from the roadside café when the coach stopped in the night. Rashid avoided the question and pointed to a dark blue car parked nearby, half in the road, half on the footpath.

'Do you like my car, Ahmad?' he said.

'The policeman's looking at it,' Ahmad replied.

'Is this your car?' the officer asked Rashid as they walked over to the vehicle. 'It's parked illegally.'

Rashid took a few notes from his wallet and pushed them into the top pocket of the man's uniform.

'I could arrest you for bribery. This is the new Islamic Republic, you know,' the policeman muttered.

'Let's forget it, eh?' Rashid answered nonchalantly as he opened the back door of the car for Zahra.

Ahmad scrambled ahead of her into the back seat and she followed him, moving his sneakers off the cream leather and telling him to sit down. Before they pulled out into the traffic, Rashid leaned out of the car window and gave the policeman another handful of banknotes. A wave of exhaustion swept over her and she closed her eyes. The car swung into the traffic, then stopped suddenly at some lights. She opened her eyes and saw Rashid, concern on his face, looking at her in the driving mirror. Were she and Ahmad going to be a problem for everyone? She closed her eyes again.

'Thanks for this!' Rashid said quietly to Firzun.

Her eyes fluttered open in time to see Rashid pat a small leather bag on Firzun's knee.

'Not much is getting through with the Soviets on the border,' Firzun answered.

'The movement needs money and so does Nasim's group. We've got to fight them—they're getting stronger every day. We've officially been the Islamic Republic of Iran for over six months now!'

Rashid's words washed over her and she wondered about his wife Nasim and her 'group'. In Afghanistan, Soviet troops patrolled the borders and there'd been sporadic anarchy in the streets of Herat. Here in Iran, religious vigilantes patrolled the coaches, elected ministers were in prison and Rashid needed money to fight the government. She stared, unseeing, out the window. Had Firzun brought her from one tinderbox to another?

They drove through grey streets, opening into wider city roads. As they crossed the city, she saw the large stores she remembered. The men hadn't changed but the smartly dressed women had gone. The few women she saw were swathed like her: in black chadors and headscarves. In spite of her fears and misgivings, she felt a thrill of excitement when the sky cleared to a bright blue and she glimpsed the Alborz mountain range that ringed the city. Tehran was bigger and richer than Herat and a well of hope sprang inside her. Ahmad pointed and chatted.

'I remember how well you speak Farsi,' Rashid said, his eyes observing her from the mirror. Firzun started to answer for her, but she interrupted him.

'Yes, I was a teacher in a private school for girls, and of course my mother ...'

'I'm so sorry, Zahra Khanoum, I'd forgotten what happened.' His eyes met hers briefly in the mirror again.

The car slowed down and they turned off the main avenue into a quieter tree-lined road. She saw a coffee shop with *La Parisienne* written on the window in gold letters. Women in chadors sat inside drinking and talking. Rashid turned right and stopped in front of a set of high bronze gates. He sounded the horn and the gates swung open. She tried to remember the house from last time, but it had been night-time then. She looked out at the long sweep of drive, which led to the two-storey house. She hadn't even realised then that it was painted white. As they struggled out of the car, Ahmad tugged her hand.

'Mummy, look, a water thing ...'

She turned and looked at the fountain, which splashed into a large pool in the middle of a lawn surrounded by colourful flowerbeds. A smart, grey-haired man greeted them from the shaded marble-paved veranda.

'Welcome, welcome, Firzun Agha ... and Madam. It's been such a long time ...' He shook Firzun's hand joyfully and ushered them forward.

'Habib, my friend,' Firzun replied warmly. 'This is my wife Zahra and our son Ahmad,' he said proudly.

Zahra shivered and bit her lip. So now the lies begin, she thought.

Mojgan—Habib's wife—and the housekeeper came forward and greeted them with a torrent of words. She remembered Zahra very well, she said. That sad business about her mother ...

'Rashid Agha and Nasim Khanoum live in the upstairs apartment now. Downstairs is empty, master and mistress are in America. *Mashallah!* God bless your son, what a beautiful boy!'

'My daddy's gone,' Ahmad told them. Zahra glanced at the smiling couple but they hadn't heard him.

'Shush,' she said quietly as they were ushered into the house. All the doors leading off from the wide hall were closed, except one. The dining room door was open a fraction and she glimpsed one of the plush chairs. She felt a piercing stab of sadness; she would never forget that evening or the room. She looked up and saw Nasim at the top of the stairs, observing her. She had hardly changed, Zahra thought, though she wore her hair lose, not scraped into a French pleat, and the thick make-up was gone.

'Firzun, welcome back! And Zahra, how lovely!' Nasim exclaimed.

She brushed her dark hair away from her face and ran quickly down to greet them all, shaking Firzun's hands warmly. She wore jeans and a brilliant white tee shirt with a long blue scarf looped loosely round her neck. She turned to Zahra, sympathy in her eyes.

'Welcome, Zahra! We meet in sad circumstances again. I'm so sorry about your husband. It must have been a terrible shock,' she said quietly as she shook her hand and kissed her briefly on both cheeks.

In two days, Zahra thought, I've deteriorated from a woman like Nasim, polite and well dressed, to a wretched widowed refugee.

'Oh, and you're a mother as well now, Zahra!' Nasim exclaimed.

She knelt down to Ahmad's height and took his small hand in hers.

'Hello darling, what a handsome boy you are! I've got some special slippers for you.'

To his delight she helped him into a pair of red Mickey Mouse slippers.

She smiled fondly at Zahra and handed her a pair of light cream ones. They followed Nasim up the thickly carpeted stairs and across a landing, which smelled of furniture polish and flowers. She ushered them into a spacious living room and Zahra stared around in amazement. She'd forgotten the huge living spaces wealthy people took for granted.

Three white sofas were arranged around a coffee table opposite a wall of windows, which gave an uninterrupted view across gardens and houses to the mountains she'd seen from the car window. The sunlight picked out the subtle colours on the brown crags—metallic blue, streaks of yellow, and deep shaded black.

'Your house is as beautiful as ever, Nasim Khanoum,' Zahra said sincerely.

Nasim smiled, showing her perfect even white teeth. 'Thank you, Zahra, this is only the upstairs apartment. My parents used to live downstairs—my father had lung problems and couldn't manage the stairs.' She sighed. 'They're in the States now ... Anyway, please take a seat and we'll have some tea. You must be hungry and tired after your trip.'

Zahra sat tentatively on one of the white sofas and looked round the room. One wall held tightly packed bookcases and on the opposite wall was a fireplace with an unlit log fire. There were photographs everywhere of weddings, babies and groups of well-dressed people. It all appeared untouched by the effects of the revolution and the changes she'd seen. But Firzun had told her that Nasim and Rashid still organised political meetings and it was probably still a very dangerous occupation.

She looked round for Firzun; he was standing with Rashid near a dining table large enough to seat eight people. Rashid selected a paper from the pile, which covered the surface, and handed it to Firzun, who frowned as he read it.

'Firzun knows his way round this house.' Nasim smiled fondly across the room at the men. 'He lived with us for five years, while he was studying.'

Zahra was surprised. Firzun had never mentioned that. She sipped the tea put in front of her and finished her chicken sandwich.

'I'll get Mojgan to take you to the room we've fixed up for you and Ahmad,' Nasim said. 'By the way, you know that Mojgan and Habib believe you're Firzun's wife?' she said quietly.

Zahra nodded and allowed herself to be steered towards the wide landing where Mojgan was waiting. She followed the woman into a large room with two single beds. Sunlight spilled into the room from a picture window that overlooked the garden. Mojgan smiled when Zahra admired the room and the view.

'The bathroom is this way, madam.' Mojgan threw open a door to the marble tiled ensuite bathroom. It was twice the size of her living room in Herat.

'Madam left some of her nephew's clothes out for Ahmad, and some toys.' Mojgan indicated a large box. 'And ... some things for you too.'

Zahra nodded, unsure of what she was expected to say.

'Your bag's here,' the housekeeper continued, pointing to where Zahra's bag stood on a piece of newspaper spread out over the blue carpet.

'Can I help you unpack, Zahra Khanoum?'

'Thank you, we're fine,' she answered quickly.

Mojgan cleared her throat. 'Nasim Khanoum told us about your husband dying suddenly of a heart condition last year. I'm so sorry to hear that,' she said hurriedly.

Zahra drew a quick breath, but before she could speak the other woman rushed on. 'Nasim Khanoum says Agha Firzun married you a couple of months ago and took on the boy. We're so glad.' She smiled indulgently at Ahmad. 'God bless him.'

Zahra felt as if she was staring open mouthed at Mojgan. Who'd concocted this elaborate lie?

'We loved Firzun Agha when he lived here, so courteous and polite, one of the family he was,' Mojgan rattled on. 'Then after the car crash the other year, just before Nasim Khanoum's wedding, when he saved Rashid Agha's life, the family couldn't do enough for him. Still, I'd better let you sort yourself out, if you don't need me.'

When she'd gone, Zahra sat down heavily on one of the beds, taken aback by what the housekeeper had said. She wondered how long Firzun intended to stay here and what she was supposed to do with her time. At least Nasim and Rashid knew the truth about Mahmoud's accidental death. Perhaps eventually they'd let her know about the lie they'd come up with.

After an early lunch with Nasim, she took Ahmad back to the bedroom for a rest. She didn't remember falling asleep, but when she woke with a start and looked at the bedside clock it was seven o'clock in the evening. She showered and dressed quickly, then unpacked their things. She woke Ahmad and showered him. Holding Ahmad's hand, she walked hesitantly into the main salon. Mojgan smiled up at her from where she was setting a cloth and plates on the floor for the evening meal.

'Doctor Maryam Milani is coming this evening,' she commented.

Zahra remembered Maryam vaguely from ten years ago. She'd been a medical student then and vociferous about women's rights. Zahra didn't relish listening to political arguments; she was still tired from the journey.

The conversation that evening *had* revolved around the politics of both Iran and Afghanistan. Guests had filtered in until there were fifteen people sitting on the floor, arguing and coming up with plans. It seemed that they were relying on her cousin, Firzun, to lead their counter-revolutionary group.

She lay awake later that evening, trying to make sense of her new situation. She was a widow pretending to be her cousin's wife and she wasn't sure why. Even though Mahmoud had been a terrible husband, she'd at least had some legal status. Now she had no idea what would happen to her, how long she and Ahmad could live here or when, if ever, she could go home.

Mahmoud wouldn't have fit in here, she thought suddenly; he was dispensable. Her heart quickened, remembering what Firzun had said in the mountains. 'He's dead. You're free of him.'

She looked across at the other bed, where she could see her sleeping son in the faint glow from the night-light. If she could give him a better life, then her recent sufferings had all been worthwhile. When she finally fell asleep, she dreamed that she was in a desert, watching vultures assault a body—Mahmoud's—tearing at his face, his chest, his limbs, and destroying him as she had longed to do so often.

7

MOURNING

Zahra woke with a start and looked round the strange room. Ahmad was tugging at the heavy curtains. She remembered with a shock that they were in Rashid and Nasim's house. In Iran! She jumped up, afraid he might damage something, and pulled the curtains open slowly. She blinked in the dazzling brightness and looked down at the garden below, dappled in sunlight. Pink flowers moved gently against a wall, and the spray from the nearby fountain arched in a rainbow across the grass. She stared at the green lushness, so different from the brown landscape she'd watched from the coach window, and a rush of tears tore through her body.

'Wait there till I call you, Ahmad. Play with your toys.' She tried to keep her voice steady as she grabbed some clothes and ran to the bathroom where she buried her face in a towel so that he wouldn't hear her sobs. As she showered, tears poured down her face unchecked.

'It's shock ...' she told herself. She pulled on the robe from behind the door and wrapped her hair in a towel. When she rubbed her hand across the steamy mirror, a miserable creature stared back at her. Hastily she splashed cold water on her face and dried it with the towel from her hair. She put on some makeup and a long-sleeved cream top and navy pants from the pile Nasim had left for her.

Ahmad didn't notice her distress as she showered and dressed him; he was too interested in the huge bathroom. After she'd dried her hair, she took Ahmad's hand, walked across the landing and quietly pushed open the living room door. Nasim sat alone at a small table near the window, waiting to oversee breakfast for them.

'Did you sleep well?' she asked solicitously.

'Thank you, yes.'

After breakfast Nasim found more toys for Ahmad, and then led Zahra to a sofa.

'You know that you're welcome to stay here as long as you like,' she began, patting Zahra's hand gently. 'A neighbour of mine runs a kindergarten from her house. She says she can take Ahmad.'

'He'd like that, he went to kindergarten in Herat,' Zahra replied, still feeling disoriented.

'You know ...' Nasim paused. 'We think it's best that no one knows Mahmoud's death was so recent, God rest his soul. We'll tell everyone that Firzun married you a few months ago and that Mahmoud had a heart attack last year.' She smiled.

Zahra nodded, and decided not to tell Nasim that Mojgan, the housekeeper, had already blurted out the lie. It crossed her mind again that things would be easier here without Mahmoud.

'Firzun will look after you and Ahmad, Zahra, and we'll take care of you as well. Mahmoud's accident was *terrible*. I do understand how you feel ... such a shock,' Nasim said quietly.

Zahra thought guiltily of the wave of relief that had swept over her when the men rolled her husband's body into the crater. She wondered if Firzun had told Nasim and Rashid about Mahmoud's violence towards her. The idea that they might know filled her with shame and she could hardly look at Nasim.

'Nasim, I want to work. If there's anything I can do.' She paused and met Nasim's eyes, not sure of what there was to do except go with them on any protest marches they were planning.

'There's always work, Zahra, thank you. Let's wait a while, after your seventh day of mourning is over,' Nasim replied. She glanced out the window. 'It's sunny outside and not too hot at the moment. Why don't you sit in the garden? Habib can put the umbrella up to give you some shade.'

Nasim opened the French window that led on to a wide terrace, and Zahra followed her down to the outside steps to a garden, cajoling Ahmad to come with them. At the bottom, they waited while Habib arranged the furniture and put up the large sun umbrella. Nasim motioned Zahra to one of the chairs set round a wrought-iron table. Ahmad rode off confidently down the path on a tricycle Habib had found for him.

'There *is* something you can do, Zahra,' Nasim said slowly. 'Not right away, of course. Do you remember Karim Konari?'

Zahra's heart leapt. How could she ever forget *him*? The memory was interwoven with her embarrassment about being so gauche, but also her anguish when she'd learned about her mother's death. Firzun had mentioned in passing that Karim had gone to the States. Was he back? Nasim was talking and she tried to focus.

'Karim's grandmother is terminally ill,' Nasim was saying. 'He got back from the States last week. He'll be living in the family home to be close to her. Esmat—his mother—is very busy and needs a companion for her mother-in-law. Someone to read to her, listen to her ... it's a live-in position.'

Zahra's mind was in a spin. A live-in position? In Karim Konari's house?

'If that's all right, of course,' Nasim added hastily. 'You can always say no, don't feel obliged ...' She stood up and dropped some glossy magazines on to the table without waiting for a reply.

'You need to rest now, Zahra,' she said, smiling down at her.

Zahra sighed. The air was warm and the sky a clear bright blue. She closed her eyes, listening to the click of Ahmad's tricycle as he peddled round. She wondered if she should write to Fatima and the teachers at the school ... but they all thought she was in Kabul. She picked up one of the magazines and frowned. The reality of her life hit her again. Mahmoud was dead. She was free! Ahmad was free! She felt relieved, but suddenly lonely, and wondered if she would ever see her women friends again. She thought of the job proposal, living in the Konari house. How long would Karim be staying, and did he have a wife and family in America? Maybe they were with him and Nasim had forgotten to mention it. She felt her head spinning again.

Nasim had had promised to help her through the proscribed mourning period, the third day, the seventh, the fortieth ... She didn't want to pray for Mahmoud's soul, but it seemed she had no choice. She closed her eyes, then opened them suddenly. The money! The money Mahmoud had withdrawn from their bank account. Where was it? Had Firzun got it? Had he taken Mahmoud's wallet from his body—or was it still there in his jacket pocket in the shallow grave at the bottom of the crater? She shuddered; she had half of the money but if Firzun had the rest of it she was determined to get it from him. She was angry with herself for not paying more attention.

She closed her eyes again, thinking of what Nasim had said: a job, a live-in position. Did Nasim want her out of the house for some reason? She wondered what Karim Konari would look like now. She couldn't imagine meeting him, let alone living in his mother's house.

Nasim's rapid footsteps on the outside stairs interrupted her thoughts. 'I'll come to the mosque with you tomorrow, Zahra. Let's say ten-thirty?' Nasim said as she sat down.

'Thank you,' Zahra replied reluctantly.

'I'm so sorry, Zahra, it's all, well ... it seems to have happened so quickly,' she said, reaching for her hand.

Zahra frowned, wondering whether *she* should tell Nasim the truth about Mahmoud's violence before Firzun did. She obviously didn't know. I can't, she thought as she looked at the sophisticated woman opposite her, it's humiliating.

A sense of unreality swept over her as she drank the tea she'd been given and half listened to Nasim talking about the neighbours —how so many of them had gone overseas to Israel or America, how she would point out the empty houses tomorrow on their way to the mosque.

'By the way,' she said suddenly, and Zahra forced herself to pay attention. 'Don't dress Ahmad in his Mickey Mouse tee shirt tomorrow—it's too American for the regime. They might stop us in the street.'

As they got ready for the visit to the mosque, an eerie feeling swept over Zahra. She felt that when she walked out the gate, she might step into a time warp and be in Herat, not Tehran. She shook her head and blinked, trying to clear her brain, trying to orientate herself.

'I find it so hard to wear these clothes.' Nasim sighed as she took her chador off the peg near the door and handed Zahra's to her.'I used to go out in jeans and a tee shirt this time last year. Now all women are forced to wear strict Islamic dress in public. I *swear* it won't be for long. We're going to fight for our right to dress as we please!' She pushed her hair under her black scarf and fastened her chador.

Zahra followed Nasim down the drive, holding Ahmad tightly by the hand. They'd lived in the old part of Herat and he was unused to city traffic. Nasim opened a side gate next to the huge wrought iron ones that shielded the house from the road. The street was wider than Zahra remembered and shaded by tall plane trees. She looked round at the high sand-coloured walls that lined both sides. Blossoms from the flowering trees, which hung over the walls, lay scattered before them on the footpath like petals from a wedding.

'Well, our suburb is called Elahiyeh and this is Maryam Street ... named after our friend Maryam! Her grandfather owned a lot of this land,' Nasim said with a smile. 'Most of the houses are the same size as ours.'

Enormous, Zahra thought. A little further on, Nasim pointed one out.

'This is where the Konari family lives. So if you take the job you won't be far away.'

Zahra caught a glimpse of another huge mansion through the gates as they walked past.

'And that is where Farah Khanoum runs the kindergarten,' Nasim said, looking down at Ahmad and pointing to another house as they passed.

'Farah's kindergarten in the city was closed down because she refused to spend hours teaching the Koran to the children.' Nasim lowered her voice, even though the footpath was deserted. 'Now she runs this clandestine one in her house. She staggers the times the mothers bring the children in case the authorities are watching the house.'

A sense of unreality washed over Zahra again—why would the authorities watch a kindergarten? She didn't have time to ask because they turned the corner into a wider, busier road. At the bottom of the hill she saw a small mosque, white and domed with one minaret. When she looked at the brown mountains behind it, a feeling of nausea swept over her. She tried to push her memories of Mahmoud's dead face to the back of her mind. But they haunted her dreams and were never far from her conscious thoughts.

'These are our local shops,' Nasim was saying as they walked down some wide steps past a shop with spices displayed in sacks and a small general store. A man sat on a stool outside a shop with cooking pots hanging round the door, mending an aluminium pan. He smiled at Ahmad and said, '*Mashallah*'—God protect him—as they passed.

'We didn't go skiing as usual this year. Things have changed so much,' Nasim said with a sigh. 'The shah's palace is in the next suburb, Tajrish, though of course he's gone. All the foreign embassies are there, except the US embassy—that's down town.'

The overload of information was making Zahra's head spin and she felt hot in her black clothes as the sun rose higher in the sky. She looked down at Ahmad; he had his hand over his ear and a pained expression on his face. Yellow taxis passed them, honking and swerving through the traffic, and a huge red bus puffed out diesel fumes.

After the noisy streets, the courtyard of the mosque was calm and quiet. A few women dressed like them in black chadors sat on benches in the shade, chatting to each other and passing round bags of nuts. As they walked across the courtyard, an older man dressed in a grey shirt, grey trousers and shoes grey with dust, motioned them towards the women's washing area. He pulled back a heavy blue vinyl curtain as he ushered them through, turning his face respectfully away from them.

Zahra was glad that there were no other women to witness her hypocrisy as they washed quickly and she sluiced the exposed parts of Ahmad's body. She was annoyed with herself for not bringing a small towel. The grey man was hovering around when they emerged.

'Women go in that door,' he said, waving a green feather duster towards the mosque.

'As if we didn't know,' Nasim said irritably under her breath as they slipped off their shoes at the door of the mosque.

They left them on the wooden shelves under the watchful eye of another grey man then walked inside, blinking in the dim light. Zahra looked round in surprise; the women's part of the mosque had been sealed off with a high wall, denying the women the sense of space that the large domed area usually afforded.

'Our mosque in Herat just has a separate area for women,' she whispered to Nasim although there were no other women around.

'The *regime* did this in all the mosques,' Nasim replied, looking annoyed. 'It used to be open here too.' Then she smiled. 'Anyway,

I've brought a few books and toys for Ahmad, so why don't I sit over there? You can say your prayers in peace, you poor thing.'

Sitting on the thick red carpet, Zahra prayed reluctantly for the soul of her tyrannical husband. The mosque was quiet and calm and she closed her eyes. Resting back on her knees, she remembered the first time he'd been violent towards her. It was less than a month after their wedding.

A teacher's meeting at work had run over time and when she'd arrived home, he was pacing the floor of their flat. He'd ignored her greeting and apology, so she went straight to the kitchen. She hadn't been aware that he was behind her until he'd grabbed her hair and twisted it sharply against her head. Her eyes had watered as she struggled to get away.

'Mahmoud, stop!' she'd protested.

'Why isn't the food ready?' he'd growled in her ear.

She'd tried to turn round, but he'd shoved her hard in the back, pushing her thigh into the handle of the oven. She'd yelled out in pain. After he'd eaten the food she'd served him in silence, she'd waited for him to apologise.

'You hurt me, Mahmoud,' she'd said eventually.

He'd ignored her and she'd gone back into the kitchen with her own food. He'd followed her, grabbed her arm and swept her plate onto the floor.

'Don't do that again!' he'd barked.

'Mahmoud!' Terrified, she'd tried to pull away, but he'd gripped her other arm and given her a fierce shake.

'Learn your lesson then, school teacher!' he'd shouted, releasing her and slamming out of the kitchen. Stunned and scared, she'd cleared up her broken plate. She'd leaned on the sink, staring at the dirty crockery, trying to stop trembling, wondering what on earth to do. He was calm and pleasant the next day as if nothing had happened. She'd tried to talk to him, but he'd raised his palm and stopped her each time.

'Forget it, Zahra. Just behave from now on,' he'd said finally.

It had taken a few more beatings to make her 'behave', especially in bed. The first time she'd refused him, he'd held her down against the mattress, his arm across her chest and forced himself violently into her. From then on, her life had become a living hell, brightened only by Ahmad's birth eighteen months after they were married. Her appeals to the family had always received the same answer.

'You're not bringing disgrace on this family with a divorce,' her Aunt Mina told her. 'You've made your bed, now lie on it!'

Defeated and miserable, she'd gone home. Firzun had supported her but couldn't get his mother to change her mind.

Zahra finished her prayers and joined Nasim, who was sitting quietly on the floor, looking through a picture book with Ahmad. The day was warm and clear, and on their way out of the mosque they passed people in the courtyard getting ready for midday prayers. She took a deep breath as waves of relief washed over her. *God forgive me, I'm glad he's dead!*

During her first week, Zahra got used to the coming and goings at the house and after her second visit to the mosque, she asked Nasim if she could help with anything. Nasim smiled and put her pen down, motioning Zahra to a seat.

'Do you remember what Maryam said about women suffering violence in their marriages and losing custody of their children?'

Zahra nodded, dreading what was coming next.

'Well,' Nasim continued, 'as a lawyer, I've represented many women who've killed their husbands. Some abused wives are pushed too far.'

Zahra looked away, thinking guiltily of the times her hand had closed over the handle of the kitchen knife, and she'd imagined killing Mahmoud while he slept.

'Anyway, a group of us send out letters to members of parliament. The religious people who've taken over haven't dismissed the government ... yet. I need someone to copy the same letter by hand, and make it look personal. That's one job.'

Zahra nodded—it sounded easy enough.

'The other is a letter to women about the march on Thursday, the first of November. I've got a Roneo duplicator downstairs for those. And,' she smiled, 'I've invited some women over next week. I'm sure you'll enjoy meeting them.'

'Oh yes,' Zahra said, but she dreaded meeting Nasim's smart friends.

'One last thing.' Nasim moved a few papers around on her desk. 'I'm waiting to hear from Esmat Konari about the job, if you're still interested. Remember? Companion to her mother-in-law?'

It seemed a far cry from fighting for women's rights, Zahra thought, but there didn't seem to be a choice, so she smiled again and nodded. Nasim cleared a space on the dining table and Zahra got to work.

She put her pen down, trying to imagine a future as a companion to an old lady. It was a comedown from her prestigious job at Herat Girls' College. But then she thought about Karim Konari and it blanked out her concerns. If he was living in the same house, she would have to deal with the situation. But what if she felt the same rush of attraction for him that she'd felt when she was seventeen? The thought of seeing him again was both disturbing and strangely exciting.

8
VISITORS

The following Tuesday morning, Nasim's friends arrived in a flurry of kisses and boxes of sweets. They all complained about wearing the chador, but when Nasim suggested they come on the march in support of women's rights, only a couple of them looked mildly interested. The others shrugged and shook their heads.

'Someone has to take a stand,' Nasim said firmly.

'Be careful, Nasim. My brother says people are being arrested for dissent, thrown into prison, even executed,' one of her friends said nervously. Nasim ignored her.

Zahra went to the kitchen to help Mojgan with tea and cakes, and when she came back into the room the women were leaning forward and talking in low voices. She heard Karim's name and someone laughed and said 'playboy'. They stopped talking when they saw her.

'Esmat Khanoum needs help and I think Zahra's the perfect choice, aren't you?' Nasim said with a smile as Zahra sat down.

'As I was saying,' she continued. 'More of our rights are going to be taken away from us. 'The decency police and the Revolutionary

Guard aren't a joke. They're thugs who harass women and we should protest or we'll lose everything.'

It didn't surprise Zahra that none of the women looked either interested or enthusiastic. They'd obviously had no experience of a violent marriage. She thought of her own life—what freedom had she had? 'If you try to leave me, I'll kill you,' Mahmoud had threatened, and she believed him. And as for Aunt Mina ... so much for women's *or* family solidarity!

The next day was bright and sunny again, and after she'd taken Ahmad to the kindergarten she settled down at the outside table. She'd copied nearly ten letters and was sealing an envelope when she heard the doorbell ring, then Mojgan's distant exclamations of delight. A few minutes later, Nasim called excitedly to her from the terrace.

'Zahra, Karim Konari's here! Come and say hello.'

She collected her papers and walked up the outside stairs. Although she tried to be calm, her heart was thumping hard against her ribs at the thought of seeing him again. Nasim held open the French window for her, pointed across the room and smiled. He had his back to her and was talking to Rashid and Firzun at the far end of the salon. Before he could turn round, she rushed to her bedroom, dumped her papers on the bed and did a quick check in the bathroom mirror, surprised at how well—and happy she looked.

She'd tied her hair in a plait to keep it out of the way while she worked and was wondering whether to loosen it when she heard Nasim's voice calling her. She quickly dabbed some lipstick on her mouth and hurried towards the salon. The first person she saw was Karim; he was sitting on the sofa, listening to Rashid. He looked relaxed and at home, as if he'd sat there many times before. They were all drinking large cups of American coffee.

He looked up when she came into the room; their eyes met and her heart lunged again—he'd hardly changed at all! She looked round for Firzun, but he'd gone.

'Here you are, Zahra!' Nasim beamed, putting her cup down. 'Let me *re*-introduce you to Karim Konari. Remember I mentioned his grandmother ...'

Karim stood politely and reached across the coffee table to shake her hand. 'Hello, Zahra, how are you?' he asked in his mellow voice.

Over the years she'd tried unsuccessfully to recollect this voice, but as soon as he spoke she knew she'd never forget it again. His handshake was both firm and gentle, making her feel like her seventeen-year-old self.

He was as tall and good-looking as she remembered him from ten years ago. He looked confident and comfortably wealthy in his light coloured polo shirt and smart blue jeans.

'I'm avoiding California at the moment,' Karim replied to a question from Rashid as he sat down. Zahra was wondering why, when he turned to her.

'So, Zahra.' His light honey-coloured eyes met hers briefly across the table. 'I believe you might be my grandmother's new companion.' He picked up his coffee cup and smiled his dimpled smile as she sat down opposite him.

'If your mother ... rather, Esmat Khanoum finds me suitable, I ...'

She dug her nails into her palms, determined to pull herself together. She wanted to stop being overawed by his fashionable looks, his thick, longish hair and that she owed him money for her airfare all those years ago ...

'Well, grandmother would love someone to talk to,' he went on. 'My mother's really busy.' He looked at Nasim.

'Karim's mother owns a fashion label and several boutiques called "Madam Leila" *and* she's the Managing Director of the family department store, Arezoo. Did I ever mention that, Zahra?' Nasim asked.

Zahra cleared her throat. 'No, I don't think so.' But she remembered Firzun's barbed comments about the Konari family wealth on her first visit to Tehran.

'Well,' Karim laughed, 'she says she's fed up with selling village gear, you know, scarves and chadors!'

He stopped suddenly and looked slightly embarrassed. He glanced at Zahra, then picked up his coffee cup again and took a sip.

Oh my God, does he think I'm a villager? she thought. Heaven knows what his mother's like—she's probably in the fashion magazines every month!

She would turn the job down, she decided. She didn't fit in with people like him. What if he found out about Mahmoud and how he'd treated her? She blushed with shame, then realised Karim was asking her a question.

'I'm sorry?'

'I said, I believe you're fluent in English?'

She nodded, dreading him testing her English. Her mind had gone completely blank.

'I studied English and Persian Literature at university,' she managed to say. He might think I look like a villager but I'm *not* a mute, she thought.

When he smiled, she remembered his even, white teeth and that his smile reached his honey eyes. She longed to just sit and talk to him like an equal.

'She'll *love* you, I know she will.' Karim turned to Nasim, his smile faded and he sighed. 'Grandmother ... she hasn't got long.'

'I'm sure that meeting Zahra will make her feel much better,' Nasim answered.

Zahra stared at her, wondering how to tell her she'd changed her mind.

'Well,' Karim glanced at the bulky silver watch on his wrist, '*Madar djan* is expecting me for lunch, so I must say goodbye.'

'I'll see you out,' Nasim said. 'Though you know you're welcome to stay here for lunch ... No, I suppose not!' She laughed when he pulled a comical face. Zahra stood as he shook hands with them all, then Nasim escorted him towards the stairs.

'I'll get on with my work,' Zahra said to Rashid as she stood up. He smiled his usual distracted smile and nodded.

As she was walking across the landing to her room, she heard Karim say her name. She stopped and looked down the stairs. He and Nasim were standing in the hall with their backs to her. Karim had his head on one side, listening intently to Nasim. Zahra moved round to the railing, just close enough to be invisible to the speakers below.

'Yes, I'm sure she'll take the job,' Nasim was saying.

'Mother will be *really* relieved,' he replied.

'My friends have told her you're a playboy!' Nasim reached up and patted Karim's face. Their casual intimacy fascinated Zahra. She watched jealously as Karim put his arm round Nasim and hugged her to him. No man in Herat would *ever* touch another man's wife like that unless she was his sister, Zahra thought. How different these people were!

'Playboy!' he laughed. 'Those days are long gone.' He released Nasim but kept his arm across her shoulders. 'I won't lay a finger on Zahra.' He laughed. 'Though *madar jan* might suggest she updates her hairstyle.'

'That's not important,' Nasim replied. 'Just remember that she's married.' The lie tripped neatly off Nasim's tongue.

'Oh yes, to Firzun the Afghan gangster,' he answered.

Listening on the landing, Zahra instinctively put her hand to her hair and grasped her plait. His casual remarks about her had stung. And Firzun might have his faults, but he wasn't a gangster, as far as she knew ...

'So what's the situation with Nancy? Are you still married?' Nasim asked quietly, shrugging Karim's arm off her shoulder.

Who's Nancy? Zahra wondered, holding her breath, unable to drag herself away.

'It's over,' he said with a sigh. 'It's our secret, Nasim. For God's sake, don't say anything—if mother found out I'd never hear the last of it.'

'Locked in the vault, Karim,' she replied seriously.

Zahra inched forward when Nasim opened the outside door. The bright sunshine flooded into the hall and picked up gold flecks in Karim Konari's hair as he stood, still talking earnestly to Nasim. Zahra sighed as she looked at them. Two beautiful people, so *cosmopolitan*: him in his smart casual clothes and Nasim in her jeans and light grey top, which fell in loose folds over her body.

Suddenly she remembered walking home from the cinema in Herat with her mother. Each week Firzun—the man Karim had reviled as a gangster—had dutifully escorted them and met them again afterwards. If it was an American movie they reminisced for days about the lovely houses, the heart-stopping love story and the beautiful people ... people like Karim and Nasim. It made life with Aunt Mina slightly more bearable.

Zahra looked down at the empty hall, choked by the memory. Would she have married Mahmoud if her mother hadn't died? Of course not, she would have protected Zahra.

She walked back to her room and gathered the scattered papers together. She felt alienated, desperately alone, and humiliated by Karim's comments about her appearance.

Did the new job mean that Nasim, and probably Firzun and Rashid, wanted her out of their politically charged house? It seemed there was no choice; she had to take the job and move. But she'd stay out of Karim's way. That wouldn't be too hard in the huge house she'd seen the other day. Anyway, according to Nasim, Karim was out most of the time.

Zahra clenched her hands, crumpling the letters she was holding. She couldn't bear any more humiliation.

9
DOUBTS AND FEARS

Zahra's belief that she was in the way at Nasim and Rashid's house had begun the previous week. She'd woken suddenly in the middle of the night to the sound of voices whispering on the landing. She'd crept to her bedroom door and listened. Rashid was saying something about the Revolutionary Guard taking over a police station.

'Can you do it?' he'd asked, then she'd heard Firzun's voice.

'No problem, I've got plenty of explosives.'

Rashid had then said something about an attack on the American embassy. As they'd started to walk away, Firzun had muttered vehemently, 'We'll be ready for them.'

After they'd gone, Zahra had sat on the edge of her bed in the dark. This was serious anti-government activity. They risked arrest, prison or death for it. She'd gone back to bed and lain awake, turning over everything in her mind, trying to make sense of it.

She had still been awake when the dawn prayer call echoed round the suburb. Firzun must have an escape plan, but how would they get out? Over the mountains? By plane? Where would they go? America? England? She would have to cope in another foreign country. Finally, after resolving to talk to Firzun, she'd fallen asleep.

Two days later she still felt edgy. On her way back from the kindergarten, she bought a newspaper. Her heart pounded when she read the banner headline on the front page, above a photograph of a former building that was now a heap of rubble: *'Our pious leader vows to punish the enemies of the state!'* She read the story quickly as she walked along. She reread it twice in her room, her hand across her mouth.

A bomb had blown up a police station, killing six Revolutionary Guard officers and two policemen. She stared in disbelief at the photograph; had Firzun done this? Then she remembered what Mahmoud had said to him before they left: 'So you botched the job at the Soviet Consulate and you're on the run ...'

On the day she'd arrived, Mojgan had told her that Firzun and Rashid were best friends at university. When pressed about the accident before the wedding, Mojgan had told her that Firzun had saved Rashid's life when someone deliberately ran their car off the road at high speed. Were he and Rashid still on some sort of 'hit list'? Maybe Firzun was a wanted man in this country as well as in his own. She stared again at the newspaper photograph, her skin prickling with fear and her head ringing with unanswered questions.

She bought a newspaper every day from then on and scanned the blurry newsprint photographs of anti-government demonstrations, looking for Firzun's face in the crowds, but she never saw him. When she read the headline: *'Traitors routed by the Revolutionary Guard'* and saw photographs of people being hustled away, arms behind their backs, heads bowed, she felt terrified. The following day the newspaper had a picture of the US president, and in thick black script the heading: *'The USA is the enemy of our people.'*

She read the story underneath the picture with mounting alarm:

'The USA and Israel are in league with the former shah to cheat our people and only the great Ayatollah can save our country. The Revolutionary Guard have arrested hundreds of people disloyal to the great leader, saviour of our country. Since he took control from the corrupt regime of the royal family, many reforms have been made to

our laws. The scourge of alcohol has been eradicated in keeping with the new laws, and many people have been punished.'

More shocking still were the pictures of the beaten faces and bodies of people who had been punished for drinking alcohol. As the days went on, the newspapers had more photographs of anti-American demonstrations in the streets. She hadn't yet had a chance to talk to Firzun about the stories. By now, the pictures of people burning the American flag and effigies of President Carter had become more numerable. She shared her anxiety about the demonstrations with Nasim.

'They're a long way from here, Zahra. Don't worry, you'll be safe with the Konari family,' she answered blithely.

Nasim's remark reminded her of something she'd heard her say quietly to Firzun the day after they'd arrived. 'Zahra and Ahmad will be better there, Firzun. I'll fix it ...'

'Okay, when she's pulled herself together ...' he'd replied, then jerked his head in her direction to warn Nasim not to say anymore.

So, it seemed, everything had been well planned in advance—everything—maybe even Mahmoud's death. Perhaps Nasim was right; she and Ahmad *would* be safer living with the Konari family.

'Well, we can see Esmat Khanoum at ten o'clock this morning,' Nasim told her at breakfast the next day. 'By the way Zahra,' she added, 'you don't need to worry about Karim. He's hardly ever home and he's not a playboy!' She laughed.

Zahra looked up from cutting Ahmad's melon into small pieces and smiled.

'He's an architect, a *very* good one,' Nasim went on. 'He built them—*himself*—a beautiful house in the States, near Boston.'

Zahra glanced down at Ahmad again, pretending she hadn't noticed the slip.

'He's got a Masters from MIT—Massachusetts Institute of Technology,' Nasim hurried on. 'He's working here now, until his grandmother passes, I expect,' she said sadly.

Zahra wanted to hear more, hoping that Nasim might mention the American wife, but she stood up.

'Anyway, the Konaris are only two houses away, remember? You can visit here whenever you like,' she said, indicating the direction of the other house, invisible to Zahra across the wide lawns.

'Rezvan Khanoum, that's the old lady, has cancer but she's still lucid,' Nasim rushed on. 'She likes to talk about the old days. Her late husband was an officer in the Persian Army.' Nasim raised her eyebrows. 'They were personal friends of the shah and shahbanu.'

Personal friends of the royal family! Zahra felt overwhelmed and she dreaded meeting Esmat and Rezvan Konari, who had moved in such illustrious circles. But then the shah and his family were in exile ...

'How many people live in the house?'

'Well, Karim and his parents, Esmat and Abbas—he's an executive in an oil company—then there's a nurse who comes every day.' Nasim counted on her fingers. 'Tahmineh and her husband Amir, the housekeepers and their niece, Shirin, who helps out. Two gardeners, someone to help with the cleaning—quite a few people actually!'

'Have they got room for me and Ahmad?'

'Oh yes, the house is much bigger than this one!'

Zahra had calculated that Nasim's apartment had five bedrooms and the apartment downstairs at least four, as well as several bathrooms, and a small flat for the live-in housekeepers. The Konari house must be the size of a small palace!

'The family department store is the Persian Harrods, if you've heard of that,' Nasim was saying. 'Esmat's running it at the moment —her parents are in the States, and so is her daughter, Karim's sister. You won't see the family very much.' She smiled.

Zahra looked down at Ahmad, still pushing his melon pieces round his plate, and tears welled in her eyes.

'I *do* understand, Zahra,' Nasim said kindly.

Zahra took a deep breath. 'If Esmat Khanoum approves of me, I'm happy to take the job,' she said.

Nasim sighed ... with relief? Zahra wondered.

'But you can still come here and help me. You're part of the team now,' Nasim assured her. 'I'll tell Esmat what I've told our servants here,' she rushed on, 'that Firzun married you when your husband died a while ago. She won't ask questions.'

'And what about Ahmad?'

'When he's not at kindergarten, the housekeeper's niece, Shirin, can keep an eye on him.'

'Thank you, Nasim.' Zahra looked up and smiled.

'Wonderful!' Nasim answered. 'Wonderful!'

Zahra looked closely at her; she was full of nervous energy, smiling and turning her rings round on her fingers. She can't wait to get rid of us, Zahra thought, it *is* all part of a plan. She shuffled Ahmad ahead of her to their room. The story about her husband had been worked out carefully, and the overall picture was beginning to get clearer. They would be out of the way while the others carried on their subversive activities. She and Ahmad were Firzun's ticket out of Iran if he had to leave quickly under his assumed name of Mahmoud Ghafoori. She felt annoyed with them all—she didn't like being lied to, or used.

'By the way,' Nasim said as they got ready, 'Karim's got a separate apartment at the top of the house, but honestly, you'll hardly see him.'

In spite of Nasim's assurances, Zahra felt nervous. She hardly saw Firzun, but she felt protected while they were in the same house.

'I think we're decent women now, don't you?' Nasim said with a sigh. Zahra adjusted her chador and nodded with a faint smile. She helped Ahmad into his sneakers.

'Daddy's not there, is he?' Ahmad looked at her fearfully.

'No, just Nasim Khanoum's friends. Daddy's gone away, remember?' she answered quietly.

'I think we'll walk,' Nasim said as Habib opened the door for them.

Zahra relaxed as they walked down the driveway, enjoying the feeling of the warm sun on her back. Nasim stopped at the open gate.

'Don't look at them!' she said suddenly.

But Zahra was already on the footpath, watching the open jeep as it drove slowly along the opposite side of the road. Drivers in the trail of traffic behind it honked irritably. The four bearded men in the car ignored them.

'They've got guns, Mummy.' Ahmad looked up at her in alarm.

'It's all right, Ahmad,' Nasim told him. 'You can walk between us.' She took his other hand in hers and they quickened their pace.

As the jeep crawled along the kerb, the occupants stared at the people on the footpaths. Zahra gasped as one of the men suddenly leaned out of the jeep and aimed a rifle at a taxi driver behind them who was leaning on his horn. She felt terrified. What if the man shot the driver and Ahmad saw it? He'd suffered enough violence in his short life already. The taxi driver took his hand off the horn. The driver of the jeep suddenly accelerated with a screech and drove away at high speed.

'Idiots!' Nasim said angrily.

She stopped in front of a set of high bronze gates and pressed the bell. As they swung open and clicked shut behind them, Zahra looked up the driveway. From its deep front veranda to the large glass cube perched on the third floor, the house loomed in front of them. It was everything she'd dreaded: a small palace. Totally unsuitable for a battered wife and her traumatised child.

A smiling woman stood waiting for them on the veranda in front of a highly polished double front door.

10

THE KONARI FAMILY

'Zahra, this is Tahmineh Khanoum, Esmat's housekeeper,' Nasim said, introducing the women to each other. Before Ahmad could wriggle away, Tahmineh knelt down and hugged him against her floral bosom.

'*Mashallah*! Welcome, welcome!' she beamed as she adjusted her white headscarf. 'Please, come this way.'

Zahra stifled an exclamation as they followed Tahmineh into the house—the entrance hall looked like a house from a Hollywood movie. A huge Persian carpet partially covered the parquetry floor and a display of flowers stood on a central table, flooding the circular atrium with their heavy scent.

'Look, Mummy,' Ahmad whispered.

She followed his gaze to the multi-coloured glass dome high above them in the ceiling, from which shards of light patterned the pale walls. She wondered if Esmat Khanoum would appear from one of the many closed doors around the atrium. Or maybe she'd appear at the top of the wide carpeted staircase, whose wrought-iron railings curved up to a landing and a balcony on the next floor.

'Madam will be with you soon,' Tahmineh assured them.

She took their chadors and headscarfs to a cloakroom at the side of the front door and handed out leather house slippers.

'Oh, look at my hair!' Nasim said, running a comb through the loose brown tangle as she checked her reflection in the cloakroom mirror.

Zahra tried not to think of Karim's comments as she adjusted her plait and smoothed her curling fringe, then helped Ahmad into the Mickey Mouse slippers he'd brought with him. She smoothed her hands over her black dress, glad that Tahmineh had given her matching black house slippers.

'I'll bring some tea,' Tahmineh told them as she opened a set of double doors and stepped aside for them to go in. Zahra stopped in amazement on the threshold, and Nasim smiled back over her shoulder at her.

'Isn't it a lovely room? Esmat has *such* good taste!'

Zahra's gaze swept over the cream leather sofas and chairs arranged casually near a huge white fireplace. Another display of fresh flowers stood in the empty grate and their scent filled the room.

A large coffee table was stacked with glossy magazines. On either side of the fireplace, photographs in silver frames were arranged on the floor-to-ceiling shelves. The most prominent one, Zahra noticed with a start of recognition, was of the deposed shah and shahbanu of Iran shaking hands with a tall man in a white military uniform. A small, exquisitely dressed woman looked on, her face wreathed in smiles. Zahra assumed she was looking at Karim's grandparents.

'I've always loved that window and those drapes,' Nasim said, pointing to the wall of French windows to the right of the door. 'Esmat loves interior design,' she went on, 'but when she had this room painted pale cream with those coffee-coloured drapes, her mother-in-law Rezvan Khanoum was extremely annoyed—she's very traditional. I shouldn't gossip!' She smiled over her shoulder at Zahra as she threw open doors to more sumptuously furnished rooms, stepping aside so that Zahra could admire the opulent decor.

Feeling slightly on edge, Zahra pulled Ahmad's hands away from a long mirror where he was making faces at himself.

Nasim was commenting on the view of the lush garden from the main salon when the door opened and a tall, elegantly dressed woman strode into the room. She held out her hand to Nasim with a smile. Zahra was in no doubt that this was Esmat Konari.

'How lovely to see you, Nasim. It's been such a long time!'

Zahra had expected the regal bearing, the tailored clothes and the gold jewellery, but she hadn't expected Esmat to be so tall that she had to bend down slightly to kiss Nasim's cheek.

'Esmat, this is Zahra and her son Ahmad.'

Esmat held out her hand. 'I'm so pleased to meet you, Zahra,' she said, giving her a quick appraising look. Her glance was enough to make Zahra painfully conscious that she was wearing Nasim's cast off clothes.

'And Ali, what a fine little boy,' Esmat said, looking down at Ahmad as if he were a small creature from outer space.

'Ahmad, madam—thank you. He's a good child.'

Zahra wasn't sure why she'd said 'madam', but Esmat smiled slightly as if she approved. She pushed back her thick dark hair, straightened her gold earrings, and smoothed her hands over her black pants. As if brushing away my handshake, Zahra thought.

'I'm sure he is,' Esmat replied as she turned to Nasim. 'Well, here's Tahmineh with some refreshments.'

She nodded to the housekeeper, who was setting delicate china teacups out on the coffee table, and invited them to sit down. Tahmineh served the tea, then took Ahmad by the hand and led him into the kitchen with the promise of cake and a soccer ball in the garden.

Esmat sipped her tea, then, putting the cup down, she said, 'Well, I'll get to the point straight away. My mother-in-law, Rezvan Khanoum, has cancer. The prognosis isn't good ...' She paused and cleared her throat.

'It's so sad,' Nasim remarked.

'Yes, we're all devastated, especially Karim. That's why he's come home,' Esmat said quickly. 'Rezvan Khanoum, as you might remember, Nasim, can be *very* demanding.' She raised her closely plucked eyebrows and a look of irritation crossed her face. 'My mother-in-law, well ... she wants someone to read to her and *listen* to her.' She sighed and looked at Zahra. 'I'm *far* too busy to deal with household matters.' She waved a hand as if pushing the household to one side. 'Now just a few questions ...'

Zahra wondered if Esmat interviewed all her staff at such high speed as the questions shot out, one after the other. To Zahra's relief, her answers seemed to satisfy the other woman. She started to elaborate on her knowledge of English and Persian literature, but Esmat interrupted.

'Yes, good, Rezvan Khanoum loves all that kind of stuff. There's a library full of it here.' She stood up and rubbed her hands together. 'Well, let's go and see her, better get it over with. She's awake,' she said briskly.

Zahra followed them across the entrance hall and up the staircase. She felt painfully aware of her plain black clothes as she walked behind Esmat in her cream silk blouse and tailored pants, and Nasim, slim and elegant in jeans and a pink tee shirt. When they reached the landing, Esmat indicated another set of stairs.

'Our son Karim has an apartment on the top floor. He designed and built it himself while he was still a student,' she said indulgently as she pointed to an unpolished wooden staircase and a bright red door.

Zahra looked up at the stairs. Karim Konari was closer to the house than Nasim had suggested. Esmat stopped suddenly outside one of the dark polished doors, her fingers on the handle. They heard a man's voice, then a deep pleasant laugh, followed by a woman's much fainter one.

'Oh, it sounds like Karim's visiting his grandmother,' Esmat said irritably. She dropped her hand as the door opened slowly. Karim's voice was very close and Zahra caught her breath.

'Take care, darling. I love you!' he said gently.

Zahra took a step back as he opened the door further. She lowered her eyes, but when he came out of the room she couldn't help but look up into his fine-looking face. It was bathed in affection. His eyes met hers briefly, held them for a second and he blinked in surprise.

'Oh, I'm so sorry, please excuse me!' he exclaimed.

His voice, refined and warm, still echoed with the laughter that lingered in the room. Zahra flushed with the embarrassment of intruding on such an intimate family moment. She looked down at the carpet, feeling gauche and uncomfortable.

'Karim, darling!' Esmat remonstrated. 'I thought you were still asleep. You missed breakfast with me!'

Zahra concentrated on the carpet.

'Sorry, Mother. Tomorrow, I promise. Hello Nasim!' he said fondly.

'More American clothes, Karim!' Nasim exclaimed.

Zahra stole a quick look at the 'American clothes': blue denim jeans, a black polo shirt with a gold embroidered motif of a man leaning down from a horse, and tan suede moccasins. She looked down again and noticed that he wasn't wearing socks, and his suntanned skin was scattered with dark hair above his ankles.

'This is Zahra Khanoum from Afghanistan,' Esmat said, forcing Zahra to look up. 'She's going to be your grandmother's companion.'

'Yes, we met at Nasim's,' he said with a smile as he extended his hand. 'Thank you, Zahra Khanoum.'

She felt as if she was looking straight into the sun on a bright day. She blushed and looked away.

'Well, ladies.' He turned to his mother and Nasim, who were deep in conversation. 'Grandmother is in fine form at the moment, so *Carpe Diem*,' he said brightly.

'What?' Esmat sounded exasperated.

'It's Latin, Mother. It means "seize the day"—don't wait. It could be the Ayatollah Khomeini's motto, couldn't it?' He finished with a laugh.

'Don't mention him in this house,' his mother replied tartly.

'See you all later!'

Zahra watched covertly as he strode down the landing towards the stairs.

'Well, here we go,' Esmat said under her breath, opening the door of the bedroom and ushering Nasim ahead of her.

Zahra glanced back, thinking she'd heard Ahmad's voice. She saw Karim standing at the top of the stairs, watching her. She looked away, disconcerted, reminding herself of the things he'd said about her to Nasim. She jumped as Esmat clicked her fingers and beckoned her into the sick room.

The windows were partially open, and through them she could see a splendid view of the brown Alborz Mountains against the blue sky. It seemed lost, though, on the invalid in a blue nightdress, who lay in the middle of a huge bed. She was propped up on pillows and her eyes were closed. A young girl of about fifteen fussed with the bedcover.

'She's very tired, madam. Agha Karim's just been to see her,' the girl said to Esmat.

'Yes, I'm aware of that, thank you, Shirin,' Esmat said with a frown.

Zahra and Nasim waited by the door as Esmat prowled round the room. She picked up a bottle of perfume from the dressing table.

'Chanel Number 5, still using that old stuff,' she remarked under her breath as she pressed the top and released a cloud of perfume, making Shirin splutter.

'Really, girl,' Esmat said impatiently. 'Don't cough in the sick room!'

'I'll get Rezvan Khanoum's lunch if that's all, madam,' Shirin said quickly, heading for the door. When she closed it, Zahra heard her sneezing on the landing.

'Mother-in-law, I've brought the Afghan woman to see you,' Esmat said loudly.

'I'm not deaf!' The old lady's dark eyes snapped open.

Nasim walked up to the bed, took the invalid's hand, and smiled at her. As Zahra waited by the door, she felt her confidence slipping. The way Esmat had said 'the Afghan woman' with a faint distain in her voice had pricked her pride. Did they look down on her so much?

'I'd like to be introduced formerly, Esmat, and please don't waste my Chanel perfume!' Rezvan said in a breathy voice.

She turned her head towards the door and beckoned Zahra forward. After Esmat had rushed through the introductions, Zahra shook Rezvan's hot papery hand while Esmat rattled out her biography.

'She studied all the Farsi and English poets and the rest of them at university. She can speak and read English. I think you'll like that,' Esmat finished conclusively.

The old lady winced while her daughter-in-law was speaking and Zahra felt an instant kinship with the dying woman. Esmat was certainly no intellectual. Rezvan assured Zahra they'd have lots to talk about, especially her life at court. She asked her if she'd seen her grandson, 'dear Karim', and when she nodded Rezvan looked pointedly at Esmat.

'We might get him engaged to a nice young woman now he's home. I'll see if I can find him someone from a *good* family, not just a rich one.'

'I can deal with that myself, thank you,' Esmat snapped.

Zahra stole a look at Nasim. But she was standing impassively as she guarded Karim's explosive secret about his American wife.

'Zahra will come and see you tomorrow morning, after she's moved in,' Esmat announced to Zahra's surprise. Apparently the job was hers by default; there didn't seem to be any other candidates.

'Zahra, a few words please.' Esmat strode to the door without saying goodbye to her mother-in-law and held it open.

'I'll stay and chat for a little while,' Nasim said and Esmat gave a brief nod.

'This way.' Esmat beckoned to Zahra. 'I'll show you your room.'

She followed Esmat past a long window with a magnificent view of the mountains, then down a narrow passage that led off the landing.

'This used to be the nanny's room when Karim and his sister were little,' she said, opening a brown painted door.

Zahra looked apprehensively into the room and was pleasantly surprised. Although it was at the back of the house, and cooking smells drifted up from the kitchen below, it was clean and bright. Esmat indicated a bathroom that led off it.

'We can fit another bed in here for your son, that won't be a problem,' she commented, leaning down and brushing a few dark spots off the white bed cover. 'The wardrobe should be big enough,' she said as she ran her hand over a chest of drawers, checking her fingertips for dust.

'Thank you, Esmat Khanoum. I ...'

'Well, you can move in tomorrow as I said to Mother-in-law,' Esmat interrupted. 'I'll show you where the library is and you can pick up something from there when you get here.'

She paused at the door and looked at Zahra. 'I can pay you a small wage.' She mentioned a sum of money. 'I can't pay you any more,' she rushed on, as if Zahra had objected. 'After all, it's an easy job. She sleeps a lot.'

Zahra felt a tinge of pleasure—her own money at last, without Mahmoud demanding it from her! She smiled at Esmat.

'Yes, I thought you'd be pleased, and of course all your meals and accommodation are free for you and your child. Personally,' she gave Zahra a tight smile, 'I think it's a pretty good deal!'

She walked onto the landing and beckoned Zahra to follow.

'Now,' she pointed, 'over there you'll see the back stairs, which the staff use. You'll eat with them at seven; we eat at eight-thirty most evenings. If we're entertaining, Tahmineh could always use extra help. I'll give you a key to the side gate. I believe you've made arrangements for Ali?'

'Ahmad, madam,' Zahra corrected again. 'He goes to kindergarten five mornings a week and ...'

'Perfect,' Esmat interrupted her. 'The mornings are when Rezvan Khanoum is *so* demanding and if she needs you in the afternoon, Shirin can look after, Al ... Ahmad.' She smiled, looking for an instant like her son. 'I believe your husband is staying at Nasim's while he's looking for a job?' she went on.

'Er ... yes,' Zahra stammered, but Esmat hadn't noticed Zahra's guilty blush. She was already walking towards the stairs.

'So it all works out beautifully. And here's Nasim,' she said over her shoulder.

'Rezvan Khanoum's fallen asleep,' Nasim said with a quick look at Zahra.

Esmat made a sound in the back of her throat and waited until Nasim joined her. Zahra followed a few steps behind, wondering if she should have taken the back stairs. Then, as if confirming her lowly rank in this household, she heard Esmat mutter to Nasim.

'Did you notice that the old witch is still turning the knife? Did you hear what she said? "A *good* family, not just a rich one." That was a direct swipe at me, and in front of a servant!'

Nasim made sympathetic noises.

'Without my money, the Konari family would have been bankrupt years ago!' Esmat muttered angrily.

Was *she* the servant Esmat was referring to? Zahra wondered, dismayed at the thought. It was another blow to her pride, and the thrill of independence she'd felt when Esmat mentioned the money evaporated. When they reached the bottom of the stairs, Esmat motioned her into the salon. Karim was sitting on one of the couches reading a newspaper. He put it aside when they came in and stood up. To her irritation, she felt her heart leap. She stopped inside the door and tried not to look at him.

'Can I offer you more tea?' Esmat asked unenthusiastically.

'No, darling, we must be going,' Nasim said. 'I know you want to catch up with Karim. And here's Ahmad!'

Ahmad, flushed and excited, came into the room with Shirin. Zahra was relieved to see him and he ran to her, babbling about the garden and a swing and a soccer ball. To her surprise, Karim came over and kneeled down at Ahmad's level.

'Hello, Ahmad. Did you find my soccer ball?' he asked quietly.

Ahmad nodded and Zahra coaxed him to say hello and shake Karim's hand. Ahmad was captivated, like her, by Karim's charm and asked if he could play soccer with 'uncle' the next day.

'We'll see,' she said, glancing at Karim.

'You've got a fine son, Zahra Khanoum,' he said.

He smiled as he stood up. She returned his smile and thanked him, and he held her gaze for a brief moment before turning towards his mother.

'So, I'll see you at ten o'clock tomorrow,' Esmat said, leading them into the atrium, completely unaware of the intimate moment that had passed between her son and 'the servant.'

'Really, all these clothes to walk five hundred metres, it's so ridiculous,' she commented as they wound headscarves over their hair and pulled chadors over their clothes. 'This Islamic government's ruining business in the store,' she went on. 'Every woman once had the right to choose how she dressed! There's one thing though.' She gave a short laugh. 'I've never sold so many black headscarves in my life, even though they mess up everyone's hair!'

Nasim sighed, but Zahra noticed she didn't attempt to recruit Esmat for her women's march. When Karim came out of the salon to say goodbye, Zahra kept her eyes lowered, but watched as his suede clad feet turned towards the stairs.

'Oh, Karim,' Nasim said, and the suede moccasins stopped. 'Come over for dinner tomorrow night? Is eight-thirty okay?'

Esmat took Zahra's elbow and moved her towards the front door out of earshot of the other two. 'Here's the key for the side gate,' she said quietly, slipping it into Zahra's hand. She indicated a closed door directly across the atrium. 'Library,' she said briefly. When Zahra looked round for Nasim, she saw her standing near the centre table with her back to them. She was saying something in a low urgent voice to Karim.

He frowned at her. 'For God's sake, be careful, Nasim!' she heard him say.

'Come on, darling, I want my son back.' Esmat strode across the carpet. 'He's been away a long time!'

'All right, *Madar djan,* I'm all yours.' He smiled and put his hand on his heart, then he touched Nasim on the arm. 'We can talk tomorrow,' he said quietly.

'Well *I* want to talk today,' Esmat replied, putting her arm possessively through his, then she released him suddenly. 'Oh, Nasim, there *was* something else I wanted to ask you about ...'

Ahmad had wandered over to the table and was touching the flowers. As Zahra went to pull him away, her eyes met Karim's again and he moved forward as if he was going to speak. She grabbed Ahmad's hand quickly and walked towards the door, afraid that Esmat wouldn't approve of her fraternising with her precious son.

'Goodbye, Zahra Khanoum,' Karim said quietly.

She turned; he was still watching her. 'Goodbye, Karim Agha,' she said formally. He smiled and headed for the stairs.

'Oh!' Esmat said in an exasperated voice. 'He's gone, and I wanted to talk to him. I'll see you later, Nasim. Karim it's lunchtime!' she called.

11

CHANGES

Firzun and Rashid had already started their lunch when she walked into Nasim's living room. Firzun looked up from where he was sitting on the floor, helping himself to the food that Mojgan had laid out on a tablecloth.

'So?' he asked.

'I've got the job and I start tomorrow,' she said, feeling a slight rush of pleasure. She sat down, took the plate Nasim offered and helped herself to salad.

'By the way, Zahra,' Firzun said casually, 'I need your passport and Ahmad's. I've already got Mahmoud's ... and his wallet,' he added.

'How did you ... ?' she began, annoyed with herself that she'd forgotten to ask about it before.

'They were inside his jacket,' he answered before she'd finished the sentence. 'I've got to get new visas for us.'

'Why did you use his passport to cross the border?'

'I had to,' he said impatiently, 'to protect you and Ahmad. And I'll use it again to leave Iran.'

'And why do we need new visas?' she continued.

He was making her feel nervous.

'They're refugee visas to get us into Australia,' he said calmly. Had she heard him right?

'*Australia?*' She put her fork down and stared at him over Ahmad's head. So this was the escape plan, a country on the other side of the world!

When he told her that they might have to leave quickly and that he had a fiancé in Sydney called Nousha Gul, she could hardly process what he was saying. She had no idea he had a fiancé, or that she lived in Sydney, Australia. Why hadn't he mentioned it?

'It didn't seem relevant. I'll be travelling as Mahmoud, of course, your husband.'

'Of course it's relevant! What's going to happen to me and Ahmad when you get married in Australia?'

'There's no need to panic, Zahra.' He put his hand up like a policeman stopping traffic. 'I've got it all worked out.'

'She's had a lot to cope with, Firzun,' Nasim interjected.

She stretched her hand across the tablecloth and patted Zahra's arm. She called Mojgan and asked her to take Ahmad into the kitchen 'for ice-cream'.

Zahra felt a flash of anger towards her cousin.

'Why do we have to go so far? Why not go to Turkey or somewhere in Europe?' she asked heatedly.

'Look,' he said with a frown, 'we'll be safer on the other side of the world. The Australian government have a refugee program; they'll give us temporary accommodation in a hostel—money and food. After a year we can get divorced and you'll be free.'

'But I'd be alone with a child in a foreign country!' she remonstrated.

'It's a Western country; divorced women live on their own in flats. You could work as a teacher again,' he said cheerfully.

'I'd be better off in Afghanistan!' she said, but in her heart she knew that wasn't true. In reality she wouldn't be able to live with her friend Fatima, she'd be forced to live with Firzun's mother, Aunt Mina.

'Zahra!' Firzun said urgently. 'I can't get out of Iran without you. I *need* a new identity. Trust me, I won't abandon you.'

Her skin prickled with fear. Supposing they were stopped at the airport and arrested, what would happen to them, to Ahmad?

'We won't be,' he said calmly when she asked. 'I'm making sure that all our papers are in order. That's why I need your passport, okay?'

'Zahra, there's work to do. Firzun's getting the paperwork done now so that you can leave easily when the work's finished,' Nasim said firmly.

'What sort of work?' Zahra asked, though she had a pretty good idea it wasn't anything with a salary.

'We want a democratic government in Iran,' Nasim replied.

'We've got to stay and fight before it's too late, before the Islamic government's entrenched, and Firzun has come to help us,' Rashid added.

'And you'll be safer at Esmat's, Zahra,' Nasim continued. 'There's a lot going on in our house.'

'But it seems so dangerous. Why risk your lives like this?'

'We're not alone, we have plenty of supporters, Zahra,' Nasim said vehemently without answering her question. 'Esmat doesn't know, but Karim's with us,' she finished.

Zahra looked from one of them to the other, remembering the whispered conversations she'd heard, the terrible stories in the newspaper about people being arrested. She felt afraid for them, and for herself and Ahmad. But at least they were trying to keep her safe, so what could she say?

After lunch she brought the passports to Firzun. He was sitting alone at the paper-strewn dining table. Nasim had taken Ahmad somewhere to read to him and Rashid had gone downstairs.

'My passport and Ahmad's.' She handed them to him. 'But what about Mahmoud's photo?' she said anxiously. 'He was wearing his glasses in it.'

Firzun put the passports in his shirt pocket and shrugged. 'I can fix that. No one looks like their passport photograph.'

She was turning to go when he touched her arm.

'Mahmoud got what he deserved, Zahra,' he said carefully. 'You're free now.'

You're free now—those were the same words he'd used in the mountains just after Mahmoud had died.

She turned back and tried to meet his eyes. 'How did he die, Firzun?' she whispered.

He looked away, his broad dark face impassive. 'He pulled a knife on me,' he said, his brown eyes finally meeting hers. 'I saved your lives, Zahra, yours and Ahmad's,' he said quietly. 'He'd have killed you in your own home, like his first wife.'

'His first wife?'

'A neighbour told me. She ran out of the flat screaming and he pushed her in the back ... She was killed in the fall.'

'Did you know that before I married him?' Zahra whispered.

'No, but I never trusted him. I saw your bruises, Zahra.'

'He always dragged me back. Your mother wouldn't help even when I had Ahmad,' she added bitterly.

'She should have taken you in.' He shook his head. 'You know how it is in our country. What can a woman's family do when men think they own their wives? There's only one way to deal with men like him.'

'It shouldn't be like that,' she whispered. She was even more determined now to support Nasim's march.

'Look, you've got your freedom, Zahra. What happened is our secret. I've helped you, now it's your turn to help me.'

Our secret, she thought. *Our vile family secret.*

He touched her arm again. 'I'm a dead man if you don't.'

Zahra lay down on her bed that afternoon as Ahmad slept soundly. What Firzun had told her had stirred up memories of her life with Mahmoud, which she'd suppressed over the years. But she'd never forget the terror she'd felt every time she'd heard Mahmoud's key in the lock. She still mourned the baby she'd lost when he'd punched her and she'd miscarried. She opened her eyes and shuddered with relief. He was dead. He couldn't harm her anymore.

She turned over the idea of living in a flat on her own with Ahmad in a Western country. It might not be so bad; there'd be no one telling her what to do. No Mahmoud hitting her and then turning on Ahmad. Maybe she *could* get a job, decorate the flat the way she wanted ... She'd had to be strong when she was a teenager—she would find that strength again. She could still be that person.

She was packing their few belongings with Ahmad when Nasim knocked at the door. She came in with armfuls of clothes for both her and Ahmad.

'You can say no, of course,' she said brightly, 'but I haven't even worn some of them.'

She wants me to be a 'suitable' person to work in the Konaris house, Zahra thought, then chided herself for being ungracious. It probably wasn't Nasim's idea—she could imagine Esmat saying: 'Could you smarten her up a little, Nasim? She'll be around in the main part of the house.'

The dawn prayer call woke her with a start on their final morning at Nasim's. Zahra glanced across at Ahmad curled up in his own bed. She lay on her back, listening to the prayer call and the repeated phrase *Allah u Akbar* as it echoed through the streets. The singer had a beautiful voice, melodic and sincere. She washed quietly and returned to the bedroom. For the first time since she'd been to the mosque, she prayed, saying the sacred words under her breath as

Ahmad slept on. When she finished she rested on her heels, feeling sad but spiritually cleansed.

At breakfast, Nasim told her there'd been a delay. Esmat's manicurist had been stopped on her way there by the decency police. They'd taken all her make-up and nail varnish and questioned her in the police station for hours. Nasim's face flushed with anger.

'How dare they arrest someone for doing an honest day's work?'

When they finally got going, Nasim insisted that she went the five hundred metres to the Konari house in the car.

'I'll miss you!' Nasim said sincerely. 'I'll call about the march. You are coming, aren't you?'

'Of course ... and thank you for everything, Nasim.'

She got in the car, breathing in the smell of new leather—a smell that would always remind her of arriving in Tehran, a widow and a free woman. When the driveway gates to the Konari house swung open and closed silently behind the car, she felt a pang of loneliness. She squeezed Ahmad's hand and smiled at him. Tahmineh was waiting for her at the side entrance and welcomed her profusely, grabbing both of the suitcases Habib put down. Zahra followed Tahmineh up the narrow back staircase. On the landing she breathed in the musky rose smell of the house, and she wondered briefly where Karim was. The house, as before, was deadly quiet and seemed deserted.

'Here we are!' Tahmineh led her along the narrow passage to her room and opened the door. 'I've cleaned it thoroughly for you.' She put Zahra's small bag down, pointing to a space for her suitcase. Zahra could still detect faint cooking smells drifting in from the open window, but there was also a pleasant smell of rosewater.

'Well, I hope you'll be very comfortable here,' Tahmineh said, squeezing past Ahmad on her way to the door.

'I'm sure we will,' Zahra said sincerely.

Tamineh smiled from the doorway. 'When you've unpacked, come to the kitchen for lunch and meet Shirin. Madam will see you soon.'

She closed the door, and Zahra looked round the small room and smiled at Ahmad.

'Do you like it?' she asked. 'That's your bed there.'

He nodded, crawled up, and sat against the pillows. She took off her black chador and headscarf, shook out her hair, and looked round the room. I love it, she thought. It's my space—mine and Ahmad's—and I feel safe here.

Next to each bed was a small, highly polished bedside cabinet with a lamp on it, and although the extra bed had reduced the space in the room, she didn't care. After she'd unpacked quickly and hung her new clothes in the wardrobe, she tied her hair in a knot at the nape of her neck, vowing never to be seen with a plait again, and went down to the kitchen.

Tahmineh had her back to her and was calling out to her niece. While she waited for the other woman to notice them, Zahra looked curiously round the large kitchen. Like the rest of the house, it was well proportioned. A long wooden table with chairs at one end doubled as a preparation area and a dining table for the staff. A large gas stove complemented the fuel stove, above which drying herbs hung from a ceiling beam. A television set was perched incongruously on a corner table. Cupboards lined the wall opposite the door, and next to them stood an enormous refrigerator. Tahmineh moved a boiling kettle deftly across the fuel stove that abutted the outside wall, then turned and saw Zahra.

'Zahra Khanoum and Ahmad!' she exclaimed.

She put a plate of chicken and meat kabobs, rice and salad on the table, motioning them to help themselves. The young girl Zahra had seen the previous day came in from a door at the back of the kitchen.

'This is my sister's daughter, Shirin. She's fifteen. She can take Ahmad to kindergarten when you're busy,' Tahmineh said as the teenager sat down at the table with them.

'We played together yesterday, didn't we, little brother?' Shirin said.

A loud jangling bell made them all jump.

'That'll be madam. They've finished lunch early.' Tahmineh bustled out of the kitchen and came back with a nod.

'She'll see you when you've finished lunch. Abbas Agha, her husband, is home at the moment, so you'll get to meet him.' She nodded importantly. 'We'll look after Ahmad.'

Although Tahmineh protested that she should finish her lunch, Zahra jumped to her feet. She didn't want to keep her new employer waiting.

12

THE LIBRARY

Esmat was in the atrium talking to a short stocky man in a dark business suit. He glanced across and inclined his head to Zahra as she walked towards them.

'This is my husband Abbas Agha—this is, er—Zahra Ghafoori from Afghanistan. She's going to be *Madar djan's* companion ...' Esmat rushed through the introductions.

'Welcome, Zahra Khanoum, I'm pleased to meet you.' Abbas smiled and shook her hand. His voice was like Karim's, deep and melodic with a polished accent.

'My mother will love ...' he began, but Esmat interrupted him.

'I'll see you later, darling, I'm sure you're busy.' She dismissed him with a nod.

He excused himself and headed for a room further round the atrium and closed the door with a faint click.

'So!' Esmat said brightly, rubbing her hands together. 'I'll show you the library and you can choose a book for Rezvan Khanoum.'

She headed off across the vast space, then threw open one of the double doors into a large room, beckoning Zahra to follow. Zahra stifled a gasp as she looked around at the bookcase-lined walls. When Esmat flicked the lights on, the room was bathed in a rosy glow from several lamps.

A rosewood baby grand piano stood to the left just inside the door. The shiny keys caught the light and a book of music was propped on the stand, waiting for someone to play it. Several comfortable leather armchairs were arranged near the shelves with tables and lamps next to them. Zahra followed Esmat to a table long enough to spread out several volumes. Esmat tutted and drummed her fingers on it as she surveyed the closely packed bookcases that lined the walls.

'All this dusting!' She sighed. 'This lot won't be going with me to the States.'

She waved her hand towards the shelves and the strong smell of her newly polished nails made Zahra catch her breath. She wondered when Esmat planned to go overseas, but she didn't ask. She was a servant, after all.

Esmat curved her fingers carefully round the handle of a half concealed bookcase. When it rolled out smoothly from the wall it created a division in the room, blocking the view of the door.

'These are all old. Don't touch the ones inside the glass doors, they're very precious.' She gave Zahra a tight smile.

Zahra looked at the books half hidden behind the glass and wanted desperately to get them out and have a look. Maybe some of them were the original copies of works she'd studied at university.

'Anyway, I'm sure you'll find something to interest my mother-in-law,' Esmat announced. 'She spent a lot of time in here with Karim, my son ... helping him, or so she said.' She pursed her lips.

'Who were her favourite authors?' Zahra asked.

'Oh, I don't know, she'll tell you.' She shrugged. 'Karim can make a list.'

They stood in silence looking at the bookshelves, then Esmat walked to the door. As Zahra followed her, she felt a stab of envy;

Esmat was so self-assured, so confident, so *privileged*, she thought. The other woman turned suddenly.

'Don't forget, staff dinner is at seven o'clock, family at eight-thirty.'

She glanced round the shelves and raised her eyebrows. 'Good luck!' She closed the door behind her with a snap.

Zahra stood in the room, breathing in the perfect silence. Why feel envious? she thought. I'm alone in a paradise of books! She sat down carefully on the edge of one of the leather armchairs, half expecting someone to come in and order her out. She sighed as she tried to organise her jumbled thoughts. *Are* we safer here than at Nasim's house? she wondered. Her eyes moistened when she thought about Ahmad. For his sake she had to trust Firzun. At least I'm close to my mother here in Tehran, she thought. Although she had no idea where she was buried. Perhaps Firzun knew ...

What did the Konaris think about the new regime? she wondered. If Karim thought what Nasim was doing was dangerous, surely his family would too. But hadn't Nasim said he was 'with them'?

She stood up and walked round behind the bookshelf Esmat had rolled out, longing to open the forbidden glass door. She found the poetry collection and ran her fingers along the spines of the aged leather-bound books. There were books in classical Farsi, modern Farsi, English and French, and she recognised some of her favourite classics by European authors: Jane Austen, the Brontë sisters, George Elliot, Flaubert, and Zola. There were volumes of poetry by Persian poets: Hafez, Attar, Omar Khayyam and Rumi. On another shelf she saw several copies of the holy Koran with commentaries next to each one.

She felt as though an invisible force was pulling her towards the forbidden glass bookcase that held the antique books. The doors were stained glass with a polished wooden surround. She moved closer and traced a finger round the recurring lead motif of tulips on the red and blue glass. She peered through the panes, holding her breath. Surely that wasn't ... She gasped. A complete set of the books of Ferdowsi's *Shahnameh, The Book of Kings*—the classic cornerstone of Persian literature, stood side by side on the top shelf. They were early editions, she thought in amazement—they must be worth a fortune!

She hurried to the end of the bookcase and looked round it; the room glowed emptily. Back in front of the glass doors she turned the key carefully. The door creaked loudly as she guided it open. The noise made her jump and she looked guiltily over her shoulder. She took down one of the volumes of the *Shahnameh*, closed the door to stop any dust getting on the books, and twisted the small key in the lock. She turned the pages reverently, hardly daring to breathe. The little book must have been at least three hundred years old. The script was ornate and almost too hard for her to read. The illustrations of people in a garden—men in long robes and turbans—had no perspective. She pored over the small volume, her shoulders aching with tension, her ears tuned to the slightest sound.

When the door of the library opened, she started violently and nearly dropped the book. She put her hand on the key to the glass fronted case. She crept to the end of the bookcase and risked a look, hoping to see Tamineh Khanoum.

To her dismay, Karim Konari stood in front of the piano with his back to her. He'd thrown his light grey jacket on a chair and rolled up the sleeves of his blue business shirt. He was idly turning the pages of the open music book. As she watched, he loosened his tie with his left hand while he leafed through the music. She stepped back behind the bookcase, wondering what to do. Then she heard a faint creak as he sat down on the piano bench. He was going to be here for ages! And she was trapped with the precious book in her hand. He began to play very quietly.

She recognised the piece at once: Beethoven's 'Moonlight Sonata'. In an instant she was back in her flat in Afghanistan, listening alone to this same piece of music. Without warning Mahmoud had slammed open the front door, his face like thunder. He was home early from his card game. He didn't look at her, but walked over to the record player and tore the record off the turntable. The arm and stylus ran across it. It was ruined.

'Western rubbish,' he had yelled while he spat in her face. He grabbed her arm, took out his knife, and slashed the point backwards and forwards over the disc then threw it across the room. She was devastated; she'd saved for months and he'd ruined it in an instant.

Mahmoud was now dead, she thought as she stood transfixed, listening to the beautiful music flooding the room. It was a backdrop to her terrible memories. Tears welled in her eyes. She reached up to return the book to the shelf, any shelf, but blinded by the tears she misjudged the distance. It slipped from her fingers and fell with a loud smack onto the wooden floor. Dismayed, she grabbed it, checking frantically for damage. The piano music stopped abruptly and Karim's footsteps were close. She reached up again, trying to replace the book.

'Let me help you, Zahra,' he said, taking the volume from her unsteady hands. The glass door creaked loudly as he slipped the book back in place and turned the key in the lock.

She forced herself to look up at him, hardly able to bear the expression of concern on his fine face. She brushed away the tear trickling down her cheek.

'I'm sorry,' she stammered. 'It's such a beautiful book.' The words came out in a strangled sob.

He smiled. 'Yes, it's nearly three hundred years old.'

He pulled a white handkerchief from his pocket and handed it to her without a word. She dabbed at her face, turned away from him and blew her nose, feeling foolish and vulnerable.

'You must have some sad memories of Tehran,' he said.

His voice was low and kind and she felt more tears rising. She tried to take a deep breath, but instead it came out as a sob and she buried her face in his handkerchief. She forced herself to look at him.

'I never thanked you properly for ... I wrote ...'

'It was the least I could do,' he interrupted. 'You were so young ...'

She covered her face again. He stepped forward and put his arm round her shoulders. She tried to pull away, shocked by the intimacy, but he pulled her closer and wrapped his other arm round her back. She could smell the freshness of his clothes and feel his hard chest through his shirt. She relaxed for a moment and leaned on him, trying to control the tears. Then she pulled away, half expecting him to crush her then shake her hard for what she'd done. She was no longer the innocent virgin he'd met all those years ago; she knew the power that men had to hurt women.

'Oh Zahra, how could I?' he said releasing her. 'I had no right ... please forgive me.' He stepped back.

'Books for your grandmother,' she blurted out, unable to meet his gaze. She was overwhelmed with shame at her weakness. While he selected the books, she waited near one of the armchairs.

'I'm ...' She looked up at him as he handed her a small pile of books. In the soft light she saw again the concern on his handsome features.

'I understand,' he said gently. 'It can't be easy for you.'

She longed for him to put his arm round her again, but instead he strode to the door and opened it and stood waiting for her. As she passed him, he touched her lightly on the elbow and guided her across the atrium without speaking. He pushed the kitchen door open with his shoulder and stood aside to let her pass.

'Tamineh Khanoum!' he called. 'Zahra's a little upset ...'

'I'm fine, really, thank you,' she whispered and hurried into the kitchen, feeling acutely embarrassed. Tamineh rushed over.

'It's all right. Thank you, Karim Agha,' she said.

When he'd gone, she fussed around Zahra and made her sit down at the table.

'You didn't finish your lunch, Zahra,' Tahmineh admonished as she handed her tea and a plate of cookies. '*Noush-e djan.* Enjoy!'

Zahra nodded, wiping away the remaining tears with Karim's handkerchief. It smelled of him, of fresh linen and almonds. The scent she'd inhaled as she leaned on his chest, the scent from many years ago. Deep inside her body she felt the stirring of the intense longing she'd felt then, but hadn't fully understood.

13

FATHER AND SON

Karim closed the kitchen door and hit his forehead with the heel of his hand—he'd forgotten where he was again! Hugging women, touching women, particularly from places like Afghanistan—was *completely* out of order. How could he have forgotten? And she's married, he reminded himself.

He looked down at his shirt and rubbed the damp patch where she'd leaned against him. He'd always felt useless, even irritated, when women wept all over him, and plenty had when he'd finished relationships. But this was different; Zahra's distress had touched him deeply.

He would never forget seeing her ten years ago, an innocent wide-eyed school girl in floods of grief-stricken tears in Nasim's dining room. How he'd longed even then to take her in his arms and comfort her. All he could do was throw money in her direction, he thought bitterly. Now fate had brought them together again. But destiny had played a trick on him. She'd been widowed young, Nasim told him, and then she'd married her cousin. Even so he had felt a rush of desire when he'd held her in his arms.

As he walked up the stairs, he thought about Nancy and how

obsessed he'd been by this beautiful American woman. Obsessed by her lithe tanned body, long blond hair and crystal blue eyes. She'd grabbed him during the countdown at a New Year's Eve party and on the stroke of midnight she kissed him deeply and pressed her half naked body against his. He ran his hand down her bare back, returned her kiss and was lost. His friends tried to warn him. 'She's a gold digger,' his best friend Husayn had said, but Karim ignored him.

Things were so different in Iran, he thought. Yesterday Nasim had politely shrugged his arm off her shoulders and reminded him she was married. Even when he was at Tehran University, his fellow female students had kept behind an invisible line—everyone knew the rules. Friends yes, boyfriend/girlfriend okay, but definitely no sex before marriage, unless you were engaged and if you could get away from your family somehow.

In the States there didn't appear to be any rules. Before he married Nancy, she'd been a siren—flirting, teasing, kissing him—but even she'd made him wait for three months before she slept with him. By then he'd been nearly out of his mind with lust for her. He'd even brought her to Iran to meet his parents—what a disaster that was! When they got back to the States, Nancy told him she was pregnant and collapsed at his feet, begging him to marry her. She came from a good Catholic family, she sobbed. They would disown her if they knew.

Lies, he thought angrily. He'd married her, intending to tell his parents eventually, but there was no baby. She'd made a mistake, she told him, and overnight she turned from a sexy blond to an ice maiden who demanded her own bedroom. The only thing that warmed her up was the promise of spending money on a grand scale.

His long bouts of celibacy were broken when she cajoled and wheedled and asked for more cash. Most of the time he lived in hope, still obsessed with her, but she kept her door firmly locked.

He'd hired 'escorts' on occasions, but found the experience humiliating and empty.

He'd never forget the day Nancy had come home flashing a diamond ring at him and told him she was engaged. When he'd remonstrated that she was still married to him, she waved a paper in his face.

'Not for long, honey. I'm divorcing you!'

'On what grounds?'

'You'll find out soon,' she called airily from her room. She threw the contents of her wardrobe into a suitcase and he'd leaned hopelessly on the door jam, begging her not to go.

He didn't contest the divorce the following year. She cited him for adultery with 'escorts'—she'd hired a private detective to follow him. He managed to salvage some of his money and property, if not his pride. He swore his friends and his sister to secrecy and came home to a dying grandmother, a job at his old firm and his country, which had changed in the blink of an eye. He knew that as soon as his grandmother passed, his mother would renew her efforts to find him a 'suitable' Persian wife.

'No more American girlfriends,' she'd said tartly at dinner the other night.

He went up to his own apartment and looked out of the window. Zahra's little boy was playing in the garden with the housekeeper's niece. He watched them for a while, smiling at the boy's antics as he ran for the soccer ball. He sighed; he wanted to get married and have kids, but his experience with Nancy had left him shaken. And now that Zahra had come back into his life, he wasn't interested in meeting the women his mother was lining up. He changed into casual clothes and went down to his grandmother's room. The nurse opened the door quietly and ushered him in.

He was still shocked by the change in his beloved grandmother. This once vital woman lay against the pillow, looking pale and thin. She smiled at him and stretched out her hand. He sat down next to the bed, took her hand and raised it to his forehead. She patted his cheek, moistened her lips, and told him she'd had some morphine and would fall asleep soon. When he reminded her about Zahra coming to read the next day, she raised her eyebrows.

'I've met her,' she said. 'I'm glad she's not one of your mother's relatives!' She smiled weakly at her own joke.

'Grandma!' he rebuked her with a laugh.

Esmat had forbidden anyone in the family to mention her Afghan grandparents and she always passed off comments people made about her unusual green eyes. The retail empire that Esmat now managed had started as a stall in Tehran's main bazaar. Her marriage into the Konari clan, one of the city's leading families, had been a triumph for her wealthy parents with their lowly origins.

'Can you say some of the Ghazals of Hafez for me, Karim?' his grandmother asked.

He took her thin hand in his and began to recite:

'*Deep in my heart's ocean many priceless pearls are there,
It's a pity if they remain unpierced, unstrung to compare!
Who speaks about the pain of grief that one can express?
It's a pity, for the pain of deep sorrow one cannot share!*'

He looked at his grandmother. She had slipped into sleep. He pondered the deep sorrow Zahra had suffered when she was so young. In his mind's eye, he saw her expressive dark eyes moist with tears and he imagined her reading to his grandmother in her gentle, cultured voice. He'd lied to Nasim when he'd told her that he didn't find Afghan women attractive. He had been deeply attracted to Zahra the first time he'd seen her ten years ago when she was only seventeen and he was twenty-two. Maybe the attraction was due to his ethnic heritage, he thought, like his light-coloured eyes. Something that could never be changed.

Zahra the woman was even more beautiful, with her high cheek bones, but the dark eyes had lost their innocence. There was a shade of wariness about them. He was still irresistibly drawn to her. He shuddered when he recalled her soft body against his. And now she was married—he'd lost her again.

It seemed ages since he was home. On his last visit his grandmother had been as bright and busy as usual, arguing with his mother and still trying to organise the household. It was before the madness had overtaken Iran, and just after Nancy had left him.

The nurse came in to check on her patient. He took the hint and left the sick room, nearly colliding with Tahmineh outside the door. She didn't give him a chance to ask about Zahra.

'Your father wants to see you in his study,' she said breathlessly.

He looked at his watch—wasn't it too early for his father to be home?

'Where's your mother?' his father asked as soon as he saw him.

'Out, I think,' he answered.

Abbas sat down in the large leather chair Karim remembered from his childhood, motioning him to the opposite seat that faced the rear gardens.

'So, *Baba djan*, is there a problem?'

'Look at this.' He waved the daily newspaper in Karim's face.

'More demonstrations outside the American Embassy,' Karim read out loud, glancing at the photograph of the huge crowd.

'I think it's time to leave,' his father announced.

The bald statement shocked Karim out of his introspective musings. 'This is a bit sudden. I've only just got back!'

'Life here is getting worse by the day,' his father went on, ignoring him.

'The new regime wants the shah sent back here to stand trial for crimes against the people, don't they?'

His father snorted. 'He'll be safe in New York soon, according to my sources, and that's where he'll stay. The American president knows that any member of the royal family would be tried and executed if they set foot here.'

'According to the *New York Times,* four million people welcomed the Ayatollah at the airport in February!'

'They'll live to regret it,' his father answered tersely. 'The Americans are thinking of closing their embassy soon.' He poured a measure of whisky for each of them. 'You know crowds of militants got over the embassy walls a couple of months ago, don't you?' He handed Karim a crystal glass.

Karim nodded. 'I read about it in the States.' He looked from his glass to his father. 'It's a bit early for this, isn't it?'

'Drink it while you can,' his father said gloomily. 'We live in an Islamic State now—eighty lashes is the punishment for drinking alcohol.' He sighed and raised his glass in a mock toast.

'Everything's much worse than I thought.' Karim sipped from his glass. 'Those kids driving round with loaded rifles give me the creeps.'

'Last year was terrible—strikes, gunfire in the streets ... those students who were killed when they protested about the government ... you missed a lot of it,' Abbas replied. 'One minute we were exporting oil, the country was rich, had a secular government. Now it's total chaos.'

Karim raised his eyebrows. 'Shah out, Khomeini in.'

'It won't be long before your mother is ordered to stop work because she's a woman.'

'Surely not!'

'All the women in my office got the sack. Oil production's almost non-existent now. My job's gone.'

'Your job?'

'There'll be a world oil shortage soon. My company's being run by clueless village idiots employed by the government.'

Karim was tempted to tell his father about the counter-revolutionary group to give him some hope. But in his heart he knew that there wasn't any.

'All our friends are leaving,' his father went on. 'We'll be joining them as soon as possible.' He sighed. 'If it wasn't for your grandmother, I'd leave next week. There's no future here. The new regime is entrenched.'

Karim's heart sank; this was his home, he loved the place, his roots were here, not to mention his closest friends. His father was talking as if they would never come back.

'I've been to the US embassy to update our visas. Is yours okay, son?'

'I've got a green card. I'm on a leave of absence from my job in the States.' He leaned over and squeezed his father's hand. 'I'm here to help, *Baba djan*—after—when she passes, you and mother can go. I'll stay here and sort things out.'

To his surprise his father picked up a sheet of paper from his desk. 'Thanks son, I've got a list ready,' he said. 'Basically you'll need to sort this house and the beach house. Amir can help. I sold a lot of our properties last year and transferred the money to the States …' His voice broke and he put his head in his hands. 'How did this happen to our beautiful country?'

'Who knows, Baba, but surely it can't go on forever?'

'Your mother and I weren't bad people, but now we're the enemies of the new State. The newspapers call us leeches, supporters of the shah's regime.' He stared at Karim in bewilderment.

Karim looked past him at the pictures on the wall. There were photos of his father and mother with the shah and shahbanu and another of his parents with the American ambassador.

'It might be an idea to pack those away.' He pointed to the photos. 'They could be used against you as evidence that you are a supporter of the old regime.'

'You're right, son.' Abbas unhooked the pictures and put them in his desk cupboard. 'Never underestimate fanatics, eh?'

For the first time, Karim noticed how much his father had aged in the past couple of years.

'I'll get on to this as soon as possible,' he promised, indicating the list.

'Thanks, son.' Abbas checked his watch. 'I've got to put a call through to the parent company in the States. They want to know when the oil's going to start flowing again.' He raised his eyebrows. 'How many different ways are there of saying *never?*'

14

THE FIRST DAY

Zahra woke early the following morning from a fitful sleep. She got out of bed quietly and opened the curtains. In the pale light she could see part of the garden. The house was deeply silent. She leaned her forehead against the cold windowpane. She felt cut adrift as if she was floating in a void, unable to put her feet on the ground. An image of Karim crossed her inner eye and she said his name out loud under her breath and sighed. If only things were different!

Ahmad stirred in his narrow bed and she knelt down next to him. He was sleeping soundly, clutching his Mickey Mouse soft toy. She moved to stroke his hair but stopped—she didn't want to wake him too early. She showered and dressed and when she came out of the bathroom he was wide awake, seemingly quite happy and settled in his new home.

'Can I play soccer today with that man?'

'Karim Agha,' she corrected. 'Maybe.' She ruffled his hair. Showered and dressed, they walked down the dark stairs to the kitchen where Tahmineh was already busy. When she saw Zahra, Tahmineh launched into the day's arrangements as she served breakfast.

'Shirin will take Ahmad to the kindergarten this morning while you read to Madam—Rezvan Khanoum, that is,' Tahmineh told her. 'Then after lunch we all have a nap. It's hot outside already.'

Zahra nodded and offered to help with any household chores. Tahmineh smiled with relief. Her fifteen-year-old niece was only helpful to a point, she said. Agha Karim's return and Rezvan's illness had put more work on her shoulders and she'd be glad of an extra pair of hands. Alone in her room after breakfast, Zahra turned to the pages she'd marked to read to Rezvan. She hadn't seen Karim that morning, so assumed he'd gone to work early. As she crossed the landing, she heard Esmat's voice floating up the wide staircase from the salon.

She knocked on the sick room door and the nurse opened it with a smile.

'Madam's looking forward to seeing you,' she said, indicating the invalid propped up on her pillows.

Rezvan looked better than she had the previous day and her eyes were bright with anticipation when she turned to greet Zahra. She was wearing a white nightdress with a high embroidered collar and her long dark hair, streaked with grey, had been carefully arranged on the pillow. She motioned Zahra to a chair by the bed and raised her eyebrows expectantly.

'I thought we might begin with Hafez,' Zahra told her.

'Yes, excellent choice.'

Zahra smiled and as she began to read, she heard Rezvan sigh.

'City of the heart,
God preserve thee!
Pearl of the capitals thou art,
Ah! To serve thee ...'

She paused in her reading, but Rezvan moved her hand slightly for her to carry on. When she'd finished, Rezvan asked if she'd ever visited Shiraz, the poet's city. When Zahra told her reluctantly that it was her mother's birthplace, and that her mother had died on a visit to Iran, a flicker of interest crossed the old lady's face.

'May God give you patience,' she said, the customary comment for those who had suffered a loss.

She thanked Rezvan and changed the subject. It wasn't hard to encourage her to talk about 'those beautiful people', the beloved royal family.

'You know,' Rezvan said in her breathy voice, 'we went to balls and parties nearly every night. Once, I was in Paris and I saw the future shahbanu in a beauty salon, just after her engagement was announced. I called out "Congratulations, Farah Khanoum!"' She turned her head and looked at Zahra. 'She smiled and thanked me. She was thrilled to hear her own language. When I met her after she became the shahbanu, she remembered me ...'

Zahra was entranced by the fairy tale world Rezvan described. A world of love and Dior gowns and beautiful children. Rezvan talked about the brilliant life she'd had, how their exotic country was admired throughout Europe. The effort of speaking had exhausted the old lady and she lay back on her pillows with her eyes closed. She sighed and a single tear slid from the corner of her eyelid.

'They've all gone,' she whispered.

Zahra picked up a handkerchief to dab away the tear, but Rezvan took it from her.

'I can do that, dear.' She shook her head sadly and the large dark eyes met hers. 'Last year was so terrible; there was fighting in the streets, and now we have fanatical people in charge. How did that happen?' She sighed as she motioned Zahra to continue reading.

'This is Hafez writing about Shiraz,' Zahra said quietly. 'The Lesson of the Flowers.'

"Twas morning, and the Lord of day
Had shed his light o'er Shiraz' towers,
Where bulbuls trill their love-lorn lay
To serenade the maiden flowers

Like them oppressed by love's sweet pain
I wandered in a garden fair;
And there to cool my throbbing brain,
I woo the perfumed morning air.'

She paused, overcome by the sentiment in the poem and the beauty of the words. When she'd finished 'The Lesson of the Flowers', she read a few more poems and eventually Rezvan drifted off to sleep. Zahra sat and leafed through the familiar pages, reading a few of her favourite poems, and marked some to read next time. She wondered what to do and whether Rezvan would wake suddenly and ask her to read again, but she seemed to be in a deep sleep. Zahra stood up cautiously and looked round the spacious room. A collection of framed photographs in gilt frames on a small table caught her eye. Unable to contain her curiosity she tiptoed over to them. She glanced back at the sleeping woman. Her eyes were closed and her breathing was slow and measured.

Most of the pictures were formal and posed: Rezvan elegant in a long sheath dress that glittered with sequins, her arm through that of a tall man in a white uniform with gold braid and medals. There was another of Esmat and Abbas at the same event. Gingerly she picked up a photograph of Karim, smiling at the camera, hands on hips. He was dressed in a white tee shirt, shorts and leather sandals and standing near a large white house. In the background, she could just see a strip of sand and a distant blue line of sea. Zahra concentrated on the photograph, trying to memorise it, and sighed when she recalled the words of the poem: '... oppressed by love's sweet pain.'

When the nurse, Mahtab, opened the bedroom door quietly, she nearly dropped the heavy frame onto the table. Her hands shook as she replaced the photo. The nurse smiled at Zahra, glanced across at the bed and joined her at the table.

'Aren't they wonderful?' she whispered. 'I love looking at them—Rezvan Khanoum had an amazing life.'

Mahtab picked up the photo of Karim, pointed to the house and told her the family called it a beach house, but it was really another mansion.

'They always spend the summer there on the Caspian Sea. I went with them last year to look after ...' She jerked her head at the sleeping invalid. 'Anyway,' she dropped her voice to a whisper and raised her eyebrows, 'they told me in the pharmacy that a couple of years ago Karim Agha had brought an American girlfriend with him.'

'Really?' Zahra hated gossip but she longed to hear more.

'Yes.' Mahtab pursed her lips. 'There was a terrible family row—the girlfriend sunbathed topless on the beach—nearly naked, they said in the pharmacy! Esmat Khanoum called her a prostitute and Karim stormed off back here with the blond woman. What do you think?'

Zahra shook her head. 'I don't really know ...'

She longed to ask if the nurse knew the woman's name but Mahtab, with a final raise of her eyebrows, turned away to see to her patient.

Zahra collected her book and left, closing the door quietly behind her. Out on the landing she shook her head, annoyed with herself for listening so eagerly to gossip. There were more important things in the world, in her life, she reminded herself, than whether her boss's son had an ex-wife in the United States.

Back in the kitchen, she asked Tahmineh if she knew what the family planned to do in the next few months.

'I think they'll all go to America when ... when she passes. We'll go back to the village and take over the family shop,' Tahmineh said sadly. 'Although Madam says we can live in this house as long as we like.' She shook her head. 'The city's getting too dangerous for us though.' She unhooked a calendar from the wall and handed it to Zahra.

'Karim Agha sent this to us. He's always been thoughtful,' she remarked. 'America looks like a lovely place,' she said over her shoulder as she opened the kitchen door.

Zahra flipped to the cover page. 'Beautiful North America' it said in English, and underneath in her own language it said: 'Dear Tahmineh and Amir, I hope you enjoy the pictures of this lovely country. Turn to the month of September and you'll see Boston where I have a house. All my love, Karim.'

She stared at the script and imagined him writing it at his desk in his American house. Was his wife Nancy chatting to him as he wrote? She admonished herself for slipping into fiction again. She flicked through the pages quickly. Tahmineh was right; America did look beautiful. She replaced the calendar, forcing herself to stop thinking of Karim and to think of something else. She was still worried about Firzun and she wanted to know more about the refugee visas and his plans for their future in Australia.

She jumped when Tahmineh burst into the kitchen.

'If you're looking for Ahmad, he's outside playing soccer with Karim Agha! Shirin hasn't had a chance to take him to the kindergarten yet.'

Surprised, Zahra looked out of the window. Sure enough, Ahmad was squealing and running after a soccer ball. She flung the door open, forgetting about her headscarf and called him to her.

'You're a champion, Ahmad!' Karim shouted.

He picked the boy up and swung him in the air. When he put him down, Ahmad ran across to his mother, laughing excitedly. Karim's hair was tousled, his face bright and happy. Seeing him so uninhibited, so alive, her heart started to race and she found it hard to breath. Is this what falling in love felt like?

Karim walked over to her. 'I haven't hurt him, Zahra!' He put his hand on his heart and made a comical face.

'I've got to get him to the kindergarten.' She smiled and pushed Ahmad ahead of her through the kitchen door.

Ten minutes later when she emerged with Ahmad, she saw Karim running down a set of outside stairs she hadn't realised existed. He pointed to a huge glass rectangle secured to the top of the house. 'My apartment,' he said proudly.

A wooden deck projected across the rear terrace of the original house and a metal staircase led down to the garden. This was the first time she'd seen the impressive apartment from the outside. He fell into step with her down the side path and asked her if she had settled in. Their eyes met and she looked away quickly.

'Yes, thank you. I read to your grandmother today. She liked the poem you chose.'

She felt him turn and smile down at her again, but she looked away, checking that Ahmad wasn't walking on the flowers.

'Well, parting is such sweet sorrow ...' Karim smiled directly at her. 'Have a good day, Zahra, and you too, champ!' Karim called to Ahmad as he got into his low silver sports car.

They stood back as he drove carefully out of the gates, then she heard him rev the engine and take off up Maryam Street. She walked along, pleased that at least she recognised *that* particular quote—from Shakespeare's *Romeo and Juliet*.

The house was silent when she returned. She could hear Tahmineh and Shirin far away up the main staircase and she decided to slip into the library and phone Firzun. She opened the library door cautiously, but the room was empty. Esmat Khanoum had left in a noisy flurry earlier and gone to work. Abbas, as usual, had left very early, and she'd seen Karim go, so there was no one to disturb her. She selected a couple of books for Rezvan and walked over to the phone. She had her hand on the receiver when she heard the library door open behind her. She snatched her hand away and fiddled with one of the books.

Karim hadn't noticed her and said 'Oh!' when she greeted him.

She'd seen him go to work. What was he doing back so soon?

'I left some drawings behind. I think they might be in here,' he said as if reading her thoughts.

Her heart was thudding, certain he'd noticed her hand on the phone. He smiled and took the book she had opened hastily. He congratulated her on her choice of Keats' *Ode to a Nightingale*.

The light was behind him and she couldn't read the expression on his face. She felt acutely embarrassed, remembering the last time they were in the library together. She wished he would go, release her from the attraction she felt every time she saw him. Instead he pulled a chair out for her to sit down and he sat opposite her with only a small table between them.

Karim started to read in English, '*My heart aches ...*' He paused for a moment without looking up. Then he finished the first stanza in his perfect English.

'You read English so well, I could never ...'

He interrupted her and pressed her to read to him in English. 'Read stanza number six,' he said and frowned. 'It's ... when I read it, I think of grandmother ...'

Karim passed the book across to her with a slight smile, and as she took it his fingers brushed hers. She felt completely overwhelmed by him. He was the most striking, sophisticated man she had ever met in her life. She breathed in to steady her voice and began to read:

'*Darkling I listen; and for many a time*
I have been half in love with easeful Death
Called him soft names in many a mused rhyme,
To take into the air my quiet breath ...'

Zahra looked up at him; he was frowning but he nodded for her to continue.

When she finished reading he didn't speak; their eyes met briefly and he looked away. She saw the pain in his and knew he was thinking about Rezvan. She wished he hadn't asked her to read that particular stanza.

Karim sighed and stood up, shattering the hypnotic mood the poem had created. 'Thank you,' he said brusquely. 'I think I left the drawings upstairs.'

She pushed back her chair and stood up startled by the sudden change in his manner. When he got to the door he turned abruptly.

'Your English is very good, Zahra. Enjoy your day.'

When Karim had gone, his aftershave lingered in the air. Zahra stood in the library, feeling totally unnerved by her latest encounter with him. She'd vowed to avoid him, but he seemed to be everywhere in the house, threatening her sham marriage. She needed to get back on track and see Firzun. That would bring her down to earth. She'd phone him and insist he accompany her and Ahmad to Friday prayers the following day. They needed at least to have the appearance of a family.

15

FRIDAY PRAYERS

On Thursday, Karim spent a frustrating day at the architectural firm where he had a temporary position. He was finding it hard to get used to the easy-going work ethic of his own country. Compared with the intensity of the New York and Boston offices where he'd worked, this place was like a school camp.

That evening when he took his seat on the sofa at Nasim and Rashid's, he had a feeling of déjà vu. Before he'd gone to the States, his friends had been rallying support to rid the country of the oppressive regime led by the royal family. Now they were determined to topple the regime that had taken its place. When he pointed this out, Nasim answered quickly.

'Look, we're angry. Why shouldn't our country have a democratic government like hundreds of other countries in the world? Isn't it time?'

'I don't know.' He shrugged. 'Maybe it's the geographical position of Iran or the inertia of our history.'

'Totally misguided, Karim,' Nasim answered as if she were in a courtroom. 'Well,' Rashid, always the peacemaker, ventured, 'let's agree to disagree as usual.'

'I'll help you as much as I can,' Karim promised, 'as long as it's nothing illegal.' And if I'm here, he thought.

The most interesting part of the evening was when Firzun made an appearance. He was dressed in work clothes and covered in some sort of white dust. Once again, the other man's educated accent surprised Karim when they met. He made non-committal noises when Firzun thanked him for taking care of his wife and son. Firzun showed a flattering interest in Karim's architectural skills—he wasn't sure why.

He wondered exactly what the Afghan was up to. During dinner, when he commented that Firzun's degree in chemical engineering might be useful if anyone wanted to make a bomb, he was acutely aware that he'd made a gaff of some sort. His remark was greeted by a moment's silence, and when he looked at his old friend Maryam, she seemed taken aback, as if he'd inadvertently spilled the beans about something. He felt annoyed that his old friends didn't seem to trust him.

It added to his suspicion that they were lying to him about something. But they were open enough about what they planned to do in their campaign against the regime. Nasim was determined to go ahead with her women's march, and if radical student groups took over the American embassy, they vowed to recapture it from them. In your dreams, Karim thought.

He sensed that there was something else, that they had another secret they weren't sharing with him. He suspected it concerned Zahra and her son. They'd told him about her deceased husband and her new marriage to Firzun readily enough, so what were they hiding? As always they parted as friends; after all, he'd known them all his life.

As he walked home, he wrinkled his nose—the street smelled of putrefying garbage. This would never have happened in the past. The servants in the big houses kept their sections of the street clean and there was a regular garbage collection. Had it always been gloomy and badly lit? Maybe he'd been spoiled in the States, with its brightly lit suburbs and flashing neon signs in shopping centres. When he got home, he looked up and down the road, wondering if someone had followed him, then wondered why the thought had even crossed his mind.

The lights were still on in the salon, so he let himself in the small gate and walked down the side path; he couldn't face being interrogated about his evening by his mother. As he put his foot on the outside staircase up to his apartment, he turned and looked up at Zahra's window. A faint glow filtered through the curtains and he sighed, wondering if she was reading in bed. He felt tempted to call up to her window, throw a few bits of gravel at the panes just to see her surprised face and her long hair cascading over her shoulders. He pulled himself together and made a decision based on what he'd heard at Nasim and Rashid's. Tomorrow he'd go to Friday prayers at the local mosque to get an idea of 'opposition' thinking.

Zahra, as Karim had guessed, was reading in bed, her hair tied in a loose plait. She wanted to go to Friday prayers, but for a different reason. If she prayed and made her peace with God, maybe she would no longer have the terrible nightmares about being lost in the mountains. When she'd phoned Firzun, she was thankful that he'd agreed to go with her. She closed her book, and as she turned off the light she fancied she heard Karim running up the metal staircase to his apartment. She lay awake and thought about the events of her day.

Rezvan Khanoum had not had a good night and her smile of greeting that morning had been tinged with pain.

'I wish that God would take me soon,' she'd said as Zahra approached the bed.

'I pray that God will ease your pain,' Zahra had replied.

As she sat down on the pink velvet chair near the bed, Zahra had glanced across at Karim's photograph, still in the position she'd left it, with its subject frozen forever at his beach house. She'd looked down at the poetry book and started to read quietly. Rezvan Khanoum had laid with her eyes shut as the words washed over her. When Karim had come as usual to see his grandmother, Zahra had excused herself, feeling his eyes follow her as she left the room. A few minutes later, he'd called her back, asking her to join in a discussion he and his grandmother were having about a particular book.

'I'm sure you've read this,' he'd said with a smile.

Rezvan had been delighted to have a 'proper conversation at last'.

At one point Zahra had forgotten where she was, and told Karim he'd completely misunderstood the author's intent. Rezvan had laughed breathily, saying she agreed with Zahra. Karim's eyes had met hers and he'd spread out his hands in a smiling gesture of defeat.

Zahra sighed and pulled her thoughts back to arrangements for the next day. If Firzun came to the mosque with her, it would validate the lie that they were married. She knew that if she were newly widowed and lived in a strict Muslim family, she'd be confined to the house for over four months. But there was no one here to disapprove of her behaviour. Only Firzun and his close friends knew the truth about Mahmoud.

The attraction she felt for Karim disturbed her. How long could she stay, she wondered, with him in such close proximity? He was bound to realise how she felt. As she drifted off to sleep she could still hear his voice in her head, reciting Keats' poetry in English.

Karim had breakfast with his mother, who was full of plans for 'afterwards', which he supposed meant when his poor grandmother died. Fortunately one of her garrulous friends telephoned and she dismissed him. He settled down in his airy apartment to work on a drawing for a client and lost all sense of the time. When he heard Ahmad shouting from the garden, he was surprised to see it was nearly midday. He moved over to the window and saw Zahra bundled up in her chador and scarf. Firzun was walking alongside her, still in his workman's jacket. Ahmad trotted along between them wearing a crocheted skullcap and a yellow tee shirt. He watched them until they rounded the corner of the house, wondering about Zahra's marriage of convenience as he had many times before.

The sound of the *azan-e zohr*, the midday call to prayer, floated through the window. He had time to get to the mosque as he'd planned, if he moved fast. He ran down the stairs two at a time, nearly colliding with his mother, who was just coming out of the salon.

'Sorry, can't stop! I'll explain later.' He kissed her briefly on both cheeks, pulled on his outdoor shoes, and slammed out of the door.

In the mosque courtyard, he saw Firzun leaving the washing area. Zahra was already on the steps of the mosque undoing Ahmad's shoes. She turned and said something snappy over her shoulder to the man who minded the shoes before she headed into the building. He didn't look too pleased—serve him right. Karim recognised him from when he was a kid and his grandmother took him to Friday prayers. The man used to wave his green feather duster around even then and try to boss the women. His grandmother had given him short shrift too.

He washed quickly, walked up the steps to the mosque and put his American shoes on a low shelf. The officious man made a comment about a lot of people coming today, as he moved them along and flicked them with his duster. Karim was surprised to see that the mosque was crowded. As he eased himself on to the end of a row, he saw Firzun standing three rows ahead of him.

The prayer call had stopped and while he waited for the prayers to begin, Karim looked around. The once shabby mosque had had a costly makeover: new tiles, a fresh coat of paint and new thick wool carpets on the floor. This was a wealthy suburb, but the wealthy weren't very religious, so who was paying? During the prayers he thought about Zahra. He was achingly aware of her at the back of the mosque with the women. He stumbled over the words of the prayers and pulled himself together.

After the devotions finished, he sat cross-legged with everyone else and watched as another Imam ascended the pulpit steps. He was dressed in a flowing white robe over which he wore a long-sleeved black gown. From under his black turban, wisps of grey hair escaped and his grey beard showed he was *Haji*, a man who had made the pilgrimage to Mecca. He glared at the congregation, then his voice rang out round the mosque.

'In the name of God, the Compassionate and the Merciful,' he began, 'evil walks amongst us and the evil ones seek to destroy us.'

The sermon that followed was not a moral discourse, but an attack on the president of the United States and its people—'the sons of Satan', as well as the deposed shah—'the fornicator, the doer of evil.' The ranting continued with the Imam urging the 'warriors of the faith' to get up and fight. There was a lot of talk about 'vengeance' and the 'wrath of the Almighty' and 'the fires of hell'.

Suddenly it was all over. The Imam stepped down and Karim tried to reassemble his scattered wits. It looked like his friends were right. The religious zealots might be crazy enough to attack the American embassy. Was this a message? Permission? He looked across at the youths who lounged round the walls of the mosque. They were jumpy and hyperactive and Karim wondered how much dope they'd smoked. In the past, someone would have told them to be more respectful in a place of worship. But now the other male worshippers avoided them. No one wanted to get shot by a trigger-happy youth.

Karim stood on the steps and pulled his shoes on slowly. Out of the corner of his eye he saw Zahra bending to tie up Ahmad's sneakers. Firzun stood nearby and was staring across the courtyard when Karim joined him. Some of the young men from the mosque had gathered in small groups. As the two men watched, they collected automatic rifles from a pile guarded by a giant in a flak jacket. With their rifles and bullet belts slung over their shoulders, the youths strutted across the courtyard and out of the main gate.

'Well, religion and politics, what a mix!' Firzun commented quietly.

Karim said nothing as he watched Zahra walk towards them with her son. Her black chador flowed round her body in the slight breeze. Ahmad returned Karim's greeting enthusiastically, but Zahra smiled and looked away. When he invited them to join him at 'Yam Yam', his favourite ice-cream shop, Firzun declined and took his leave—gracefully, Karim had to admit.

Even so, he felt unreasonably let down by the rebuff. He tried to catch Zahra's eye, but she wouldn't look at him. They walked together across the courtyard and out of the mosque. When Ahmad tripped on his trailing shoelace, Firzun stopped to fix it and Karim seized the opportunity to talk to Zahra.

'I've managed to get a paperback copy of the *Shahnameh* for you to read to Grandmother,' he said quickly. 'I'll leave it in the library.'

She thanked him and apologised for Firzun's rebuff. She stepped aside and took Ahmad's hand as Firzun rejoined them. Outside in the busy street they shook hands and went their separate ways.

16

A HOUSE CALL

The weather was pleasant and Karim walked home leisurely, his shoes still warm from being in the sun. He pushed open the side gate and let himself in the front door. The house was completely silent. A cold lunch had been laid out for him in the small dining room. In spite of the sunshine, he felt gloomy and a bit lonely. After lunch he drifted into the library; he hadn't played the piano for a few days and it always cheered him up.

Karim found the paperback copy of the *Shahnameh* and put it on a table. He looked at the piano and felt an overwhelming need to play, to lose himself in music and forget the disturbing things he'd heard in the mosque. He took his copy of the *Goldberg Variations* from the music cupboard. Bach would definitely clear his head, he thought as he sat down on the piano bench. He could forget about everything for a while. He sighed; the only woman he really liked was married to someone else; moreover, he was stuck in Tehran indefinitely. He remembered what Maryam had said the previous evening, about the new draconian adultery laws—the woman could be stoned to death and the man hanged—what a medieval punishment! He shuddered—things were never *that* bad under the old regime.

He opened the music, placed it on the stand and scanned it. He'd need to concentrate to get through it all. His mind couldn't wander to thoughts of Zahra while he played—or Nancy for that matter. He took his hands off the keys. Nasim had slipped him a letter from his ex-wife the previous evening. As instructed she'd written care of his friends. He pulled the note out of his pocket and re-read it. It was penned in her usual childlike scrawl.

'Thanks for the big bucks, hon—outa sight! Some heavy stuff going in your neck of the woods so keep on keeping on. Besos, Your Foxy Mama Nancy.

PS California is well hip. Hi five to your mother—what a POW!

Irritation overwhelmed him, especially when he read the final swipe. POW was a pointed degrading insult aimed at his mother: 'a piece of work'. How typical of Nancy to write almost entirely in slang too.

'What an idiot I was,' he said out loud. At least she'd attached the decree absolute this time.

He ran his eyes across the music and stared at the page. He couldn't stop thinking about Zahra. She was so contained, so secretive. He shrugged; perhaps if you were a refugee, you learned to keep your mouth shut.

He had almost finished playing when the sudden jangling of the front door bell shook him out of his reverie. At this time of day he knew the housekeepers were resting. He got up from the piano, walked into the atrium, and opened the front door. Two well-dressed young men stood on the doorstep. They greeted him politely. If he'd been in the States he'd have taken them for Mormon missionaries. Each wore a dark suit, white shirt and green tie, and each had a neatly trimmed beard. They both carried an official-looking clipboard.

'We're just checking the names of everyone who lives at this address, sir. If you could tell us, then we can tick them off our list and be on our way.'

The taller man smiled pleasantly when he asked the question. Even so, Karim felt uneasy. Their lips smiled but their eyes were hard.

'I'd like to see some identification, if you don't mind,' Karim replied.

'Of course,' the second man answered smoothly, fixing Karim with a stare as they handed him their cards. They'd been issued by the Department of Religious Affairs and Karim felt unnerved. He had no idea that such a department existed, and why would this particular department need to know such information? Wasn't that the job of the electoral office—if there was one?

'Religious affairs?' Karim queried.

They waved away his concerns and told him that a lot of departments had been amalgamated and they were now charged with surveying all the houses in the street.

'The names?' the first man prompted him, his pen hovering over the clipboard. Karim drew a breath and gave them the names of his father, mother and grandmother. Both men nodded and put a tick next to a printed name. He was just about to recite the names of the household staff when Amir touched his elbow and asked if he could help.

'And you are?' one of the men asked.

Amir told them his full name and his birthplace.

'So, in addition to the family, how many servants live here?' one of the men said. Amir looked at Karim.

'Three,' Karim replied and gave their names.

'We don't seem to have your name on the list, sir,' the taller man said with a supercilious smile at Karim.

He told them his name and that he'd recently arrived from the

United States. When they asked to see his passport and entry visa stamp he had difficulty controlling his irritation, but he went to the safe in his father's study and brought it back to them. He was glad Amir was blocking their entrance into the atrium. If he'd left them alone he was sure they'd have wandered into the house.

He waited while they laboriously thumbed through his passport, turning it this way and that to read the stamps. As they were both copying details from it, Karim glanced down the driveway. To his surprise, Firzun was standing at the front gates. As Karim watched, he turned swiftly, swept Ahmad up from the footpath, and with his other hand propelled Zahra down the road away from the house. Amir cleared his throat—he'd seen them too. The strangers, to Karim's relief, had not.

The men looked up and returned his passport without comment.

'And there are definitely no other people living here?' the shorter man asked.

'No.'

'Well, thank you for your help. God be with you,' they said and turned away slowly. They walked back down the driveway and let themselves out the side gate. They'd hardly gone before Amir hurried down and locked the gate behind them.

'Let's make sure it stays permanently locked, Amir,' Karim said when he came back. Amir nodded. 'And thank you for not mentioning Zahra. It looks like her husband isn't too keen to meet anyone from the government.'

'Yes, sir. Can I get you anything?'

Karim shook his head and left Amir to close and lock the front door. He returned his passport to the safe, then went to the library and sat down at the piano again. He felt rattled; what had those Mormon lookalikes *really* wanted? He stared at Bach's *Goldberg Variations* on the music stand. It looked impossibly difficult. He felt so rattled that even a C major scale would be a challenge.

Where was Zahra? And what the hell was Firzun up to?

Firzun knew the city well and after they'd said goodbye to Karim, he took Zahra and Ahmad for lunch in a huge restaurant that he claimed had been an official's house a couple of centuries ago. They sat cross-legged on wide divans and ate the food that had been set out between them on a tablecloth.

'I didn't want to spend time with Karim Konari,' Firzun commented as they ate and drank. When she didn't answer he went on. 'He looks at you as if you were a single woman.'

She felt herself blushing. How typical of Firzun to be alert to nuances of behaviour in other people! Her cousin was watching her closely.

'That's a shocking thing to say,' she retorted. 'I'm a respectable woman, Firzun, and it was you and the others who put me in this situation with the Konari family. Now you're suggesting that I'm in some sort of moral danger!' she snapped. He had the grace to look uncomfortable before he shrugged and finished his tea.

'Nasim hasn't told Karim the truth about Mahmoud, has she?' she asked. He shook his head.

'She won't gossip. It might compromise the group.' He helped himself to a piece of bread. 'We'll be leaving soon anyway,' he added casually. 'I've just got a bit more work to do in the city.'

Zahra felt a spasm of unease as she looked across at his intense face. What sort of work was he talking about? She hadn't forgotten the bombed police station.

She leaned towards him and said quietly, 'This isn't our country, cousin. Why risk your life for Iranians? Let them fight their own battles.'

'They need me, Zahra,' he muttered. 'I can look after myself. All you have to do is be ready to leave at short notice.'

They finished their meal in silence, then Firzun lifted Ahmad from the divan and on to the floor. 'Ice-cream time, Ahmad!' he announced.

Zahra followed them out onto the noisy streets. The best ice-cream shop was in the bazaar, he told her over his shoulder as she pushed through the jostling crowds trying to keep up with him.

The city bazaar was huge and even busier than the streets. She felt a pang of homesickness when she smelled the familiar tang of the spices in their open sacks and saw the glittering gold shops. It was full of women dressed like her. She had difficulty keeping up with Firzun when he turned suddenly from one passageway and into another. Sometimes, as they pushed through the crowds, she noticed people who looked like Afghans and to her surprise, several of them greeted Firzun.

Suddenly the narrow passageways of the bazaar opened into a wide courtyard with a pool and fountain in the centre, where people sat around on benches drinking tea. The arches that supported a large glass dome above the pool were decorated with intricate blue and yellow mosaic work and the light from the dome cast sparkles on the water. She looked around smiling at this unexpected oasis. The doorways of the carpet shops were also decorated with brightly coloured tiles. Young women in chadors sat laughing and chatting among the pots that had been set out on the steps of a pottery shop. The ice-cream parlour was crowded, but to her surprise the proprietor knew Firzun and found them a table outside.

'I used to meet my university friends here,' Firzun informed her. He pointed to the dome. 'Seventeenth century,' he added.

She longed to stay in this quiet space, watching Ahmad dabble his hands in the water with the other children. The whole area was a pleasing octagonal shape and shards of sunlight picked out intricate details on the tile work. But as soon as they finished their ice-creams, Firzun was on his feet again and she followed him back along the brick-floored passageways. She promised herself she'd come back to look at the scarf shops. One place she passed had nothing but black material stacked up to the ceiling. Outside the shop, a row of dummies displayed identical chadors. There was bright dress material for little girls, and as she passed Zahra wondered sadly if she would ever have any more children. She'd love to have a daughter to dress in frilly sparkly clothes ...

She sighed when she thought of her life in Herat. There, thanks to the communist government, she'd worn a Western style suit for work, skirts just below the knee and a light headscarf—but only to placate Mahmoud. Here in a large capital city, women had lost the right to dress as they wished. How easily people could be terrorised by young zealots and religious old men! But then, she'd been terrorised by her husband in her own home. It seemed a long way back to Elahiyeh, and Firzun carried Ahmad for most of the way.

When they reached Maryam Street, he put the child down and, impatient at their slow progress, he set off at a faster pace ahead of them. He stopped suddenly at the gates of Karim's house, turned and rushed back. Sweeping Ahmad up in his arms, he propelled her forward past the house.

'Don't look, don't speak!' he hissed. 'Keep moving!' He looked round quickly at the parked cars and exhaled loudly. They reached a corner and he pushed her round it and down another street. 'Turn left here!' he ordered. He hurried her along a rutted unsealed road behind the houses in Maryam Street, urging her to keep moving. Finally he stopped and put Ahmad down. He asked Zahra if she was all right as she stopped to catch her breath.

'Did you see them?' he demanded, and she shook her head. 'Two of them at the front door.' He took a deep breath and his eyes met hers.

'They're looking for me! I'll have to lie low. Hopefully Karim didn't mention you and Ahmad.'

He reached inside his jacket and pulled out a small leather pouch. 'Our passports with the new visas,' he said, pushing them at her. 'Keep them on your body, it's safer than leaving them in the house.'

She grabbed his arm. 'I'm scared. Who are those men? Why are they looking for you?'

Although she had a good idea why they were after him, she wanted him to tell her, to come clean about his activities.

'Stop worrying, Nasim and Rashid will sort it.'

'Firzun, whatever you're mixed up in, please don't take any risks!'

'Just look after the passports, okay?' He frowned at her as he pushed against the high wooden gate into the Konari garden.

'It's locked!' he said in exasperation. 'Have you got a key?'

She handed him the key to the front gate; to her relief it opened the back gate as well and he stood aside to let her through.

'Keep the passports on you all the time,' he said, and with a brief nod he was gone. She locked the gate, hoping she'd remember the way into this back lane. She could always use it if she wanted to avoid walking along the street.

As she picked her way along the garden paths with Ahmad, she glanced up at Karim's apartment, but there was no sign of him. Once inside the safety of the silent kitchen, she helped Ahmad to remove his shoes. Her hands shook as she pulled at the ties on her chador and unfastened her coat and scarf. She hustled Ahmad up the back stairs and settled him for a nap. She hid the passports beneath her underwear in a drawer next to her bed. Next time she went out, she'd put them in the money belt she'd made. She lay down and stared at the ceiling, wondering when she would ever stop feeling frightened.

17

POLITICS

A gentle knock on the door woke Zahra from a fitful doze. It was Tahmineh, telling her that Rezvan wanted to see her.

The invalid was sitting up in bed. She didn't want to be read to, but was happy to reminisce about the past.

'Such wonderful parties, Zahra,' she said dreamily. 'We had a glittering life!'

Although she smiled as she listened and made the right noises, Zahra's thoughts wandered. She'd been invited to dinner at Nasim's, without Ahmad this time—maybe Nasim would tell her more about what was going on.

To her relief, Rezvan's nurse came into the room and interrupted the the older woman's monologue. The doctor had arrived.

'It will be good for you to see your husband,' Tahmineh commented when Zahra told her she was going out for dinner.

Zahra sighed; she'd seen enough of her tense cousin for one day. But she did want to see Nasim and find out how the campaign was going. She also wanted to see Karim and ask him about the men Firzun had been so keen to avoid.

'Well look at that!' Tahmineh exclaimed. 'Karim Agha's playing soccer with little Ahmad. What a good father he'd make!'

It wasn't exactly the right place to talk, but she had no choice. She pulled her scarf over her hair and went outside where Karim was showing Ahmad how to shoot goals. He gave Ahmad a few instructions, left him with Shirin, and walked over to Zahra.

'They wanted to know who lived here,' he said before she could ask. 'I didn't mention you and Ahmad. It's none of their business.'

'What if they see us coming and going?'

'They'll think you're visiting. I'm pretty sure they're not watching the house—Amir would have mentioned it,' he replied. 'Don't look so worried. Your papers are in order, aren't they?'

She knew he was trying to reassure her, but he too looked agitated. Her papers were in order, she thought. Everything was fine except that her cousin was impersonating her dead husband!

'I'm sorry ... we'll be leaving soon,' she said. 'Firzun's arranged visas for another country.'

He looked startled—she shouldn't have told him that. To her relief, the soccer ball whizzed past them and he turned and ran for it. She grabbed hold of Ahmad, thanked Karim, and hustled her son indoors before Karim could ask her any questions.

She went back to her room and while Ahmad was playing with his toys, she took their passports out of the drawer, sat on her bed and looked through them. There were four: hers, Ahmad's, Firzun's and Mahmoud's. So Firzun had access to two passports in different names—how convenient! But did he intend to leave the country the way he entered it, as Mahmoud?

She took a deep breath and opened Mahmoud's passport. She gazed at his photograph, hardly able to believe he was dead. The image of his face with the gold-rimmed glasses blurred before her eyes and she shivered. She wanted to tear the pages out of the passport and fling them in the garbage, but she closed it quickly and put it to one side. She flicked through her own passport and stopped at the page with a pink visa. It had a row of numbers across the top and her name. Underneath she read 'refugee processing visa' and another number. She ran her fingers over the badge at the top of the small page: two strange animals on either side of a crest. One day she might know what this meant. She put the passports back into the pouch and pushed it beneath her underwear. There was no need to take it to Nasim's with her.

She checked her watch, it was getting late and she had to get ready. As she walked onto the landing with Ahmad, Karim emerged from his grandmother's room.

'Oh, Zahra,' he said. 'I found Ahmad's jacket.' He handed it to her with a smile.

Once again she felt the electrical charge pass between them. He opened his mouth to speak but before he could, she thanked him and said quickly, 'I've been invited to dinner at Nasim's.'

'I'm going too! I'll give you a lift—really, it's no trouble, Zahra,' he added when she objected. 'I've left the book on the piano, by the way.'

Was he trying to arrange a meeting in the library? she wondered as she agreed reluctantly to the lift. She was deeply attracted to him and it both worried and annoyed her. She wished he'd leave her alone and not be so kind. He believed she was married, so why didn't he treat her with respect? But maybe Karim Konari already knew what she was thinking. Perhaps he'd laugh about it with his sophisticated friends and they'd smile and shake their heads at her silly crush.

He drove her the short distance to Nasim's in his low silver sports car.

'It's a Ford Mustang,' he said proudly as she got into the passenger seat. 'I brought it over from the States a few years ago.' He smiled and closed the door. When he got into the driver's seat, his nearness nearly overwhelmed her. He grinned at her. 'Comfortable? I have to admit, Zahra, I love this car!' He turned on the engine and they glided out the front gate. Within two minutes they were pulling up outside Nasim and Rashid's front door.

This was the first time she'd come in the front door at night at Nasim's house since she'd visited as a teenager. The house was brightly lit, just like it had been ten years ago, but as she stepped over the threshold, it felt like a lifetime. She looked down at the parquetry floor, not wanting to see the rooms on either side of the front door, unused now but redolent with memories. Karim guided her gently by her elbow and when she looked up, she knew he remembered as well.

'Chauffeur driven by the boss!' Firzun commented when he greeted her in the upstairs living room—he must have been looking out the window.

'Maryam's here, as well as a couple of other friends, Zahra.' Nasim gave her a quick hug. 'I'm so glad to see you! Rashid's over there, Karim.' She smiled at him.

A large cloth had been spread out on the floor and Mojgan was placing dishes along it as people took their places, sitting cross-legged with ease and passing the food to each other. Zahra looked covertly at them, wondering if they were the same people who had lounged around downstairs the first time she'd come. She remembered the sophisticated women drinking wine, smoking and flirting. What would their lives be like now? They had lost most of the rights they'd had then. How did they feel?

Zahra listened attentively to the conversation, glad that she'd kept up to date with the changing political scene. At one point Karim mentioned the men who had called at his house that afternoon.

'They're wooden-headed idiots in that department,' someone said dismissively, and the conversation moved on. She noticed Karim shrug in answer to a question from the man sitting next to him.

'They're about to make a move,' Firzun announced. There was a sudden deathly hush in the room. 'The sermon in the mosque today was a call to arms. It won't be long now.'

'I went to the American embassy today. The crowds are getting bigger, and they're burning effigies of the shah and the American president,' Rashid said.

'Someone's whipping them up,' Firzun commented. 'I wish they'd do something so we can take them on.'

Zahra glanced round; everyone was listening just as they had when Firzun was a student. Although his reckless bravery alarmed her, she felt the familiar stab of admiration for him. *So this is his work. He's a leader, but of what? A group of rebels?* A terrible thought struck her—what if he was arrested and put in prison? She'd have to escape to Australia on her own ... that's if she wasn't arrested as an accomplice. What would happen to Ahmad? She pulled her attention back to the conversation. Nasim was talking about the march for women's rights.

'It's on Thursday the first of November,' she announced. 'A thousand women across the city have signed up. It will be a great show of solidarity!'

The women in the group applauded. Nasim looked across at Zahra. 'Yes?'

Zahra nodded and feeling suddenly very tired, she caught Nasim's eye. 'Excuse me, Nasim, I must leave now. I'm very tired.'

'Of course,' Nasim said kindly.

Karim got up, which prompted Firzun to scramble to his feet.

'I'll take her back,' he said, jerking his head in the direction of the patio door. 'We'll go along the lane—you can carry the flashlight, Zahra.'

Karim resumed his place without looking at her. As they left, another passionate political argument started up.

They picked their way along the dark lane with Firzun chatting amiably.

'Did you look at the visas? Nousha says Sydney's a beautiful place, with beaches and sunshine. Much better than Herat!' To Zahra's surprise, he laughed out loud.

'Will the crowds overrun the American Embassy?' she asked, avoiding the subject of Australia and 'Nousha'.

'Not the crowds, Zahra, radical students. We think they might be stupid enough to take hostages this time.'

'What? American hostages? Surely not!'

'Well, if they do, we'll just go in and release them!' He laughed again.

His flippant attitude alarmed her. He seemed different tonight, she thought, as she said goodnight to him at the kitchen door. His earlier tension had been replaced by a contagious energetic restlessness. He was like a wild animal ready to spring on its prey, and he made her feel restless.

18

A VISIT FROM THE MINISTRY

The days settled into a routine. Karim always visited his grandmother alone before he went to work, then Zahra read to her. He came again in the evenings and often joined in as she read or he chatted with his grandmother about his working day. At these times Zahra rose to leave, but he often motioned her to stay.

'Grandmother will get bored with my monologue soon, won't you, my dear?'

Often he'd come in the library in the morning as she was choosing a book, dressed immaculately in his business suit. She found it hard to suppress the deep attraction she felt for him whenever they were together.

'I just thought I'd drop in before work,' was his usual excuse when he wandered in. 'I remember Grandmother loved these short stories,' and he'd hand his selection to her.

She chided herself constantly for thinking that maybe he felt the same as she did. Sometimes their eyes met and once when they were alone on the landing, he'd moved towards her and stretched out his hand.

'Zahra ...' he'd said, but she'd shook her head and turned away.

While she sat reading in the evenings, occasionally glancing at Karim seated on the opposite side of the bed, Zahra's heart went out to him. Rezvan was never going to recover. After a particularly prolonged fit of coughing, she saw the hope die from his eyes. Sometimes the nurse turned her away from the door and told her the poor old woman was too sick.

As October progressed and the plane trees that lined Maryam Street turned from green to a riot of red and yellow, Zahra knew that soon she'd have to move back to the tension of Nasim's house. The previous day she'd read about another bomb attack on an army post and wondered fearfully if Firzun had been involved.

On the morning that things took a dramatic turn for the worse, she had decided to take Ahmad to kindergarten herself. Rezvan was too sick to see her, so went to Nasim's afterwards. Nasim had mentioned that the women who'd signed up for the march needed a reminder.

It had rained the night before. The side path of the house was damp and slippery with fallen leaves, and Amir told her to leave via the main gate.

As she walked along the footpath, she was aware of a car sliding slowly past her in the gutter. She glanced at it and felt uneasy when one of the two men inside looked up at her. Suddenly the car accelerated and stopped a few houses further along from Nasim's. As she came level with it, someone wound the window down and a man's voice said quietly: 'Good morning, madam.'

Ahmad jumped and stopped talking.

'May I speak with you for a minute, please?' the man continued politely as he got out of the car. Her scalp prickled with terror. Who were these men? Government officials, gangsters or just men harassing women in the street? She ignored him and carried on walking quickly, but he followed her.

'I am from the government, madam,' he called out. 'We can talk here on the footpath or you can get in the car.'

She turned and looked at him. He was only a little taller than her, dressed in a brown suit with a white shirt and green tie. His face was puffy and pale, as if he spent a lot of time indoors. As she looked away from him at the footpath, she noticed a bulge of fat hanging over his belt.

'I prefer to talk here,' she said, raising her eyes, her throat constricting with fear. He showed her a card in a greasy plastic cover. It looked official enough and she just had time to read his name, Jafar Azari, before he returned it in his pocket.

'I'm from the Department of Religious Affairs,' he said piously. 'I have some questions for Ahmad.'

'Ahmad?' Fear gripped her—how did he know her son's name? And what on earth was the Department of Religious Affairs? Why did they need to question her son?

The man crouched on his haunches with difficulty, looked Ahmad straight in the eye and said, 'Hello Ahmad, my name's Jafar. Can you tell me where you come from?'

Ahmad looked uncertainly up at her.

'Don't ask Mummy,' Jafar said with forced jocularity. 'I'm asking you.'

'Over there, that house.' He took his fingers out of his mouth and pointed back to the Konari house.

'No, Ahmad, where did you come from before that?'

Zahra's fear was replaced by a seething anger. How dare he question her son?

'I've got our papers with us,' she cut in sharply. 'They show where we're from.' She remembered with a sick lurch that the papers were forgeries, good ones, according to Firzun, but still fake.

Jafar stood up and put his hand out for her bag. Reluctantly she gave it to him. He rummaged in it and threw her lipstick, mirror and comb in the gutter. Then he pulled out the documents. He read them slowly, glancing up at her and then down at Ahmad as he flicked over the pages. Her heart was beating with a loud thick thud against her ribs and a lump rose in her throat. It threatened to choke her. As she watched him turn the papers over, she remembered the passports hidden in her room and Firzun's warning, which she'd forgotten, to keep them with her in case the house was ever searched. Thank God, she didn't have them with her!

Jafar returned the documents without comment, an impudent expression in his dull brown eyes. It reminded her of the looks Mahmoud used to give her.

'Can we go now?' Ahmad asked plaintively. She kneeled down and put her arms round him.

'Stand up please, madam. Keep quiet and don't help him. Look at me, boy,' Jafar barked. 'What's your daddy's name?'

'Daddy,' Ahmad whispered.

'The name your mummy calls him,' the man said impatiently. Ahmad shook his head.

Jafar made a hissing noise through his teeth and tutted. He crouched down on the footpath opposite Ahmad. 'Is it Firzun?' he asked sharply.

Zahra knees felt weak. How on earth did he know about Firzun?

'My husband's name is Mahmoud, as it says in our papers,' she said, trying to control the tremor in her voice. 'Ahmad is five years old, he doesn't know his daddy's name.' She squeezed Ahmad's hand hard willing him not to say anything.

'Shut up, woman.' Jafar looked up at her.

'Is your daddy's name Mahmoud or Firzun?' he asked Ahmad.

Ahmad looked up at his mother, confused and frightened. 'He's called Mickey Mouse,' he said suddenly.

'He's joking. You're frightening him,' Zahra blurted out.

'I don't hear anything funny,' Jafar said, standing up with difficulty. 'Mickey Mouse is American Zionist propaganda. How does he know about Mickey Mouse?'

'I've got books and some slippers,' Ahmad volunteered.

'Shut up!' Jafar glared at Ahmad, who buried his head against his mother.

Zahra said nothing, horrified by the sudden dangerous turn in the conversation.

'Is this Western propaganda in that house?' He moved a step closer to her. 'Look at me, Mrs Ghafoori!' She lifted her eyes and looked him full in the face. 'Possession of Western books, alcohol and Zionist American propaganda are offences against the State,' he said loudly.

She was conscious of people passing them on the pavement, their footsteps quickening away.

'Your name wasn't on the list. Are you a servant in that house?' He pointed to the Konari mansion. When she nodded, he said, 'We'll search it immediately and see what else we might find.'

Jafar snapped his fingers at the driver and pointed to the house. She squeezed Ahmad's hand.

'Keep quiet,' she muttered in her own language. She could hardly suppress her rage when she looked down at her son's stricken face. Jafar motioned her to walk ahead. A cold wave of fear ran down her back when the driver revved the engine and drove ahead of her. He waited in the front of the gates with the engine running.

'Open them,' Jafar said impatiently.

She could feel his menacing body behind her, almost touching her coat.

'I haven't got a key.'

Jafar pushed her in the back. 'Then ring the bell!'

She stumbled forward, a feeling of dread twisting her stomach. How could she warn the family? The house was full of non-religious 'propaganda', from Esmat's *Vogue* magazines to photographs of Karim's parents with the deposed shah and shahbanu. Would the whole library be classed as propaganda and confiscated along with Ahmad's Mickey Mouse books? And what about all the alcohol? She knew the punishment for drinking it was eighty lashes.

She felt faint as she waited for the gates to open and relieved that Jafar hadn't noticed the side gate overhung with branches. She peered through the bars at the house but there was no sign of life.

'Right, if they don't open up we'll drive straight through,' Jafar announced. He pushed the bell with his thumb and left it there. The other man revved the car and at the first deafening blast of the horn, the gates swung open smoothly.

Zahra pulled Ahmad out of the way as the car screeched up the driveway. Jafar took her elbow and propelled her up to the porch. Esmat was waiting for them at the front door.

'Good morning,' she said with icy politeness, holding the front door half open.

'Mrs Konari. You're breaking the law and this house will be searched.'

'Breaking the law, who says so?' Esmat replied coldly.

'The Ministry of Religious Affairs. My name is Jafar Azari and this is Ali. Is your husband Abbas home, and your son Karim?'

Esmat flicked a contemptuous look over the men.

'My husband and son are at work,' she replied. 'Agha Azari, I am Esmat Konari. I own Arzoo, the oldest department store in the city. We are a God-fearing family, so I can't imagine what you want.'

Zahra felt terribly afraid for Esmat as she stood tall and straight in the doorway. Her coffee-coloured satin top had a high neck and long sleeves and reached to her thighs. She wore discretely loose cream pants, and had thrown a matching cream headscarf over her hair. She could not be accused of breaking any religious dress codes. Looking at her, Zahra's spirits rose. Esmat hardly ever dressed like this at home. Had she, by some miracle, been warned about Jafar?

'I've been questioning your servant here. She's confessed to having seditious non-religious books in her possession. We have the authority to search this house.'

'Whose authority?' Esmat enquired, looking at Jafar as if he were a cockroach washed up by the rain on her doorstep.

'The authority of the new Republic!' Jafar shouted, pushing past her into the hall.

'How *dare* you barge in here. I'm phoning the police!' Esmat snapped.

The driver seized Esmat by the arm and pushed her roughly into the salon. Jafar grabbed Zahra and dragged her after them, with

Ahmad clinging desperately to her clothes. Esmat squirmed furiously, but the driver was strong. He threw her roughly onto the couch. She jumped up, but he pushed her hard in the chest and she fell back with a sharp cry.

'Now, let's hope we understand each other,' Jafar said quietly. 'You will stay here while we search the house. If we find anything, you and your family will be questioned further at headquarters.'

Zahra glanced fearfully at Esmat sitting furious and silent on the couch, then she noticed that there were no magazines on the coffee table. She looked surreptitiously round the room. It had been cleared of all incriminating items. Thank God, someone must have warned them.

'You can keep the kid with you.' Jafar grabbed Ahmad's arm and pushed him towards the sofa. He sobbed and hung frantically to his mother's coat. The man lifted him by his arm and threw him roughly on the couch next to Esmat, where he wailed loudly for his mother.

Jafar strode into the atrium where the driver had marshalled Tahmineh, Amir and Shirin.

'If you're hiding anything and you have anything you want to confess before we search the house, do it now,' he declared.

Zahra felt lightheaded. All she could think about was her son crying quietly onto Esmat's expensive clothes, and the leather pouch hidden in her underwear drawer. She wouldn't give this animal the satisfaction of a confession. She would think of something, but her mind was blank. If they found the passports, she was sure they'd hustle her down the stairs and push her into the black car.

'Sir,' Amir's voice shook as he spoke, 'this is a house of God-fearing people. You won't find anything which breaks the law.'

Jafar ignored him and went back into the salon.

'I insist on accompanying you through my house.' Esmat stood up. 'My mother-in-law is an invalid. She mustn't be disturbed.'

He loosened his tie and pointed to Zahra. 'She can do it. You stay here and shut up.'

'You have no right to speak to Esmat Khanoum like that!' Amir said, his voice quivering with anger.

'Shut up, old man.' The driver grabbed Amir's arm, shook him fiercely and dragged him into the hall. Tahmineh shrieked and rushed at him, pulling at the man's jacket until he turned and gave her a violent push, sending her sprawling on the floor. Zahra ran forward and helped her up, too frightened to speak.

'You,' Jafar turned to Zahra, 'come with me. The rest of you stay here. Ali watch them!' he barked at the driver.

Ahmad's wails followed Zahra as she left the room. She knew from her life with Mahmoud that no amount of pleading or appeals to a bully made any difference. She burned with rage as Jafar pushed her ahead, firing questions at her about the family. Had she ever seen them drinking alcohol? Looking at Western magazines? Playing Western music? She shook her head.

'Where's your room?' he said, and she pointed down the passage. He marched ahead and pushed the door open. She glanced at the windowsill—most of the Mickey Mouse books had gone! Jafar snatched up the last two and waved them in her face. She felt a glimmer of hope—had they managed to clear the whole house?

Jafar pointed to the small chest of drawers near her bed. 'Open them!' he ordered.

So this was it. Firzun was right. She should have kept the passports on her body. Instead they were beneath her underwear in the drawer he was now pointing at. Then she remembered Mahmoud. He had torn her things from the wardrobe, ripped scarves and shawls, smashed her make-up, but he had never touched her underwear. He considered it 'unclean'.

She turned to Jafar and said calmly, 'Agha Azari, my intimate garments are in the top drawer. No man has *ever* touched them. It's a shameful thing for you, a religious person, to even think of handling my undergarments.'

She looked straight at him and saw a look of revulsion cross his face. She'd beaten him!

'I'll decide what's shameful,' he spat at her. 'Pick them up yourself and move away.'

She scooped up the small pile of underwear. Her fingers ached as she gripped the leather wallet underneath. After a cursory look in the other drawers, he told her to put her things back and left the room, still holding the Mickey Mouse books. She wanted to launch herself at him, tear at his face and kick him. She could easily break one of the drawers over his head, she thought, knock him senseless, punish him, *destroy him* for hurting her son.

The nurse stood outside Rezvan's room and silently opened the door, revealing the sleeping invalid. Jafar walked round the room, looked under the bed and pushed past the nurse on his way out. He looked in every room, opening drawers and tipping out the contents. She followed him into Karim's apartment where he pushed things aside and opened cupboards. Downstairs he tore through Abbas's study, scattering papers, but to Zahra's relief he didn't find any alcohol.

He demanded the combination of the safe from Esmat, but she said she didn't know it. For a moment, Zahra thought Jafar was going to hit her, but she dropped her defiant attitude and said simply, 'That is my husband's business. You'll have to telephone him and ask.'

He checked in the library, which had been almost cleared. He helped himself to an expensive leather-bound atlas, putting it under his arm. He went through the kitchen, opening drawers and cupboards. While he was searching the housekeeper's small apartment off the kitchen, she noticed that the wine racks were completely empty. He grabbed Ahmad's Mickey Mouse slippers from where he'd left them near the door.

'These will be taken as evidence and then destroyed!' he announced.

If she wasn't so terrified, she thought, she would laugh in his face. A child's slippers and story books—evidence of subversive activity? It was ludicrous. For the time being he seemed to have forgotten about Firzun, she thought with relief.

19

KARIM TO THE RESCUE

As she followed Jafar through the house, Zahra hated herself for going with him as if she was his accomplice. He'd found nothing but the Mickey Mouse slippers and two Mickey Mouse books. She shuddered with relief. All the photos, books and alcohol had been cleared and hidden in the time Jafar had been interrogating her on the footpath. No wonder Tahmineh had looked so dishevelled when they arrived. Jafar was panting by the time he returned to the salon. Everyone was waiting quietly, exactly as he'd left them, but Ahmad wailed loudly when he saw his mother.

'Get him out of here,' Jafar ordered.

Shirin took Ahmad gently out of the door, promising him chocolate cookies. He turned pitifully to his mother and pointed to his arm where Ali had dragged him to the sofa. She squeezed her nails into her palms to control the rush of blind rage that swept through her. Esmat stood up, her mouth set in a firm line.

'So did you find anything?' she asked.

'I did, Mrs Konari. These!' Jafar held up the Mickey Mouse books and slippers. Mickey, with his big white grin and silly yellow shoes, looked more ludicrous than usual.

'We know people like you break the law and drink alcohol and read filthy American books,' Jafar announced in a louder voice. 'I know you've hidden everything now, but if I brought a team here and searched this house properly, we'd find something. We could lock you up for a long time, Mrs Konari, you and your whole family.'

He walked towards the salon door where the driver was waiting for him. He turned suddenly and stood in front of Zahra.

'By the way, Zahra Khanoum. Where *is* your husband? Why isn't he living here with you?' he asked. Zahra stepped back, taken off-guard by the sudden question.

'It wasn't convenient to have him here,' Esmat said coldly.

'Quiet!' he snapped. 'She can answer.' He turned to Zahra. 'Well, where is, what's his name again ... Mahmoud?'

'He went back to our home town yesterday to try to sell some of our things,' she lied. 'I expect he'll return in a few days.'

'And where will he stay then?'

'With friends, I think.'

She raised her eyes as little as possible while she spoke to him, but when she did, he was staring at her.

'He'll stay with friends, *you think*.' He continued to stare. 'I don't believe you. I think he's here somewhere. I want to talk to your husband, whatever his name is, *when he gets back*,' he said sarcastically.

She didn't raise her eyes from the carpet. She was terrified. He knew about Firzun. They were looking for him, but he'd slipped through their fingers. If only Jafar realised how near he'd got to catching her cousin. For all their surveillance, they'd mistaken the house. They thought he was here with her. The Konaris were of minor interest to the authorities, she was sure of that. Their target was Firzun. Her guilt overwhelmed her. She was responsible, through her cousin, for all of this. Her hands shook as she clenched them at her sides.

Jafar stood without speaking and when she didn't reply, he said, 'Fortunately for you, I haven't got time for further questioning now.

You and your husband are on our list. I have to warn ...' He stopped mid-sentence as the salon door flew open and Karim stood in the doorway.

'Get out,' he said quietly.

'And you are?' Jafar said imperiously.

'You know who I am,' Karim snapped. 'Now leave my parents' house before I have you arrested or before I kill you.'

Jafar walked up to him; he hardly reached Karim's shoulder. 'I'm from the Ministry of Religious Affairs,' he said arrogantly. 'We don't take threats from anyone.'

'I'm asking you politely to leave my house,' Karim repeated.

Zahra hardly recognised his voice. It was thick with fury and menace.

Jafar drew himself up and faced Karim. 'We have the authority to search any house we want. You're lucky we only found a couple of items.' Jafar raised his chin and waved Ahmad's books and slippers in Karim's face.

Karim grabbed the 'items' and threw them on the floor.

'So you've finished your search and those were the only items you found,' he said coldly. 'I'm asking you again to leave us in peace.'

'Be very careful, Agha Konari. You and your family—people like you are enemies of the new regime.'

Karim walked to the front door without replying and held it open. 'Goodbye, be assured we are not breaking the law.'

Zahra watched as Jafar and the driver strolled out the door and Karim locked it after them.

'Thank God you're here, thank God.' Esmat ran to him as Karim came back into the salon. He folded his mother in his arms. 'Is the door shut and locked?' she asked. 'And the gate?'

'I'll double check it mother,' he said gently. 'I believe this book belongs in our library.' He put the atlas on the table. 'Right everyone,' he went on briskly, 'thank you for what you did. I'm going to organise security for the house so this won't happen again. I should have done it weeks ago,' he added quietly.

Esmat took a deep breath and started barking out orders for tea. She wanted everyone back in five minutes so she could talk to them. She motioned to Zahra to stay. Alone together in the salon, the two women stared across the carpet at each other. Zahra covered her face with her hands. Esmat stood like a furious frozen statue.

'I'm so sorry, so sorry, Esmat Khanoum,' she whispered. 'I couldn't stop them.'

'How dare they!' Esmat screamed suddenly, and Zahra took a step back. 'How dare they do this to my house. I'm complaining to the police, to the Ministry, to whoever is in charge. I am not going to let this pass. They assaulted me and a child. They terrorised all of us and trashed my home. No one has the right to do that!'

'Okay mother, let's all just sit down now,' Karim said as he came back into the room and led her to a sofa. Tahmineh pushed open the door and put a tray down on the coffee table.

'If we hadn't cleared everything away, madam,' Tahmineh lowered her voice to a whisper, 'including the alcohol, we'd have all been arrested and punished.'

'Alcohol, yes, bring me a gin and tonic—with ice—I need to calm my nerves,' Esmat replied, regaining some of her composure. 'Thank you, you all did a wonderful job.'

Zahra glanced across at Karim, who raised his eyebrows and gestured to the door with his head. Gratefully, she followed Tahmineh out to the kitchen. When the door was shut, Esmat started to shout again.

'Mickey Mouse books! Mickey Mouse! These people are insane,' she yelled.

'I'll tell Amir to get her drink,' Tahmineh said hastily to Zahra.

In the kitchen, Ahmad fell on his mother in floods of tears. She soothed and rocked him on her knee and stroked his hair. She only half listened to Tahmineh's account of how she'd seen the men talking to her in the street and anticipated what might happen. She'd run through the gardens to warn everyone.

'Thank goodness, here's Abbas Agha home from work,' she said breathlessly. 'He'll stop Madam doing anything foolish.' Tahmineh filled up a bowl with ice-cream for Ahmad, just as Amir came in after delivering the gin and tonic.

'Madam wants to see you, Zahra.'

When she returned miserably to the salon, Esmat was sitting on the sofa, alternately sipping from a tea cup and a tall glass. She looked up when Zahra came in.

'Right, Zahra, I want you to go into the library and write down *everything* that happened from when you were stopped to when those animals left my house. I shall go and complain personally to the Ministry.'

'I couldn't stop them, I'm so sorry. I'll pack up and leave today, madam,' Zahra stammered, too embarrassed to look at the family sitting on the plush sofas.

'Oh no you don't!' Esmat said sharply. 'I can't cope with mother-in-law as well as all of this nonsense. You stay right here. *I'll* be complaining to every government minister I can find.'

'We'll talk about that later, not now,' Abbas said quietly.

'That's the spirit, Mother.' Karim raised his eyebrows at Zahra and put his arm round his mother's shoulder. Zahra felt a stab of jealousy towards Esmat; she longed to have Karim's arms around *her*, his soothing, comforting voice against *her* hair. She felt deeply alone.

'Here.' He disengaged himself from his mother. He walked across the room and handed her Ahmad's Mickey Mouse books and slippers. 'It might make the poor little guy feel a bit better,' he said with a smile.

Zahra took Ahmad's precious possessions, feeling a sense of loathing, as if Jafar's damp fingerprints were still on the books and all over the slippers. In the kitchen she wiped them over with a cloth before she gave them back to Ahmad. Tahmineh had hidden the rest of his books at the back of the fridge and as he ate his ice-cream he turned the pages, seemingly recovered from his ordeal.

When Nasim arrived at the kitchen door, she listened politely to

Tahmineh's account of the morning, made soothing noises and then excused herself and went through to the salon.

'It's a disgrace,' Tahmineh declared after she'd gone. 'Decent people like her having to visit via the backdoor.'

Tahmineh was getting the lunch ready when Nasim put her head round the kitchen door to say goodbye.

'Amir said he'd drive me home.' She smiled at them. 'Zahra, the rally begins at Azadi Square, near the tower, at ten o'clock on Thursday morning. You're still coming, aren't you?'

'Yes, of course.'

'That's the spirit,' Nasim answered. 'We won't be defeated by these people. We'll stand up for our rights!'

'Be careful, Nasim Khanoum,' Tahmineh warned. 'You don't want stir up any violent men.'

'We'll be fine,' Nasim said breezily. 'I'll pick you up at nine-thirty on Thursday, Zahra. We'll show them!'

Zahra walked slowly up the back stairs with Ahmad. Tahmineh's comment had unnerved her. Maybe the women's march wasn't such a good idea after all.

20

THE MARCH

When Zahra opened the curtains on the morning of the march, she saw with dismay that it was raining—not much, but enough to make the footpaths slippery. She went over Nasim's final instructions in her head.

'We won't be breaking the law,' Nasim had said on the phone. 'We'll wear our headscarves and chadors. This will be a passive protest. We walk up to the tower carrying banners proclaiming our rights under the original constitution. We won't give the authorities any reason to get violent with us like last time.'

Last time? Zahra wondered.

'Our leader will address the crowd, then we'll walk around the tower and disperse.'

Nevertheless, Zahra felt nervous. She hadn't forgotten Maryam telling her that since the new government had come to power, women had lost most of their rights. Surely that would include the right to protest in public?

Karim came into the library while she was sitting at the long table finishing off yet another 'report' on Jafar's visit for Esmat.

'How's Ahmad today?' he asked, pulling out the chair next to her.

'He's all right now, thank you.' She smiled at him. He was dressed casually, which meant he was working from home. He returned her smile and leaned towards her.

'So are you reading to grandmother today?' he asked, indicating a book she'd put on the table.

'Yes, later today.' She hesitated and took a breath. 'I'm going to the women's rally at Freedom Square this morning with Nasim.'

'What! You can't be serious?' he exclaimed.

'I promised Nasim I'd go—I owe her a lot.'

'Zahra, believe me, it's not safe—there are bands of aggressive men out there, armed with guns. They won't allow women to protest. They want all of you to stay at home.'

'That's why I'm going,' she said firmly.

He might be her employer's son, but he had no right to tell her what to do. She wondered if Esmat would approve, but she wasn't around. She'd left early to continue her crusade against the Ministry of Religious Affairs.

'You're not taking Ahmad, are you?'

'He'll be at kindergarten.'

'And what does your husband think about this?' Karim asked irritably. 'Is he going along to protect you?'

She shook her head. It crossed her mind that for her, the words 'husband' and 'protect' didn't belong in the same sentence. She heard him take a breath and then he shrugged.

'Have it your way, but if there's any trouble, get out quick.' He reached in his pocket, took her hand and folded several banknotes into it. He held her hand closed over them, his mouth set in a determined line.

'No!' she protested, trying to release herself from his warm grip.

'Take it. You might need a taxi to get home, Zahra,' he said.

She accepted the money reluctantly, he could be right. 'Thank you. I don't know the city very well. I'll give it back if I don't need it.'

'You *will* need it if you have to get out of there quickly. I don't want it back, okay? Use it to get Ahmad something.'

His honey-coloured eyes held hers as she picked up her writing and stood up quickly.

'Zahra, I care about you very much,' he said quietly as he got to his feet. He reached round her waist with his left hand and steadied the chair she'd toppled. For the first time she noticed the slight dent and lighter skin on his third finger where his wedding ring had been. He'd worn it on his left hand in the American fashion. She moved away from him.

'I'm married, Karim.' She was tempted to say 'and so are you' as she looked up at him.

'And he's Ahmad's father, I know,' he answered.

She wanted to shout at him, 'You're so wrong!' but she avoided his gaze, knowing that he sensed something wasn't right.

'Zahra, from the minute I saw you ten years ago ...' he began. His voice was low and warm as he reached for her hand.

'Please!' She pulled away. 'You mustn't talk to me like that, Karim. I'm not that schoolgirl now!'

He stepped aside and as she passed him, she heard him take a deep breath.

'Okay, I understand,' he said in a controlled voice. 'I'm sorry. I shouldn't have said anything.'

She didn't trust herself to reply. She swept up her writing things from the table and, clutching the book against her chest like a shield, she hurried towards the library door. She forced herself not to look back.

As she walked across the atrium, she heard a car stop outside the front door. Her heart lurched. Had Jafar returned with armed men this time? She paused as Amir opened the front door to Nasim, who was swathed in a chador and huge headscarf.

'I'm a bit early, Zahra, but we need to leave in ten minutes,' she said brightly. 'I'll say hello to Esmat.'

'Mother's not home,' Karim remarked as he came out of the library. 'I'd like a word with you though, Nasim.'

Zahra hurried to the kitchen, wondering if Karim was going to try to talk Nasim out of going to the rally too. Her head was in a spin when she thought about what he'd said to her. So he felt as she did—what had he said? *'The moment I saw you ten years ago ...'*

In the kitchen, Ahmad was ready for kindergarten and he and Shirin were just putting on their outdoor clothes. As she kissed him goodbye, a terrible fear clutched her heart. If she was arrested, she might never see him again. Her resolve wavered as she watched him walk down the garden path with Shirin. She reminded herself that she was going on the march for herself, for Ahmad, and for every woman who had been terrorised by a violent man.

She had never seen Azadi Tower, although Tahmineh had told her about it. 'All marble, Zahra, sweeping up to the sky!' But her description had fallen far short of the reality. It was magnificent. Their driver negotiated the car slowly along one of the wide roads that circled the tower. From the back seat Zahra, enveloped in her headscarf and chador, gazed in amazement at the monument.

'It was built in 1971.' Rashid turned round from the passenger seat. 'It used to be called Shah's Tower. The shah had it built to remind people of his achievements. The new regime changed the name to Freedom Tower.'

Zahra gazed at the inverted Y-shaped edifice. Freedom seemed in short supply at the moment, she thought.

'The marble represents the mountains around Tehran,' Nasim added. 'You can walk through the archway from one side of the gardens to the other. A lot of people contributed money to build it,' she went on. 'I never thought I'd be protesting here, though.'

'There they are, Nasim. They haven't let you down.'

Rashid pointed to a gathering crowd on the grass area of the square that surrounded the tower.

Zahra looked at Rashid, who was smiling at his wife in the back seat. Why didn't he warn Nasim like Karim had warned her? On the contrary, he was excited—fervently committed to her cause.

'Where would you like me to stop, sir?'

Rashid gave directions and Habib swung the car off the expressway and into a side street. Carrying their banners, Zahra stayed close to Nasim and Rashid as they dodged the traffic on the busy road. Within minutes they were walking through the gardens surrounding the tower. She followed them towards a large group of women, who all greeted them warmly. Someone told Nasim that the numbers were far short of the thousand they'd expected.

More women arrived, until Zahra estimated that there were about one hundred altogether. She felt nervous. It would be easy for the police or government guards to break them into smaller groups and push them around. Someone told her that if she was wearing make-up, *they* would use it as an excuse to arrest her. But maybe *they* didn't need an excuse; protesting against the government was enough.

Nasim's voice rang out above their heads. 'Walk slowly towards the gateway and then stop.'

Someone pushed Zahra in the back as Nasim ordered them to start marching. She saw Nasim coming towards her, but then she turned and was swept into a row ahead of Zahra. The rain had eased to a drizzle and it was beginning to soak through her scarf. She pushed her hands into her pockets to keep them dry.

Nasim called out: 'Link arms! Let's go!'

As they moved forward they chanted, 'Freedom for women! Don't change the law!' Zahra joined in, marching towards the gateway with the others. She felt exhilarated and free as they marched in step.

'We won't wear a scarf, we want democracy!' they shouted every few steps.

She was in the centre of a row, holding on to the arms of women on either side of her. Up ahead she saw the gateway through the throng of headscarves. She looked to her right and left as she marched. No police, yet. Relief swept through her. They were shouting louder now and heading for the entrance to the tower. Just before they got there, they planned to stop and Nasim was going to give a speech.

Zahra tramped forward, repeating the refrain. Then somewhere in the distance she heard other voices. Was it more women? The sound was coming from the other side of the gateway and she was being pushed towards it.

'I thought we were going to stop!' she called out, but her words were drowned out by a tidal wave of men's voices.

'Death to the communists! God bless the Ayatollah, saviour of our country!'

The column of women slowed and she stumbled forward into the woman in front. Then she saw them: a huge mass of men carrying posters with pictures of various clerics. 'Death to America! Death to the shah! God bless our sacred leader!' they chanted.

The men marched through the archway and headed straight for the women. Their feet tramped in unison, like soldiers, like a human tank rolling forward. The women at the front started screaming. Someone yelled, 'Get out, get out! Run!' The women on either side let go of her and she staggered trying to keep her balance.

Shots rang out and the screaming intensified. The men were shooting in the air. She was being pushed harder by the people behind her. Her one thought now was to stay on her feet. Ahead of her, women were falling onto the ground. As the marching men reached the front lines they divided and surrounded the women in a pincer movement. They pushed at the sides of the women's group, squeezing them together. She couldn't breathe.

'Link arms again, link arms!' she yelled.

The woman next to her staggered forward and started screaming. Someone managed to drag her up, but the screaming got louder.

'Don't stop!' Zahra yelled, dimly aware of police sirens, of being pushed into the coat of the woman in front. She could smell the rain-damp cloth as she stumbled, clawing and clinging at the woman's back, trying not to fall. Suddenly she felt two hands grasping her arms.

'I've got you, Zahra!'

'Karim!'

She felt his arms half lifting, half dragging her through the mass of bodies. He pulled her head against his chest.

'My God, I thought you'd gone!' he choked. 'I thought you'd gone!'

She looked up as he pulled her clear. The groups of men were moving towards the gateway, still firing rifles in the air.

'Don't look round!' Karim ordered.

She threw her head back and took in gulps of air. Rain spattered her eyelids. His face was close to hers. He bent his head and she saw his eyes were anxious ... concerned for her.

'What happened?' she gasped.

'You were nearly trampled, Zahra,' he said breathlessly. 'God knows ... The ambulances are there now, keep going!'

'Ambulances! Where's Nasim?' She tried to twist round but he stopped her.

'She's okay. Rashid's got her. Keep walking, don't look back.'

She felt nauseous as he half dragged her across the wet grass. The police were trying unsuccessfully to redirect the cars and buses off the expressway, and she stumbled as he bundled her through the honking traffic. Amir was at the wheel of the Konari vehicle.

'God save us!' he gasped when he saw her dishevelled muddy clothes.

Karim eased her into the back of the car and tucked a blanket round her, then got into the front passenger seat.

'Let's get out of here,' he said to Amir.

She craned her neck to see out the window as they joined the speeding traffic round the square. She glimpsed women lying on the ground and others being carried on stretchers to waiting ambulances. Suddenly she was sobbing.

'It's shock, Zahra. You're safe.' Karim looked over his shoulder. 'Those bastards planned this!' she heard him mutter as he passed her his handkerchief.

She curled into the corner of the car, unable to control her trembling body or her tears. Finally the car swung into the driveway. He helped her out and put his arm round her as she staggered up to the front door. Tahmineh was waiting for them, clutching her hands to her throat.

'She's okay, Tahmineh. She needs a hot drink. I'll bring her to the kitchen.'

Zahra leaned against him. His arms tightened around her for a fraction, but it felt safe, like something she had wanted for a long time. He pushed open the kitchen door and led her to a chair. As he left, she glanced up at him gratefully and their eyes met. He searched her face, shook his head and said her name quietly, then he was gone.

Tahmineh helped her take off her outdoor clothes and sat her down at the kitchen table. She remonstrated about the foolishness of marching in the streets while she fussed over her. The kitchen was warm but she shivered as she drank her tea. Eventually she excused herself and went to her room. She lay on her bed, her heart beating fast as images of the march criss-crossed her mind. She could see the woman in front of her and hear the men's shouts, then she was falling, grasping, terrified. If Karim hadn't grabbed her she would have been trampled, injured or killed. To calm herself, she replayed the car journey back in her mind, reliving Karim's closeness. She realised she needed him but it was a need, she knew, that could not be requited.

She stood under a hot shower, still shivering with fear and cold. Slowly the events of the march and the horror of what had nearly happened to her lessened. She was alive, but how many women hadn't survived? She dried her hair and dressed quickly, then sat on her bed. Once again she felt comforted when she remembered the feeling of Karim's arms around her, and she tried to push the memories of stumbling and falling to the back of her mind. She felt a wave of despondency; she had to avoid him if she could. He was a threat to her future, to Firzun's plans to escape. And anyway, how could anything happen between her and Karim? She thought about his American wife and his recently removed wedding ring. Although he'd told Nasim his marriage was over, he hadn't said he was divorced. There was every chance he'd return to the States and pick up his old life again.

21

THE FIRST SUNDAY IN NOVEMBER

Karim had been working on a drawing for half an hour and was already bored with it. He wandered over to the small kitchen area in his apartment and made his second coffee of the day. He flicked the television set on and frowned at the screen. He recognised the street outside the US embassy immediately; he'd been there on plenty of social occasions with his parents. Although it was still early—the dawn prayer call had woken him up—the crowds at the embassy gates were six deep. As one they fell silent, preparing to pray. Men and women with their hands outstretched in front of them waited for the cue from a distant Imam, who was out of camera shot. Karim watched for a few minutes, put his coffee down and headed for the bathroom.

By the time he'd showered and shaved, the prayers were over. Karim stood watching the TV in his bathrobe, rubbing his hair dry with a small towel. There was a general scuffling and eventually a sea of banners arose across the crowd: 'Death to America', 'God bless the Saviour of our Country.' Huge posters of the stern turbaned man whose image was plastered over buildings everywhere swayed in the light breeze. The TV camera closed in on a group burning an American flag and another, an effigy of the American president. A television reporter was bawling into a microphone, his voice coming in snatches: 'The Ayatollah ... not commented ... approves ... students will take action ...'

The camera swung towards the chained and padlocked gates of the embassy, still standing firm against the weight of the thrusting mob. No one had attempted to scale the walls yet because of the barbed wire. Karim stared at the television set. He was looking at a country on the brink of anarchy—*his* country. He ran his hand through his hair—he felt completely powerless.

The TV coverage stopped and switched suddenly to a serious bearded young man intoning the news in a studio. Behind him was a huge portrait of the Ayatollah Khomeini. Their leader had a message for all women, the newsreader went on: they should stay at home and out of politics. He mourned the death of two women after a recent protest march. He cautioned other women not to question the authority of the new laws or their husbands.

Karim threw his towel at the TV screen. 'Sanctimonious, hypocritical bastard! Twelve women, not two! Twelve!' he shouted. Maryam had found out the numbers from the morgue and phoned him. He stormed into his bedroom and got dressed in a frenzied state.

It was too early to go down to breakfast, so he flicked through the TV channels—forgetting there were only two, and they both had the same pictures. He peered at the screen and wondered if Firzun was somewhere in the surging mob doing a bit of 'intelligence' work. He switched the television set off and went down to his grandmother's room, but when he tapped lightly on the door, the nurse opened it a fraction and told him that her charge was still asleep. He wandered down the main staircase feeling at a loose end. There was no sign in the silent house of his parents or anyone else. The salon doors were open and Tahmineh had already pulled back the drapes on the grey, drizzly day. He sighed and switched on the large colour TV his mother had installed there the previous year—against his grandmother's express wishes. He heard a slight noise behind him and turned round.

'Good morning, Karim, sir,' Tahmineh greeted him. 'Breakfast is ready in the small dining room.'

She let out a startled cry when a picture emerged on the television set behind him. 'Oh it looks terrible!' she cried. 'And with Zahra nearly trampled to death the other day, I don't know what's going to happen, I really don't.'

'How is Zahra?' he asked, suddenly remembering last night's dream. He'd been carrying her lifeless body from Revolution Square and calling out for help. Tahmineh assured him that she was all right. She was lucky she wasn't one of the women who had been trampled to death or the injured ones in hospital under police guard. She left the room still tutting.

He turned back to the TV set and the pictures of the surging mobs. At the edge of the crowd, he could see long distance coaches disgorging men who instantly joined the throngs. He picked up the phone and dialled Rashid's number. Nasim was fine, no ill effects, his friend told him. When Karim asked him about the protests, Rashid sounded excited—according to their informants, the students were going to make a move on the embassy today!

'We're ready for them!' Rashid said fervently. He promised to call later.

Karim replaced the phone and stared unseeing at the television set. Surely the students wouldn't be stupid enough to storm the American embassy? Didn't they know they'd be violating international law?

On his way to the breakfast room, he heard Ahmad running down the back stairs and Zahra's voice telling him to be careful. He walked quickly across to the kitchen and opened the door. She started when she saw him.

'How are you, Zahra?'

'I'm still a bit shaken,' she admitted. 'Thank you again for ...'

'Oh Zahra,' he cut in, longing to grasp her hand. She still looked terrified—he knew what an awful experience it had been for her. Her damned husband should have been there looking after her! He excused himself and headed for the breakfast room. His mother was there already and wished him good morning as she poured his tea and piled food on his plate. While he ate she talked non-stop.

'Now! I want to tell you about my latest visit to the Ministry.' She laid her hand on his wrist. When she paused for breath, he mentioned the US embassy and that the crowds might break in. Esmat scoffed.

'They wouldn't dare. What nonsense, they're just hotheaded students!' she said dismissively.

'Don't be too sure, Mother—turn on the television,' he replied as he stood up. 'Sorry, I've got to go to work.'

He rang the bell, and when Amir appeared he ordered the car.

'*And,*' his mother continued as if he hadn't spoken, 'I've been referred to yet another religious person in the Ministry ...'

Amir put his head round the door and Karim got up, kissed his mother goodbye, and followed Amir into the atrium.

He stared out the car window as they edged into the traffic. Crowds outside the US embassy were nothing new—American television stations had given a lot of coverage to the events earlier that year. The walls had been breached by demonstrators and they'd been repelled with tear gas by local police and the US Marines. He remembered watching the marches and demonstrations from the comfort of his American living room. But now he was here, and especially after the house search and the women's march on Thursday, he felt somehow that he too should be involved in trying to stop his country sinking into chaos.

The office was quiet and soporifically warm. He drew and measured, his mind totally focused, hardly noticing his colleagues arriving. Just after eleven o'clock, he was drinking his morning coffee when a voice shattered the peaceful hum of the workplace. Mehdi, the owner of the firm, rushed out of his office.

'They've overrun the US embassy and taken the Americans hostage,' he shouted. 'It's on TV!'

Karim followed the architects and clerical staff into Mehdi's small room and craned his neck to see the television set.

'Students have seized the American embassy,' a reporter yelled. In the background the crowd was roaring the Ayatollah's name.

'The students are demanding that the Americans return the shah to stand trial.'

'They've taken hostages!' The reporter's voice was nearly inaudible. 'A hundred people were in the embassy. The students climbed the walls then ran to the main building and overpowered the guards. I can smell tear gas. They say that the Ayatollah approves! I can smell burning!'

Eventually Karim returned to his workstation, overwhelmed by a sense of unreality. What the hell were these people thinking? Did they expect the US to do *nothing*? Just sit around and watch? Those hatchet-faced military men in the Pentagon would be on high alert. They'd be sending in the US Air Force within hours and bombing his city.

His phone rang—Nasim.

'Karim, what do you think?' She sounded breathless and overwrought.

'They've invaded the American embassy, Nasim!'

'I know, Karim. We can't believe they're so stupid.'

He wasn't sure who 'they' were: the Americans for not protecting the embassy or the students for invading it.

'Firzun phoned, Karim. He wants you to meet him in Bijan Alley just behind the embassy. He needs an interpreter.' She lowered her voice. 'He thinks he can rescue some of them.'

'What!'

'You'll do it, won't you? I know you're with us. It's urgent—he's waiting.'

When he didn't answer she whispered, '*Please*, Karim.'

He sighed and shook his head. 'I'll do it for you and Rashid, Nasim.'

'Thank you, Karim. I've got to go.'

He put the phone down, feeling irritated. Of course Firzun would be in the thick of things. How typical! He expected Karim to drop what he was doing and rush halfway across the city. He looked round the office and noticed that Mehdi had moved the television set into the main office. Work was over for the day as far as he could see. He might as well go, he thought as he pulled on his jacket and raincoat. He decided not to call Amir; he didn't want the family car noted by someone like Jafar. This was his business. He phoned the concierge desk and ordered a cab, told his distracted boss he was going to continue working at home, and headed for the exit. The taxi was waiting for him when he got to the ground floor, but when he told the driver his destination, the man wanted triple the usual fare to go anywhere near the American embassy.

'Too dangerous, sir. I don't want my windows smashed.'

'Okay, okay, just get as near as you can,' Karim agreed impatiently.

Bijan Alley, he remembered, was where cars waited in line to go through the back gates of the American embassy. His family had always been invited to official receptions: American Independence Day, Thanksgiving or Christmas Eve. He had sat in the back of the car dressed in his best clothes and his sister in a frilly party dress. His grandparents and parents were honoured guests, friends of the royal family. His father was an important person in the oil industry, a friend of America. And now they were enemies of the new Republic.

He glanced out of the taxi window at the wet greasy streets where people were still going about their normal business. Two women in voluminous black chadors and headscarves pushed a child along in a stroller. A shopkeeper lifted a box of fruit and took it into his shop out of the rain, and several men sat inside a teashop drinking tea and talking. The early morning drizzle had turned to rain, and Karim regretted leaving his umbrella in the office. As they neared the embassy compound he saw smoke. Had they already torched the building?

The taxi driver stopped. 'No further,' he said.

Karim handed him a bundle of notes, got out of the taxi, and walked quickly towards the noise. He huddled into his raincoat, turning the collar up against the rain, and pushed through the crowds. Through the mass of bodies and people carrying huge pictures of various clerics, he could see that the building was still intact. The smoke was coming from near groups of men who were burning American flags. The noise was deafening, and men and women almost hoarse from shouting moved forward towards the gates in waves.

He shoved his way through with difficulty and headed in what he thought was the direction of Bijan Alley. When he got closer to the railings, the embassy grounds were swarming with men and women protesters. The men looked like the ones he'd seen in the mosque—some wore jeans, others khaki camouflage gear. He stood aside quickly to let a large group of chanting women go past, indistinguishable from each other in their black chadors. They all carried banners with pictures of the Ayatollah. Several of them wore laminated pictures of him on strings round their necks.

Karim pushed on; in places the crowd was six deep. Men yelled, women shrieked and the smell of burning was overwhelming. He looked round again, trying to remember the route Amir took and the railing he'd always pointed out because it was twisted into a fancy shape like barley sugar. Should he turn down that way or further on? He paused, but was pushed forward by the swell of the crowd and found himself squashed against the railings. He followed their metal lines until miraculously he found the twisted one.

He turned a corner and was suddenly in a deserted street—Bijan Alley! He stood irresolutely, trying to orientate himself and recover from the shock of being alone so abruptly. He looked around the deserted street. How stupid to expect Firzun to be here, waiting for him. Revolutionaries keep moving, don't they? Firzun had probably forgotten what he'd said to Nasim and was out there mingling with the mob! The quiet of the alley was eerie compared with the cacophony that he could still hear from the other side of the embassy compound.

Karim pressed on grimly down the empty street. The apartment blocks on either side looked deserted, their windows shrouded with lace curtains or closed Venetian blinds. The inhabitants were probably glued to their TV sets or out in the crowds. He followed the curve of the street to the right and was relieved to see one of the back entrances to the embassy ahead of him. It looked abandoned. No smart Marines stood on guard near the gates. They must be round the front, or worse—they'd been captured. He heard a slight noise and turned to look back up the empty street, feeling vulnerable and exposed. He walked on, but before he'd taken a couple of steps, someone hooked his arms violently behind his back. He couldn't move and pushed backwards, trying to free himself, his heart pounding in his chest. A voice he recognised hissed in his ear: 'Don't speak! It's me, Firzun.'

22

BIJAN ALLEY

Firzun pulled him into a passage between two apartment buildings. A smell of rotting food made him catch his breath. He shook off his captor.

'What the hell ...' He stopped and turned round.

Four roughly dressed Afghan men in jeans and thick jackets regarded him with interest. Firzun put his finger to his lips, then one of the men flattened himself against a wall, edged forward, and looked cautiously round into the street. He inched back into the safety of the hiding place and raised four fingers.

Karim felt every muscle in his body tense up when he heard a bewildered voice say in English, 'Okay, so what do we do now?'

Firzun raised his eyebrows. 'What are they saying?' he whispered.

'They're from the embassy. They don't know where to go,' Karim translated. 'They're suggesting someone's house or the Swiss embassy.'

They all kept back in the shadows as the group walked past the entrance to the small alley. Karim edged to the corner and watched them. They looked glaringly conspicuous as they wandered down the street in an untidy bunch, so *American*, right down to the guy with the crew cut.

'Can't we do something?' he muttered to Firzun.

'Not yet, wait!' Firzun edged forward to the entrance of the alley, then pulled back.

Someone was chanting: 'C...I...A! C...I...A!'

Karim pushed Firzun out of the way and peered round the wall. A group of about fifteen young men was marching towards the Americans. He stepped back quickly as the shouts got louder. He risked another look and caught his breath; was he was going to witness a massacre?

'C...I...A! C...I...A! C...I...A!' The chant echoed round the empty street as the mob surrounded the men.

'Look, the embassy's yours, do what you want with it,' one of the Americans shouted.

'Shut up! Shut up! Walk, hands up!' someone yelled in English.

Karim backed deeper into the gloom with the Afghans, nearly losing his balance as he slipped on cabbage leaves and potato peelings. He watched in disbelief when the crowd passed. The Americans had their hands on their heads as the mob pushed them forward.

'We've got them all now,' a voice said.

'No, some got away in a car, but we'll get them.'

'Now they'll see who's boss in our country!'

'Death to America!' they repeated as they marched.

Firzun was right, there was nothing they could do. The voices got fainter and he risked another look into the street in time to see the captives marched past the empty guard posts and through the gate of the embassy compound.

Firzun broke the silence and snapped out orders: 'Wait, then leave in twos. Karim stay with me.'

As the Afghans slipped away, Karim heard a loud roar in the distance. They were probably parading the captives to the crowds. It was time to get out of Bijan Alley.

Karim followed the other man into the street and towards the embassy. He could hear the sporadic roars long before he got there. He had difficulty keeping up with Firzun as he pushed through the dense crowd. Eventually he couldn't move and he craned his neck, trying to get a glimpse of the Chancery, the main embassy building. It looked like an American high school, a flat-fronted three-storey brick building with steps leading up to the double doors. From where he was standing, he was relieved to see that it seemed untouched.

'They've got an important hostage,' a man in front of him shouted over his shoulder.

The damp-smelling mob parted for a second and he saw an American man standing on the front steps of the Chancery. He was very tall and dwarfed the small bearded men who held him. He was also blindfolded, his hands tied behind his back. Karim watched horrified when one of his captors put a gun to the man's head. A hush fell over the crowd. Then a sound, a low rumble, rose slowly to a roar all around him. 'God save our Ayatollah! Down with America!'

Suddenly Firzun was there, pulling him through the mob by his coat sleeve. The rain was falling now in vertical sheets, drenching everyone, but no one seemed to care. Karim managed a last look at the American, wondering who he was and how the hell he must be feeling. The man's dark hair was plastered to his head and the rain ran unchecked down his face.

'We can't help him,' Firzun muttered, jerking his head to the right for Karim to follow as he ducked and weaved through the roaring crowd. Occasionally he looked back with a grin to check that Karim was still with him. They got to the busy highway and dodged through clogged traffic to the other side. Firzun turned down a narrow street and stopped outside a small café.

'Best food in town,' he said. 'Please ...' He stood back and ushered Karim through the door. There were no other diners. A swarthy man stubbed out his cigarette and got up from behind a cash register.

'*Salaam alaikum*, Firzun, brother. Welcome ...'

'Karim Konari, *alaikum as-salaam*,' Karim replied.

The man beamed and then spoke rapidly in Dari to Firzun. He showed them to a traditional wide couch covered in rugs and large cushions. Karim shrugged off his raincoat, jacket and shoes, and took his place opposite Firzun, mirroring his crossed legs. A young waiter brought hot wet towels for their hands and laid a plastic table cloth between them. Karim pressed the towel to his face, trying to block out the image of the captured American.

He dragged his thoughts back to the present. The picture on the small television set flickered silently in the corner, showing the captors taking their hostage inside. At least he was still alive! Firzun lit a cigarette and puffed columns of smoke towards the ceiling.

'Okay, so why am I here?' Karim demanded as he helped himself to salad and bread.

'All in good time. Try this,' Firzun replied.

He pushed a dish of aromatic meat towards Karim while the waiter heaped rice on their plates. Karim tore a strip of bread from the warm loaf in front of him.

'What do you think they'll do with the American?'

Firzun shrugged as he blew out another column of smoke, then ground his cigarette into an ashtray.

'Those guys who've got into the embassy are stupid, but they're not total idiots. They won't kill anyone ... yet.'

'How do you know that? I thought they were going to blow that guy's head off on national TV just then!'

'They won't, they're just students.' Firzun shrugged. 'I've got people in the embassy, I know what's going on,' he added.

Karim realised that he'd seriously underestimated the Afghan. The guy was a hardened veteran. When Firzun told him there were about eighty hostages, he was appalled but didn't doubt that the information was correct.

'The Americans won't take this lying down!' Karim remarked.

'Maybe. I'm pretty sure they'll never send the shah back here, however long these guys hold the hostages.'

Karim sighed. The current president was a peacemaker; he was probably in the Oval Office right now being browbeaten by the military, ordering him to bring in the Marines. They'd be itching to get going. What had happened was provocative, dangerous ... insane. The ball was in the court of the USA. He shrugged, there was no point in speculating. What was that Chinese proverb? 'Let me not live in interesting times.' Not for the first time he wished he'd stayed in the States. But then he would never have seen his grandmother ... or Zahra again.

He looked across at Firzun, curious about his background. Nasim and Rashid had seemed loathe to share that with him. He shook his head as Firzun pushed a dish of food towards him. He needed a large whisky, he thought, not Afghan food.

'Thanks for helping with the interpreting,' Firzun said, taking a piece of bread. 'You could be very useful to us.'

'How? I don't know a thing about your organisation, or you for that matter.' Karim watched Firzun closely, wondering whether he might get the truth from the horse's mouth, and why he even cared.

To his surprise, Firzun was happy enough to talk about his six years at Tehran University. He was involved in the politics of Karim's country as well as his own and dedicated to a fairer system of government in both. He rattled out the information like a salesman. He was adamant that he was a socialist, not a communist.

'So, you're a freedom fighter,' Karim summarised. 'I've met you before, remember? Zahra's mother?'

'Oh yeah, the plane tickets. Thanks.' Firzun frowned. 'She gave me a letter for you, I forgot ...' He shrugged.

Karim sighed. Typical. 'So what are you doing here? Why aren't you in Afghanistan?'

Firzun hesitated before he answered. 'I'm a wanted man in Herat Province.'

Karim stared at him—a wanted man who drags his wife and child along with him? Firzun kept on talking through mouthfuls of food. He'd been informed on after the last job he'd done and had to get out. The Soviets had him on a 'wanted' list. His counter-revolutionary organisation here had cells on high alert all over Tehran. They'd been waiting for something like the embassy invasion to happen. Now they were planning to release the hostages as fast as possible.

'Have you got an escape plan?' Karim asked.

When Firzun told him his escape route would take him to Sydney, Australia, he was stunned.

'Australia? Why not Europe?'

'It's the furthest place I can think of.' Firzun looked straight at him.

Karim glared across the table. 'What about your wife and son?'

Firzun stopped eating and observed Karim with a slight smile. 'You seem very interested in Zahra. Did she tell you that we're first cousins?'

'First cousins?'

'But Ahmad isn't my child,' Firzun continued smoothly. He told Karim about Zahra's husband's sudden heart attack the previous year. He'd married her to please his mother; widows were a drain on families. 'It's an Afghan thing. We won't be having any kids together, if you get my meaning.'

'So, why are you telling me this?' Karim asked.

Firzun shrugged. 'I'm grateful to you for rescuing her the other day. She's a very beautiful woman, as I expect you've noticed.' He smiled again.

'She was nearly killed in that crowd,' Karim replied irritably.

'And you think I should have stopped her or been there?'

'Yes I do.'

'Well, now you know why she won't listen to me. I'm her second husband *and* her cousin. We grew up together.'

Karim couldn't quite see the logic in Firzun's statement, but then he couldn't imagine Zahra taking orders from anyone. Independent—one of the things he loved about her.

'Her main concern is Ahmad,' Firzun went on. 'That's why she's agreed to go with me to Australia. I wouldn't leave her behind.' Firzun returned Karim's hostile glare with a shrug and carried on eating.

The food was good and they ate in silence while Karim digested the crumbs of information Firzun had thrown him. The bastard knew he liked Zahra, Karim thought angrily, and he was just the sort to use her as a bargaining tool.

'Are you with us or not, Karim?' Firzun asked suddenly. 'After all, it's your country we're fighting for,' he added.

'Of course I'm with you.' He met Firzun's intense gaze.

'Good. We're going to get those Americans out of there—fast.'

'It's a suicide mission,' Karim snapped.

'I call it a challenge,' Firzun said calmly. 'Look, we need proper plans of the American embassy complex. You're an architect; can you get your hands on them?'

'Probably not, foreign embassy plans are classified documents,' Karim told him. 'For obvious reasons ...'

Firzun gave him an intense stare. 'There's always a way.'

'I'll do what I can,' Karim replied reluctantly.

'Welcome to the group,' Firzun said. He put his hand out and Karim shook it.

Immediately Karim's thoughts went elsewhere. He wanted this man's wife, Firzun didn't deserve her. As if he'd read his mind, Firzun told him he needed another favour. Karim tensed; wasn't getting the plans enough?

'If I get captured or killed, can you look after Zahra and Ahmad for me? Get her out of here, maybe escort her to Australia? I've already sorted the visas. I know your family's well connected. You've got more freedom of movement than most people.'

You mean we've got enough money to pay bribes, Karim

thought. 'You know our house was searched, don't you?' He frowned at Firzun.

'The idiots who turned over your place were looking for Nasim and Rashid ... and me. I expect you realised that,' Firzun said nonchalantly. 'Anyway, since your mother complained to the government, they've cleared off.' He smiled slightly, then raised his eyebrows. 'You haven't answered my question.'

'Of course we'll look after them,' Karim retorted. And he would marry Zahra and take her and Ahmad to the States. Forget Australia.

Firzun shook his hand again. 'Thank you, Agha Karim,' he said formally. He stood up suddenly and, waving away Karim's offer to pay, he threw a few banknotes on the table.

Karim followed him out into the wet street.

'There's a taxi stand over there.' Firzun jerked his head and shook Karim's hand. *Khodafez*,' he called over his shoulder as he walked away.

Karim waited at the deserted taxi rank for several minutes, then started walking. He couldn't be any wetter than he was already. As he walked in the darkening damp afternoon, he thought about the American captives. He knew Firzun was right; any rescue mission had to be swift. When he eventually found a taxi, he sat in the back staring sightlessly out the window. He had no idea where he was going to find the plans to the United States embassy compound.

23

PLANS, DECLARATIONS AND HUBRIS

Esmat's shrill cry alerted everyone in the house. 'Zahra, Tahmineh, Amir, anyone!' she shouted.

Zahra ran out of the kitchen.

'Quick! Come and and look at this,' Esmat called.

Zahra gasped out loud when she saw the blindfolded American diplomat on the screen. Tahmineh, puffing from her run across the atrium, shrieked and threw her apron over her face.

'They're holding a gun to that man's head,' Esmat whispered. 'They're going to kill him. On national television!'

'God save us!' Amir exclaimed.

Zahra suddenly remembered Ahmad in the kitchen, probably watching television. When she got there she was relieved to see that the television set was off and Shirin was reading to him.

'I'll be back soon,' Zahra told her, returning to the salon just as Tahmineh was coming out.

'Madam's very upset,' Tahmineh said, pursing her lips as they crossed on the threshold.

Esmat was standing next to a sofa. When she saw Zahra, she

pointed to the television set. 'This is madness. *Madness!*' she shouted.

After the American man had been hustled back inside the building, the mob cheered and chanted and surged forward through the gates. The next picture showed men on the walls surrounding the embassy and hanging on to the railings.

'Right!' Esmat announced. 'That's it, I'm leaving. My country's been overrun by bandits. My house has been invaded and now lawless mobs are running round the city!'

When Tahmineh came back with tea, Esmat barked out orders. 'Suitcases, ocean trunks, boxes ...' She ordered the crockery to be packed and for Zahra to take some boxes and pack up the library. 'Except the antique books, Karim can see to those.'

After Tahmineh had scuttled off with Amir, Esmat turned to Zahra. 'Could you have a quick look in Rezvan's wardrobes, Zahra?' she said quietly. 'I'm sure she's hoarding loads of stuff. Wait till she's asleep and that nosy nurse isn't around.'

'Yes, of course, Madam.'

Esmat finished her tea and stood up. 'Let's get started.' She swept out of the room.

A minute later she was back.

'Come with me now, Zahra. I think she's asleep. The nurse has just gone into the kitchen.'

The rest of the afternoon passed in a haze. Cases and boxes were brought out and moved up the back stairs to Esmat's bedroom. Some of the dresses in the wardrobe were counted before Rezvan stirred and looked as if she would wake up.

Karim arrived home, causing his mother to exclaim about how wet he was, and Zahra heard him run up to his apartment. A little later he knocked on the kitchen door, his hair still damp.

'Zahra,' he said urgently, and she turned from putting soup into Ahmad's dish. 'Can I speak with you a minute?'

She indicated Ahmad.

'I'll wait in the library.' He smiled at the boy.

She handed the soup dish to Shirin and walked slowly to the library, uncertain about being alone with Karim. She knocked and walked in without waiting for him to call out. She expected to see him sitting at the piano or looking along the rows of books. Instead he was pacing the room. He indicated the chair where she'd sat before with a small table between them. He sat opposite her. She kept her eyes lowered, not wanting him to see the longing she felt for him.

'I expect you've seen that drama at the American embassy?' he began.

'Yes, your mother has started packing.'

'Zahra ...' He hesitated. 'Firzun told me about your first husband.'

She felt physically sick and put her hand to her throat. Why on earth would Firzun do that? What reason could he have for confessing to a murder?

'What did he say exactly?' Zahra asked, her mind racing with possibilities.

'Well, he told me that your first husband died of a heart attack last year and that's why you got married,' Karim said. 'I'm so sorry for your loss.'

She was furious with Firzun. Why was he repeating the lie without telling her? She took a deep breath. She felt that she was staring at Karim like a mad woman.

'I've just seen him. He asked me to take care of you and Ahmad if anything happens to him here.' His voice was gentle, concerned. 'I promised him I'd take you to Australia, but ...' he rushed on, 'I could take you to the States with me *now*, this week. You could divorce him ...'

Zahra gasped and he reached across for her hand, but she pulled hers away. Not only was Firzun repeating the lie, he was organising her life without consulting her! And now Karim was making everything a thousand times worse. She pushed the chair back and stood up. She desperately needed to get out of the room, get away from Karim—away from all the lies.

'Zahra, please wait!' Karim jumped to his feet, took her arm and held her gently. 'I'm very fond of you and Ahmad ... more than fond,' he said.

'I can't divorce my husband and come with you to America. This is madness!'

'I'm sorry,' he said, but he pressed the point. 'Would you come with me *if,* God forbid, anything happens to Firzun?'

She stared at him. 'If anything happens? What's he planning to do?'

'Well, I think he's planning to rescue the Americans.'

She covered her face with her hands. 'I knew it. I knew it. He said he would!'

She wanted to tell Karim the truth—that she was trapped, that she had to be there to help her cousin escape. A shiver of anger passed through her when she thought of her cousin manipulating this good man. She looked up into his handsome features, full of concern for her. He led her back to the chair and she sat down reluctantly.

'I can help you, Zahra.'

'How can I go with you? What about your American wife?' she blurted out.

'How do you know about her?' His voice was abruptly harsh and angry; she hardly recognised it.

'I ... overheard ...' She started to get up again.

'Wait!' he answered tersely. 'I'll tell you. My *ex*-wife is alive and well and probably has another new boyfriend. She's living in an apartment in California, which *I* paid for. I got the final divorce papers a couple of days ago.'

Zahra breathed hard. She had him wrong. 'I'm so sorry,' she said, sinking down into the chair.

'So now we know each other's secrets,' he replied.

He leaned towards her, his hands outstretched on the table. 'If you were free ...' he began.

'I'm *not* free!' she interrupted him.

'Just give me some hope,' he entreated.

Hope, she thought, *hope*! This is what she'd longed to hear since she'd first seen him ten years ago, and now she was turning him away. She told him that even if she felt the same, there was no future for them together. She stood up again, but he stepped in front of her.

'Firzun told me about the letter you sent me. I never got it. I'd have written back. Things could have been so different!'

Tears welled in her eyes, if only he knew *how* different.

'Let me just hold you, Zahra, please.' He caught her arm and drew her to him, folding his arms round her. She leaned against him, feeling his strength. Being with him felt so *right*. An untapped well of desire flooded through her body. He kissed her hair, then turned her face up to his as his mouth sought hers. She sank into his deepening kiss, but she forced herself to pull away.

'I'm not a loose woman, Karim, we mustn't ...'

'Why not?' he asked huskily. 'You must know I love you, Zahra.'

She pulled away from him more firmly and walked to the door.

He caught her hand and kissed it. 'I've never felt like this before in my life,' he said quietly.

'Neither have I,' she replied, glad at last to tell him the truth.

She smoothed her hair down and as she reached for the door handle, his hand closed over hers. She looked up at him and shook her head before she opened the door and slipped out into the deserted atrium.

The evening was closing in. Zahra flicked the light on in her bathroom and splashed water on her face. Her reflection in the mirror looked bright and feverish. She didn't want to dwell on the undelivered letter, what was the point? She closed her eyes, but she couldn't dispel Karim's image from her thoughts and she touched her mouth where he'd kissed it. *He'll think I'm an adulteress and have no respect for me.* But he had told her he loved her. These were the words she'd longed to hear him say since she was seventeen. And she had to turn him away.

When she got to the kitchen, her little group had already started dinner. While they ate, Tahmineh chatted volubly about the day's events and only stopped when Zahra gave a pointed look towards Ahmad.

She took Ahmad up to bed, and when he fell asleep she turned on the television and muted the sound. All the channels were replaying the day's events. She shuddered as she watched screaming women snap the chains on the embassy gates with bolt cutters. Then they waved pictures of the Ayatollah at the cameras. With the gates hanging open, men and women poured across the compound. Some of them smashed the basement windows of the main building with rifle butts. Zahra switched the TV off and got ready for bed, but sleep eluded her. She couldn't guess what would happen next—no one could. One thing was certain, Esmat had made up her mind. She'd said she was leaving the following week.

'But you'll still have a job, Zahra, until Rezvan ... passes.' Then she'd added, 'After that there'll be plenty to do. You can help Tahmineh pack up the house.'

Esmat had then taken a deep breath.

'So! I'm being forced out of my own country by this *rabble!* I'll have to live with my daughter in America. I hope no one there will think I'm one of those awful revolutionaries. I won't be back in Iran until there's a decent government again.'

With an irritated toss of her head, Esmat had quit the room.

The next morning as she read to Rezvan, Zahra watched her covertly. She was weakening by the day. She was conscious enough to enjoy listening, but now it was an effort to speak. After she'd slipped into sleep and the nurse had gone, Zahra followed Esmat's instructions and rechecked the wardrobes. She looked guiltily over her shoulder a few times. She counted all the closely packed dresses in their muslin covers, then quietly left the room.

At the bottom of the kitchen stairs, she opened the door into the atrium and listened. The house was silent except for the distant drone of the television set in the salon. She crossed the wide space, opened the library door and stopped. Karim, his back to the door, was talking on the phone. He turned and smiled at her, motioning her to continue what she was doing. There was no escaping him, and she wondered why he wasn't making phone calls from his apartment. She looked along the rows of books for the one Rezvan liked, trying not to listen to Karim's raised voice. He was speaking to Rashid and she guessed he was asking about Firzun.

'What do you mean he's not there? Where is he?' He listened, then went on, 'I haven't been to work yet.' He listened again. 'Okay, tell him I called, would you?'

She watched out of the corner of her eye as he drummed his fingers on the desk.

'Okay, this evening then.'

He was dressed for work in the grey suit, light blue shirt and tie he was wearing the day she'd first seen him playing the piano.

'Zahra,' he said softly, and she turned to him. Their eyes met briefly and he took a step forward. 'Zahra, about last night ...'

'Please ...' Had he changed his mind?

'I meant every word I said.' He took her hand.

His felt cool and firm against her skin, but she pulled, slowly, away from him. This had to stop, she told herself.

'Please don't say any more, Karim.'

'I understand,' he murmured, but continued to look at her as she opened the door.

After she'd put the book in her room, Zahra ran down the back stairs and told Tahmineh she was going to Nasim's. Tahmineh, transfixed in front of the television set, hardly said goodbye as they left.

'I won't be long,' she said to Tahmineh's back.

Once in the street, she took a deep breath. The rain had cleared and it felt good to be walking. There was a tang of a clear winter chill in the air and she wondered how soon there would be snow on the distant mountains ahead of her. She walked quickly, trying to avoid the damp leaves that had collected in large clumps at the edge of the footpath.

Nasim greeted her warmly and immediately ordered tea and asked after Esmat. She wasn't surprised to hear that Esmat was packing and assured Zahra that she was always welcome in her house.

'Thank you, Nasim,' she answered, relieved that Nasim had offered before she'd had to ask. 'I wanted to speak to Firzun, but apparently he's not home.'

'Only to some people! Here he is,' she said as Firzun strolled into the room. She smiled at them and slipped out the door. Zahra could hear her light footsteps crossing the landing to her bedroom.

She watched Firzun as he took a seat opposite her. He seemed edgy.

'Did you come to see me?' he said, looking at his watch then back at her.

'The Konaris are packing up. Esmat Khanoum is leaving at the end of next week and I'll have to come back here, Firzun.'

He nodded distractedly. 'I expect you've heard about the siege at the American embassy,' he commented.

'Yes, of course and ...'

'We're going to get them out,' he announced. 'A counter-raid if you like. Keep it to yourself, of course. Konari knows.'

She didn't tell him that he'd already told her. 'I think it's a crazy idea. You could be killed!'

He shrugged his shoulders. 'I did tell you that's what we'd do.

Anyway, I've arranged for you to be taken care of. I expect Karim Konari couldn't wait to tell you that.'

'Yes.' She frowned at him. 'You didn't need to repeat the lie about the heart attack though.'

'Would you rather I told him the truth?' Firzun said calmly, blowing a smoke ring at the ceiling. 'I've fixed things up for you ... just in case, Zahra.'

Mollified somewhat, she nodded, but his reckless plans frightened her. She fought against the feeling of powerlessness that threatened to engulf her again. She took a deep breath and appealed to her cousin.

'Firzun, *please* don't do this. Apart from Ahmad, you're my only family.'

'It's what I came here for.'

'I thought you were escaping from the communists!'

'That too. Look, if something does go wrong—and it won't—but *if* it does, the Konaris have money and contacts. Just be thankful.'

A flare of anger shot through her body and she gripped her hands together. 'What if you're arrested and the authorities find out you're posing as Mahmoud? They'll arrest me too, then what would happen to Ahmad?'

'Zahra! I *am* Mahmoud. I've got a passport and papers to prove it. They might be looking for Firzun, but he doesn't exist. I'm Mahmoud Ghafoori, family man.'

She glared at him; his suave answers made her feel impotent and afraid for him, afraid for all of them. She reminded him that the men who'd raided the Konari house had asked about Mahmoud *and* Firzun. He'd been here at university, surely there was a record of him somewhere—photographs?

'We can get the Americans out,' he went on as if she hadn't spoken. 'Good planning and they'll be free in a couple of days.'

'A couple of days!' she echoed.

He leaned towards her. 'We'll be out of Tehran before *Ashura*,' he said quietly.

Ashura, the religious day of mourning, was in a few week's time, she thought nervously.

'We could still go home, live in a different city.'

'For God's sake, Zahra! I've told you before. We can't go home! The Soviets are about to invade Afghanistan. *We* go to Australia or *you* go somewhere with Karim Konari, okay?'

She leaned her forehead on her hand, feeling defeated, and looked up at him. 'Is there anything I can do?'

'Just get real and be nice to Karim Agha. Your life might depend on it.' He smiled at her and raised his eyebrows.

'He's a decent man, Firzun, and I'm a decent woman!' she said firmly.

'I know that, Zahra,' he replied.

She tried one last final plea. She begged him not to risk his life, but he gave her a look of exasperation and stood up.

'Zahra you know nothing! *Nothing*! I could change the course of history in this country. This is what I *do*!' He threw his arms out as if speaking to a crowd.

She gathered her things and rose slowly to her feet. 'You sound like a dangerous lunatic, Firzun,' she told him.

'No, I'm an invincible warrior, Zahra!' he countered. 'Now excuse me, I have to make plans.'

24

THE ARCHIVE

When Karim pushed open the heavy glass doors of his workplace on Monday morning, the usually quiet architect's office was buzzing with conversation. His boss Mehdi hovered round him while he took off his coat.

'They've still got them all locked up there in the embassy,' he commented.

'So I believe,' Karim replied.

'Come into the conference room, I want a word.'

Karim followed his small, fastidiously dressed boss, wondering if he was going to be asked why he'd shown up an hour late for work.

'You've lived in the States, what's your opinion about this?' Mehdi asked as Karim sat down. He waved his hand towards a TV set, which was running footage of the embassy invasion on a loop.

'Bad for business?' Karim ventured.

'Absolutely,' Mehdi said as he watched the TV. 'I might have to lay people off.' He flashed a gold-toothed smile. 'Not yet though.' He lit a cigarette and blew smoke out of the side of his mouth like a gangster. 'I've heard in some places people who've had links to the royal family have been purged, summary executions, that sort of thing.' His eyes met Karim's.

Karim nodded, wondering if that was the reason he'd been summoned. Mehdi rambled on, asking Karim what the Americans would think. Would they bomb Tehran, invade the country? When Karim said they'd probably negotiate, Mehdi looked disappointed.

'See that building there near the back of the compound?' Mehdi waved his cigarette at the screen. 'We designed that a few years ago.'

'Really?' Karim commented, trying to sound uninterested.

'Yes, and you know what? The Americans never picked up the final copies of the plans.' Mehdi blew out another stream of smoke.

Karim's heart plunged and started to pump faster; he couldn't believe what he was hearing. 'Aren't they classified documents?'

'Of course they are. They're locked up every night in the archive room, with all the other plans we've ever produced.' He waved his cigarette at Karim. 'That's the trouble with the Americans; they're careless—too busy worrying about oil contracts.'

Was this Mehdi's point? Americans are stupid and careless, now their embassy has been invaded and it served them right? Karim sighed. He was relieved when Mehdi's phone rang and he gave Karim a dismissive nod as he picked it up. Karim went back to the main office, feeling stunned. The plans for part of the US embassy complex were here! Had Firzun known that already? Surely not. But he was crafty, Karim thought, *and* he knew a lot of people.

As he worked, Karim considered the conversation with his boss. Did Mehdi know he wanted the plans? Was he, Karim, being set up? If he copied the plans, would someone arrest him as soon as he left the building? Was Mehdi one of Firzun's group, but wanted to keep his hands clean? Karim's head ached as he leaned over his drawing board. He was determined to get the plans; he wanted Firzun's group to succeed. He wanted the Americans to be released.

He glanced quickly across at the archive room. Through the open door he could see architectural drawings in flat files hanging on racks in the cool, dry room. He sighed, hoping that they'd retained the majority of their lines. This was old technology, subject to fading; he'd be lucky to get a clear copy, but there must be negatives somewhere.

There was no way he could ask one of the assistants to get the embassy plans for him. Someone, *everyone*, would want to know why. He'd have to wait until they all went home this evening, then get into the room and have a look. It was going to be a long day. As it dragged on, he walked past the room several times. In the afternoon he saw Ebrahim the office assistant moving the files along as if he too was looking for something. Karim stood up and stretched, then walked casually towards the room. When the other man saw Karim watching him, he asked if he needed anything.

'No, no, I'm fine,' Karim responded, trying casually and unsuccessfully to see past Ebrahim. He strolled back to his drawing board.

The sky outside the huge windows darkened and one by one his colleagues packed up and headed for the door.

'Don't overdo it, Karim,' one of them joked as he passed Karim's workstation.

Ebrahim was the last to leave. Karim watched him covertly from his desk as the man quietly made his way round the office, covering computer screens and locking the boss's office. Karim drew, measured, consulted, then saw Ebrahim shut and lock the door to the archive room. Damn! Would it sound suspicious if he asked it to be left open? Yes, it would!

'I can lock up, Ebrahim,' Karim said as the man hovered near his desk.

The other man wished him goodnight and reluctantly left him a set of keys.

'Please don't forget to lock the office door and give the keys to the janitor on the ground floor, sir,' he said. The poor man looked worried. He was probably scared of losing his job if he made a mistake.

Silence descended on the office and for the first time Karim was aware of the honking horns and heavy diesel buses on the street below. He hurried out to the reception area and locked the main office door. Outside the archive room, his heart rate increased with each key that didn't fit. Finally the door swung open.

The filing system was impeccable and he was terrified of disturbing it, but where to start? Mehdi had said 'a few years ago' 1974? 75? 76? The room was stuffy and although he was in his shirt sleeves he soon felt hot as he carefully moved the large files along the rack and squinted at the tiny characters on their labels. He undid his cuff links, rolled up his sleeves and loosened his tie. Was the room making him clammy or was it his nerves? Anger welled up when he thought of Firzun and his dangerous plan. He dismissed him from his mind and tried to focus. He moved the large files along carefully, afraid of knocking one off the rack in his haste. He was at the April 1976 section now and the smell of old paper from some of the plans was catching in his throat. He left a gap, and as he walked back to the main office he heard a clatter as the files slid along the rail.

He turned back fearfully—they were all intact, but something caught his eye. The stars and stripes of the American flag! Someone had painted a tiny flag on the folder containing the September 1976 drawings. What luck! He unhooked the drawings and took them into the main office, laying the huge folder out on a table. Yes, this was it! The US embassy drawings! They were beginning to fade, but all he had to do was find the negatives and copy them on the dyeline printer, put them and the drawings back and go home. To his surprise, he found the negatives quickly and with an overwhelming sense of elation and relief, he headed to the copy room.

It was locked and none of the keys worked. While he was fiddling with the lock, the negatives slid from his fingers and scattered on the floor.

'What the hell!' he said out loud. Frustrated, he hit the wall with his fist. The door flew open with a crash and he swore as he picked up the slippery negatives, then fought the copier for every reluctant copy. He put everything back and carefully closed all the doors.

Exhausted and sweaty, he packed the papers into his sports bag. He phoned home and asked Amir to come and pick him up.

Fumbling with the keys again, he let himself into the boss's small bathroom, scrubbing at his hands to get rid of the dirt and dust. When he looked in the mirror, a wild man with loosened tie and rolled up sleeves looked back. He had a black smudge on his face that he wiped off irritably with a wet handkerchief. He rolled his sleeves down, fixed his cufflinks quickly and looked in the mirror again, feeling more like his old self.

'You clever bastard!' he said out loud to his reflection. As he rode down in the lift he did a mental check, although he was sure he'd left no clues. He congratulated himself on executing the perfect crime, as nondescript as it was.

He was surprised to see that Amir was already at the desk, chatting to the concierge.

'The roads are deserted Karim, sir. I got here quickly,' Amir explained. 'Can I take your bag?'

Karim's fingers tightened on the sports bag in his left hand. 'Just the briefcase, thanks,' he said and followed Amir to the main door.

'Excuse me, sir!' the concierge ran after him. 'The keys, sir?'

He fumbled as he handed them over, his heart hammering against his ribs.

'Thank you, goodnight, sir. See you in the morning, *Enshallah*.'

'Goodnight ...' He'd forgotten the man's name.

'*Enshallah*.' —God willing.

The familiar remark suddenly struck fear into Karim's heart. Did the man mean: 'As long as you're not arrested before you get home?'

He shivered as Amir opened the door and he walked out into the damp night air. He felt as if he'd escaped without detection from a gulag.

At home Karim showered, changed and managed to avoid his mother.

Esmat was entertaining again, judging by the sounds of indignant voices coming through the salon door. He could hear the television droning in the background as he collected his coat from the cloakroom and pulled on his outdoor shoes. He checked his watch then opened the front door, surprised to see that it was already nine-fifteen. He headed for the side gate, and when it clanged shut behind him he glanced back just in time to see the salon curtains twitch open slightly. He sighed; he'd have to get used to his mother checking on him again and made a mental note to use the back stairs from his apartment in future.

He turned and walked towards Rashid's house, toting the bulky tennis bag. Firzun had also requested a few cartons of duty-free American cigarettes, which made it even more difficult to handle. The footpaths felt slippery and greasy with the recent rain and the street lamps seemed gloomier than usual, he thought. Perhaps the new government was trying to economise—God knows they'd had enough power cuts since he'd arrived. The trees dripped on his hair. A car passed on the other side of the street, its headlights illuminating the build-up of leaves and rubbish in the damp gutters.

He jumped when another vehicle screeched out of a side street. The headlights on full beam dazzled him momentarily. He was within sight of Nasim and Rashid's house and he lowered his head and walked on resolutely. The jeep passed him at speed, spraying his jeans with leaf litter, then reversed slowly back along the gutter. He quickened his pace, clutching the bag under his arm instead of letting it swing awkwardly from his shoulder. The jeep kept up with him and he glanced round quickly—was it Firzun? It was slightly ahead of him now, then it stopped and four bearded men jumped out. They were silhouetted against the headlights and each had a machine gun aimed at Karim's chest.

'Hands up! Put the bag down.'

He dropped the bag and felt his heart pumping blood rapidly

round his body. He could see the lamps on the gatepost of Rashid's house only metres away as his skin crawled with fear. He was transfixed by the reflection of the pale street light, which flared off the bullets strung on belts round the men's waists.

'What's in the bag, brother?'

His nerves were taut as violin strings. The speaker moved nearer and Karim saw his face. The lad looked about sixteen years of age with a thin wispy beard. He was toting an AK47, and it flashed across Karim's mind that if the safety catch was off and the kid waved it at him it would start firing on its own, cut him to bits, and take out the wall behind him at the same time. The teenager's mates stood alongside him, their guns pointed at Karim's chest. He felt a cold sweat down his back and his mouth was so dry he could hardly form any words.

'It's ...'

'... none of your business, friends!' another voice answered.

Firzun had already grabbed the youth from behind and knocked his gun to the ground. Every muscle in Karim's body froze in anticipation of a volley of bullets when it hit the footpath, but it lay there silent and harmless. He pulled his gaze back to Firzun, who was holding the kid round the throat with a pistol to his temple. His voice was calm, almost conversational.

'This is my beat. Clear off,' he said. 'Put your weapons down and get back in the jeep.'

'We're keeping the streets safe!' one of the kids said, his voice high with fear.

'Don't kill me, please!' the captive begged.

'Put the guns there, nice and gently, and he gets to go home to his mum.' Firzun indicated the footpath. 'Good boys,' he said as they put the rifles down.

He pushed his captive into the jeep with his mates. The driver crashed the gears as the jeep screeched off.

'You okay?' Firzun asked.

Karim was too shaken to speak, and now that he owed Firzun his life he disliked him even more.

'Let's go.' Firzun grabbed the bag. 'Pick up some of the guns, check the safety catches first. I'll take the rest.'

Firzun slipped through a gap in the hedge at the side of Nasim's house, and after he'd checked the weapons, Karim followed him across the sodden garden with his awkward bundle.

'Got to show them who's boss!' Firzun said to Karim.

The light from Rashid's front porch made his grinning face seem ghoulish. Karim grunted, still shaken.

'There's going to be plenty of live ammo around soon,' Firzun remarked.

Not near me, Karim thought. What the hell had he gotten into here?

'Got the drawings?'

'Yes.'

'Good man, you were quick!' Firzun waited for him, holding the door open with his back.

Habib met them in the hall. He glanced at the rifles and inclined his head slightly, his face impassive. 'They're waiting for you upstairs, when you're ready, Karim, sir.'

25

PREPARATIONS

Firzun took the rifles from Karim and jerked his head at the door that used to be the dining room of the downstairs apartment. Karim pushed it open and was flabbergasted when he saw the large dining table had been pushed to one side and was stacked high with weapons. There were about twenty men sitting on the floor smoking, and the room stank of their acrid cigarettes. They were all swarthy like Firzun—Afghans.

In spite of the large group downstairs, when he got to the living room Nasim and Rashid were alone.

'You look like you need a drink. Bourbon?' Rashid handed it to him.

'The holy hotheads stopped him.' Firzun came quietly into the room and jerked his head in Karim's direction. 'Anyway, let's look at what you've got.'

Karim unfurled the drawings on the table and anchored them on either end with a couple of heavy books. He explained that the only detailed plans he had were of the new building his company had designed.

'That's okay,' Firzun interrupted, waving crumpled papers at him. 'I've got drawings of other parts of the compound from the guys on the inside. You can fix them up later.' He stuffed the papers in his pocket.

'Do you know where the hostages are?' Karim asked.

Firzun stabbed a finger at Karim's plans. 'We know twenty-five of them are here. So, talk us through.'

They listened intently as Karim explained the layout of the building, its exit and entry points, the position of the power boards and the plumbing. He felt an odd surge of excitement. Firzun's confidence that his outrageous plan would work was contagious.

'Okay,' Firzun said, straightening up. 'Can you draw up clear floor plans from these?' He pulled the crumpled sketches from his pocket and handed them to Karim. They felt warm where they'd been close to Firzun's body.

A distasteful thought crossed Karim's mind: Zahra had shared a bed with this man.

'I'm getting all the groups to meet here tomorrow evening,' Firzun said. 'We'll have the Americans out by Thursday night, before they get shifted to different places.'

'It's Tuesday tomorrow. Isn't Thursday night a bit soon?' Karim objected. 'Thursday night before they shift them to other locations,' Firzun repeated.

'He's right, Karim,' Nasim said as she handed him sheets of drawing paper.

'I need copies of the consular building plans as well as good copies of the rough ones,' Firzun called out over his shoulder as he headed for the stairs.

'I can copy the main plans, Karim. I finished my architecture degree, eventually.' Rashid grinned at him.

While they worked, Rashid told him about a group who called themselves 'The Brotherhood'. They were a group of young radicals and they were behind the storming of the embassy, not ordinary students. They had contacts in high places and the Ayatollah had endorsed everything they did since he came to power.

'What about those people who searched our house?'

'The Brotherhood was behind that, Karim,' Firzun said decisively, coming back into the room. 'If you need a reason to join us, you've got one.'

Karim ignored the remark.

'Why didn't the Americans open fire on them when they overran the embassy?' he asked.

'And give them some martyrs?' Firzun shrugged. 'Thursday marks five days since the capture of the hostages,' he went on. 'We know the students are going to read out a list of grievances tomorrow. They blame the CIA and other Western powers for stealing our oil. After that they might release the Americans. Probably not, though—they're drunk with power.'

'We've got fifteen people on the inside. They come in and out as they please, so we know exactly what's going on,' Rashid commented. 'There's no control—no one really knows who's who—at the moment.'

'We've got to move fast. The Brotherhood will get organised soon,' Firzun said.

'If you blow it, what'll happen to the hostages?' Karim asked.

'We won't *blow it*, we can't afford to,' Firzun said dismissively.

Karim stood up; he needed to get away and clear his head. He wanted to take the rest of the drawings home where his equipment was better. Firzun gathered up the completed plans and told him he'd done a great job. He cautioned him to lock the drawings up in a safe. Their eyes met for a second; there was something about the Afghan that unnerved him. He's a cold bastard, he thought. Poor Zahra!

Rashid suggested he use the back lane. 'Firzun can go with you,' he said as he handed Karim his overloaded sports bag.

Karim demurred, but they insisted, and he dutifully followed Firzun down the outside stairs.

The two men walked in silence along the rutted lane where Firzun's flashlight lit up the puddles and muddy holes. Karim checked his watch; the small glow from it gave him a sense of reality as he followed the wavering flashlight ahead of him.

'It's too late to say goodnight to Zahra and Ahmad, but you're welcome to come tomorrow,' Karim called out quietly.

Firzun stopped and turned round, his expression unreadable in the torchlight. 'Some other time,' he said.

He turned away, and as Karim followed the bobbing flashlight, his earlier irritation rose to the surface. Why would the great leader bother himself with his chattels? If Firzun got killed, there wouldn't be 'some other time'. The Americans had a good word for people like him: *asshole*. Karim loathed him, but when they reached the back gate to his house, he shook Firzun's hand and wished him goodnight.

Karim woke at the usual time the next morning, still feeling tired. He'd worked on the drawings until two o'clock, listening to the rain battering down throughout the night. He took the plans out of the safe and rechecked them quickly, being careful not to spill his first coffee of the day on them. He glanced at his watch and wondered if his grandmother was awake. Zahra was on her way to the sick room when he got to the bottom of his apartment stairs, and she turned when she heard his step.

'Good morning, Zahra,' he said quietly. 'Is Grandmother well enough for you to read to her?'

He moved nearer, inhaling Zahra's familiar fresh citrus scent. Why would such a beautiful woman waste herself on a thug like Firzun? he wondered. Then he remembered her story—she'd obviously had no choice.

'She's weaker every day,' Zahra replied sadly.

She rested her fingers on the door handle without looking at him, then opened the door and stood back to let him go first. He was shocked when he saw his grandmother, who seemed to have deteriorated overnight. She was propped up on her pillows and looked as if she was clinging to life by a thread. He sat down next to her and held her hot hand with its papery skin. He kissed it and raised the fragile fingers to his forehead.

'Karim.' Her voice was faint. 'Zahra will read to me this morning. You must go to work, dear boy.'

He looked across to where Zahra sat in her usual place, an open book on her lap, her eyes lowered. She'd tied her hair in a knot in the nape of her neck, he noticed. He felt a lurch of desire—tendrils of hair had escaped and were curling round her cheeks and across her forehead. He longed to kneel at her feet and wind her hair round his fingers and across his lips.

'I'll stay for a minute,' he said. Zahra looked up and he raised his eyebrows, indicating his grandmother. She nodded and the tendrils of hair fell forward again as she looked down at the book.

'Hafez. Your favourite, Madam: "The Rose and Nightingale".' She started to read.

'I walked within a garden fair
At dawn to gather roses there;
When suddenly sounded in the dale
The singing of a nightingale.'

When Zahra stopped reading, she glanced at Rezvan. The old lady's eyes were closed and there was a faint smile on her lips.

'Paradise is a garden,' Rezvan said quietly.

Karim looked across at Zahra. Their eyes met and she bit her lip. He saw a tear trickle slowly down her cheek. His own eyes were moist; he was overwhelmed with grief.

Zahra cleared her throat and began the second verse. '*Alas he loved a rose, like me ...*' but Rezvan started to cough and gasp for air. Zahra jumped up and rearranged the pillows to ease her breathing.

'I'll get the nurse,' she told Karim.

He nodded, unable to speak, feeling as if a lead weight was pressing down on his chest. He held his grandmother's hand in his as the cough subsided and her breathing eased. In his head, he'd always known she was dying, but now in his heart he believed it. His love for Zahra was futile, and within days both of their lives would be changed forever. At this fragile moment, he knew that his life without Zahra would be a life half lived. When the nurse came in, he left the room with a final look at his grandmother. He went downstairs to the breakfast room and sat with his father.

'I sit with her every morning before I leave,' Abbas said despondently, folding the newspaper he'd been reading and putting it to one side. 'It can't be long now.'

Karim shook his head and helped himself to coffee.

'I feel like there's a dark shadow over everything,' Abbas sighed.

Before Karim could answer, he heard a heavy thump on the ceiling. Overhead things were being moved around and, above all the noise, his mother's raised voice was loud and clear. She was packing in earnest.

'I've booked a flight for your mother next Wednesday,' his father said. 'I'll start winding up our affairs here.'

His mother was obviously anticipating Rezvan's demise within the next week. But if that didn't happen, he knew she'd go anyway, even though one of her duties as a female member of the family was to wash and prepare the body of the deceased for burial. Perhaps she'd decided to opt out. He told his father he'd stay as long as necessary to settle the family affairs.

'I'll be here until … until she passes,' Abbas replied.

He was relieved to get to the office and away from the escalating dramas at home. When he acknowledged the concierge's morning greeting, he remembered with a jolt that he'd committed an act of industrial espionage the previous evening. He rode up in the lift, took a deep breath, and pushed open the double glass doors to the company's office. He nodded to a few of his colleagues as he took off his coat. Most of them were working at their drawing boards. Everything appeared normal, he thought as he glanced round on his way to his desk.

Ebrahim materialised at his side, making him jump. 'Tea or coffee, sir?'

'Er, yes, tea, thank you, Ebrahim,'

He watched as the man walked away. The doors to the archive and copy rooms were wide open. There was nothing in Ebrahim's behaviour to suggest anything might be wrong or out of place, yet ...

'Good morning, Karim. Lost anything?' Mehdi's voice behind startled him.

He turned round sharply to where his boss was standing, an odd look on his face.

'This is yours, isn't it?' Mehdi opened his hand and Karim stared at his own gold cufflink. Where on earth had he dropped it, and why hadn't he missed it last night?

He forced a smile. 'Where did you find that?' he asked casually, dreading the answer.

Mehdi paused and raised an eyebrow.

For God's sake ... say it! Karim thought.

'Found out!' Mehdi said triumphantly.

Karim stared at him, speechless.

'I found it in my washroom.' Mehdi gave him a stern look, then grinned.

Karim stifled his sigh of relief. Everyone in the office knew that Mehdi was pathologically clean and never let anyone else use the pristine washroom attached to his office. In his haste to wash his hands the previous evening, he'd forgotten. He remembered putting the cufflinks back in a rush; one of them must have slid out and landed on the floor. Thank God he hadn't dropped it in the archive room! How many more clues had he scattered around?

'Anyway, once is okay,' Mehdi was saying amicably as he laid the cufflink carefully on the desk. 'How are things at home?'

Mehdi, Karim remembered, was a well-known hypochondriac

and easily distracted by talk of health issues. He told him about his grandmother and relaxed as Mehdi gave his medical opinion.

Karim nodded his thanks, and Mehdi drifted back to his office. He stared unseeing at his drawing, then scooped up the gold cufflink and shoved it in his pocket with a shaking hand. Suppose he made a mistake on the drawings? The weak link in the group who put everyone in danger! No, I'm a good architect, he told himself. I don't make errors in my work. He sighed and drained the small tea glass.

He tried to concentrate, push the images of the teenagers in the jeep to the back of his mind. Was someone watching him? Following him? Had Mehdi or Ebrahim been asked to keep an eye on him at work? If so, they would be watching him more closely now since he'd stayed back alone in the office last night. He tried to shake the thoughts away, but they were slowing his thinking and disturbing his concentration. If it hadn't been for his grandmother, he would never have come back from the States. Trying to live a normal life here was impossible.

He was glad when the day finally dragged to an end. He dined with his parents, then slipped quietly out of his apartment down the outside stairs and headed for the back lane. He carried a flashlight and a sports bag crammed with drawings, which he'd double-checked. He felt like some sort of fifth columnist.

26

THE BRIEFING

Once again Karim successfully negotiated the back lane and his friends' garden with a flashlight. The side door was shut, and when he rang the bell he was surprised to hear Habib's voice on an intercom asking him to identify himself. Rashid was waiting in the hall and Karim commented on the increased security.

'Firzun suggested it,' Rashid answered. Firzun again!

The upstairs living room was packed with people. Dark skinned men in rough camouflage gear lounged on the sofas. Others in jeans and sweatshirts sat on the floor or round the table. The plans he'd copied were stuck on one of the walls. The smell from the Afghan's cigarettes made him catch his breath, and he squinted trying to see through the haze. Someone opened a window and a rush of cool damp air filled the room. Firzun emerged from the throng and grasped his hands.

'Thanks for coming,' he shouted over the din. 'Everyone's here.' He waved his hand over the crowd, his eyes darting round feverishly.

Karim saw Maryam with a small group of women and he gave her a brief wave, then Firzun raised his hand and silence fell.

'Welcome, friends. Tonight it's the overall picture. Tomorrow night, final briefing for each cell at the safe houses. Then we unite to strike a blow for democracy!'

Everyone cheered.

'Okay, updates,' Firzun announced. 'The American president is still taking advice. Apparently they think it's too risky to mount an air-strike from the bases in Turkey.'

A few people asked questions, then he went on.

'The Soviets are monitoring everything with their spy satellites. We're sure they're going to invade Afghanistan before the end of the year.'

A low murmur rose from the groups of Afghan men. Would Firzun take on the Soviet army next? Karim wondered.

'So, it's up to us,' Firzun exhorted them, holding out his arms with palms turned to the ceiling like a prophet. 'We'll smash the enemy and free the hostages!'

The audience shouted their agreement, hands raised above their heads as they applauded.

Karim felt a grudging admiration for the stocky Afghan as he paused dramatically and regarded his troops. He half expected Firzun to give some sort of salute. Instead he held up his hand.

'We've got accurate numbers now—sixty-six hostages, men and women. They're in groups, spread out across the embassy compound in four different areas.' He pointed to the charts on the wall and indicated the areas with a long wooden pointer. 'At the moment there's no set routine for guarding them. Karim here has fixed up the floor plans for us. He'll explain them.'

He lowered his voice and the atmosphere in the room changed to calm attention as people shifted on the floor.

'We can move much sooner than we thought. Over to you, Karim.' Firzun thrust the pointer at him.

Karim took a deep breath and looked round the room at the silent group. A little earlier he'd felt elated—this would be a triumph of democracy. But now his elation was evaporating. Could they really rescue sixty-six hostages from the embassy without casualties? He forced himself to focus on the plans, first checking that his listeners had their own copies.

'The compound stretches over twenty-seven acres,' he began.

He carried on talking, showing where all the entrances and exit points were, the open areas that would be dangerous to cross. He pointed out the chancery building, office buildings, motor pool and four residential cottages. He moved on to the floor plan of the new consular building, explaining the layout in detail.

He glanced at Firzun, who nodded for him to continue.

'Path to large warehouse, deputy chief of mission's residence, ambassador's house and gardens, path from the house to the main chancery building ...' He tapped each one with the pointer. 'Any questions?'

He managed to answer some, but referred the tactical ones to Firzun, then handed the pointer back. Firzun reviewed the deployment for each group.

'Blue group will come in through the Roosevelt Gate,' he began.

A murmur spread through the group, but Firzun raised his voice above them.

'Yes, it's seething with people day and night—that's the best cover we've got. It's chaotic there, there's no checking system.'

The young men in jeans at the back of the room nodded, and Karim looked more closely at them. They were his countrymen, in their early twenties, possibly university students. He wondered if they'd done their mandatory military service and could handle a weapon. He looked at the rest of the men. The Afghans looked as if they'd had weapons grafted onto their bodies at birth.

Firzun's orders were precise. Each group would have a different colour armband. The hostages had been tied to chairs for a long time and wouldn't be able to walk easily. Some of them had been interrogated; they'd be agitated and on their guard. He circulated pictures of the main leader, who maintained that all the Americans were spies.

'Shoot him on sight,' he ordered.

Good God, he looks like a demented pirate, Karim thought when a copy of the photograph came his way.

'What about the outside lights?' someone asked.

'Our men on the inside will cut the floodlights dead at midnight,' Firzun explained. 'Most of guards are very religious—they pray three times a day. They'll see in holy Friday with prayers at midnight. There'll only be a handful of students guarding the hostages. When the lights go out, that's the signal to attack.'

He looked around for more questions. Each man would be equipped with a side arm, a knife and a sub-machine gun.

Karim's attention wandered. So far no one had suggested that he join them on the raid. He was as fed up as everyone else with the new regime and the Ayatollah, and he wondered whether to volunteer. What the hell did the regime think they were doing attacking the US embassy? He had done his national service—albeit in the Air Force as a pilot—but he knew Firzun would consider him an amateur.

He pulled his attention back and listened as Firzun outlined the overall plan. They'd take the freed hostages out of the rear gates of the embassy to army style trucks. Next stop was a private airfield, where a plane chartered in the name of a group of businessmen would fly them to Ankara, Turkey. The group commanders and the second in charge would go with the hostages.

'The Turkish and American secret services know about the operation,' Firzun concluded.

Karim stared at him—the plan was audacious. Who had funded a private jet? He saw Firzun glance at Rashid when he mentioned the plane—wealthy Rashid was in this up to his neck. The flight was risky; it would take over an hour to get into Turkish airspace. The plane could easily be shot down.

'What if the hostages put up a fight?' someone called out.

'There'll be an English speaker in each group,' Firzun answered. 'They can tell the captives they've got no choice. Once they're in the trucks, you disappear.'

He beckoned Maryam forward and she stood next to him, pushing her thick curly hair away from her face. Quickly and efficiently she outlined basic first aid for wounds. If anyone needed treatment, they were to come to the Laleh private hospital, where she'd be on duty in the emergency room.

'If you go to a public hospital, you'll get arrested,' she finished brusquely. She smiled a brief professional smile and returned to her seat.

'Rescue the injured, leave the dead,' Firzun added. He took a breath. 'Okay, I need the group leaders to stay behind. Everyone else, meet in your safe houses tomorrow at 2200 hours. We *can* do this; we *must* do this. Good luck! When we meet again, it'll be as victors after our great battle!' He raised his right arm, fist clenched. 'To victory!'

Karim didn't join with the other male voices as they mirrored the salute and fighting words. He got up to leave as they ran quietly down the stairs, their muted voices drifting up to him from the stairwell. Firzun strolled over to him.

'It's daring, but it'll work if everyone keeps their cool.' Firzun sounded confident.

It's a suicide mission, Karim thought. He said goodnight and turned towards the door, but Firzun stepped in front of him.

'Beer?' he asked casually.

'Okay.' Karim sat down reluctantly on the sofa and accepted the beer. Firzun took a seat opposite him with a can of soft drink in his hand.

'You're coming with us, aren't you?'

'Me?'

'I need an English speaker and a medic in my group.'

Karim knew the geography of the compound by heart, it made sense to go. He realised suddenly that he *wanted* to go. Since Jafar's invasion of his parent's house and Zahra's treatment on the march, his anger towards the regime had escalated. He was ready to change from a bystander to a participant. He was surprised that Firzun thought he was good enough. He looked across at the other man, bright eyed and confident. The arrogant bastard might just pull it off! He took a deep breath, conscious of the other man watching him intently.

'Count me in,' he said. 'I'll be there.'

'Good man!' Firzun leaned across the table and shook his hand.

When he looked up, Nasim was watching them, an odd look on her face. Did she have misgivings as well? His elation evaporated and he felt sick of the whole business—sick of the upheaval that the Afghan had brought into his life and of the upheaval in his country. He wanted to leave and go to a place where he could walk along a street without being harassed by religious zealots in jeeps, where women were respected, and the police needed a warrant to search your house.

Firzun's voice broke in on his thoughts. 'Come here at 2200 hours tomorrow for a final briefing. Wear warm dark clothes. I'll give you an armband—we're the green group.' He laughed suddenly, a short barking sound. Karim struggled to see the joke.

'We'll go from here to the laneway off Bijan Alley. Our target is the consular building, the one you got the plans for.' When Karim said nothing Firzun continued, 'You can handle a gun, can't you?'

'Yes. Where did you get all the weapons?'

'Black market. It's a booming trade in the city now.' Firzun grinned. 'I brought plenty of stuff with me to pay for them.'

'Stuff' could only mean one thing, Karim thought with a surge of anger. If he'd crossed the border from Afghanistan with enough raw opium to equip forty fighters and fund trucks, then he'd put Zahra and Ahmad's lives on the line. The Mujahedin never took prisoners, they executed everyone. If the raid tomorrow night was successful, they were in danger. If it wasn't ... It didn't bear thinking about. He felt edgy; the whole plan was madness.

'What if you're captured, or the plane isn't there ...'

'That won't happen,' Firzun replied dismissively.

Karim stood up. He wanted to go home and clear his head. He wished Maryam goodnight.

'A democratic country with free elections is worth fighting for, isn't it?' she asked him.

Maryam was right, but he still felt a deep sense of dread when he thought about the raid. Nasim and Rashid shook his hand, and to his relief they didn't offer Firzun as an escort. Nasim touched his arm.

'Send my love to your parents and your grandmother. It'll be all right, Karim. I know it will.'

He didn't answer. He doubted that anything would be all right from now on. Maryam handed him his flashlight, pulled back the heavy curtain, and opened the door to the veranda. The damp air stung his face as he ran down the outside stairs of the apartment. The rain had cleared and he stopped in the lane. When he gazed up at the millions of stars in the clear night sky he felt insignificant and terribly alone.

Karim opened the back gate to his own garden. To his surprise, the house was brightly lit although it was past midnight, and he was forced to step around a pile of packing cases in the atrium. Cautiously he pushed open the door of the salon. Wrapped packets were piled up on the dining room chairs and there were boxes on the long table—the departure preparations were in full swing. He sat down heavily on the sofa and wondered how quickly he could get out if Firzun's plans went wrong. Thank God he had a Green Card, but then again, he might end up in Australia with Zahra and Ahmad.

Upstairs, the door to his parents' room was wide open and several large cardboard boxes stood outside on the landing. He looked into the bedroom and blinked at the chaos. His mother was kneeling, stuffing clothes into a half full suitcase she'd thrown open on the floor. She stood up when she saw him and pushed her hair back off her agitated face. His father, in his dressing gown, was standing helplessly at the end of the bed.

'There was a news report on TV tonight,' he told Karim. 'Apparently there's a list of families who were close to the royal court. They —people like us— are going to be investigated.'

'Investigated? By the government?'

Abbas shrugged, then turned to his wife. 'Esmat, *please* can we get some sleep?'

'Father's right. Do this tomorrow,' Karim told his mother.

Tomorrow ... tomorrow night he might be dead or in prison. Dresses, shoes and handbags would be irrelevant. He said goodnight, shut the door, and walked along the landing to his grandmother's room. He stood at her bedside, listening to her shallow breathing, thinking how small and frail she looked in the huge bed.

'God protect you, Grandmother,' he whispered.

He closed the door quietly. He longed to see Zahra, to reassure himself she was alive and safe. As if in answer to his thoughts, she appeared ghost-like ahead of him.

'Zahra!' he whispered, and she turned, startled by his voice.

She clutched at the neck of her long dressing gown. 'Karim!'

He walked over to her and she backed away, stumbling over Ahmad, who was clinging to her clothes.

'The banging woke him up,' she said. 'He thought it was a monster. I brought him out to show there wasn't one.'

'No monsters, Ahmad, just my mother.' Karim kneeled down in front of the boy and ruffled his hair.

'Thank you, Karim, goodnight,' Zahra whispered.

'Goodnight, Zahra.' He wanted to gather them both in his arms. 'No monsters,' he said again as she turned away.

He ran up the stairs to his own apartment. He could smell the citrus tang of her hair long after he'd showered and lay sleepless in his bed. He dozed fitfully until the *azan-e-sobh* echoed round the suburb. He lay on his back, wondering if this would be the last day of his life.

27

THURSDAY, 8 NOVEMBER

Karim was relieved to go to work, to get away from his mother and the turmoil she'd created at home. He wanted to put the hostage situation to the back of his mind, but it was the only topic of conversation in the office. As usual Mehdi, his boss, lingered by his desk. The American president had refused to return the shah, who was sick anyway, so the hostages were stuck, he informed him. Karim made a non-committal noise.

'Do you think the Americans will invade us?' Mehdi asked.

'I have no idea,' Karim replied, finally forced to look up from his work.

'There's been no word from the Ayatollah again,' Mehdi commented before he drifted back to his office.

Karim looked around and noticed he wasn't the only person who couldn't concentrate. Everyone seemed uneasy. People were chatting and pointing to stories in the newspapers. There was an edgy feeling of expectation in the city too, as if something was about to happen. Or could he be imagining it? Well, they wouldn't be disappointed tomorrow. It was a bleak thought. By lunchtime he'd had enough and decided to go home. Things there might have calmed down at bit.

He was wrong. His mother's exasperated sighs punctuated lunch in the breakfast room. She shuffled lists around while she ate and glared at his father.

'Really, this is all too much!'

'Be lucky you can leave, Esmat,' Abbas replied.

Eventually she excused herself and went upstairs. There was a loud thump overhead and his father shrugged. Karim decided to visit his grandmother, and was pleasantly surprised when Zahra opened the door. The room was in chaos; dresses and jewellery were draped over every chair and on the bed. His grandmother was sitting up in bed, talking in a bright feverish manner to Zahra. She motioned impatiently for her to bring out even more evening dresses and hold them up so that she could see them.

'Oh, Karim *djan*, we're having such a lovely time!' Her brown eyes sparkled with some of their old fire and she held out her hand. 'I feel so much better today!'

He took her hand in his. It was unnaturally hot, but still he felt a rush of hope—she might recover.

'I'll come back this evening before you go to sleep,' he promised.

He glanced across at Zahra, but she had her back to him. He watched for a minute as she tried to find a place in the tightly packed wardrobe for the dress she was holding.

He spent the rest of the day putting his affairs in order. He left letters for his parents, sister and grandmother. Now and then he paused and stared out at the mountains. He stuffed five hundred American dollars in an envelope and wrote a heartfelt letter to Zahra. At the end he scrawled, 'Read Shakespeare's Sonnet Number 29, and think of me.'

He locked everything in his wall safe behind the Picasso print. Hopefully it was the first place they'd look if he was killed. He stood up and stretched; he knew what he really wanted—needed to do. An afternoon hush had settled on the house as he walked quietly down the stairs and opened the library door.

It was as soporific as usual in the rose-coloured library. He played the piano for a while and immediately felt calmer. He closed the piano lid and sat breathing lightly, staring unseeing at the music in front of him. The library door opened slowly and Zahra came in carrying some books. She started when she saw him, but he stood up, took the books from her, and put them down on the piano. His first instinct was to pull her to him and hold her close. Instead he reached for her hand. She took a step back, averting her eyes. He wondered if she knew. Should he tell her?

'Zahra, Firzun ...'

'Is it tonight?' she asked quietly.

'Yes.'

At last she looked up at him her eyes fearful. She put her hand to her throat. 'How do you know?'

'I'm going as well.'

'You!' she said angrily. 'How did *you* get involved?'

'I can keep an eye on Firzun for you.'

He'd expected her to be pleased by his commitment but he was wrong.

'You could all be killed! What about your parents, your family obligations here?'

She gripped her hands together in front of her. She was concerned about him, but what about her husband?

'This whole business is madness!' she said. When she looked up at him, her face was flushed and her eyes bright.

'Look, Zahra, Firzun's done his homework. We'll get the Americans out.'

The fretful look she gave him was almost unbearable. He put his arms round her and she leaned on his chest.

'It's all ... all ... too much,' she choked.

'We'll be okay, Zahra,' he whispered as he moved her closer. She didn't resist as he kissed her hair. He knew she didn't believe what he said—he didn't believe it himself. She pulled away from him and he let her go.

'I'd like to play soccer with Ahmad,' he said suddenly.

'He's in the garden. He wouldn't have a nap today.' She attempted a smile. 'I'll come with you.'

At dinner he told his parents he was going out later. To his surprise his mother didn't object.

'You've been good parents to me,' he said suddenly, and as Esmat stood to leave the room, he gave her a hug. She smiled at him, surprised.

Why had he agreed to go tonight? he asked himself angrily. Zahra was right; he was their only son. He *did* have family obligations. But he'd given his word. The dye was cast.

He visited his grandmother as he'd promised. The room smelled of the delicate late roses Zahra had brought in from the garden that afternoon. He stared down at his grandmother; she looked like a fading rose as she lay sleeping peacefully on her pillows. The lively woman he'd seen that afternoon had slipped away again. He knelt at her bedside and put her small hand to his forehead.

'Goodnight, Grandmother,' he said softly.

The old lady's lips moved. 'God protect you, Karim darling,' she whispered faintly.

Her eyes fluttered open for a second and she smiled at him, then they closed. He laid her hand back on the counterpane and a wave of sadness swept over him. He lingered by her bed. He longed for her to open her eyes again and smile, but she didn't. At the door he paused for a last look at her before he headed for his apartment. He was halfway up the stairs when he heard Zahra's light step on the landing. She hadn't seen him.

'Zahra!' he called quietly.

She looked up, startled. 'Your mother wants to see me,' she whispered.

He ran down the steps. She looked calm and relaxed as she waited with downcast eyes for him to speak. Maybe she's said her prayers, he thought, and accepted whatever fate is in store for her husband and herself. He seized her hands impulsively and she looked round in alarm.

'Not here!'

'I've just said goodnight to Grandmother,' he said, without releasing her hands.

When she met his eyes, he saw his own sadness mirrored in hers.

'I'll watch out for your husband, Zahra, I promise you!'

Her face was tense and worried. 'You should know ...' She hesitated and took a deep breath.

'What should I know, Zahra?'

'Ahmad really admires you,' she said quickly. 'I'll pray for you, Karim.'

She wished him goodnight. He watched as she walked towards his mother's room, her back straight and head held high. At the top of the stairs he turned as he was opening the door of his apartment. She too glanced over her shoulder and their eyes met briefly.

'God be with you,' she whispered.

He stood with his hand on the door handle watching her, but she didn't turn round again. What should he know? Not just about Ahmad, surely?

Once in his apartment, Karim moved quickly. It seemed like he'd had all the time in the world and now it had melted away. He changed into a black tracksuit and sneakers, then pulled on a thick jacket. He glanced at his watch and caught his breath. It was nearly ten o'clock and he was due at Rashid's in half an hour, earlier than the rest of the group, whose arrival times had been staggered to avoid suspicion. He paused at the door to the back stairs and looked round the apartment. Would it be for the last time? He left the door on the latch—he might need to get back in quickly. The night air felt cool and damp as he ran down the metal stairs.

Nasim and Rashid's living room smelled of acrid Afghan cigarettes. A sick feeling of dread settled on Karim's chest.

Rashid was waiting for him, dressed in jeans and a black jacket. 'I'm going now, Karim,' he said. He raised his arm in a clenched fist salute. 'Victory!'

As he embraced his friend and wished him luck, Karim felt even more certain that the whole scheme was madness. He heard Rashid running down the outside stairs, then in the distance a car engine started up. He turned and joined the Afghans. They were hunched round the dining table, poring over the plans of the embassy compound.

Firzun looked up and stretched his hands out in welcome. 'Karim Konari, the twelfth man,' he said.

The group gave a greeting, then Firzun went over the plan of attack. A minibus would drop them in Bijan Alley. They'd get in the building at the rear entrance. The insiders would open the door. The attack would be simultaneous, at midnight. Karim asked about resistance.

Firzun sniffed. 'Deal with them,' he said shortly.

'They've got twenty-five hostages tied up.' Karim looked at one of the Afghans.

'Bolt cutters?'

The man nodded.

About fifteen students were guarding the hostages. Most would go and pray at midnight. They had a couple of AK47s.

Firzun handed out green armbands. 'Put them on now,' he ordered. 'Put the headgear on later.'

Karim felt a weird sense of unreality. Would he really be there in just over an hour? What had possessed him to agree to this dangerous mission against an armed opposition? He forced himself to concentrate.

'... to drop their weapons,' Firzun was saying. 'Ashraf and Mohammed keep them covered. Everyone else untie them—Karim, tell them they're being moved. We're friends. There's no choice.'

The minibus had the name of a university on the side, Firzun continued. If it was stopped, they would say they were going to relieve the students. Speed was essential. Keep talk to a minimum. Run the hostages across the open area, make them get in the trucks. The drivers would be armed.

'Karim, go with any injured to the Laleh hospital; a taxi will follow the truck. All the trucks will rendezvous at the airstrip and when everyone's on board the plane will take off. Dump everything —balaclavas, weapons, armbands. There'll be minibuses to drop you off near taxis with Afghan drivers.'

'It's 2300 hours. Check your watches,' Firzun ordered. 'We go in fifteen minutes.'

Karim felt nauseous as he followed his group downstairs to get their weapons.

In the downstairs dining room, guns and knives were lined up on the long table. An Afghan in a flack jacket handed out revolvers, knives and machine guns. The Afghans handled the weapons with expert ease.

Firzun passed Karim a gun belt to fasten round his waist. He checked the revolver he was given and shoved it in the holster. He reached for a machine gun.

'Just a side arm and knife,' Firzun told him. 'You're the medic.'

He collected a balaclava from a pile and pushed it in the pocket of his American jacket. The pack of medical supplies he'd slung across his body felt bulky and awkward. More men came into the room to collect weapons. They spoke in low voices—already at battle stations.

'Green group. Any questions?' Firzun looked round at the silent men.

Karim heard the sound of an engine, and through the dining room window he could see the dim lights of the minibus waiting in the back lane.

'This is it, may God be with us,' Firzun said quietly, adding something in Dari that sounded to Karim like 'freedom for our country as well'.

The Afghans replied, but he didn't understand them. He followed them into the familiar hall, past the empty kitchen and out the back door. His heart thudded in his chest as he walked with the others through the garden. The bus was a dark shape, hardly visible with only its parking lights on. He ducked down and scrambled into a seat at the back. The driver revved the engine and the vehicle lurched forward along the back lane. His mouth was dry and he felt sick with apprehension. No one spoke.

28

THE RESCUE

Karim was squashed inside the vehicle with the other men, taking him back to the misery of his national service training camp. There was the same damp smell and feeling of tension. But then *he'd* been in charge, not Firzun, and it was only a practice mission. Now, in this jolting claustrophobic minibus, he asked himself again why the hell he'd been persuaded to come. He looked out the window; it was pitch black outside. The minibus lurched into potholes in the back lane and the men were knocked against each other. Finally it swung left and he saw the dim lights of Maryam Street. When they pulled out onto the road, he felt a rush of adrenalin. Maybe it wasn't madness—they *could* do it! And he was involved. He was striking a blow for democracy!

He patted the revolver at his side several times. He didn't want to use it, but he would if necessary. From his seat at the back he observed the hunched figures of the other men. They were talking quietly in their own language. What was in it for them? Was this some sort of practice for a war in their own country? The traffic was light and the driver picked up speed. Trucks rushed down the opposite side of the highway, heading off across the country on long-haul runs. An overnight coach passed on its way out of the city. The bright interior lights were on and he caught a glimpse of people standing up, organising bags or settling into their seats. For a brief second he wished he was on it, not here in this stinking minibus. Finally Firzun turned from his front seat and whispered orders in his abrasive voice.

'We're here! Balaclavas on. Keep quiet.'

Karim pulled on his balaclava. His skin recoiled from its damp heaviness. His nerves felt taught, attuned to the faintest sound. The bus stopped.

'Bijan Alley. Out, out ...' Firzun whispered.

The outside lights of the embassy compound were a dull yellow, but across the grass the building blazed like the coach he'd just seen. He stumbled out with the others, his feet slithering on the greasy footpath of Bijan Alley. It was completely deserted. He ran with them into the narrow passageway between two apartment blocks where he'd been the other day. He looked up apprehensively. Dim lights flickered through the blinds and curtains of some of the apartment windows, but no one was looking out. On a distant radio, the insistent voice of a cleric droned verses from the Koran. There was a smell of old onions. Above the pounding of his heart he heard a baby wailing. He checked his watch—three minutes to midnight. His heart was beating slower now and he touched the comforting bulk of the revolver again.

He breathed out, then in, sharply, when Firzun hissed, 'Go! Go! Go!'

Karim ran out of the passage with the others in single file, keeping close to the walls of the street. As they neared the embassy gates, the outside lights went off suddenly and he staggered in the abrupt darkness. It was on! His heart raced as he ran. He could hear his own jagged breathing.

The few guards at the gate scattered like ants. He saw the Afghans in front of him grab them and silently drop their bodies on the grass. He didn't look back but surged forward with the others towards the building. They all kept low in the shadows, away from the lighted windows. He ran quickly, crouching until they reached the wall. Firzun pushed open a rear door. He beckoned them to follow him into the service passageway. Three men were waiting for them, crouched low—Firzun's 'insiders'. They pulled on balaclavas and took their machine guns, huddling close to their leader, whispering and pointing. Firzun signalled and everyone stopped and hunkered down.

Karim knew the layout by heart: a two-metre wide passage, exit door either end, two lavatories on his left, cleaner's room between. The windows to the right looked out onto a grassy space, the embassy gates and Bijan Alley. The yellow painted passage was well lit. To his left, the double swing doors moved slightly in the draught from outside. Beyond the door, the hostages waited in ignorant limbo ... so close.

Firzun squatted below the door and pushed it open slightly. He squinted into the room, then he crawled back to the group. When he spoke, his voice was muffled and rapid. Karim strained to understand him.

'Hostages on the left, six students playing cards, four guns between them, two women. Watch them, they'll run for help. Ready? God be with us. Go! Go! Go!'

The room plan flashed through Karim's brain as he crashed through the door with the others—large square room, high counter on left, desks behind. The room had been ransacked; papers and files were scattered everywhere. He blinked, dazzled by the light. His eyes strafed the room and he saw the hostages through a pall of cigarette smoke. They were sitting or lying on makeshift floor mattresses. Half of them were blindfolded; each tied to a partner, two women with straggling matted hair, men unkempt, unshaven.

Everyone started yelling.

'Oh my God, what the hell ... Help us!' some of the Americans called out, struggling to stand. The women students screamed and ran towards another door.

'Stop or I shoot,' Firzun bawled. The women dropped to their knees, wailing, clinging to each other, their black chadors pooling round them.

'Weapons on the floor. Against the wall. Hands on the wall. Move!'

The students sprang to their feet, startled, terrified, scattering playing cards and cigarettes. No time to reach for their weapons.

'Hands up, hands up!' Firzun yelled.

They threw themselves spreadeagled against the wall, shouting curses. Karim ran forward and shifted the guns away from them with his foot. He ran across to the hostages. The Afghans were already there, slashing the bindings and pulling off the blindfolds. Suddenly one of the students ducked away from the wall. He snatched a revolver from the floor.

'Sons of Satan!' he shouted, firing the gun with a shaking hand. He missed and the bullet lodged in a door frame.

Karim grabbed his sidearm, but before he could use it, Firzun levelled his weapon and fired. The student crumpled to his knees, clutching his chest. With a terrible scream he fell face forward at Karim's feet.

'Jesus Christ! Another bunch of crazies,' one of the Americans yelled.

'Son of a bitch! That's Sami, you bastards,' a woman screamed. She staggered to her feet.

'Stay there,' Karim ordered in English.

'Get them out, now!' Firzun bellowed.

Karim and the Afghans dragged the hostages to their feet. 'Hurry up. Get moving!'

The Americans rubbed their wrists and ankles; they were disorientated. The blindfolded ones blinked in the light.

'What the hell's going on?' A man grabbed Karim's arm, but he shook him off.

'Shut up, we're getting you out.'

'Who the fuck are you?' another American demanded, swaying on his feet.

'Pigs of the shah!' one of the students yelled. 'You're dead. We'll kill you all.'

One of the Afghans knocked him to the ground with the butt of his rifle.

'On the floor,' Firzun roared at the students. He turned to Karim. 'Get them out. Go! Go! Go!'

Karim pushed the stumbling hostages towards the door. He was yelling now like everyone else. 'Move! Move! Out the door!'

One of the Americans looked over his shoulder. 'Who are you?' he asked in Farsi.

'A rescue party. Keep moving.'

The man hesitated and Karim pushed him hard in the back.

'What the hell, pal?' the man shouted in English.

'For God's sake, shut up and get going.'

Firzun strode towards them. He pointed his submachine gun at the group. To Karim's amazement, he spoke in English. 'Do what you're told. Move!' The group huddled together and shuffled towards the door at a snail's pace.

'These bastards are gonna kill us!' someone said.

Karim gaped. 'What the hell's wrong with you? We're the rescue party!'

They were terrified, why wouldn't they be? But they wouldn't go through the damn door. 'We're getting you out!' he shouted at them. They seemed to be walking on the spot, shuffling and reluctant. The students against the wall yelled obscenities and threats. Out of the corner of his eye he saw the black chadors move.

'The women!'

'Stop or I'll shoot!' Firzun yelled.

The women had struggled to their feet. One of them glanced over her shoulder before she ran through the far door, her chador flying round her body. The other crumpled to the ground when a single shot from Firzun's revolver hit her leg. She clutched her knee, screaming a long high-pitched screech as she collapsed. Blood oozed slowly onto the floor.

'Bastard, pigs!' the students cursed.

Firzun turned to the American hostages. 'Move faster!' he ordered, waving his gun at them. They didn't hesitate or argue.

Karim marshalled them along, using his gun to show them the way to the corridor. Two of the Afghans ran down the passageway to secure the outside door. He glared at the Americans. The women were sobbing, their hands clasped over their mouths. The men looked dazed. The Afghans brought up the rear, urging everyone along with machine guns. Why hadn't someone turned the damn light out? Karim was furious. The place blazed like a Christmas tree! They were sitting ducks! The enemy must have heard the gun shots.

'Put the lights out!' he shouted. Someone aimed a rifle at the neon tube and it exploded in a shower of glass. The women screamed.

'Christ almighty, they'll get us killed!' one of the men said.

Karim recognised his accent—Boston—how ironic! 'Move and shut up!'

He heard an engine revving and his heart lifted. They were nearly there—albeit covered in shards of glass, crunching it underfoot.

'There's a van waiting, keep going!' he ordered.

'Where to?' one of the Americans demanded.

'A plane to Turkey!'

'We're better off here,' a different voice whined.

'What the hell's wrong with you?' Karim felt desperate. 'We're getting you out!'

'Look, pal, this is American soil, we're safe here. I'm a marine ...'

'Then obey orders, shut up and keep moving.'

He tried to keep calm, but he felt furiously angry with them. Why did they want a debate about being saved? The man stopped and stepped forward menacingly. He was a head taller than Karim and well built. Over his shoulder, Karim saw the outside door swing open ahead and felt a surge of hope.

'You're free!' he said.

The marine swore at him, but turned to the open door and kept walking. They were metres from the gate and the trucks. He could just see the last two Afghans as they backed out of the reception area, keeping their machine guns trained on the students.

From the darkness outside, a voice screamed. 'All of you, hands up. Sons of Satan! Surrender!'

A blinding flash lit up the no-man's land from the outside door to the gate. A group of men was waiting for them, machine guns trained on the doors and windows. Bullets sprayed below the window. The outside lights came on suddenly, temporarily blinding everyone and lighting up the passageway. The hostages backed up against the wall, their hands raised above their heads.

'God help us,' one of them said quietly. Some of the group crossed themselves.

In the distance Karim heard more gunfire.

'Don't shoot! Don't shoot!' an American man yelled in Farsi.

Karim put his hands up and walked carefully with the Afghans towards the outside door.

Firzun stood with his gun raised above his head. 'Mohammed—Ashraf, cover me and take a couple of them out fast. The rest of you, run for the van, forget the hostages,' he hissed.

Karim swallowed. His mouth was dry and naked fear made his hands tingle and his scalp creep.

'Don't shoot, we surrender,' Firzun shouted.

It was enough to distract the men outside. One of the Afghans silently opened a window in the passageway. His first shots hit two of the men in the garden.

'Go!' Firzun yelled.

Karim ran across the grass, head down. He couldn't see the truck. Had it cruised down Bijan Alley? Was it there at all? The clatter of machine-gun fire bombarded his ears. Behind him he heard more gunfire from the reception area. Someone staggered forward in front of him and fell on his knees. He saw the green armband and hoisted the other man's left arm round his neck. He looked down—Firzun! Blood was gushing from a wound in his leg. He was a dead weight and swung sideways from Karim's neck and back to the ground.

'Leave me! I'm hit,' Firzun gasped, clutching his leg. 'Save yourself!'

Karim stared at him wildly—Zahra's husband! If he died, she'd be free. He hesitated. The firing started again.

'Help here, quick!' he called out.

One of the Afghans ran back and hoisted Firzun's other arm round his neck. Together they stumbled across the grass, dragging the wounded man. Karim's knees buckled under the weight as he lurched forward. He saw the truck coasting backwards to the gate. They hauled Firzun's inert body towards it. Karim's chest was bursting as they lurched forward under fire from their pursuers. He risked a look back and saw two of the Afghans in the lighted corridor with their hands up alongside the Americans. Men with pistols and submachine guns were herding everyone into the American embassy visa processing office. The rescue mission had been a total rout. And now he was a wanted man.

29

THE WOUNDED

Karim was sweating, staggering with the weight of the injured man, and his heart thumped low and hard in his chest. His breath came in laboured gasps as footsteps pounded behind him and gunfire lit up the darkness. He expected any minute that he'd be hit, his legs would give way, and he would crash to the ground with his load. He kept his head down and with the help of the other man, they dragged Firzun towards the gate, the van, safety. Suddenly Firzun's body swung heavily to one side. The Afghan who was supporting him dropped to the ground. Karim glanced sideways; half the man's head was shot away. Fighting his nausea, he didn't look back. He half dragged, half carried Firzun the last hundred metres.

He could see armed men waiting for him at the back of the truck. One of them ran forward and helped him pull Firzun into the vehicle. The other returned fire as bullets ricocheted wildly off the outside. Someone pulled Karim up. He collapsed onto the floor of the truck, gasping for breath as he peeled off his balaclava. Before he could get to Firzun, he was thrown against the side of the vehicle as it screeched off down the road, zigzagging to avoid the bullets. One of the Afghans pulled the canvas flap down as it sped round a corner.

Karim heard Firzun groan and he dragged himself upright. He staggered towards him, feeling disorientated and sick. They'd laid Firzun out along the floor, taken his balaclava off, and put a jacket under his head. The injured man's eyes had flickered open, then closed. Karim took a deep breath and looked round. In the gloom he saw three other figures—only three? They'd left with twelve. He pulled a flashlight from the first-aid bag and knelt unsteadily next to Firzun.

'Shine this on his leg, someone,' he ordered. 'Driver! Go to the Laleh hospital!'

'Okay, sir!' the man answered.

The truck swerved as it changed direction. One of the Afghans steadied the flashlight as Karim slit open Firzun's heavy trousers with shaking hands. The bullet had torn through the skin and muscle below Firzun's knee. It was slippery with blood, the wound a sodden bloody mess. It reminded him of the lamb he'd seen slaughtered in a village when he was a child—raw and open. He swallowed, feeling sick again. Firzun was semi-conscious and groaning with pain. Karim wiped away the blood and peered at the wound—it looked bad.

'For God's sake, don't die on me!' he muttered.

He disinfected the area and applied the tourniquet quickly. With the help of the other men he packed it and tightened a pressure bandage round the area. The seeping blood slowed and suddenly Firzun's body went limp.

'Shine the flashlight on his face,' he ordered.

'Allah, save him!' the Afghan whispered.

Firzun's face was deathly pale. Blood oozed out over Karim's hands as he knelt unsteadily in the swaying vehicle, pressing on the wound. He ordered them to check the pulse in Firzun's neck.

'Faint,' someone said. Blood was still seeping from the bandage and onto the floor. Karim crouched over Firzun, willing him to live. He looked round and asked if there were any others injured.

'Seven missing,' a voice said.

In the dim light their faces looked young and scared. A wave of anger swept over him. Seven from his group dead or captured, including the man who'd turned back to save Firzun. And him, their leader, clinging to life by a thread ... for what? Was Rashid dead too? Had the other groups failed like them?

'We can't go into the Laleh hospital!' someone said.

'Why not?' Karim snapped.

'They'll know we're Afghans. They'll be looking for us.'

He glanced at the unconscious man and his blood soaked leg. '*I'll* take him into the emergency room.'

He talked to them, trying to reassure these young victims that they were all right—that they'd got away with it. But they were all wanted men, they knew that—and so was he. He looked out the window. Where the hell where they?

'Get a move on!' he called to the driver.

He looked down at Firzun's face, his thoughts racing. If he dies, she's free, he thought again. The mantra repeated itself in time with his heartbeat. Firzun dead—Zahra free. A feeling of intense cold swept over him. It was like kneeling next to a pillar of ice and he shivered.

Don't wish him dead, Karim. Every life is precious. He heard his grandmother's voice in his head as clearly as if she were there speaking to him.

Tears welled in his eyes and he turned round, convinced that she was standing behind his shoulder, watching him. Then she was gone and there was nothing but the throbbing of the engine, the streets outside and finally, thank God, the Emergency sign of the hospital. He looked down again at Firzun. The other man opened his eyes and met his.

'Thanks, Karim,' he whispered as his eyes flickered shut.

'We can't wait long at the hospital,' a frightened voice said from the darkness.

'Leave if you have to,' Karim said.

He squinted through the windscreen; no police cars—yet. They'd get here eventually. They'd be checking all the hospitals for gunshot victims; he knew that and so did the Afghans.

The truck pulled up slowly outside the Emergency entrance. He kneeled and tightened the bandage on the injured leg, then ordered the Afghans to help him get Firzun out of the truck. One was already opening the flap. Karim jumped out and the Afghan hoisted Firzun's inert body over his shoulder. He staggered under the dead weight. They supported Firzun until they got to the entrance.

Karim's knees buckled when they left Firzun with him. He pushed open the double glass door, and as the truck cruised away towards the back of the building, he yelled out: 'Help, quick! He needs a doctor.'

Nurses in chadors ran towards him. One of them grabbed a gurney. A young doctor in a white coat was close behind. They helped Karim unload Firzun onto the trolley.

The doctor tutted. 'You should go to the public hospital.' He sounded irritated.

'No time ... we stopped to change a tyre ... a car hit him.'

When Karim spoke the doctor looked surprised, as if he'd expected to hear a rough worker's accent. Karim glanced down at his clothes—he was covered in mud and blood. God knows what his face looked like. The doctor started to ask more questions, but before he could answer Maryam came striding down the corridor towards them.

'Car accident,' Karim said.

Maryam nodded.

'Is he the only injured?' the other doctor asked.

'I'll see to this. I'm the duty surgeon,' Maryam said dismissively.

Her colleague shrugged and walked away as she snapped out orders to the nurses.

'Prep him for theatre. Don't touch the wound, leave that to me.'

'We need details, his name ...' one of the nurses began.

'Do it later, just get him ready,' Maryam said sharply. 'Call him Davar for now. I'll be there in a minute.'

The nurses raised their eyebrows at each other, then set off down a long corridor.

Maryam motioned Karim to one side, her eyes fearful. 'What happened?' She spoke in English, keeping her voice low.

He shook his head. 'We didn't get them out.'

The enormity of what they'd done overcame him. He shoved his shaking hands in his pockets.

'You're in shock. Go home, lie low,' she whispered. She pointed to a door behind him. 'Go that way. I'll be in touch.'

'I used a tourniquet and pressure,' he stammered. 'I did my best ...'

'Good. Leave it to me, he'll be okay. Get moving before the police come.'

He pushed the exit door open with his shoulder. Maryam's shrewd eyes met his and she shrugged. We blew it, he thought as she pulled the door shut behind him. To his relief, the truck was still there and it coasted slowly up to him. He hoisted himself in and collapsed next to the other men. He leaned back against the cold metal wall, feeling completely drained.

'They said he'll be okay,' he told them as the truck swung out of the hospital gates.

In the reflected light from the hospital he saw that they looked relieved but they didn't speak.

'Too dangerous to go down the main streets,' the driver said out of the darkness.

They dropped him on a corner. A taxi with an Afghan driver was waiting as Firzun had planned. Karim gave him directions to his home and asked him to go down the back lane.

After a few hundred metres the driver stopped. 'Too many potholes!'

Karim got the message and fumbled for money.

The man waved it away. 'Paid already.'

Karim got out onto the rutted lane, stepping back as the driver swung the cab round. After the taillights disappeared it was pitch black in the lane. He pulled the flashlight from the first-aid bag, which was still slung across his body. The beam was weak and intermittent, but enough for him to get his bearings. He knew he was several houses away from Nasim and Rashid's back gate.

Keeping near the fences he started to jog towards it. Then he heard the sound of an engine—someone was crashing the gears of a diesel vehicle. It was behind him in the lane and moving fast. He looked round desperately and ran to a large bush near a back fence. He clawed the branches away and curled himself behind it, pulling his coat collar up, wishing he still had the balaclava.

For a second he saw the open jeep before its headlights blinded him. It was bouncing down the lane over the potholes, spraying mud and stones into the fences as it passed. He saw the outlines of four men, teenagers by the sound of them, all armed with machine guns trained on the backs of the houses. Just before it passed him, it hit a large pothole and the kids were bounced out of their seats. The vehicle passed within a metre of him, but they didn't see him. He saw them punch the driver's shoulder.

'Yeah, Mehran! Mad boy. Yeah, faster! Faster,' they whooped.

He watched the taillights dip up and down as the yelling got fainter. He half expected the jeep to flip with them still urging the driver on. He watched until it got to the end of the lane, then crawled out of the bush. Branches snapped against his face and twigs caught in his hair. The wind picked up as he ran alongside the back fence, heading for the faint light of his friend's house. A rush of relief swept over him. He knew Nasim and Rashid had left the back gate open. Once inside he'd be safe.

The jeep was coming back. It raced along, swerving past potholes, plunging into them, then sideswiping the fences. When it ran onto the fields on the other side of the lane, the driver revved the engine. Karim heard mud spraying into the puddles as the passengers yelled obscenities. The lights were on full beam and lit up every hiding place. They dipped forward, sideways, up and down as the crazy madman at the wheel roared back up the lane. Within minutes it would be on him and they'd have a quarry to chase—a man-rabbit caught in the headlights.

Karim hunched low against the fence, his hands splayed as he felt for the gate. He could smell the fumes from the jeep and hear the occupants yelling and laughing. He was sweating now in his heavy jacket, pushing desperately against the fence. The wind whipped overhanging tree branches against his face and then it started to rain; a heavy drenching downpour, soaking the wood. As the jeep closed the gap between them, it skidded in the mud. Any second now the lights would pick him up, a pathetic scrabbling spread-eagled creature with nowhere to hide.

30

DEATH AT MIDNIGHT

Suddenly the wood gave way, the gate swung open, and Karim fell forward into the garden. He turned, still crouching, and shut the gate very slowly, afraid that any abrupt movement would catch someone's eye and they'd be on to him. As it swung shut, he saw the lights pass by through the fence palings. The gate was almost two metres high, but he stood with infinite care. He could still hear the jeep, revving through the mud, the driver crashing the gears. The youths were laughing like lunatics and shouting 'Rain! Rain! RAAAAIN!' He prayed the jeep would stay upright. If they survived a crash they'd be banging on the fences and they'd find the gate. He had to keep moving.

The driving rain soaked his hair and clothes and rivulets of icy water dripped down his back. Karim ran through Nasim and Rashid's garden, still keeping low. There was another gate in the fence to the next garden and another into his. They'd used them when they were kids. But could he find them in the dark? His breath was coming in sharp gasps as he forced himself to move faster. Pictures flashed through his brain as he ran. He could hear the woman's screams when the bullet hit her leg. He saw the terrified faces of the American hostages, the shattered head of the Afghan who had helped him with Firzun. He could still feel Firzun's blood seeping through the bandage, through his fingers, staining his hands.

Karim stopped and leaned forward, his hands splayed out on his knees. He looked up, still breathing hard, fighting his rising nausea. A faint light filtered through the curtains of an upstairs window in Nasim's house. Should he go in and tell them about Firzun? No, it was too dangerous. He had to get home, clean up, pretend everything was normal.

In the distance he saw his home. Another light shone through the trees, but the wind blew the rain into his face, temporarily obscuring it. There was an empty house and another vast garden between him and safety. He pushed back his wet hair and focused on the light that he knew was in his grandmother's room. It was like an unreachable mirage. He staggered on, thrashing through the trees. He followed the damp fence wood along with his hands, splinters catching at his fingers. Finally he found the gate; he tried to prise the latch open, but it was rusted shut. He threw his shoulder against the old wood. The gate splintered, gave way and collapsed into the next garden.

He trod heavily across it and pushed his way through the shrubbery. He tripped on tree roots and the long wet grass clung to his ankles. He was running stealthily now, like a thief through the overgrown garden of the empty property. He'd dropped the flashlight ages ago and his breath came in ragged gasps. But the dim light was still there, guiding him home. He headed in what he thought was a straight line. Again he had to feel along the wet fence and when he found the gate into his property, he thanked God it wasn't locked. At last he was in his familiar garden, and he saw the shape of the outside stairs to his apartment. His pants were heavy and wet against his legs, thick with dried blood. He half ran, half stumbled up the steps.

Karim staggered into his flat and ran across the living room, tearing off his clothes in a frenzy, leaving them where they fell. In the bathroom, he turned the shower to maximum. He stood in the pounding jet and soaped his hair and his body, scrubbed fiercely at his arms, torso, legs. The water cascaded over his head. He could hardly breathe. He spluttered and cursed. When he closed his eyes, he felt the motion of the truck as it lurched round the corners.

He turned off the water abruptly and leaned with both hands flat against the tiles. He got out of the shower and vomited into the toilet bowl. At the sink, he washed out his mouth and splashed his face with cold water. He wrapped a towel round his waist and stood in the silence, watching the rivulets of water run down his body.

'We botched it! Bloody waste of lives!' he spat.

He pulled another towel off the rail and dried himself quickly, punishing himself with its roughness. He dropped the towels on the floor and pulled on his bathrobe. He grabbed a hand towel and rubbed it through his hair. A question pounded insistently in his head: 'What now?'

Karim caught his breath. Someone was thumping relentlessly on the door of his apartment. His stomach knotted with fear. He called out and his mother answered. He opened the door cautiously. She was fully dressed.

'It's Grandmother ...' she began.

'What ... ?'

'She passed peacefully. We tried to find you.' His mother put her hand out and grabbed his arm to steady him.

'No, she can't have ... She was happy today ...' He felt sick and his head swam.

'Your father's sitting with her.' Esmat's voice seemed to come from a long way away. 'I'll get your clothes out.' She tried to push into the room.

'No!' He took a breath. 'I can manage. I'm coming.'

She tried to stop him, but he closed the door and flicked the lock shut, then buried his face in his hands. She hadn't waited for him! Why? Something inside him shattered and he leaned against the door, sobbing quietly.

His mother thumped on the door panels. 'Karim, don't lock me out!'

'I'm coming!'

He staggered across the room, scooped up the blood-soaked wet clothes and stuffed them in the wardrobe. His mother rattled the handle and called his name again through the door. He pulled on a clean tracksuit, took a deep breath, and opened it. She pushed past him, remonstrating with him as soon as she got inside.

'Karim, where were you? I rang Nasim and she said you were out with Rashid and some friends. Then we rang all your friends and no one knew.' She shook his arm, her voice accusing and tearful. 'You should have been here. Why weren't you?'

He couldn't speak, but she didn't wait for a reply.

'The nurse called us, her breathing ...' Her voice was anguished and distressed. 'It was a terrible rattling sound.'

He wanted her to stop but she wouldn't.

'We sat with her until the end—just after midnight.'

He nodded mutely—midnight—when he was creeping across the grass at the embassy.

'You have to say goodbye,' his mother said. 'For God's sake, Karim, where *were* you?' She glared at him.

He had lost the power of speech, struck dumb, but she didn't seem to notice. She turned to go, beckoning him impatiently to follow her down the stairs. He felt dizzy, his brain was numb, hardly able to process the information. Finally she stopped outside the open door to his grandmother's room and turned to him.

'Pull yourself together, Karim,' she said sharply.

The light that had led him home glowed in the corner by the window. He went in slowly. On the opposite side of the bed, his father sat with his head in his hands. He stood up when he saw his son and indicated the bed. Rezvan lay with her hands crossed on top of the sheet. She looked pale and serene. Karim knelt down at the side of the bed, tears trapped in his throat. When he took her hand, it was icy cold.

'I heard your voice,' he said quietly. 'You spoke to me in the van!'

The air was still full of the scent of the roses, which Zahra had put on the windowsill earlier that day ... yesterday. Zahra! His brain jolted back into consciousness. She didn't know. He had to tell her! He jumped when his father touched his arm. Carefully he replaced the cold hand and his father drew the sheet up and under the dead woman's chin. The two men embraced; they stood at the side of the bed and prayed together for the soul of the departed. Karim prayed for his grandmother and the young men whose brief lives had been snuffed out.

Karim caught his breath as he repeated the final words. When Esmat met them on the landing, her initial anger had evaporated and she patted him on the arm.

'Thank you, Karim. Your grandmother had a long and happy life. Phone your sister in Boston, your father's not up to it.' She thrust a piece of paper in his hand. 'I'll organise the funeral for later today,' she said over her shoulder as she led his father to their bedroom.

Karim walked slowly down to the library and sat in one of the winged chairs, staring sightlessly at the wall. He felt lightheaded, incapable of picking up the phone. He looked at the library clock ticking away the minutes. It was six in the evening of the previous day in Boston. He longed to have yesterday back, to change everything, to insist that Firzun came to his senses and cancelled the raid.

Finally he stirred himself and dialled the number for the international operator. It crossed his mind that the regime might have blocked overseas calls, so when an efficient-sounding male voice asked for the overseas number, he gave it in a rush and had to repeat it. He listened distractedly to the familiar hissing and whirring of the international connection. A woman's voice with an American accent asked for the number, and the operator in Tehran repeated it in English.

'Connecting you, caller,' the American woman said.

On the other side of the world his sister's phone rang. 'Hi, this is Soraya,' his sister answered brightly in English.

His heart leapt when he heard her voice. 'It's Karim, Soraya,' he said in their own language. 'I ...'

'Karim! Is everything okay?' she interrupted him.

'Grandmother passed away a couple of hours ago.' He tried to keep his voice steady.

His sister burst into tears and Karim heard her husband Nadir's voice in the background. He came on the line and asked what had happened.

'Sorry for your loss. May God give you patience,' his brother-in-law said, mixing his condolences. 'Hey, Karim,' he said in a low voice, 'we just got a news flash on TV. Some crazies tried to get the hostages out. What's going on?'

'No idea,' Karim lied.

'Sorry, guess you're busy with family stuff. Soraya's good, it's a shock, but she's looking forward to seeing her mom.'

'They'll be with you next week.'

'What about you, Karim?'

'I'll get there as soon as I can. I'll call later, Nadir, got to go.'

'Sure, you sound dead beat. Take it easy.'

After they'd said goodbye, Karim stood up and stared unseeing at the bookcases. How was Firzun? Would he was be making the journey to Paradise with his grandmother tonight? He looked at the clock. It was too late to wake Zahra and tell her. He picked up the phone again and dialled Rashid's number. He answered on the first ring. Relief flooded over Karim—Rashid was alive!

'It's Karim. How many got out?' He was trembling.

'Two or three from each of the cells.' His friend's voice was flat, emotionless.

'What about the Americans?'

'Still there, Karim. Firzun's okay, Maryam phoned.'

Karim urged him to leave the country; the plane would wait if they called. Or go by road over the mountains across the border to

Turkey and ask for asylum. Nasim was listening on the extension phone.

'We can't abandon Firzun,' she interrupted. 'You saved his life, Karim.'

When he urged them to get out while they could, they were adamant that they would stay.

'We'll be martyrs for the cause if we have to,' Nasim said firmly.

'You should go, Karim,' Rashid interposed. 'Go tonight while you can!'

'Grandmother passed.'

They were fulsome in their condolences.

'Is the funeral today?' Nasim asked and when Karim said yes, she hesitated a fraction. 'We might need to ask you a small favour. Firzun can't stay in the hospital. Look, we'll talk later—just go to bed now. May God give you patience.'

She hung up the phone.

'Rashid?' Karim expected the line to be open, but the phone was dead.

What now? What the hell did they want now? A wave of furious anger swept over him. He was angry with everything and everyone. The stupid idiots who had destroyed his country, his grandmother for dying, his friends for using him, and Firzun for being married to Zahra. He thumped his fist down on the telephone table.

'Shit! Shit! Shit! Damn everyone!' he shouted out loud.

He stopped and listened; there were voices in the atrium and the sound of footsteps.

Now what? He opened the library door in time to see Tahmineh's back retreating up the main staircase. She was carrying white linen cloths over both arms. A wave of grief clutched his heart, making him shiver. The women of the house were preparing his grandmother's body for burial. He waited until he heard a door close upstairs, then made his way stealthily to his apartment.

31

AFTERMATH

Zahra woke suddenly. She heard Tahmineh whispering her name through the bedroom door as she knocked. She opened her door apprehensively. Was this bad news about Firzun—about Karim? It was almost a relief when the sobbing woman told her that Rezvan had passed half an hour ago and that Esmat wanted them both to help wash the body. While Zahra got dressed, Tahmineh fetched Shirin and they moved Ahmad into his mother's bed. Shirin still half asleep crept into Ahmad's.

Zahra followed Tahmineh down the back stairs and helped her collect rosewater, camphor and winding sheets. They'd been ready for a while in a special cupboard in the kitchen, but Tahmineh still wanted to double-check everything. While they waited to give the family time together, Tahmineh related the events of the night.

Zahra's hands trembled as she listened to the other woman's ramblings. When Tahmineh said that 'Mr Karim' had come home very late, Zahra clenched her hands together in silent prayer. He was alive! But she still didn't know what had happened to Firzun.

Finally Tahmineh decided it was time to start. 'I'm going up the main stairs just this once,' she said.

Zahra preferred to use her usual route to the first floor. She didn't want to see Karim yet. She couldn't deal with any more bad news. To her relief the landing was deserted. She walked across to Rezvan's room and joined Tahmineh and Esmat to begin the ritual washing of the old lady's body.

As they performed their tasks, she glanced occasionally at Esmat, but the other woman avoided making eye contact. Her lips were pursed and her face was blank during Tahmineh's tearful recital of verses from the Koran and prayers for the dead. '... *Every soul shall have a taste of death, in the end to Us shall you be brought back ... Nor does anyone know in what land he is to die ...*' Tahmineh intoned. Esmat's sighs punctuated the procedure, but under Tahmineh's direction she went through the motions. Occasionally she patted her hair into place or checked her earrings.

Then the ritual washing of the body three times. After each washing, Esmat disappeared into the bathroom and they waited, listening to the gushing water. Zahra imagined her feverishly scrubbing her hands with Rezvan's rose-scented soap. When she came back into the room, she wiped the palms of her hands across her thighs several times, as she'd done when she first shook hands with Zahra.

Before they finally shrouded Rezvan in the winding sheets, they dabbed rose water on her forehead, nose, hands, knees and feet, the parts of the body that had been used in prayer. Tahmineh reverently crossed the dead woman's hands on her chest, then Rezvan was covered forever. Zahra waited until Esmat left the room, then she said goodnight to Tahmineh, who was standing by the bed saying another prayer.

So it's finished, Zahra thought as she closed her bedroom door. She envied Ahmad and Shirin's innocence as they slept quietly in their beds. She tiptoed to the bathroom and soaped her hands thoroughly, trying to wash away the smell of camphor, which Tahmineh had added to the water for the third and final washing. As she showered, her vision was hazy with tears, and after she'd pulled on her long white cotton nightgown she leaned again the wall and cried.

Ahmad grunted in his sleep when she moved him across her bed, but when she closed her eyes sleep eluded her. She lay wide awake next to her son and allowed herself to think about Karim. He was alive, but only he knew what had happened. She felt agitated. Was Firzun alive? If she was she a 'widow' for the second time, what would she do?

A sliver of light from the landing still shone under the door. She swung her feet onto the floor and hastily pulled on her dressing gown. She glanced at the sleeping children, then opened the door quietly. If no one was around, she could phone Nasim from the library. Whatever the time, she *had* to know.

She heard his step on the stairs before she reached the landing. He glanced towards her room as he passed and started.

'Zahra!'

'Is Firzun all right?' she whispered.

He looked round. 'He's injured. Come up to my apartment and I'll tell you more.'

She shook her head. 'I'm in my night clothes.'

'All right, the kitchen. Everyone's in bed.'

He led the way down the kitchen stairs and she followed him carefully in her long clothes. A small lamp burned in the corner of the warm silent room. She looked across at Tahmineh's apartment, but no light shone under the door and everywhere was still. The clock ticked loudly and she glanced up; it was nearly three o'clock! She pushed some fuel into the stove. When it caught, she sat down opposite Karim at the wooden table and looked across at him.

'God give you patience,' she said, putting her hand on his.

He nodded distractedly. 'I still can't believe it.'

In the dim light, she could see scratches on his cheek and dark shadows under his eyes. She lifted his hand; there were brown stains under his manicured nails.

'It's blood,' he said shortly, following her gaze. She raised his hand to her lips and kissed his fingers.

'What happened?' she asked again, frightened by the way he looked. Had her cousin survived? As if he'd read her mind, Karim spoke calmly.

'Firzun was shot in the leg. He's in hospital, he'll recover. The raid was a disaster. The Americans are still there.'

His hazel eyes met hers, heavy with exhaustion as he related the events of the night. He put his head in his hands and she leaned across and touched his hair. He grasped her hand in both of his. He searched her face and told her again about the dead student, the dead Afghans.

'I wasn't here when my grandmother died.'

'You were the last person she spoke to before she slipped into a coma,' she said, trying to reassure him.

He took her other hand and held it tightly, looking directly into her eyes. A wave of love for him flooded through her. 'Thank you, Zahra.'

She let her hands lie in his.

'They mustn't know where I was,' he said, his eyes searching her face.

'I know.'

'Everyone's in danger now.' His voice was dull. She stared at him, trying to hide her fear. 'The police and the Revolutionary Guard will search the hospitals and then the houses.'

'How long can Firzun stay in the hospital?'

'We'll have to get him out—he'll go to Nasim's.'

She watched his anxious face, looking desperately for any sign of hope. Stupid Firzun, she thought. Stupid, stupid man! He's put everyone in danger. She clenched her fists inside his cupped hands.

'I can't believe she's gone,' he said again, his voice thick with emotion.

She moved her hands from his and their eyes met briefly as she stood up. 'I have to get back to Ahmad ...'

'The funeral's later today.' He sounded distracted, distant.

'I know. She's ready.'

He pushed his chair back, and as she turned towards the door, he pulled her to him and put his arms round her. This was wrong—she should move away, but when he held her close to his chest, an enormous sense of relief swept over her. Thank God he'd survived! This was where she felt safe, held by him, leaning into him just as she had after the march.

She felt his hand move inside her robe and then her nightdress, and gasped when he cupped her breast gently and ran his thumb across the nipple. She didn't stop him—didn't want to stop him. She wanted to savour the moment and the weakening sensation deep in her body. Gently he pulled open her clothes and lowering his head. He kissed her breasts, cupping each in turn. He ran his tongue over each nipple. Her body buckled against him and she grasped his hips, pulling him closer to her. Her whole being ached for him. He released her breasts and pushed his hands into her loose hair, then kissed her deeply on the mouth. She felt his hardness against her. She pulled away from him as a sudden terrible memory of Mahmoud's rough thrusting swept over her.

'Stay with me tonight, I need you.' His voice was ragged with desire as he reached out for her.

She released herself and took a step back. She shook her head. 'No, we mustn't—this is too much,' she said as she gathered her clothes together. She looked up into his face and her heart contracted. She reached out, stroked his cheek and whispered his name. He took her in his arms again and kissed her. She was weak with desire and longing for him.

'I love you, Zahra. I love you with every fibre of my being.' He stroked her hair and touched his fingers across her lips.

'I love you too, Karim,' she whispered. 'I have to go ...'

She opened the door, then turned back to look at him. In the lamplight, he looked younger and more vulnerable than she'd ever seen him.

He caught her hand and kissed the palm. 'Zahra!'

She covered her mouth to stop her saying his name again; she knew if she did, she'd grasp his hand and ask him to follow. She closed the door and hurried up the stairs to her room. She climbed into her bed next to Ahmad and put her arm round his small body. She fell asleep, luxuriating in the smell of Karim on her skin, the taste of him on her lips.

Ahmad tapped her cheek and peered into her face. 'Hello Mummy, wake up!'

With a rush she remembered that overnight her whole life had changed again. She looked at Ahmad as he snuggled up next to her. She stroked his hair, trying to quell the desperate feelings that threatened to engulf her. She dreaded the next few days.

Karim! She flushed with embarrassment when she thought of their intimacy last night. Why on earth had she been so weak? What point was there in encouraging him in his declaration of love? She was going to be dragged halfway across the world by her crazy revolutionary cousin. She felt sick with anxiety; suppose Firzun had died overnight. What would she do then? And if he was all right, how would they get him into Nasim's house? What would happen to her and Ahmad, and worse ... how soon would they have to leave the comparative safety of the Konaris'?

She half listened to Ahmad telling her about another of Mickey Mouse's adventures as she got up, showered herself and then him. She dressed in black pants and sweater, and with Ahmad's hand in hers, they went down to the kitchen.

When she opened the door, she wondered how her life would be now that her usual routine and her job were finished forever. She no longer belonged here. She joined Tamineh and Shirin at the table. Both were red eyed and distressed, their food untouched on their plates in front of them.

'I can't believe it, Zahra, I just can't believe it,' Tahmineh said as she went to the stove for the tea. She poured out two glasses with a shaking hand.

'God give you patience,' Zahra answered automatically.

'God be praised,' the other woman replied tearfully, putting the tea down for Zahra and Shirin. 'Madam was so kind to me, so kind.' She sniffed and wiped away a tear. Ahmad pulled at his mother's sweater and asked in a whisper why Tahmineh was crying. She told him that the nice lady she used to read to had gone away.

'Like Daddy?' he asked.

Zahra looked sharply at him. 'Yes, but we don't talk about him, Ahmad, remember?' she said quietly. She glanced at Tahmineh, but she was refilling her tea glass.

'When you've finished, Ahmad, you can go to our room,' Zahra told him. She got up when she heard a light tap on the kitchen door.

'Yeah! Uncle Karim.' Ahmad jumped up when he saw Karim. 'Can we play soccer?'

'Ahmad, come here!' Zahra called sharply.

Karim wished them all good morning and tousled Ahmad's hair. 'We'll play soccer soon, Ahmad. I need to speak to your mummy first.'

He held the door open and motioned Zahra into the hall.

'Is it Firzun?' she asked, trying to keep her voice steady. She felt too embarrassed to look up at him.

'Yes, he's all right, but I think you should go round and see Nasim about arrangements for you and him as soon as you can.'

His dismissive tone made her heart sink. Was he trying to blot out what had happened last night? Was he wondering how he could take back what he'd said? But his next words dispelled the doubts and made her feel guilty and selfish. She looked up into his strained face.

'The funeral's set for three o'clock at the local mosque,' he told her quietly. He massaged his temples with his fingers and ran his hand distractedly through his hair. 'They're coming to collect her soon. It may be better if Ahmad isn't around. Please excuse me.' He turned away. 'I have to look after my parents ... lots of arrangements ...'

'Of course.'

'Zahra,' he said, turning back to her.

A quiver ran through her body.

'*Enshallah* your husband will recover quickly.'

'*Enshallah.*'

As she pulled on her outdoor clothes, she promised Tahmineh she'd be back to help her prepare food for the guests when they came back after the funeral. She bundled Ahmad out the door, but as she walked along the street her anger towards Firzun rose to the surface again. They were now in an even worse situation than before! How did he expect to get out of the country soon if he was badly injured? She strode along quickly and almost ran up to Nasim's door in her haste to get some news.

32

FIRZUN

Nasim answered the door herself, explaining that Mojgan and Habib had gone to Friday prayers.

'We failed, Zahra. But thank God our men survived,' Nasim said quietly as she took their outdoor clothes and hung them on a hook.

Ahmad ran ahead of them up the stairs and was setting up the toy train tracks around the floor by the time Zahra sat down on the sofa. She tried to swallow the sense of dread rising in her throat as Nasim handed her a glass of tea on a china saucer.

'So, tell me ...' she said nervously.

Nasim gave her a summary of the events of the raid, and she tried to take it all in. When Nasim told her Karim had saved her cousin's life, she interrupted her.

'He saved Firzun's life?'

Nasim nodded. 'Karim's a hero, Zahra. He went back for him.'

The same crippling feeling of fear that she had felt in the mountains overwhelmed her. Suppose he'd died? Her hand shook as she held the tea glass in its saucer. Nasim took it from her and put it on the table.

'Where is he now?'

'He's in the Laleh hospital where Maryam works.'

'Is that safe?'

'No. All the hospitals are being searched for people with gunshot wounds,' Nasim said. 'Don't worry, Zahra. We're moving him today. Karim's agreed to let him stay in his apartment.'

'I thought he was coming here! What about Rezvan's funeral? You can't ...'

Nasim waved away her objections. 'I've just phoned Karim and cleared it with him. The funeral's a good cover. We know the house will be entirely empty.'

Zahra was appalled. How could Nasim be so callous, using Rezvan's funeral as a cover to smuggle a fugitive into someone's house? Surely Karim had objected.

'If the authorities find Firzun there, they'll arrest everyone!' she expostulated.

'It was Karim's idea,' Nasim said defensively. 'Anyway if your "husband" is in the house, sick or not, your reputation won't be compromised. You can stay there after Esmat and Abbas leave.'

Zahra felt like laughing in Nasim's face. 'He's *not* my husband. I'm living a lie! I can't stay in Karim's apartment with Firzun!'

Nasim held up her hand. 'We've got an Afghan male nurse from the hospital to look after him. You and Ahmad can stay in your own room. We have no choice, Zahra,' Nasim insisted. 'You'll have to give an excuse for not going to the funeral. We need your help to do this,' she concluded.

Zahra shook her head. 'No, I ...'

Nasim kneeled down in front of Zahra, took her hands and clasped them in both of hers. She looked desperate. 'Firzun's a wanted man; they *know* about him, Zahra. Someone's watching our house. It's not safe here.'

'But neither is the Konari house, and neither are you!' Zahra objected.

'Yes, it's safer there for a while. Esmat's still got influential friends.'

'But what if Firzun dies? What about me?'

'He won't,' Nasim said dismissively.

'But if he does!' she shouted at Nasim and pulled her hands away from her grasp.

'Maryam says he's out of danger,' Nasim said calmly with a faint smile as she stood up. 'Zahra, we all have to make the best of things.'

Zahra felt impotently angry and turned away from Nasim. People like her were lucky; they had both passports and money. They could leave easily, but what about the others they'd recruited for their cause? Were they making the best of things? They were either in prison or dead. And what about her and Ahmad? she thought again.

Nasim sat back on the sofa and continued to outline her plan for later that day. Her eyes were bright and excited. She was convinced that the regime could be beaten. She promised Zahra she'd tell Esmat later and say that Firzun had the flu and needed to be in isolation.

'We have to look at the bigger picture, Zahra. We're fighting for democracy here,' Nasim went on.

'I don't *want* to look at the bigger picture,' Zahra said.

Nasim sighed. 'I know, darling, but you've contributed to the cause enormously by supporting Firzun. He'll be well soon and then you can help him escape.'

Zahra looked away; she couldn't trust herself to answer politely.

She still felt angry on her way back to the Konaris' and she felt frightened again. She kept her head down as she walked along with Ahmad, but something caught her eye and she glanced sideways. A dark-coloured car with tinted windows was parked further up on the opposite side of the road. Fear enveloped her—was Jafar back? The car looked similar to the one he'd kerb crawled in.

She quickened her step, then froze with fear when a man's voice said cheerfully: 'Hello, little man, how are you today?'

She looked up, then averted her gaze, wondering if her guilt and fear showed. Two young bearded men dressed in military style clothes and with rifles slung across their shoulders were smiling down at Ahmad. Before he could answer, she grabbed his hand, squeezed it hard, and pulled him to her side. He knew by now that a hard hand squeeze meant he mustn't speak. Did they know about Firzun? Were they following her?

'God bless you, Madam, and your son,' the men said politely and walked on.

Her legs felt like lead. She didn't dare look back, but kept walking faster and faster. She dragged Ahmad along and, ignoring his loud protests, rushed past the Konari house. At the final house in the street, she turned left and stopped. A high wall shielded the house from the road.

'Wait, Ahmad!'

'But Mummy ...'

She surveyed the small side street they were in. It was completely deserted and the two houses on either side of it seemed empty. She walked back to the corner of the street and peered round the bricks. The men who'd spoken to them were still there in the distance. They were leaning down and talking to the occupants of the black car. Her mouth felt dry and her heart started racing again.

'Are we going the secret way?' Ahmad asked.

'Yes, if that's what you call it.'

He ran ahead of her down the side of the grey brick wall and beckoned her excitedly. He disappeared round the corner and she hurried to catch up with him. It was the same lane Firzun had rushed her down when he saw the men at Karim's door. She took more notice this time; the lane was wide enough for a car to travel down one way. Several times she had to avoid large potholes and deep tyre tracks. Every few seconds, she glanced nervously over her shoulder as she walked. On her left were the backs of Maryam Street's huge houses. On her right all she could see were scrubby bushes and brown empty patches of land. Through the trees around the houses, she saw the glint of water from swimming pools.

Ahmad ran ahead, kicking at pebbles. He turned frequently to make sure she was following him. Eventually he stopped. 'Here we are! I told you!'

They were at the end of the Konaris' garden. She got out her key, but Ahmad said excitedly: 'Shirin and I go through here. It's a secret way.'

He pushed aside a few fence palings and jumped through. She put the gate key back in her pocket and followed him. Ahmad ran past the swimming pool and the rose garden, then across a wide lawn. From there she could see the back of the house, with its French windows and wide terrace. She looked up at the rectangle of glass that belonged to Karim's apartment, half expecting to see him standing at the window, but everywhere was deserted and silent.

Ahmad ran ahead of her towards the kitchen. Through the steamy window, she saw Tahmineh moving from the stove to the sink and back again. She sighed. The Konari house was now as familiar as her own home had been. But it was a house in mourning, and she had more lies to tell.

During their quick lunch, Tahmineh briefed her about the funeral arrangements and suggested that Shirin take Ahmad to the kindergarten for the afternoon session. Zahra agreed gratefully. She didn't mention Firzun.

At half past two, she stood respectfully next to Shirin and Tamineh at the front door as the family got into their car. Shortly afterwards a taxi arrived to take Tahmineh and Shirin. It had hardly left before a dark blue BMW came slowly through the gate. She couldn't see the driver through the tinted windscreen and she felt a tinge of alarm. Was this Rashid's car or the one she'd seen in the street? She put her hand to her throat and the driver flashed the headlights twice. She ran back into the house and pressed the button to close the gates, then rushed back to the front porch. The car doors were already open.

'Take it carefully!' Maryam was saying.

Rashid stood at one of rear doors. He looked up and gave Zahra a reassuring smile. A bulky man waited at the other door.

'I need help this side,' he called to her in her own language.

Firzun lay on the back seat, one leg propped on the seat, the other sprawled on the floor. His face was white and his head lolled against a pillow. She was aghast—he looked close to death.

'Zahra, go and open all the doors for us!' Maryam called, struggling with a long tube leading from Firzun's hand.

She was out of breath by the time she got up to Karim's apartment. She turned the door handle too quickly and stumbled into the room with the fresh sheets she'd put outside his door. She could hear the voices of the two men behind her as they slowly carried Firzun up the stairs and Maryam urging them to keep him steady. She stood in the middle of the room, looking round helplessly. Where was the bedroom? She saw the edge of a bed through the door directly ahead of her and ran across the apartment, pushing chairs and rugs aside to make a pathway for them.

She had just remade the bed when the Afghan nurse and Rashid staggered into the room with their burden. She stood aside as the men gently laid him down.

He was wearing a green surgical gown and his leg was bound up just below the left knee. The tube taped to his hand led up to a bag of fluid that Maryam held aloft before securing it on a lamp stand.

'This will have to do,' she said, looking anxiously at her patient as she adjusted the tube in Firzun's hand. 'Call me if you need me,' she told the nurse.

'We've got to go, Maryam!' Rashid urged.

'He'll recover, Zahra. He's very strong,' Maryam called over her shoulder as Zahra ran down the stairs after them.

Rashid stopped at the porch and turned to her. 'Thank you for your help, Zahra. Firzun's very brave and he's lucky he's got you.' He shook her hand and smiled at her. 'God bless you, Zahra,' he said sincerely.

She smiled back at him, wondering how such a kind man could be a revolutionary.

'Hurry up, Rashid,' Maryam called. 'The funeral starts at three.'

Zahra opened the gates and watched Rashid swing the car down the driveway. It paused just beyond the gates, its indicator flashing. When it turned into the street towards the mosque, she closed the gates behind it.

She stood in the atrium, letting the silence of the house settle on her for a minute. She looked at the stairs to Karim's apartment, straining her ears for any sound—nothing. Zahra went to the kitchen and started on the food preparation; she'd been told that fifty guests were expected. Tahmineh came back from the funeral, her face tear-stained and mournful, but she changed quickly from her funeral clothes to her working ones and took over. Shirin arrived a few minutes later with Ahmad and promised to keep him occupied when the guests came.

Making her excuses to Tahmineh, Zahra ran up the back stairs, trying to stem the tide of panic she felt about the hidden invalid. The family were due back any minute, but she decided to take a chance. She ran up the stairs to Karim's apartment and knocked on the door. The Afghan nurse opened it.

'He's sleeping, do you want to see him?' he asked.

She nodded and followed him into the bedroom. Firzun lay on his back in Karim's bed, his eyes closed in his sallow face. She gasped involuntarily and took a step back.

His eyes flickered open and he smiled faintly at her. 'Zahra!' He gestured her nearer.

The door clicked shut as the nurse left them together and she moved closer to the bed.

'If I die, say the *Namaz-Meyet* for me,' Firzun whispered.

'*Enshallah*, I won't need to say the prayers for the dead.' She tried to keep her voice steady.

'We're blood, Zahra, don't abandon me,' he rasped. 'God forgive me for what I did to Mahmoud.'

'Don't talk about it!' she said urgently.

'I've done my best for you and Ahmad,' he gasped. His eyelids flickered closed.

'I know—I'm grateful.'

With a parting look at her cousin, she walked quickly through Karim's living room and nodded to the nurse.

'He *will* recover, Zahra Khanoum,' the man said to her retreating back.

'*Enshallah* !' She turned to him, knowing he'd seen the alarm on her face. At the top of the stairs she paused. The sound of voices and car doors slamming drifted up from the atrium. She went to her own room, her mind in turmoil. What would she do if Firzun died? Or suppose he started talking in his drug-induced sleep—talking about Mahmoud or their 'marriage'?

She checked her make-up in the bathroom mirror and sighed. She looked terrible, but who among the guests would notice her? She took a deep breath and walked slowly down the kitchen stairs. She was welcomed into the flurry of activity, and helped Tahmineh and Shirin arrange sandwiches and cakes on large platters while tea bubbled away on the stove.

A bell rang from the salon.

'They're all here!' Tahmineh announced as she hoisted a tray of food and headed for the salon.

Zahra started to collect the dishes as the final lingering visitors were being ushered out the front door. Karim was sitting alone on the couch in the empty room.

'I've moved out of the apartment,' he said when he saw her.

She stopped what she was doing and walked over to him. 'How can I ever thank you for saving Firzun's life?' she said quietly.

He looked up and their eyes met.

'I did it for you,' he told her. 'Ahmad needs a father and you need a husband.'

'You were very brave, Karim.'

She turned away, unable to bear the pain in his eyes.

Once again she lay awake, reflecting on the snatches of conversation she'd overheard while serving the guests. The Revolutionary Guard were tightening their grip. Women were being stopped in the street and their make-up forcibly removed by female Revolutionary Guards—'using spittle!', an outraged woman reported. Zahra overheard a tall boney man telling Karim earnestly that there was a war brewing between Iran and Iraq. As if things weren't bad enough, Zahra thought.

She closed her eyes. She wanted to leave; Iran had become a frightening place. The house settled into silence and she began to drift off to sleep. Suddenly she jerked awake. From somewhere in the house, Karim was yelling her name.

'Help! Zahra, anyone. Help!'

For a minute she thought she was dreaming, but it started again.

'For God's sake, someone help me!'

She jumped out of bed, pulled on her dressing gown, and glanced at Ahmad. He was fast asleep. She opened her bedroom door and ran to the top of the main staircase.

'Zahra! Help me!' Karim yelled up to her.

He staggered forward to the bottom of the stairs. He was cradling a woman in his arms. Her long legs were swung over his right forearm and she had her arms round his neck. Her long white satin gown was streaked with mud and clung to her body. Her wet hair was plastered to her head and she was sobbing, her face turned into his chest.

'It's Nasim! They've arrested Rashid,' Karim gasped.

33

IMPRISONMENT

Esmat, swathed in a purple satin robe, raced out of her room. She grabbed Zahra's arm and propelled her down the stairs to the atrium, barking orders as she ran.

'Karim, go to the kitchen! Put her in a chair near the stove. Zahra, get a blanket.'

Tahmineh appeared in the atrium and Esmat shouted at her: 'Tea, soup, something hot ... now!'

The kitchen was still warm as Zahra helped Esmat wrap the blanket round Nasim's shaking shoulders. Her drenched white satin dressing gown clung to her body and her bare feet were covered in soil. Her face was scratched and bleeding and there were leaves and twigs in her sodden hair. She shook with the cold and her breath came in wheezing sobs.

'They've arrested Rashid!' She half rose from the chair.

'Don't talk, drink this,' Esmat told her. Nasim took a few sips of tea from the cup Esmat held to her lips.

'They broke into the house ...' Nasim stared wildly round at them. 'They dragged him away! I escaped—but Rashid ...' She howled like an animal.

Esmat put her arms round her. 'You're staying here tonight, Nasim,' she said quietly. 'Tahmineh, sort out a guest room, find some clothes for her. I'll get her in the shower. Karim, go and tell your father what's happened. We'll sort things here, then we'll go to the salon.'

Zahra's mind was in turmoil. The Revolutionary Guard had found Rashid, but Firzun had eluded them! If they discovered him here, in this house, they'd arrest everyone. Her eyes met Karim's as he turned to go. She knew he was thinking the same thing. He looked shocked and exhausted as he stepped forward to help his mother get Nasim up the stairs.

'Bring the hot drink, Zahra.' Esmat snapped her fingers at her.

She went up the back stairs and put the hot drink on the night table. While they settled Nasim, she ran to her room and pulled on some clothes. Karim was waiting outside the closed door of the guest room.

'Firzun's got to know about this, Zahra. I don't care how sick he is.'

'What will they do to Rashid?' She searched his face, seeing her own anxiety mirrored in his.

'I don't know. I'll wait till I've heard Nasim, then I'm going to see my lawyer,' he replied. He ran down the stairs and she could hear him talking to his father.

Esmat open the guest room door and beckoned her in. Nasim was sitting on the bed, staring at the wall, dressed in some of Esmat's clothes. She didn't move when Zahra came in.

'Stay with her for a minute, I'm going to get dressed,' Esmat said.

As soon as she'd gone, Nasim turned suddenly and grasped Zahra's wrist. 'They want Firzun!' She put her hand over her belly. 'I'm twelve weeks pregnant. I don't want to lose the baby!' she sobbed. 'Oh God! What will they do to Rashid?'

Before Zahra could answer, Esmat came back into the room.

'Okay, Nasim,' she said briskly. 'You can tell us everything in the salon.'

Abbas and Karim were waiting for them when they finally got downstairs.

'We heard shots,' Nasim began. She broke down and covered her face with her hands. 'I need your help ... we've got to get him released!'

'We'll sort something out,' Esmat said.

'You heard shots ...' Karim prompted.

'There was a huge crash. They shot the lock off the main gates and drove in. They smashed down the front door and then they were in the house.' She put her hand to her mouth.

'What about Habib and Mojgan?'

'They're at a village wedding. We were alone.' She looked round the group with terrified eyes. 'Rashid locked the living room door. He pushed me out onto the back terrace and he told me to run and get help. I ran down the back stairs and hid in the garden. They shot the door open and burst in ... they smashed all the windows. They hit Rashid in the face, handcuffed him ... pulled a hood over his head, pushed him out of the door. The others ran through the rooms, banging open the doors ... looking for me ... for ...'

Zahra met Karim's eyes and looked away quickly. Mixed with her terror, she felt overwhelmed with shame and remorse. Her cousin should have been arrested, but he'd escaped.

'Karim's lawyer friend will fix this up,' Esmat announced, breaking the stunned silence.

'I'll call him.' Karim stood up and Zahra heard him running up the stairs to his apartment.

'All right, Nasim,' Esmat said, 'time for bed. We'll check out your house tomorrow.' She signalled Zahra and together they helped Nasim up to the guest room. 'Esmat, they'll let him go, won't they?' Nasim asked.

'Of course they will. We've still got some standing in this city,' Esmat replied. 'Karim will demand that they release him.'

Esmat had just closed the guest room door when Karim, dressed in his outdoor jacket and holding his car keys, hurtled down the stairs from his apartment.

'Zahra!' He grasped her hand. 'I told Firzun. He's still groggy but he understood. Get ready to leave.'

'Where are you going?'

'To see my lawyer—he'll meet me in the city.'

He slammed the front door and she heard the car engine leap into life. The wheels sprayed gravel from the driveway onto the porch. The gates clanged shut and the car screeched out into the night.

The city streets were deserted and Karim felt a frisson of fear as he parked near Zak's office. His footsteps rang on the empty pavement as he walked up to the building. He half expected a jeep full of armed maniacs to come screeching round the corner. His lawyer questioned him closely about Rashid's activities. When Karim told him about Rashid's involvement in the rescue mission, Zak took a long drag on his cigarette.

'They'll have taken him to the Evin prison. They hanged six Afghans this morning for their involvement in that botched rescue,' he said. He looked directly at Karim. 'If you were there, I don't want to know.'

When Karim handed him the money his father had forced on him, Zak looked relieved.

'Bribe money, thanks,' he said. 'Look, Karim, I know how they operate in the Evin. They beat people, get a confession and give them a quick "trial". Then they hang them.'

Zak's stark statement shocked him.

'You'll get him off though, won't you?' It was a stupid question and he knew it.

'This isn't the States, Karim,' Zak replied. 'There's no rule of law, just total mayhem with a bit of Sharia law thrown in. Let's hope I can persuade the right people. This money might save his neck. I'll go over there now. I'll call you tomorrow.'

It was nearly midnight when Karim got back. The house seemed unnaturally quiet after the earlier drama. He walked slowly up the stairs to his old room, feeling sick with apprehension about Rashid. He knew the sight of Nasim staggering through the garden in the dark, clutching her white silk robe round her body, would haunt him for a long time.

The *azan-e-zohr*, the midday prayer call, had just started when Zak phoned. He sounded exhausted and his voice was strained.

'I represented him in front of a judgement panel of four men,' he told Karim. He paused. 'I'll know the sentence later today. I've spread the money around—hopefully it'll help. I'll come as soon as I hear.'

He ignored Karim's torrent of questions and repeated, 'I'll call when I know something.'

Karim ran up to his apartment and flung open the door. Firzun was leaning on the nurse's shoulder and a crutch, limping forward on one leg. They both stopped and stared when Karim burst in.

'I hope you're happy now,' Karim shouted at them. 'A good man is in the Evin prison, waiting for a trial verdict, thanks to you.'

'None of us is safe,' Firzun replied calmly.

'You know that both women *and* men are raped, beaten and tortured in that place, don't you?' He was infuriated by Firzun's calm manner.

'We'll be gone in a few days,' Firzun replied, looking at his injured leg. 'Good,' Karim called over his shoulder as he left the room. He ran down the stairs to join his parents for lunch.

'Remind me,' his mother said, 'did you say that Zahra's husband is in your apartment suffering from the flu?'

'Yes, he's on the mend,' Karim replied hastily. 'How's Nasim?' he asked before his mother could say anything else.

She sighed. 'She's still in shock. Have you heard from Zak?'

'The trial's over. We'll know the sentence later this afternoon.'

'So soon?' his mother exclaimed.

The cup in her hand shook as she poured his coffee. He took a sip. It tasted odd, tainted.

'We're going to take Nasim with us the States,' his father announced. 'I've been in touch with her parents. They said there's a passport in her safe in her maiden name—and she's got a five-year visa for the US too, thank goodness.'

'She won't want to go,' Esmat remarked. 'But I think I can persuade her. I'll bring her down to the salon. You can tell her what Zak said.'

Karim had never seen his mother look so scared in his life. He reached across the table to her. 'You were wonderful last night, Mother,' he said sincerely.

She smiled faintly at him as she got up to fetch Nasim.

'Can I see you in my study, Karim, after you've spoken to Nasim?' his father asked.

He nodded. 'Of course.'

He walked quickly to the library and, as he'd hoped, Zahra was silently packing books into boxes. She looked up, and when their eyes met he saw the fear in hers.

'He's been tried,' he said.

'Have you told Nasim? What will happen to him?' she whispered.

'Mother's bringing her down to the salon. He'll get a prison sentence or ...' He couldn't bring himself to say it, but she guessed.

She put her hand across her mouth, her eyes wide with fear.

He folded her shaking body in his arms. 'I'm here, Zahra. I'll protect you.' He kissed her hair and held her closer, feeling the beat of her terrified heart.

She pushed him away gently. 'Go to Nasim, she needs you,' she said shakily.

He turned away and opened the library door, then paused, giving Zahra a last look over his shoulder.

'Go!' she said. 'I'm strong.'

He strode across the atrium and took a deep breath before he pushed the salon door open.

After he'd told Nasim Zak's news, she clenched her fists angrily. 'This is a travesty of justice! Tried in one day with no witnesses! I'm going to visit him.'

She half rose from the couch. He looked away. He would never tell her that according to Zak, Rashid had been badly beaten and could hardly walk. Instead, he nodded and promised to try to arrange it.

'My father wants to see me.' He excused himself and went across to his father's study.

His half hour interview with his father made him feel like a teenager again. He unburdened himself with his confession while his father listened without comment.

'Zak used all the money you gave him, Baba. How … I can't thank you enough.' He could hardly look his father in the face.

His father sighed. 'They'll say it's treason, son. It could be a death sentence.'

'I'm sure it won't.' He tried to sound more hopeful than he felt. What if he was next? What if they came knocking on the door for him? Why chance putting his parents through so much anguish?

Esmat rapped on the door, and when he opened it she pushed a piece of paper into his hands.

'It's the combination of Rashid's safe,' she announced. 'We're all going to Nasim's house. We need to empty the safe and collect anything that hasn't been destroyed. Nasim's housekeepers are on their way back ...' She stopped mid sentence and put her hand to her mouth. Someone was ringing the doorbell.

'It's probably visitors, Mother,' Karim reassured her.

Esmat looked ready to sob with relief.

Abbas put his arm round his wife's shoulders. 'The Revolutionary Guard don't ring the doorbell, Esmat,' he said.

34

KARIM AND ZAHRA

The rain had stopped but the grass was sodden beneath Zahra's feet. She struggled through the gap in the fence Nasim must have used the previous night. She shuddered at the thought of her running through the jagged fence in the dark. The ground was awash with muddy puddles as she followed the others through the neighbour's overgrown land. When they finally got to Nasim's garden, they stopped and stared in disbelief.

The house had been ruined. Not one of the windows was intact and the thick curtains lay outside against the brickwork in bedraggled piles. Most of the panes of the French windows downstairs were missing; some had jagged edges of glass sticking out of their empty frames.

'They've destroyed the place!' Esmat whispered.

On the terrace, the glass crunched and splintered under their feet. Memories of the house in the village engulfed Zahra, and she stood inside the door trying to catch her breath. Karim turned round and came back for her.

'It's terrible,' she murmured.

'We won't stay long,' he promised as he helped her across the glass-strewn floor. 'Mother needs you, she's devastated.'

He led her out of the room, then squeezed her hand before letting it go as they walked into the hall. The others were standing together, staring at the heavy front door. It swung drunkenly on its hinges and its broken stained-glass panels lay in a mess of coloured shards on the floor.

'I'll go first,' Karim said quietly, taking a gun from his jacket.

'You don't think ...' Esmat's eyes were wide with fear.

'No, but I'm not taking any chances.'

He climbed the stairs, gun at the ready and called out, 'Hello! Anyone here?'

The hairs rose on the back of Zahra's neck as he disappeared from sight at the top of the stairs. Would there be silence and then a single shot like at the village house?

'There's no one up here, but it's a mess.' His voice was strong and clear.

'This is an outrage!' With a sudden burst of energy Esmat ran up the stairs. 'Let's get Nasim's things and go,' she called down to them.

Zahra followed Abbas up the familiar stairs to Nasim and Rashid's apartment. Muddy footprints were embedded in the wool on each step.

'They've ransacked it,' Esmat said quietly, stepping over the torn books that littered the floor.

Zahra followed her into Nasim's bedroom where bottles of perfume and cosmetics lay in a shattered pile and torn clothes littered the floor. A large photograph of Nasim and Rashid on their wedding day hung lopsided above the bed and muddy boot prints stained the gold satin counterpane.

Esmat turned to Zahra, 'What's happened to our country? Who did this?'

Tears filled her eyes as she shook her head in disbelief. Then with an impatient gesture, she flicked her hand across her cheek and took a deep breath.

'I can't salvage anything. I'll get her new clothes from my store.' Esmat looked at Zahra and her lips curled in disgust. 'Nasim can't possibly wear anything these animals have touched!'

She pointed to the clothes on the floor.

'I'll check the other rooms, Zahra. I need to make sure there aren't any valuables lying around,' she said briskly. 'Try and clear up here as best you can.'

When she'd finished in the bedroom, Zahra moved to the living room and stood in the doorway, surveying the destruction. She stepped carefully through to the kitchen. She managed to push the kitchen door open against the pile of smashed crockery on the floor. A plastic coffee mug from an American restaurant called McDonald's was the only piece still intact. She picked it up, thinking that it might be from an expensive eating place and Nasim would want to keep it.

Karim waited with his father at the top of the stairs. He had a backpack slung across his shoulder and held a large cardboard box under his arm.

'The housekeepers should be here soon.' He glanced at Amir, who nodded from where he was kneeling, screwing a hinge back on a door.

'They'll come and see us first, Esmat,' Abbas said. He shifted the box he was holding. 'Let's go, we've done all we can.'

No one spoke as they crossed the gardens to the peace and order of the Konari house.

'I know I can trust you to keep what you've seen confidential, Zahra. I don't want Nasim upset,' Esmat said quietly.

'Of course, Madam,' Zahra lied. Firzun had to know about this.

Esmat waved her away. 'I'll call you if I need anything. Ask Tahmineh to come and see me, would you?'

Tahmineh was waiting with bated breath to hear about the house, but before Zahra could speak, the bell from the salon rang impatiently.

'I told Shirin to stay at the kindergarten with Ahmad,' Tahmineh said over her shoulder as she obeyed the summons.

Zahra was still taking off her chador and scarf when Tahmineh returned.

'Madam wants me and Amir to go over there now. Nasim's housekeepers are on their way home.'

After she'd gone, Zahra sat at the kitchen table, vaguely aware of the soft ticking of the clock and the dull hum of the kettle on the back of the fuel stove. She closed her eyes, and images of Nasim's ruined house danced across her eyelids. She put the McDonald's coffee mug on the table, wondering when she should give it to Nasim. A gentle knock on the door made her jump.

'Zahra, it's me, Karim. Are you alone?' He pushed the door open and looked round the kitchen.

'Tahmineh's gone to Nasim's house,' she said, closing the door behind him.

He looked flustered. 'I need your help, Zahra. It's urgent.'

What next? Had he brought things back from the house?

'I found documents in Rashid's safe—floor plans of the US embassy, details of the raid and lists of names. He didn't have time to get rid of them. We'll have to burn them right now!'

He swung his backpack onto the floor and opened it. Stray papers fell out and she scooped them up. Their eyes met and she saw her own fear reflected in his. She grabbed an iron tool and hooked up the lid from one of the burners on the fuel stove. When she put it aside, the fire roared with the sudden injection of oxygen. He scooped up handfuls of paper from the bag and stuffed them into the flames.

She touched his wrist. 'You'll smother the fire!'

He slowed down as the chemicals in the architectural drawings sent flames rushing upwards and she stepped back. Together they watched as the fire curled round closely written lists of names, pen drawings of buildings and architectural plans. She felt his anxiety and edginess as he stood next to her. She worked rapidly with him, tearing up the larger sheets as they thrust the documents into the stove. Finally it was finished, but he seized the poker from her and raked the charred embers like a man possessed. She took it from him.

'Wait, I'll throw some kindling on!'

She reached into the basket at the side of the stove and threw the wood directly onto the flames. He picked up the flange tool and replaced the burner in its hole. The fire simmered again. In the sudden silence, the kettle burbled gently and time ticked away on the kitchen clock.

'Thank you, Zahra, thank you!' he gasped.

She looked up at him. The heat had made his face glow and his eyes were bright with relief. He gazed intently at her and took her hand.

'Zahra, things have changed. Firzun's a wanted man in this country. He could drag you down with him. Let him go to Australia on his own. I'll take you and Ahmad to America, you can get a divorce there. I promised Firzun I'd look after you if anything happened to him. Now it has—you're nearly free!'

She stared at him, completely taken aback. Had she heard him correctly? 'I'm *not* free. He's my husband and he's still alive,' she said, looking away to avoid his penetrating gaze. The word 'husband' felt like sawdust in her mouth. 'I can't desert him. He needs me to help him escape!'

'He's a selfish brute!' The words burst out and she turned away from him.

He caught her arm and pulled her towards him. 'I'm ten times the man he is!' he said fiercely. 'I want to marry you. I want Ahmad to be my son. I love you, Zahra. Remember when we kissed here the other night? We're made for each other, body and soul.'

Slowly she removed her arm from his grasp. His touch had reawakened her deep longing for him and she couldn't bear to meet his eyes.

'If you do love me, then you'll help me to leave ... with Firzun!' she said tearfully.

He took her arm again, gently urging her to look up at him. He told her how wealthy he was, how wonderful her life in America would be. He owned houses, an apartment in New York, he'd bought an architectural business ...

'Come with me,' he begged.

'I can't, Karim, he's my family. I have to help him. You know that.' She looked into his eyes. She was devastated by the longing she saw in them.

He pulled her into his arms and she didn't resist. 'I love you,' he said desperately. 'Since the day I met you. Remember *'your tiny hand is frozen?'* He smiled down at her and kissed her hair and her face. 'You said you feel the same! We belong together.'

She buried her head in his chest and his arms tightened round her. He lifted her chin gently and kissed her so deeply and tenderly that she felt her resolve melting away. She ran her hands urgently through his hair. She felt herself relaxing, falling deeper and deeper in love with him. She pulled away reluctantly and traced her fingers across his lips.

'We can't always have what we want, Karim,' she said softly.

How could he know what torment it was for her to hear the plans he had for them both? If it wasn't for Firzun, she would go to the ends of the earth with Karim, rich or poor. But Firzun had saved her from Mahmoud and they shared a terrible secret. Now she'd seen Nasim's house, she knew Karim wasn't exaggerating. Her cousin was in grave danger and he was her family. Without her, he was trapped in this country and the authorities would find him eventually. Without her, he was a dead man! She *had* to continue with this charade of marriage.

Karim reached into his pocket and pulled a folded wad of notes from his wallet. He tried to put them in her hand, but she backed away.

'Take the money, Zahra, it's for Ahmad as well. They're American dollars. You can use them anywhere.'

'No, Karim!'

'I don't trust Firzun,' he blurted out. 'He might abandon you somewhere. Please take the money, for Ahmad's sake.'

His words alarmed her, but she *had* to trust Firzun! She met Karim's eyes, her own were moist.

'How can I ever thank you ... repay you?'

She knew how, although the time wasn't right, would never be right. She heard Ahmad's voice from the garden.

'You've got to go, Karim. Ahmad and Shirin are coming.'

For a moment he didn't move. Then with a deep sigh he picked up his backpack, turned and was gone. She pushed the money deep in her pocket and leaned on the door with her head in her hands. Tears seeped through her fingers. Suddenly the garden door flew open and she held out her arms for her son as he ran into the kitchen and threw himself into her embrace.

35

ZAK'S NEWS

The afternoon and early evening crawled past slowly with no news. Karim paced restlessly round the house, trying to shake the feeling of despair that had settled below his ribs. Memories of Rashid and of his grandmother played like a tape through his brain. Now Zahra was lost to him as well.

He went to the library, but as soon as he flicked on the light he remembered Zahra had been packing up the books. He looked round helplessly at the half empty shelves. But the most precious books were still there. His parents would take them in their hand luggage. He opened the glass doors and took out the ancient copy of *Shahnameh: The Persian Book of Kings*. This pre-Islamic history of his country and its noble past told of Zoroastrian beliefs, good and bad rulers, and the destruction wrecked by invaders. For a moment he held the book close to his chest.

'This is who I am. I'm *Persian*,' Karim said aloud and his impassioned voice echoed around the empty room. 'This is my heritage. This book is my *home!*'

He opened the book at random and looked down at the page. It was where the shah, Kay Khosrow speaks to Gudarz:

'Consider how the world passes; take note of what is hidden as well as what is plain. There is a day for amassing treasure and a day for distributing it: look at our ruined frontier forts and bridges, at our crumbling reservoirs destroyed by Arfrasayab; look at our motherless children, at our widowed wives who sit alone and desolate ...'

Karim shut the book slowly and put his hand on the aged cover. The last line, *'Our widowed wives who sit alone and desolate ...'* sent a shiver down his spine. He stared at the book and thought of Rashid probably lying battered and bruised in a cold prison cell. He shuddered. A deep sense of foreboding swept over him.

He heard a car skid to a stop on the driveway and he ran to the window, pushing aside the drapes. Zak! Thank God, some news! He saw Nasim run out onto the gravel in her house slippers. Zak got out of the car and she clung to his arm, her face turned up to him beseechingly.

Karim locked the book away and looked at his watch. Eight o'clock. Zak must have spent the day at the prison waiting for a verdict. As he came out of the library and into the atrium, Zak was coming through the front door. Nasim, still clinging to him, bombarded him with questions.

'Let's sit down in the salon, Nasim, and I'll tell you everything,' Zak said.

She waited by his side as he handed his coat to Amir and greeted the family.

They sat in the salon and waited while Zak dragged heavily on his cigarette. He looked at them through the smoke.

'He's been found guilty of treason,' he began with a sigh. 'It's a serious charge. The judgement panel are still deliberating about the sentence.'

Nasim leapt to her feet and shouted, 'I'm going to see them! This is a travesty, a show trial!'

Esmat stood up and urged Nasim back to her seat. 'Let's hear everything first, Nasim.'

'The best outcome would be a minimum of twenty-five years,' Zak said, dragging on his cigarette. Esmat gasped.

'We've got to wait till tomorrow now,' Zak went on. 'Please believe me, I've done my best,' he said, looking across at Nasim.

'What *exactly* have you done?' Esmat asked.

'I'm proud of what he did,' she said defiantly, before Zak could speak.

'He planned the rescue to free the American hostages and he was there on the night,' Zak said evenly.

Esmat stared at Nasim in disbelief. '*Nasim*! Did you know about this? What was he *thinking*?'

'I helped him,' Nasim said proudly. 'Right is on our side, Esmat. No one else had the guts to stand up the regime!'

Esmat took a deep breath. 'But it was a crazy idea, *crazy*! You might have known ...'

'This isn't the time, Esmat,' Abbas said quietly.

She glared at him, but stopped talking. Zak massaged his temples with his fingertips and when he looked up at them all, his eyes were hollow and desperate.

Karim felt as if a dark cloud had settled over the room and an even darker one over him. He dreaded to think of what his mother would say if she knew he'd been there. What if she thought back to that night and started asking questions? It was bad enough that his father knew.

'If Rashid is here in prison, I'm not leaving the country,' Nasim said firmly. No one answered, and Zak stood up with a sigh.

'You've done your best, Zak,' Abbas told him.

He and Karim accompanied him to the door and shook his hand.

After his father had returned to the study, Karim stood alone in the atrium, wondering where Zahra was. He heard a faint click and saw her waiting by the kitchen door. She came forward into the atrium.

'Is it bad?' she asked, and he told her.

'What will Nasim do?' she asked fearfully.

'I don't know, but you've got to get away, Zahra.'

'I have to stay with Firzun,' she replied.

Before he could stop her, she walked quickly away from him towards the kitchen.

He waited, hoping she'd glance back, but she didn't.

When Karim got to his room, the drapes were still open. In all the upheaval Tahmineh had forgotten to close them. As he pulled them across the window, he thought he heard Rashid's voice: '*Say the Namaz Mayet for me, Karim. Say the prayers for the dead.*'

Karim shivered and admonished himself for imagining things.

The following morning the family was in the breakfast room when Karim saw Zak heading for the kitchen door. Something was wrong. Why hadn't he come to the front door? Zak's face was deathly pale and his dark eyes looked hunted as he glanced up at the house. Karim jumped up and went to the kitchen. Zak was just coming out, accompanied by Tahmineh.

'We're in here,' Karim said with a dismissive nod to the housekeeper.

When they came in, Abbas took a bottle from the sideboard, poured a measure into a glass and handed it to Zak.

'It's brandy, you look like you need it,' he said quietly.

The lawyer sat with his hands clasped in front of him on the table. He waved away Esmat's offer of food, but sipped the brandy instead. He put the glass down and took a deep breath.

'It's not good.' His voice shook as he looked at them.

Karim's heart contracted and his mouth felt dry.

'How long?' Abbas asked.

Zak looked down at his hands, then directly at Abbas. 'Rashid's dead, they hanged him at dawn.' He put his hand across his mouth, trying to stifle the terrible sob that burst out.

'Oh my God!' Esmat gasped. 'I don't believe it!'

The sense of dread from the previous evening burst inside Karim, and he felt as if his blood had turned to ice. He walked to the sideboard and poured three shots of brandy. He passed them round in a daze.

'Say it's not true!' his mother begged. Her hand shook as she took her glass.

Zak opened his palms, beseeching them to forgive him. 'I did my best. I thought I'd saved him!' He stopped and covered his face with his hands.

Karim stared at him. 'Are you sure it's Rashid?'

'Yes, I identified the ... his body,' he said. 'I failed everyone, failed Nasim, failed you ...'

'You did everything you could,' Abbas told him, but Zak continued to rail against himself. Abbas shook a cigarette from its packet and handed it to him. 'They'd already made up their minds,' Abbas said as he lit the cigarette for the other man. 'So now we have to make arrangements for the funeral.' He looked across at Zak. 'Will they release his body?'

Zak nodded. 'He's in the morgue,' he said. 'Nasim can't see him —he's been badly beaten.'

Esmat covered her face and cried quietly. 'Poor boy, poor boy,' she wept. She turned away from them towards the window and wiped the tears from her face with her fingertips.

'I'll tell her,' she offered. 'Can you find Zahra, Karim? Tell her to meet me in the atrium.'

Zahra followed Esmat up the stairs, carefully cradling brandy in a large balloon glass. She knew just by looking at Karim and his mother that the news was bad. Surely he wasn't ...

Nasim met them at the top of the stairs, dressed in dark clothes. 'I heard Zak's voice,' she said as she tried to push past Esmat and go downstairs. 'Is there any news?'

Esmat took her firmly by the arm. 'Let's go into your room, it's more private,' she answered as she steered her along. 'Wait here, Zahra.'

Zahra stood on the silent landing, holding the brandy glass, trying to keep her hands from shaking. When Nasim screamed she jumped violently, splashing brandy on her clothes. She started back as Nasim wrenched the door open.

'NO! NO! You're lying. He's not dead. Where's Zak?'

She shook off Esmat's restraining arm, pushed past Zahra, and raced down the stairs. Zahra went into the empty room and put the brandy glass on the table by the bed. She held on to it, feeling stunned and terrified. They'd killed Rashid! She had to tell Firzun! She ran onto the landing.

Karim was there, his face drained of colour. 'He's dead, Zahra!' His shoulders slumped. 'They killed my best friend. Why didn't I stop him?'

A single tear ran down his face and her heart contracted. He took her in his arms. She felt his body shaking as he held her.

'He was a good man,' he said, burying his face in her hair. She pulled away, afraid that his mother might suddenly run up the stairs and see them.

'We have to tell Firzun.' Her voice quivered with fear and she could hardly get the words out.

He took a deep breath and released her. 'I'll do it now,' he answered, heading for his apartment.

Nasim's voice reached her from the salon. She sounded hysterical. 'Why didn't you save him, Zak? Why? We trusted you!'

Zahra couldn't hear his reply, and she waited uncertainly on the landing. But Karim didn't come back. She walked slowly down the stairs, thinking that Esmat might need her. Through the half open door she saw Nasim. She was on her feet, still shouting at Zak. Zahra slipped quietly into the room and stood near the door.

'How did he die?' Nasim screamed.

Zak hesitated.

'Tell me! Tell me!' Nasim yelled. 'I want to know!'

'They hanged him, Nasim, but they ... they let me take his body.'

Nasim covered her face with her hands and sat down suddenly on the couch. Her gut-wrenching sobs filled the silent room.

Abbas took her hand and told her gently that he'd make arrangements for the funeral and that the men would wash Rashid's body.

She stood up again, swaying slightly, her face contorted with anger and grief. 'No, *I'll* do it! It's my right, my *right* as his wife! You can't stop me!' 'Nasim!' Esmat's commanding voice stopped Nasim's outburst. 'You can't wash him!'

Nasim turned furiously towards the other woman.

Esmat stood up and faced her. 'They didn't treat him well, Nasim. It's best you remember him as he was,' the older woman said quietly.

'No! No! Don't say that!' Nasim sobbed.

Esmat motioned to Zahra to help her and together they persuaded Nasim to go back upstairs to her room. She ordered Zahra to stay with Nasim while she checked on the funeral arrangements.

When the next storm of weeping passed, Nasim turned to Zahra. 'I don't want to be a widow. I'm a *wife*!' She stared at Zahra, tears coursing down her face. 'You're a widow, Zahra, you're the only person who understands,' she sobbed.

'Please, Nasim ...' Zahra begged. 'If they find out about the lies I've told!'

She thought of Karim. He'd be devastated if he learned the truth.

'Go to America with them, Nasim. Your parents can care for you. Think about your baby. It's a new life, the child will be a comfort for you.'

Before Nasim could answer, Tahmineh knocked on the door and put a stack of clean handkerchiefs on the bedside table. As she handed one to Nasim she said, 'God give you patience, Nasim Khanoum. This too will pass.'

Zahra took a handkerchief for herself and pushed it hard against her eyes, trying to stem her tears. She felt desperate. Now that Nasim's house was destroyed there was nowhere to run to. Her life, like Nasim's, was unravelling, and she too had to escape to a foreign country.

36

GOODBYES

The day after Rashid's funeral, a pall of silence fell over the house. Zahra was relieved that there was little to do except help Tahmineh with the enormous task of packing up the Konaris' possessions for shipment to America.

When she accompanied Nasim to the mosque the next day, the young widow sat huddled on the back seat of the car, nursing her grief. Zahra thought about her own forty days of mourning, now thankfully over, as she stared out the car window at the dull wet streets. She felt no remorse for Mahmoud's passing, just relief. She sighed and a wave of dread swept over her. Did Firzun really think he was going escape Iran through an international airport without detection? She shivered with fear.

At two o'clock the following Wednesday, Zahra waited at the front door with Tahmineh, Ahmad and Shirin. To her irritation, Firzun hobbled down the main stairs, leaning on a cane and holding the stair rail.

'I thought you promised to lay low for a while,' she muttered.

'I came to say goodbye to Nasim,' he said defiantly. 'They were like family to me.'

'It's too dangerous,' she whispered, but he ignored her.

Zahra looked round nervously. Esmat was already in the car, but Karim was waiting in the atrium as Nasim kneeled and hugged Ahmad.

Karim frowned at Firzun.

'Your friend has come to say goodbye, Nasim,' he told her curtly.

'Thank you for everything, Firzun.' She stood up and smiled weakly at him. 'There's always a home with us in the States, you know that.'

'Rashid was a good man and a brave fighter, Nasim.'

She bit her lip, trying to hold back the tears. She shook Firzun's hand and hugged Zahra. 'Good luck.' Her voice broke.

Karim took her arm and helped her into the car. He got into the passenger seat without a backward glance.

'Father phoned from the airport. The flight's on time, Mother,' Zahra heard him say before Amir closed the door.

She felt drained of all emotion as she waved goodbye and sighed when Tahmineh, weeping openly, came back into the house and closed the front door. Zahra started to follow the housekeeper to the kitchen, but Firzun touched her arm.

'We need to talk, Zahra. Come up in a few minutes. Don't bring the kid.'

She left Ahmad with Shirin in the kitchen and walked reluctantly up to Karim's apartment. When the Afghan nurse opened the door, she glanced quickly round the large room. The last time she'd been there was the day they'd carried Firzun up from the car, and she'd been too distracted to take in the surroundings. Now she was curious to see how Karim had lived in the two months she'd known him. On her first visit she hadn't noticed how modern and light the apartment was, compared with the traditional design of the Konari house. Bright nomadic *gelims* were scattered across the polished wood floor and the furniture was ultra modern chrome and glass. The sofas had stark orange upholstery.

'Out here,' Firzun called from a wide outdoor deck.

She sat down in a plush garden chair opposite her cousin and breathed in slowly. The air felt cool and sharp on her face in spite of the sunshine. Firzun lit a cigarette, and its semi-sweet smell hung between them on the still air.

'Let's hope they don't have any trouble at the airport,' Firzun commented.

'*Enshallah*, they'll be all right,' she replied. 'How's your leg?'

'Well enough to pass for an injured *Haji* at Rashid's funeral,' he said. When she didn't smile, he added quietly, 'Yes, well, God rest his soul. He was unlucky.'

She said nothing, hoping he'd tell her their departure plans.

'Dr Maryam's been to see me. I can get around easily now with this,' he said, tapping a dark wood silver-headed walking stick.

Zahra read the inscription on the top: '*Mashallah*'—God protect you.

She raised her eyebrows. 'A religious inscription for a socialist?'

'An old guy in the hospital passed away and a nurse gave it to me. I'm a socialist, but God's protected me so far!' He laughed.

She glared at him. 'Don't tempt fate, Firzun. Remember Rashid.'

'I know, I know,' he said. 'I can get on the plane in a couple of days,' he went on. 'Ashraf here can take out the stitches at the last minute.' He indicated the nurse as the man put a cup of coffee on the table for Zahra. So that's the man's name, she thought. Firzun usually called everyone '*dost*'—friend. Ashraf must be one of the few people Firzun trusted.

'The last minute?' Zahra sipped her coffee and looked across at Firzun. 'You never mentioned ...'

'You're coming with me to the travel agency in Antaz tomorrow. It's on the other side of the city,' he announced before she could protest. 'The tickets are ready. We're leaving early next week.'

'So soon?'

'Of course *soon*! I can't stay here much longer!' he snapped. 'Remember to call me Mahmoud in public.' He reached for his coffee. 'The travel agent's a friend of mine, but he has to sight the passengers and their passports before he can issue the tickets.' He waved his coffee cup at her. 'It's another stupid government regulation. He'll need to take a photograph as well.'

'What about Ahmad? I've got a few photographs of him.'

'Yeah, they'll do. We don't want to drag him across the city. Just bring his passport. We're leaving at nine o'clock tomorrow morning. Don't be late.'

She assumed by his tone that the conversation was finished and she stood up.

'We've got to get out fast,' he repeated. 'Just stick with me, I'll get us to safety and freedom.' He used his cane to push himself to his feet.

She regarded him steadily for a minute. He was leaning on his stick, looking like a war hero, his face suddenly enlivened by the prospect of deceiving the authorities. This was another challenge, another strike against them, but he couldn't do it without her. A wave of anger swept over her. How much did he really care about her and Ahmad?

If she told him she actually had a choice, that she could go to America with Karim, what would he do? She knew the answer: he'd remind her of everything she owed him—the extra money he'd given her over the years, her freedom from Mahmoud, a new life in a Western country. She had her hand on the door handle when he called to her. She turned with a frown; to her irritation he was grinning.

'I'll be in my *Haji* clothes tomorrow too, so you'd better look respectable and pious and keep quiet. I'll do the talking.' He paused. 'We're going by car, Ashraf's driving.' He jerked his head in the man's direction.

By car—whose car? Zahra couldn't imagine Karim lending them one of his. Asking Firzun would be a waste of time; instead she nodded and was opening the door when he called her back. Reluctantly she walked across to him.

'I might as well tell you now about the airport,' he said, motioning her to a seat. 'They'll probably question you.'

She sat down again on the edge of a chair. 'Question me? What about?' He was making her feel nervous again.

He waved his hands in the air. 'The usual stuff—where you and Ahmad were born, how long you've lived here. You'll go through the women's area and they might search you and ask more questions. If you tell the truth about most things you'll be all right. The authorities know exactly when we arrived.'

'How?' she interrupted.

He sighed and shook his head at her. 'They gave me papers at that border crossing. They're not totally stupid. Look, I've fixed everything. I extended the Iranian visas for another month. I've done a lot of running round for us ...'

'But the passport photos?'

'I'll have the glasses on, remember ...'

He pulled a pair of gold-rimmed spectacles out of his pocket. When he put them on and peered at her through the lenses, she shivered as she had the first time he'd worn them. If he trimmed his beard he would pass as Mahmoud easily.

'But aren't they suspicious of Afghans now?' she asked, thinking of the burgeoning refugee camps on the border.

'They're happy for us to leave,' he said firmly. 'They're looking for Firzun Khan, not Mahmoud Ghafoori.'

As usual she felt disturbed by his answers. 'What about Jafar and the man who searched this house?'

'They're still after me,' he said shortly.

'But what if ...?' Her heart started to race. Why did he have to live like this? She was always on edge with him.

He put his hand up to stop her. 'Enough! Take it from me, I need you and the kid to get out of Iran,' he answered. 'All you have to do is wear a chador and follow me at the airport, say nothing and keep Ahmad quiet.'

'I'm really scared, Firzun.'

He leaned forward and stared into her face. 'Don't be, cousin. I'll look after you. We came into this country legally and we'll go out legally. Once we get the tickets tomorrow, we can go.'

She wished she had his confidence, instead she just felt sick with anxiety. She stood up. She needed to be alone to think everything through.

'I've been in contact with the Australian authorities. They're expecting us, so don't worry. Don't forget—nine o'clock tomorrow!'

Zahra walked slowly down the stairs from the apartment, her disquiet replaced by irritation at the subversive life Firzun lived. All she wanted was to be an ordinary person, to buy tickets from a polite travel agent, to be ushered onto the plane like respected guests. How typical of Firzun to have a travel agent in Antaz of all places. It was the run-down suburb where her aunt and uncle had lived. The place she'd had to return to after her mother's sudden death. She sighed and turned towards her bedroom to check on Ahmad. Shirin could look after him tomorrow while she was miles away on the other side of the city.

37

A DIFFERENT FUTURE

Zahra checked that all of her hair was secured under the tight wide band and arranged her long black scarf over her head, fastening it securely under her chin. She threw her chador over her coat, covering it completely, and fastened the strings below her throat. She checked her image in the mirror—her pale face stared back at her. She looked more worried than pious.

There was a tap on the door and Karim walked in. She saw his eyes sweeping over her outdoor clothes, but before he could speak she said quickly, 'We're getting the airline tickets today in Antaz.'

He frowned. 'Isn't that where ...?'

'Yes my aunt used to live there. They're in the States now. Firzun's travel agent friend can get the tickets at a good price for us.'

She had no idea if that was true but it sounded plausible enough.

'I could fix up tickets for you ...' he began, but she shook her head.

'Firzun says we're going early next week.' She heard his sharp intake of breath.

'So soon ...' His voice tailed off.

'He has to leave as soon as possible—after what happened to Rashid.' She couldn't bear to look at Karim's face.

'How are you getting to Antaz?' he asked. 'It's about twenty kilometres across the city.'

'By car.'

Karim frowned again, then smiled as Ahmad ran down the stairs. He ruffled his hair, but before he could ask Karim to play soccer, Shirin called him and he ran back up the stairs. Karim opened the door to the hall. His hazel eyes held Zahra's.

'Take care, Zahra. There's been some unrest on that side of the city,' he said.

She felt nervous, wishing he hadn't told her that. She knew he didn't trust Firzun. She didn't trust her cousin either, but she had no choice. She waited at the open kitchen door until she heard the click of the study door when Karim closed it. She bit her lip and frowned; Karim's last comment hummed in her brain. Did he know something she didn't? She stood in the kitchen, wondering whether to go to the study and ask him. Ahmad hurtled down the stairs again, followed by the sound of Firzun's stick clunking on the bare wood. Too late now; she was about to be herded outside.

She hugged Ahmad quickly and followed her cousin and his friend Ashraf out the back door. The day was cool and blustery, and grey clouds scudded across the sky as she walked behind the two men. Instead of heading for the street, Firzun picked his way through the Konaris' garden, helped along by Ashraf. Of course he'd use the back lane, she thought, he was on the run. But where was the car? As soon as she stepped out of the back gate, she saw it: Rashid's unmistakable blue sedan. Surely not?

Firzun turned to her. 'Okay, there it is, get in.' He motioned her towards the vehicle with his stick.

'But this is Rashid's car ... How did you get the keys?'

'You want to catch a bus?' he asked, limping along beside her. 'I've always had Rashid's spare keys. Ashraf checked it out last night, made sure it had enough gas.' He shrugged his shoulders. 'Well, why not? Ashraf's changed the number plates. Better for us to use it than the Revolutionary Guards!'

He hitched up his white *shalwaar kameez* slightly and pulled his dark cloak tightly round his body as Ashraf, dressed in identical white *shalwa kameez,* long white pants, and crocheted cap helped him into the passenger seat. Firzun stuck his head out the window and shouted to her. 'Hurry up! Get in the back.'

Zahra flinched as she slid along the leather seat. How much lower could her cousin sink? This was a murdered man's car! Firzun turned round, knocking his tight rimless cap against the back of the seat.

'You don't need to worry, Zahra. The windows are tinted—no one can see us,' he remarked.

Ashraf turned the key in the ignition. The car roared into life, then settled into a gentle purr. The men exchanged delighted glances.

'BMW. German!' Ashraf laughed. 'Good car, very fast.'

'Yeah, take it easy,' Firzun warned. 'Don't draw attention to us. Switch the alarm on when we park it in Antaz.'

Zahra huddled in the back seat, too disgusted to speak to them. She was glad of the tinted windows. She was past caring who saw her, but the police might be suspicious of two religious men in a luxury car like this.

The long journey took them through crowded streets, then a busy highway. Eventually Ashraf drove down a quiet unsealed lane.

'Okay.' Firzun turned to her. 'We're leaving the car here. It should be safe near the mosque.'

As she walked behind them, the wind caught her chador and swirled it round her body. The weather unsettled her; it was threatening rain but was still dry, and the irritating wind stung her eyes and her exposed face. She followed Firzun and Ashraf as they turned onto a crowded footpath bordered on one side by small shops. Behind the shops, the walls of the local bazaar loomed dark and grey. The air smelled bad, as if a factory was belching out noxious fumes, and the footpaths were slippery from the thin veil of rain that had started to fall. She looked around feeling alien and lost. If Firzun deserted her, she had no idea how she would get back to the Konari house in Elahiye to Ahmad to Karim ...

But he hadn't deserted her; he was limping as fast as he could round the side of the bazaar and occasionally he looked over his shoulder and called out impatiently: 'Keep up, Zahra!'

Sometimes people acknowledged the two men respectfully as they passed. '*Salaam Haji,*' and Firzun and Ashraf nodded solemnly in reply. Hypocrites, Zahra thought angrily. They turned a corner to an open area at the back of the bazaar from which narrow cobbled streets branched off in different directions. On either side of the streets, small businesses displayed their wares on the damp footpaths: fruit and sweets, spices and pans. A few cars were parked half on the footpath and half in the road. Firzun pointed ahead with his stick and glanced over his shoulder again. Ashraf stood aside and she followed her cousin to a small shop.

'Okay, we're here.' Firzun dropped his calm pious act. 'Hameed, the travel agent, is a friend of mine. If there's anyone else in the shop, I'll pretend I don't know him. Just say *yes* if you got that.'

'Yes.'

'Ashraf is waiting outside in case.'

She glanced at her cousin in alarm—in case of what? But he took her arm and pulled her across the threshold. The grimy shop smelled of cigarette smoke and old food, but Hameed was clean-shaven and efficient. He took their photos 'for the customs people'. After he'd checked their passports, he handed Firzun the tickets. He passed them to Zahra.

'Put them in your bag,' her cousin ordered. 'Wait outside with Ashraf. I've got something else to fix up. I won't be long.' The phone started ringing and he waved her out of the shop. 'Stay with Ashraf.'

She stepped down into the street, wondering how he was paying for the tickets, but she was beyond caring. Everything was fixed up. They were free to leave and—her heart jolted—she would have to part from Karim. She'd hardly closed the door when it opened again and Firzun caught her arm. He looked tense and worried.

'Ashraf! Quick, take her back to the car!' Ashraf looked at him in alarm. 'I'll meet you there.' Firzun sounded breathless. 'Hang on to your bag, Zahra!'

'What's going on?' she asked.

'Nothing. Go with Ashraf—hurry up!'

Ashraf grabbed her arm and she had to run to keep up with him. She risked a quick look back. Her cousin was on the footpath, scanning the street, then he went back in the shop and slammed the door. Fear gripped her—something was wrong.

Ashraf had just opened the car door when the bomb went off. It came from the place they'd left, but seemed so near that she thought their car had exploded or an earthquake had passed beneath her feet. Loose white paint from the mosque wall rained down on the vehicle. A flock of birds, squealing in terror, their wings beating wildly, rose in formation from a nearby building. The car alarm started wailing in loud loops of sound. Ashraf flung open the driver's door and switched it off. He turned to her and grabbed her elbow.

'It's a bomb! There may be another. Go to the mosque. Run!'

She squirmed and looked up at him. 'What about Firzun? He was there.'

Ashraf didn't answer, but steered her round the wall towards the courtyard gate of the building. Ahead of her, a burgeoning plume of black smoke rose into the sky. As they ran towards the main road she heard screaming. Ashraf pulled her along to the mosque. People knocked against her as they ran yelling and sobbing, some towards the blast site, others away from it. A group of young men firing rifles into the air rushed past them. She pulled her arms into her body, clutching her chador to her neck.

'Get in here!' Ashraf grasped her arm and pushed her into the courtyard of the mosque. 'It's safe,' he gasped urgently. He steered her towards a covered walkway and pushed her onto a bench.

'I'll find him. Don't talk to anyone. Stay there, I'll come back for you!'

He was gone in an instant. She sat trembling on the bench for a couple of minutes. Where was Firzun? Was he dead? Her ears were ringing from the effects of the blast. Her breath came in sharp bursts. Had Firzun done this? She put her hands over her face. No! No! He couldn't have, could he? She had to do something—help the injured. She was culpable, he was her cousin.

She ran to the gate just as an ambulance mounted the footpath, its siren shrieking. She jumped back.

A woman pushed past her into the courtyard, blood streaming down her face. She staggered under the weight of a screaming child. 'Help me, help me!' she shrieked. 'My husband's out there! My daughter's hurt!'

Zahra caught her arm. 'Over here!' She helped the woman to a bench. The hysterical child was screaming for her father. 'Stay there!' Zahra ordered.

She ran to the washing area and soaked a handkerchief, but the mother and daughter had gone when she got back. She looked round helplessly for them.

Bloodied terrified people poured through the open gates and into the courtyard. It was raining heavily now as clerics in long robes and white turbans ran out of the mosque to help. Young men from the Madreseh—the school next to the mosque—rushed in the gates, their robes muddied by the wet ground.

Zahra pushed her way towards the exit. She glanced back at the courtyard; they were laying people out on the ground. Some were screaming in agony, in terror. She had to get out of here! She had to find Firzun!

From the gate she could see the blast site barely two hundred metres away. A couple of motorbikes lay in tangled heaps on the ground; a fruit stall was a devastated mess of singed canvas and smashed fruit. Large blood stains leaked into the wet earth. She felt sick—someone was already collecting body parts in a sack. She turned away and leaned on the wall, wretched and spat on the ground. When she looked up, she saw Ashraf dodging a fire truck and running towards her. He was alone. He didn't speak, just took her by the elbow and propelled her round the outside of the mosque away from the carnage.

'Where's Firzun?' she shouted.

He shook his head and pushed her harder.

The car was still there, intact but smeared with dust and flakes of paint. Ashraf flung the back door open and she tumbled in. He jumped into the driver's seat and gunned the engine into life. He spun the steering wheel and swung the car round. The wheels skidded on the damp road as he took off at high speed away from the blast site. As he manoeuvred the BMW through narrow alleyways, Ashraf honked and cursed at the pedestrians who had poured out of their dingy apartment blocks. Zahra glimpsed them standing around in stunned groups as the car raced past. The sound of sirens finally receded in the distance.

'I couldn't find him, Zahra. God help me, I looked!' He turned to her from the driver's seat, his face pale and drawn. 'I found this.'

He passed her something and she looked down at the thing in her hand. It was the top of Firzun's cane; the wood was burned and sticky with blood. She felt sick as she stared at the inscription: *Mashallah*—God protect. A sob caught in her throat. Firzun's luck had finally run out.

'Another funeral,' Tahmineh remarked dolefully when Zahra returned from the mosque the following day. 'God give you patience, Zahra Khanoum.'

Zahra nodded; she never wanted to hear that terrible phrase again. She sat at the kitchen table feeling stunned. The funeral had been excruciating, coffin after coffin was passed over the heads of people wailing for the dead. A mass funeral for over one hundred victims. Karim and Ashraf had come with her and then Ashraf had packed his things and left. And now she had to observe another three-day mourning period for her 'husband'.

'I've moved your things to one of the guest rooms,' Tahmineh was saying. 'Karim Agha said you weren't to stay in that cramped room a minute longer.'

She smiled, glad to be out of the room over the kitchen that she and Ahmad had shared for two months. She opened the door to their new room. Ahmad was sitting on his bed, playing a board game with Shirin.

The young girl smiled up at her and cleared her throat. 'Tahmineh Khanoum has put your husband's bag in the wardrobe,' she said.

Zahra thanked her, feeling both relieved and sad. If she saw the bag it would remind her of Firzun. He'd annoyed her, he'd been unreliable and headstrong at times, but he was her cousin, more like a brother to her—and now he was dead. After Shirin had left, taking Ahmad with her, Zahra lay down on the bed and wept.

Karim sat at his father's desk and rested his hand on a pile of folders. He only needed a few more days and everything would be tied up and finished with. He sighed; he hoped he never had to go to another funeral for a very long time. His grandmother's and Rashid's had been bad. But this mass funeral, which had included Firzun and the many others who'd been blown apart, was awful. There was no doubt that Firzun was dead, even though, like many others, his body had never been found.

He'd questioned Ashraf closely and felt sickened by what the other man had told him.

'He definitely perished, Karim Agha. When I went back I found his stick,' he'd said.

'That hardly proves it though,' Karim had objected.

'I also saw ...' Ashraf had cleared his throat. 'I saw part of his leg, Agha—no foot—but I recognised the stitches.'

Karim winced, wondering if he should tell Zahra. Only if she asks, he thought, hoping fervently that she never did. He'd supported her through the crowds at the funeral and he'd attended the mass burial. If he hadn't been with her at the mosque, he was sure she'd have collapsed like some of the other mourners.

He wrote a list of the things he still had to do and made a final decision. He rang the bell for Tahmineh and when she came he told her he wanted to see Zahra.

Zahra was waiting for him in the salon. He felt a rush of emotion when he saw her sitting on the edge of the sofa, looking abandoned and exhausted. He sat down next to her and took her hand in his. He told her what he planned and she nodded her agreement.

'We can be in New York within a week, Zahra. My apartment is in a quiet area. You can rest and relax and we'll find a school for Ahmad.'

Her eyes filled with tears as she looked up at him. 'I know we've been to the funeral but ... I can't believe he's dead, without seeing ... seeing his body. Could he have survived?'

Karim told her gently what Ashraf had said. As she sobbed, he kissed her hair and her face and held her close to his body.

'I love you, Zahra. We'll get married as soon as we can. I'll take care of you and Ahmad,' he said gently.

'I love you too. Just give me time ...' she whispered.

He stroked her hair. 'We have all the time in the world, Zahra.'

After he'd returned to his office, Zahra sat alone in the salon. Karim's words had washed over her like soothing spring water. This was where she belonged—with him.

She grieved for her cousin and eventually she would tell Karim her story. But now it was enough that they were together. They had found each other again.

GLOSSARY

Allah u Akbar
Literal meaning: 'God's mightiness is beyond description'. It is often translated as 'God is Great'. These are the first words of every prayer call from a mosque. In Chapter One it is used as a triumphant battle cry.

Khoda Hafez/Khodafez
Goodbye/Have a good journey (God protect you).

Azan-e sobh / Azan-e zorh / Azan-e maghreb
The names of the prayer calls in the Persian language: the dawn prayer call, the midday prayer call, and the final evening prayer call. In some Muslim countries there are five prayer calls a day. In Iran there are only three.

Muezzin
The man who traditionally climbed the minaret, the tower next to the mosque, and called/sang the faithful to prayer. Nowadays the prayer call is often a recording.

Salaam alaikum / War alaikum as-salaam
A greeting when meeting people.
'Peace be with you' / 'And peace be with you also.'
(Often shortened to 'Salaam'.)

Mashallah!
Sometimes used in Iran, especially by older people when first meeting a child. It means 'God protect him/her'.

Farsi
The Persian language, the official language of Iran.

Dari
A language that is close to Farsi and is spoken by people in the Iranian border regions of Afghanistan. Both languages are written in Arabic script.

bismillâh ir-rahmân ir-rahîm
The opening words of the Koran, and of Muslim prayers: 'In the name of Allah, Most Gracious, Most Merciful ...'

Khanoum
A term of respect for women, which translates to *Madam*. Used after a first name, for example Zahra Khanoom, or to attract someone's attention: 'Khanoom!' on its own.

Agha
A term of respect for men, which translates to *Sir*. Used after the first name, for example Karim Agha. In more formal use it is put before a name: Agha Karim = Mr Karim. Can also be used alone to attract someone's attention.

Gelim
A cotton rug or carpet, often called Kilim in English.

Djan
Term of endearment often used after a name: Madar djan—dearest mother.

Noush e djan
Said when offering food. Literally means *May your soul be nourished.*

Baba
Daddy/Dad

Jihad
Holy War

Ghazi
Warriors of the faith (Islam).

Pakul
A flat woollen hat worn by men.

Shalwaar Kameez
Man's long shirt.

Chador
A woman's long cape worn over her outdoor clothes. It ties at the collar with strings made from the same material. Mostly black, though some of the capes worn by Iranian villagers have flower patterns. It is worn with a black headscarf and the hair is pulled back under a band.

Shabanu
The wife of the shah. Literally 'the shah's lady'.

ACKNOWLEDGMENTS

I would like to thank the following people for their help and encouragement while I was writing *The Afghan Wife*: Persian national and teacher, Naz, who read the manuscript and for her valuable suggestions. Thanks to all the Muslim women for sharing information about Islam, and my students who told me their stories. Mehran, our male tour guide in Iran, for his patience in answering my questions. I'm indebted to my writers group for their input: Jacques Horeg, Elizabeth Llhuede, Helen Lyne, Isolde Martyn, Flick Pullman, Chris Stinson, Viv Wilson, Bea Yell and Margaret Zanardo. My book group in Sydney, thanks for your interest and encouragement and the 'mods' group: Jane Cook, Carole Cole, Shirley Graham and Kay Ryan. FW for your intellectual input and generosity, and for encouraging me to stay on track. Frances and David Lyon for providing me with a quiet place to work. Debbie Lewis-Bizley and Frances Lyon for reading the manuscript and for your suggestions. Thanks to Pauline and Warren Hill for making it possible for me to visit Iran. Thanks to Kate Morritt and Polly Price for your long and supportive friendship. To architects Ipek and Izzet Goldeli, Peter Fuller and Tim Brook for information about architectural practices in the 1970s. Louise Cox from 'Eventuality'—your organisational skills are amazing! Roslyn Russell, thank you for your continued interest in my writing career and for information about Iran. Thanks also to Susannah Fullerton OAM and Carolynn and Mal Davies for all your encouragement. Frances Coleman for hours of listening. My daughter Emma, son Adrian and his wife Kath for taking an interest when you have such busy lives; son Mark for your excellent knowledge of English grammar. I'm indebted to my husband Harvey for reading and editing the manuscript as well as for his extensive knowledge of Persian literature and language. Finally thank you Michelle Lovi, my publisher, and Sophie and Jessica for the final edits.

ABOUT THE AUTHOR

Cindy lived in a small town on the Black Sea coast of Turkey for two years where she taught English. This was the beginning of a lifelong interest in Middle Eastern culture and language. Born in the UK she emigrated to Australia in 1975 with her family. She's been an English language teacher, freelance travel writer and tour guide, in both Turkey and Sydney, Australia. Her first novel *The Afghan Wife* is a love story set against the background of the Iranian Revolution in 1979. She's currently working on a sequel.

www.cindydavies.com.au

Ingram Content Group UK Ltd.
Milton Keynes UK
UKHW041259090623
423177UK00001B/95